"Litfin has woven another fascinating narrative in his imaginative world of epic adventure. Using his keen understanding of theology and history, he has skillfully infused this novel with the grand themes of grace and redemption at every turn. There's a lesson for readers here as Teofil and Anastasia face their own brokenness and find who has the power to give strength and courage in their weakness."

DR. THOMAS CORNMAN, Academic Vice President,
Cedarville University

"*The Gift* ushers readers back into the land of Chiveis, a medieval future-world brimming with adventure and intrigue. It continues the story of Teo and Ana, exiles from their homeland, on a quest to learn more of Deu, the Creator God. While entertaining to read, *The Gift* is much more than mere entertainment. It is a call to know and love the one true God through his Son, Jesus Christ, the Pierced King."

MATT TULLY, Pastoral Assistant, Cedar Heights Baptist Church,
Cedar Falls, Iowa

"A captivating narrative that journeys into the discovery of a living religion that seems lost and unrecoverable, this tale imagines how a sovereign God might reveal its mysteries anew. Any lover of theology and Western history would enjoy watching believers uncover lost symbols and writings, piecing together the greatest paradoxes of the faith in the drama of a fictional narrative. Action, conspiracy, romance, and faith combine in a tale depicting how the treasured beliefs of Christianity might first appear to a generation that had never seen its wonders."

DR. W. BRIAN SHELTON, Vice President for Academic Affairs,
Toccoa Falls College

"*The Gift* is a powerfully written story about forgiveness and a desire to know the truth, no matter the cost. It's impossible to read this book and not develop a greater appreciation for the Scriptures and a deeper understanding of the Christian faith. Few authors touch my heart so deeply that all of their books make my favorites list, but Bryan Litfin has done it with this series."

MICHELLE SUTTON, author, *It's Not About Me* and *Letting Go*

"Litfin writes with a warmth reminiscent of Lewis, both of whom can tell drama and battles, and even tragedy, while still making the reader feel alive. His fascinating research and knowledge of Christian theology makes *The Gift* an enlightening read."

DAVID ULRICH, college student, Orange County, California

"I finished this book within twenty-four hours of receiving it! Thrilling action, sound theology, a damsel in distress—what more could you ask from a novel? *The Gift* caused me to feel deeper love for my wife, more gratitude for my children, and a renewed sense of God's mercy in the gift of Christ. Enjoy!"

DR. JAMES HAMILTON, Associate Professor of Biblical Theology, Southern Baptist Theological Seminary; author, *God's Glory in Salvation through Judgment*

"Litfin draws readers into an evocative postapocalyptic world, where the true faith is emerging from the ashes of the past—a faith the enemy is intent on destroying. A suspenseful story, skillfully woven with characters who risk their lives for loyalty, honor, and truth."

C. S. LAKIN, author, *Someone to Blame* and *The Wolf of Tebron*

"The second installment of the Chiveis Trilogy steps into a futuristic but believable world where evil is powerful. This story elicits widened eyes, shed tears, and gasps of surprise as the author reflects on the reality of our fallen world and the grace God gives us through Jesus. As Teo and Ana piece together the truth of God's perfect narrative and search for the God they have yet to fully know, I rediscovered the beauty of the gospel and saw the Savior in a whole new way."

RACHEL ESTES, college student, Denville, New Jersey

THE GIFT

Also in the Chiveis Trilogy:

Book 1: *The Sword*

CHIVEIS TRILOGY

THE GIFT

A NOVEL

BRYAN M. LITFIN

CROSSWAY

WHEATON, ILLINOIS

ISBN 13: 978-1-4335-2516-2

ISBN 10: 1-4335-2516-X

PDF ISBN: 978-1-4335-2517-9

Mobipocket ISBN: 978-1-4335-2518-6

ePub ISBN: 978-1-4335-2519-3

Library of Congress Cataloging-in-Publication Data
Litfin, Bryan M., 1970–
   The gift : a novel / Bryan M. Litfin.
     p. cm. — (Chiveis trilogy ; bk. 2)
   ISBN 13: 978-1-4335-2516-2
   ISBN 10: 1-4335-2516-X
   ISBN 13: 978-1-4335-2519-3 (ebk.)
   ISBN 13: 978-1-4335-2517-9 (pdf)
   1. Dystopias—Fiction. I. Title. II. Series.
PS3612.I865G54   2011
813'.6—dc22   2010042544

Crossway is a publishing ministry of Good News Publishers.

LB		20	19	18	17	16	15	14	13	12	11
14	13	12	11	10	9	8	7	6	5	4	3	2	1

Sed quae stulta sunt mundi elegit Deus ut confundat sapientes,
et infirma mundi elegit Deus ut confundat fortia,
et ignobilia mundi et contemptibilia elegit Deus,
et quae non sunt ut ea quae sunt destrueret,
ut non glorietur omnis caro in conspectu eius.
1 ad Corinthios 1:27–29

contents

MAP   11

PROLOGUE   13

PART ONE
SOLIDARITY

CHAPTER 1   17

CHAPTER 2   41

CHAPTER 3   63

CHAPTER 4   89

CHAPTER 5   113

PART TWO
EXTRAVAGANCY

CHAPTER 6   141

CHAPTER 7   165

CHAPTER 8   187

CHAPTER 9   209

CHAPTER 10   233

PART THREE
VICTORY

CHAPTER 11   257

CHAPTER 12   279

CHAPTER 13   303

CHAPTER 14   329

CHAPTER 15   353

CHAPTER 16   379

EPILOGUE   405

STUDY QUESTIONS   409

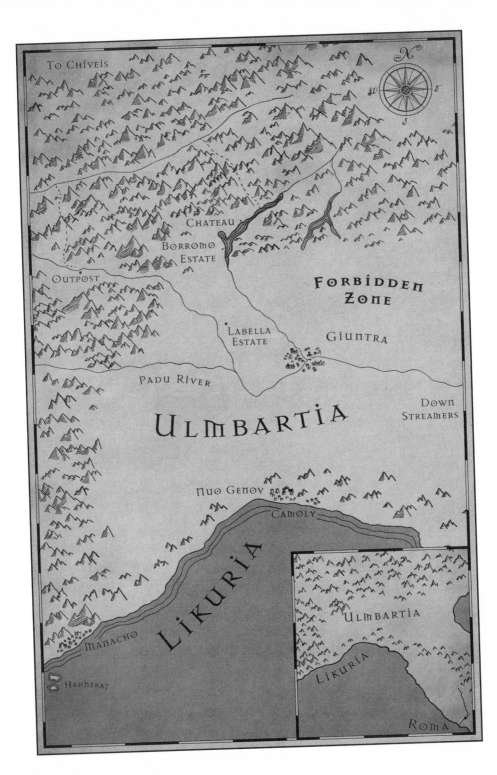

PROLOGVE

The people of the twenty-first century nearly destroyed the earth in a global nuclear holocaust. This is the story of what God did next.

The horrific war followed a viral rampage that began in the year 2042. Together the biological threat and the human conflict reduced the earth's population to a tiny fraction of its former size. The survivors viewed those who lived before the Great War of Destruction as an ancient culture whose ways were now lost. Clawing their way back from brutal chaos, the people of the postwar centuries recalled some of their former technologies and learned other skills anew. Thus, in a strange rewinding of history, the society of the twenty-fifth century became medieval once again. Men rode on horses and fought with swords; they sailed ships without engines and built civilizations without machines. And what about their religion? That too they rebuilt with little reference to the distant past—until a young soldier and a beautiful farm girl stumbled upon an ancient book.

The alpine Kingdom of Chiveis had forged a noble society when Captain Teofil of the Royal Guard's Fifth Regiment and Anastasia of Edgeton found themselves swept up in their great adventure. Anastasia was kidnapped by outsiders and relinquished all hope of returning to her home. Everyone in Chiveis feared she had been lost forever—everyone, that is, except one soldier who believed in action more than fear. Teo set out alone to find Ana in the Beyond, snatching her from the outsiders at her most desperate moment. They galloped away on a single horse into the black forest around the outsiders' village.

Although Teo and Ana only wanted to return home, circumstances led the pair to a lost city and its forgotten temple, a building the Ancients had called a cathedral. In that vast edifice of mystic beauty, Teo and Ana found the Sacred Writing of the one true God. The language of the book called him Dieu, or Deu in the Chiveisian speech. It was a name they would learn to treasure.

The recovery of this long-lost book opened up new spiritual horizons not just for Teo and Ana, but for a community of seekers who longed to know the God of the Ancients. Yet their knowledge was incomplete, for only a portion of the Sacred Writing had survived the ravages of time. Though the first Testament remained intact, the pages of the second had dissolved. The New Testament could not be found in Chiveis.

Opposed by enemies who did not want to see the religion of Deu return to the world, Teo and Ana faced the ultimate choice: to curse the name of their newfound God or be run through with a sword. Ana was willing to die for her faith, but Teo—always fiercely protective—offered her a third way. He would take her across the snowcapped peaks of Chiveis into the unknown world on the other side. Though it broke Ana's heart to leave her beloved homeland, she agreed to go. The army closed in; the die was cast; Chiveis refused to believe. And so it was that Teo and Ana joined hands and stepped into the Beyond once more.

PART ONE

SOLIDARITY

CHAPTER

1

Anastasia lay awake under a bearskin cloak, listening to the alien sounds of a land far from home. The stub of a candle hung from the ceiling of her leather tent, providing enough light to chase away the nocturnal spirits, but not the heaviness in Ana's heart.

Three weeks earlier, she had relinquished her home in the Kingdom of Chiveis. When she crossed the mountains into the Beyond, she had abandoned every person she knew in the world except one: the man who slept beside her in a bedroll on the tent floor. She sighed as she lay under her covers, contemplating a future of exile and uncertainty. It wasn't the future she had dreamed of, yet it was the will of Deu, the Creator of all things. Ana resolved to bear whatever burden he might ask of her.

She glanced over at the dark-haired man on her right. *At least I'm not completely forsaken*, she thought. Teofil had come over the mountains with her, lending his strength and encouragement when she faltered. The steady sound of Teo's breathing reassured Ana in the vastness of the unknown.

Descending from the glacier, the exiled pair had met four army scouts from a land called Ulmbartia. The men had welcomed Teo and Ana into their expedition, for the scouts too were in a foreign land, far from their own realm to the south. Warlike tribes called Rovers wandered these wild mountains, often raiding into Ulmbartia, so the kingdom had sent an expedition to seek out the passes the enemies were using. When the tall, powerful warrior Teo appeared out of nowhere, the Ulmbartian scouts readily accepted his offer to join them in exchange for provisions. Lieutenant Celso and his men-at-arms were happy to add Teo's sword to their dangerous patrols. With Ana cooking and tending the needs of the camp, the soldiers decided their mission had taken a dramatic turn for the better. Teo and Ana were assigned a tent of their own at the expense of the tracker named Bard, who was relegated to sleeping outdoors.

Ana hunched into her bedroll and gathered her blankets. Though it was high summer, a cool mountain breeze found its way into the tent and fluttered the candle's flame. Dawn was still several hours away. Ana was about to roll over when she felt something move against her leg.

She froze.

Did that really happen?

Ana lay still, trying to convince herself she had imagined the movement at her ankle. Her heart thudded. She held her breath lest she stir up the thing that had invaded her bed.

It's nothing. Go back to sleep.

Ana had decided her anxious mind was playing tricks on her when the creature moved again, sliding against her calf under the covers. It was smooth and ticklish in a revolting way. Ana's mind reeled as she realized the creature was a snake. She began to tremble as she felt it move up her leg, but she forced herself to hold still, hoping it would move past her and find its way out. Instead the creature sought the warmth of her body and slipped beneath the linen shift she was wearing. Ana clenched her jaw at the slippery sensation against her thigh. The snake paused, then glided onto the skin of her stomach. Only willpower held back the scream that clogged Ana's throat as she felt the serpent crawling up her body. *Is it poisonous?* She didn't dare move in case it was.

Time hung suspended. Ana's every sense came alive. She heard the gentle rustle of her garment and felt every undulation of the snake's muscles against her belly. Though it moved slowly, as if with painstaking deliberation, she knew the creature was coming toward her face. It was about to emerge from her neckline. Ana scrunched her eyes. *Deu, help me! Make it go away!*

For a long time nothing moved. The tent was quiet. Ana swallowed.

Maybe it's gone? Yes. It slid away from me just like I prayed. She opened her eyes and glanced down.

The viper rested in the center of her chest, staring back at her. Its yellow eyes were lidless and glassy. A forked black tongue tasted her skin.

"I'm coming for you," it whispered.

Ana exploded into a scream, snatching the snake behind its head in an attempt to hurl it away. The serpent recoiled, then struck her mouth with a smashing blow. Ana felt its fangs latch onto her lip. The hideous burn of fresh venom flooded her face.

"Teo! Help me! Get it off!" She was outside her covers now, writhing on the floor and grasping the snake's flailing body as it dangled from her lip. Though she yanked on it, the viper refused to let go. Its fangs pumped more venom into her soul.

Strong hands grasped Ana's shoulders, firm yet gentle. A familiar male voice spoke into the confusion. "You're okay! It's Teo. I'm here with you. You're safe."

"I'm coming for you," the snake repeated, then let go. The walls of the tent crowded toward Ana. The world spun in circles.

"Wake up, Ana. You're dreaming. Everything's okay."

What . . . ? Who . . . ? Where am I? Am I home in Chiveis? Relief coursed through Ana. There were no Ulmbartian scouts. She hadn't left home after all. It was just a horrible nightmare.

The space around her came into focus. A musty leather tent. A wobbly candle. A rumpled bearskin cloak. The night air cool against her skin. She looked into Teo's gray eyes. His handsome face wore a look of deep concern. His hands were steady on her shoulders.

"The s-snake," Ana stammered. "Is it gone?"

"There was no snake. You had a bad dream."

Ana put her hand to her lips. The burning sensation had vanished. She glanced at her fingers. Nothing. "Am I bleeding?"

Teo leaned toward her and inspected her face in the candlelight. "You're unhurt."

"It seemed so real. A snake was in my bed." She shuddered. "It touched me."

Teo glanced around. "The tent is tight. The mesh in the vents is unbroken. A snake couldn't get in here."

Ana felt a heavy weight settle into the pit of her stomach. The snake may have been a dream, but everything else was real. The tent. The scouts. The journey over the mountains into the Beyond. Her beloved Chiveis really was lost—maybe forever.

A draft stirred the air in the tent. Goose bumps arose on Ana's exposed legs. She gathered her knees to herself, wrapping her arms around them.

"I'm cold, Teo."

The bearskin cloak enveloped her, then Teo's arm encircled her as he held her close. Ana tucked her chin to her knees and began to cry.

"The Eternal One knows the plans he has for you," Teo said softly.

It was a quotation from the Sacred Writing of Deu. Those holy words and the strong arm around her shoulders were Ana's only comforts in the turbulent sea of grief.

◆　　◆　　◆

The afternoon sun sparkled on the water. Bard dropped the string of rabbits on a flat rock next to the stream, then retrieved a knife and cleaver from his rucksack. It didn't take him long to gut and skin the carcasses. When the job was finished he opened his padded satchel of spice bottles, cursing the Ulmbartian quartermaster who had packed several vials of unknown contents for the expedition. Though Bard couldn't read any of the labels, he knew from taste or smell what most of the bottles contained, and he left the mysterious ones alone. Locating the salt, he deposited the rabbits into a leather bag to soak in brine. By dinnertime the meat would be ready to cook, and that was a good thing, because Lieutenant Celso could be very demanding when he was hungry. The soldiers would return from their patrol in a few hours, and they would be expecting a hearty meal.

Rolling his neck to work out a kink, Bard glanced toward the camp upstream. It was a well-chosen location. The tent sites were level, water was close, and plenty of dry wood lay about. A natural stone grotto in the hillside made a cozy place for a campfire, not only catching the warmth to ease the evening chill, but also shielding the fire's light from any prying eyes that might be wandering in the woods. When he was on an expedition, Bard never let himself forget he wasn't home in Ulmbartia. He was across the high pass, deep in a Rover-infested wilderness. Danger could come from anywhere.

The expedition, Bard's sixth foray into the wild mountains as an army tracker, had been unlike any other. In part this was because they hadn't encountered any Rovers yet. Normally the soldiers would have had a few skirmishes with their enemies by now. Yet the main thing that set this mission apart was the presence of the two strangers in camp. Three weeks ago Bard and Lieutenant Celso had been investigating some Rovers' tracks when the lieutenant stepped on a branch. The sound triggered movement upstream. Several paces away, a man in foreign clothing scrambled to his feet. Bard laughed as he recalled his surprise at seeing the handsome warrior standing over his young lady-friend. They obviously weren't Rovers; their attire was too civilized. How had this strange pair found their way so deep into the wilds? The warrior had waved, so Bard and Lieutenant Celso returned the greeting. Now, three weeks later, Teofil was a mercenary in the service of Ulmbartia, and Anastasia was a far better camp cook than Bard had ever been. He grabbed the sack of rabbit meat and walked toward the tents.

Anastasia was feeding leftover scraps to the expedition's bloodhound. Though Trusty's tracking ability hadn't been needed so far, he made an excellent companion for the two guardians who were left to tend camp while the soldiers were out. The woman tossed the dog a last chunk of gristly meat, then glanced up.

"Hello, Bard," she said. Her accent wasn't quite right, but she was doing her best to learn the Talyano speech.

"Hello, Anastasia," Bard replied. He held up the sack. "See what I have?"

"In what the sack is?"

Bard broke into a wide grin. "No," he corrected, "you're supposed to say, 'What is in the sack?'"

Ana's cheeks flushed, and she shook her head with a shy smile. "I try, Bard, I try."

"I know. And you're doing well. Talyano isn't easy to speak. You've learned a lot over the past few weeks."

"Teofil is faster."

Bard pursed his lips and nodded. "He has a knack for languages like I've never seen. He's almost to the point where we can converse back and forth."

"Me too. Very soon. Watch." She pointed at the leather bag Bard was holding. "What is in the sack?"

He burst into laughter. "There you go! You're a fast learner, Anastasia of Chiveis."

At the mention of Anastasia's homeland, her face fell, and Bard immediately regretted his words. Though the other men in the scouting party didn't know it, he sometimes heard Ana crying when she thought she was alone. Sensitive by nature, Bard knew how much the beautiful young foreigner missed her home. He felt sorry for her. Unlike the macho soldiers who shunned him, the gentle woman with the sunny disposition treated him with acceptance. The pair had developed a friendship of necessity as they watched the camp while the three Ulmbartian soldiers and Teofil were on daytime patrol. Anastasia gave Bard dignified camaraderie, and he tutored her in Talyano. It was a good arrangement.

Bard opened the sack, lifting a dripping carcass from the brine. Ana's eyes lit up, and she nodded approvingly. Her hair shone golden-blonde as it caught the afternoon sun. "Good! I like ribbits," she said.

Ribbits, Bard thought to himself. *That's cute.* Anastasia was learning his language as fast as she could.

This time, he didn't have the heart to correct her.

◆　◆　◆

With their bellies full, the men reclined around the campfire in the rocky grotto they had dubbed their "dining room." Firelight flickered on their faces, and shadows danced on the walls behind them. Teo had come to enjoy the company of the three Ulmbartian soldiers, especially Lieutenant Celso, a wiry middle-aged man with a sharp tongue. The commander was a true warrior, and an excellent leader of men. Only the fourth Ulmbartian, the fair-haired tracker named Bard, remained a mystery to Teo. Bard seemed uncomfortable around the other rugged men.

One of the soldiers belched, drawing guffaws from his companions. Teo frowned and kicked the offender with the toe of his boot. "There's a lady in the camp," he said.

Ana's meal had been exquisitely prepared. She had added wild onions, mushrooms, and juniper berries to the rabbit stew, simmering the meat until it was falling off the bone. She had also made a salad of dandelion leaves and chard with an oil dressing. All the men agreed they had never eaten so well on an expedition.

Teo touched Ana lightly on her back. "Everything was delicious," he said in Talyano.

"Thanks." She smiled at him, then held up a bottle of thick, golden liquid. "This is new to me. I like it. It's good."

"There's nothing like a fine olive oil," Bard chimed in from across the fire. "It's made by the Likurians. They're always one step ahead of us."

Teo glanced up. "Who are the Likurians?"

"A wealthy people we trade with," Lieutenant Celso explained. "Their kingdom lies a few days south of ours. Likuria sits upon a vast sea whose water cannot be drunk."

"Why not?"

"It's salty. It would kill you."

"I've read of that in books, though I've never seen it."

"You can read?" Lieutenant Celso was surprised. "Few in Ulmbartia can."

"In Chiveis, Teofil was a"—Ana sought the right word—"a teacher," she finished. "Very smart." She tapped her temple.

"They can both read," Bard said to the men around the fire. "Haven't you heard Teofil reading his holy book at night? Apparently their civilization is advanced."

"Are you a priest, Teofil?" one of the soldiers asked. "In our land it's usually the religious who can read."

"I'm not a priest, but I am a follower of the true God. His name is Deu."

"Ah, the high god of the Chiveisi."

"No." Ana shook her head. "The Creator of all. The God of every-one." The men murmured at this.

"Where did you get your holy book?" Bard asked.

Teo and Ana glanced at each other, exchanging knowing smiles. He knew what Ana was thinking: *The telling of that story would take all night!*

"From those big grins, it must be a good tale," Bard said. "Come on, Teofil, tell us the story."

Teo stirred the fire with a stick, wondering where he should begin. Should he start with the first time he met Ana—when a bear attacked him and Ana's archery saved his life? Should he describe how he invited Ana to be his escort at a party in the woods, only to find she was repelled by its debauchery? She'd fled into the forest, where evil raiders captured her. That wasn't a good memory for Teo.

Ana spoke into the silence. "Captain Teofil is a hero like no other man. Enemies took me away, carried me from Chiveis. I was lost. Teofil came to me." The campfire crackled and sent up a shower of sparks. "Tell the whole story, Teo," she whispered to him in Chiveisian speech. All eyes were transfixed on him. He took a deep breath and began to narrate.

"As you can see, Anastasia is very beautiful. Outsiders from beyond our realm took her to be a queen. I alone went after her."

Teo could see from the men's faces that the story had already arrested their attention. In the best Talyano he could muster, Teo described the epic adventure he and Ana had shared. He followed Ana for four days, tracking her kidnappers to their home village. As Ana was being taunted in a feasting hall on the night of her "wedding," Teo disguised himself as a jester. The ruse enabled him to mingle among the men until he could extinguish the hearthfire, plunging the hall into darkness. In the confusion he whisked Ana away, and they escaped on horseback. But their enemies gave pursuit. Chasing the fugitives through a dense forest, they soon caught up with Teo and Ana. The enemy warriors spurred their horses and attacked. Teo did battle with four men at once, yet defeated them all. As he recounted the story to the Ulmbartian soldiers, he stood up and acted it out. The men around the campfire listened in silence, their eyes glued to him.

"The leader was a cruel man named Rothgar," Teo said. "He held me against a tree, then drew his knife." Teo demonstrated how he fought against Rothgar but couldn't stop the knife that was about to plunge into his belly. Slowly Teo drew back his arm to imitate the killing blow.

"What happened next?" Lieutenant Celso's mouth hung open, and his eyes were wide.

Teo glanced at Ana, who was staring into the fire. All the men looked at her.

"Do you want to tell it?" he asked. She shook her head.

Teo made the motions of an archer drawing a bow. "Just as my enemy was about to kill me, Anastasia shot him with an arrow. His body fell to the ground. And do you know what she said?" Teo paused dramatically. The men waited in hushed expectation.

"She said, 'You chose the wrong woman, Rothgar!'"

Everyone around the campfire burst into cheers. One of the soldiers clapped Ana on the back, and Lieutenant Celso raised his mug of ale to her.

Ana motioned to Teo with the back of her hand. "Get to the part about the Sacred Writing," she said.

When the clamor among the men died down, Teo resumed his story. He described how he and Ana had discovered a lost city built centuries ago by the Ancients.

"We know of the Ancients," Lieutenant Celso said. "The remains of their society can be found in Ulmbartia as well."

"I've never seen anything like what we discovered there."

"A temple," Ana said. "The house of Deu. Beautiful and holy."

"A man of the ancient times had hidden a book in the temple. He left . . . how would you say it? He left *tracks* for us."

"Clues," Bard corrected.

"Right, clues," Teo said. "The clues led us to the Sacred Writing of Deu. Only the first part had survived the centuries. The last pages were destroyed. So we don't know the whole story of our God."

Lieutenant Celso arched his eyebrows and held out his hands. "But surely you had records of this religion in the annals of your land?"

"No. The High Priestess of Chiveis suppressed it, on pain of death."

"So you practiced your religion in secret?"

"For a while. But Deu is a God for everyone. Eventually the time came to proclaim his name in the open."

"Then how are you still alive?" one of the soldiers inquired.

Teo didn't answer. He sat down next to Ana, whose expression was disconsolate.

Bard slapped the soldier on the shoulder. "Don't you see? They're exiles. That's why they're here. They've lost their homeland."

Teo regarded Ana as she sat beside him on a log. The velvety fabric of her gown shimmered in the firelight. Her hair, honey-blonde in the daytime, now carried a reddish tint. Twin pinpoints from the campfire shone in her eyes. As the warm glow caressed her high cheekbones, Teo found himself stunned by the overpowering beauty of the woman who had left her beloved home rather than deny Deu.

"Someday," Ana vowed as she stared into the flames, "we'll discover the rest of Deu's story." She looked up at Teo. "And then our kingdom will come to believe it."

He met her eyes and nodded. She reached for his hand, intertwining her fingers in his.

"Let it be so," Teo said.

◆　　◆　　◆

Ana awakened to the sound of an owl hooting. The moon had risen above the trees. Its pale light shone through the vents of the tent.

Ana's mind went to the story Teo had recounted around the campfire a few hours earlier. He had made her seem so brave and heroic. But now, in the dead of night, Ana didn't feel very brave. She dreaded her uncertain future.

"Teo," she whispered, "are you awake?"

His breathing was steady.

Ana sat up on one elbow and looked at Teo, noticing little details she had never observed before, like his angular jawline and the way his earlobes did not hang free. He wore no shirt, and his covers were pushed down. The moonlight illumined the contours of his body like a carved statue. Ana marveled at his powerful physique: broad shoulders, lean waist, muscular arms and chest. He was shaped just like a man should be.

In the secret corners of her heart, Ana had found it unexpectedly pleasant to sleep next to Teo in the tent. Having him close at night wasn't entirely new to her, because in the aftermath of her kidnapping she had camped with him as they made their way back to Chiveis. Although they had often been alone on those nights, with no other people around for many leagues, not once had anything sexual occurred. However, sleeping inside the privacy of a tent seemed more intimate to Ana than sleeping under the stars. Lately her nighttime thoughts had been wandering. She wasn't sure why.

The tent had originally been Bard's, and his alone, for the other three Ulmbartians preferred not to bunk with the suspiciously effeminate tracker. When Teo and Ana arrived, the tent was handed over to them. Ana knew the men thought she and Teo were sexually involved. Whenever it was time to turn in for the night, the soldiers made crude gestures to Teo with their fingers or gave him knowing winks and elbow nudges. At first Teo would protest, but now he just shook his head at their immaturity. All things considered, though, Ana was glad for their suspicions. Being viewed as Teo's woman shielded her from unwanted advances.

What if I were Teo's woman?

The thought startled her. Though Ana couldn't help but notice Teo's rugged good looks, she had always told herself he was her protector, companion, and friend—not her lover. At times she had wondered if something like that might develop, but neither of them had ever expressed such feelings. In this strange new land, however, Ana felt open to it. *But what if Teo doesn't feel the same way?* She sighed and flopped back on her bedroll.

"You alright?" Teo asked.

"Oh! I thought you were sleeping."

"Just woke up. Everything okay?"

"I'm feeling a little lonely, I guess."

"Missing home?"

"Mm-hm. It's really hard. I miss . . . Mother and Father." Her voice caught.

Teo rolled onto his stomach. The movement brought him nearer to her. "What can I do to help?" His voice was gentle.

Ana took a deep breath. "I'm scared, Teo. I need you to be with me in whatever lies ahead."

"We're both going to need each other, I think."

"Maybe. But I especially need you."

Teo rested on his elbow and leaned toward her. "Why?"

"Because I can't make it in this new land without you. I'm overwhelmed! I just want to go home, but I can't." She sniffed, wiping her eyes. "Will you stay with me? I feel so . . . so completely vulnerable."

Even in the pale moonlight, Ana could see Teo's expression change. He drew back, nodding as he stared into space.

Apprehension seized her. *I said the wrong thing! I misunderstood what he thinks!* She had no words to fill the silence.

Teo drew the covers of his bedroll around him. "You can count on me, Ana. I'll make a safe space around you. You can rest there and figure out what your future will look like. Take as long as you need."

She paused. "You're good to me, Teo."

He flashed her his usual cocky smile. "Of course I am. That's what friends are for."

Ana breathed a sigh of relief.

I can live with that.

✦   ✦   ✦

Dawn came none too soon for Ana. Nights in this wilderness were scary. She was glad Lieutenant Celso had ordered the men to be ready at first light. They were leaving the base camp for an exploration mission. Teo was sitting up in his bedroll getting dressed.

"I'm going to miss having you around," Ana said to him.

He turned and looked at her. "Oh, sorry. I was hoping I wouldn't wake you." Teo finished lacing up his first boot, then grabbed the second. "We should only be gone one night. Are you sure you'll be okay?"

"Like I said, I'll miss you, but I'll be fine."

"I don't feel good about leaving you. Part of me says not to. The other part of me, the rational part, says there's no reason to worry. There aren't any Rover tracks around here. Still, I have reservations."

"Do you have to go?"

"I'm a man under orders now. The food we're eating is earned by my service to the Ulmbartian army. We could run into some Rovers in the valley where we're going. My sword might be needed."

Ana sighed. "At least I'll have Trusty to keep me company. With that nose of his, he can smell danger a long way off."

"He's a good watchdog. And remember, it'll just be one night. Two at the most. We hope to establish a forward camp along a trail that climbs up the mountains. Lieutenant Celso thinks it might be the trail we've been searching for."

"Where does it lead?"

"Hopefully over a high pass that leads south into Ulmbartia—a different pass than the one they used to get here. The military has an outpost on the other side. If we can locate the pass from the wilderness, then go down and make the connection to the outpost, it would complete a big loop and tighten up the kingdom's borders. The Ulmbartians would know a lot more about the routes into their land. It's an important assignment."

"Daring exploits are your gift, Teo. Go find the pass, and don't worry about me."

He grinned. "Actually, I'll probably do both."

Ana shook her head with a *tsk*. She knew she could take care of herself, and she didn't want Teo to worry about her, though secretly she was glad he did.

"If you find the pass, then what?" she asked.

"Then the mission is over and we can go to Ulmbartia."

"I guess what I'm asking is, what's our plan? What's our . . . ?"

"Future?"

"Yeah."

"Here's what I'm thinking. We have to find a way to support ourselves. I'm a soldier, and the Ulmbartian army seems happy to have me. So I can earn a living by my sword, and we'll find a place to live."

"Together?"

"Well, at least near each other."

"And I could probably earn money spinning wool or something. Once we've gotten settled, we can start thinking about the bigger reason we came."

"You mean to tell people about Deu?"

"Right. And to find the rest of his book. The New Testament."

"You know about that?"

"You said it's in the table of contents of the Sacred Writing. It must be important. We should search for it in Ulmbartia."

"There's no guarantee we can locate it in this new land."

Ana sat up in her bedroll. "Maybe not. But there's one thing I *am* sure of."

"What?"

"If anyone in the world can find it, it's you."

Teo puffed his cheeks and blew out a breath. "I don't know about that. But with Deu's help, it could happen. For now, though, I'm more worried about finding the pass and keeping the Rovers off my back." He reached over and patted Ana's arm. "I have to get going. I'll see you tomorrow night, okay? Maybe you can fall back asleep now."

"No, I'll get up and see you off. Go on. I'm right behind you."

After Teo exited, Ana dressed quickly and followed him out. The men had already dismantled the other tent and saddled the horses. The expedition had brought four mounts and two packhorses, but with the addition of Teo, only one packhorse remained. It was loaded with supplies and the folded tent.

Bard spoke to Ana from the saddle. "Sorry to leave you, Anastasia. But I'm the tracker on this trip. It's for moments like this that they brought me along."

"Yeah, why else would we, Bardella?" The insult from one of the soldiers brought laughter from his companion. Bard ignored it.

"I'll take good care of Trusty," Ana said. "Or maybe he'll take care of me."

"Let's move out, men! The sky is already light." Lieutenant Celso's voice was all business.

Ana approached Teo as he began to ride away, putting her hand on his knee. "Come back to me," she said.

At those words, Teo caught Ana's eye. They broke into smiles. There was no need to answer, for each knew what the other was thinking. Long ago Teo had made a promise to Ana on the night he rescued her from the kidnappers' feasting hall. Fleeing in a driving rain, they had sheltered in an abandoned castle. As Ana lay shivering and exhausted in her bedroll, she had thanked Teo for coming to find her when no one else would. Without thinking, Teo had responded, "*I always will.*" It was a surprising remark, for at that time he hardly knew her. Even so, Ana had known it was true. And he had proven it ever since.

Teo winked at Ana, then turned his horse and prodded it into a trot to catch up to the other men. She stood alone in the clearing as Teo disappeared into the mist that shrouded the ancient trees.

A nose nuzzled Ana's hand, and she looked down to see Trusty's soulful eyes staring at her. She knelt and wiggled the bloodhound's droopy jowls. "It's just you and me now, Trusty. What do you say we get some breakfast?" As if to answer, Trusty licked her nose.

Ana grabbed a basket and left camp to forage for wildfowl eggs. By the time the sky was bright, she had located some ground nests. She was picking through them to find the good eggs when she noticed Trusty sniffing at something in the underbrush. Ana went to investigate. As her eyes fell on the round, white object under the hound's nose, her breath caught, and she stepped back. The object was a human skull.

"What've you got there, boy?" Ana's heart was beating fast as she knelt and inspected the skull. It seemed small, perhaps that of a woman or child. Tufts of hair and bits of flesh still adhered to its contours, indicating the person had died within the past few months. A few bones from the rest of the skeleton lay scattered about. Wild animals had devoured the body. Ana used a stick to roll the skull over. What she saw made her gasp.

Twin holes punctured the skull, and deep grooves were gouged into its surface.

This person was hunted as prey!

Suddenly wary, Ana glanced around the forest. Birds chirped from the branches. A squirrel ran along a limb. Sunbeams filtered through the leafy canopy. Ana uttered a nervous laugh and shook the fearful thoughts from her head. Whatever had made this kill was long gone. She picked up her basket and returned to camp, where she fried the eggs and washed them down with juniper tea.

She spent her day in the monotony of the campsite routine. Only Trusty provided any company, and Ana's conversations with him were decidedly one-sided. She mended some of the soldiers' torn clothing, wove a basket from dried sweetgrass, foraged for herbs and vegetables, and collected a supply of firewood for the "dining room." As the sun began to set, she ate a simple meal of bread, cheese, and berries, then lay on the grass and watched the fireflies dance among the trees.

When it was fully dark, Ana moved inside the comforting walls of the grotto. Crickets chirped nearby, and in the distance a wolf howled at the night sky. Ana stared at the campfire, feeling blue, missing her parents. She pictured her father, a warm and caring man who always smiled at her through his graying beard. Stratetix had often taken Ana on overnight hunting trips, and she could still recall the taste of the squirrel stew he used to cook on those campouts. Ana's thoughts drifted to her mother, Helena, the more outgoing partner in the marriage. Ana had always been proud to have inherited her mother's light amber hair and blue-green eyes, as well as her independent spirit.

Will I ever see them again?

Though she didn't know what her future held, Ana knew she couldn't return to Chiveis—not unless she was willing to deny her God.

O Deu! It's such a hard road you ask of me! I'm going to need your strength to walk it!

Tears gathered in her eyes, and she began to cry softly. Trusty's head swung around. He ambled over, laying his jowls in Ana's lap. For a long time they sat together in the stone circle, two lonely creatures in a wilderness neither called home. At last, when the sticks had burned down to embers, Ana stood up, arched the stiffness from her back, and retired to the tent.

By the light of a candle Ana undressed and set aside her amethyst earrings, then used her little comb to clear the tangles in her hair. Teo's rucksack sat in the corner. She stared at it, biting her lip, frustrated that it contained the book whose holy words she desperately wanted right now but could not have. Ana lifted the flap of the rucksack and laid the Sacred Writing on the tent floor. She wished Teo could somehow return from his mission to stretch out on his bedroll and read aloud the scriptures of Deu. It had become their bedtime ritual since they had joined the expedition: Teo would read, they would discuss the text, then say prayers before blowing out the light. Tonight, however, Ana knew there would be only silence.

The final third of the Sacred Writing had been destroyed by water, leaving the ending a mystery. Even so, plenty was left to read for anyone who knew the language. Ana thumbed the brittle pages, wishing she could decipher the words. The book was written in the Ancients' forgotten tongue. Only Teo, a part-time university scholar, could still read the archaic speech. Before leaving Chiveis he had translated several chapters of the Sacred Writing's first book, called Beginning, as well as many of the Hymns and the sweet story of Ruth. Through these new-found words of ancient scripture, Ana and Teo had discovered Deu, the Creator God.

Unfortunately, despite Teo's hard work, only one brief translation had made it with him into exile: Hymn 27. Ana slid the worn parchment from inside the book's cover, along with the red ribbon that had once bound it as a scroll. The hymn was the only portion of the Sacred Writing available in her language. Holding it toward the light, the opening lines caught her eye, and she knew they were meant for her at this very moment: "The Eternal One is my light and my salvation. Whom shall I fear? The Eternal One is the support of my life. Whom shall I dread?" Ana read the entire hymn, meditating on its message. As she reached the end, she let the final stanza become the cry of her soul:

> *Oh! What if I weren't certain to see the Eternal One's goodness in the land of the living?*
>> *Hope in the Eternal One!*
>> *Fortify yourself, and strengthen your heart!*
>> *Hope in the Eternal One!*

THE GIFT

It was a hymn to sleep on. Ana blew out the candle, and before long a deep slumber took her.

✦ ✦ ✦

A horrible sound jolted Ana awake. *Where am I?* She sat up in her bedroll, trying to climb out of her stupor. Danger was at hand, but sleep refused to release its hold. Blackness surrounded her. Outside, fierce snarling filled the air. Barking . . . growling . . . fighting—ferocious animals battling to the death.

A yelp pierced the night. Forlorn and desperate, it was the sound of a creature who knew its end had come. The other snarls intensified in bloodlust, and then abruptly the yelping ceased.

Trusty's gone.

I'm alone.

Fear gripped Ana's gut, but she beat it back and reached for the box of matches. With trembling fingers she withdrew a matchstick and struck it against the side of the box. The flame burst to life like a tiny warrior ready to do battle against the night. She lit the candle and threw aside the tent flap, holding the candle aloft as she peered outside. Shadows flitted among the trees but made no sound. Then she saw it: a pair of yellow eyes gleamed at her from the forest.

Wolves!

Ana's entire body shuddered, and she dropped the candle. Its light winked out. Frantic, she snatched the candle and ducked into the tent, striking another match. When she thrust the candle outside again, she was horrified to see that a huge black wolf had crossed half the distance from the trees to the tent. At the sight of the flame, the predator jumped back into the bushes.

A thought crystallized in Ana's mind: *Fire is my only defense.*

She glanced at the rock grotto. A dim glow illuminated its recesses, cast by the few surviving coals from her evening campfire. Nearby an extra hunting spear lay on a pile of supplies. There was no time to wait. Ana threw Teo's bearskin cloak around her shoulders and stepped from the tent. Holding the candle and matchbox in one hand and shielding the flame with the other, she began to ease across the clearing. The grass was wet under her bare feet. Beyond the candle's circle of light, several shadows slipped into the campsite, slinking low to the ground. A breeze stirred Ana's loose shift, and the candle's flame wavered.

Please, Deu! Don't let it go out!

She reached the spear, keeping her eyes on the dark forms creeping toward her. The black wolf grew bold, darting ahead, its ears erect, its tail thrust out. The thick fur on its neck stood up in a ruff.

Ana sucked in her breath as a wave of terror convulsed her. She dropped the matchbox. The top flipped open, spilling the contents on the ground. *No!* Ana crouched, staring at the black wolf as it stalked her. She could hear the low rumbling in its chest. Only the burning candle kept it from pouncing. Other stealthy shadows closed in behind the leader of the pack. Ana desperately patted the ground, feeling for a match. Her fingers found one. She thrust it into the candle's flame, then flicked the match toward the wolf. The flare-up halted the creature's advance, and Ana used the moment to grab the spear and dash inside the circle of rocks.

Flinging herself onto her belly, Ana blew into the embers of the campfire. The orange glow intensified, then a tiny tongue of flame curled up. Ana fed it pine twigs to increase the blaze. She added larger sticks and was about to add a few more but then glanced at the pile of firewood. Not much was left. If she used the supply conservatively, it might last until sunrise.

Ana could hear the wolves prowling around the campsite outside the grotto. One of them found a sack of provisions and tore it open with a ripping sound. The creatures yapped and barked as they fought over the supplies of dried venison and hard bread. *No matter—let them have it. They're not going to have me!* Ana put her back against a boulder and held the spear in her lap as she gazed across the tiny campfire. She studied the sky, trying to estimate when dawn would come.

As Ana was staring upward, the black wolf appeared in the grotto's entrance. Ana shrieked and recoiled. The fierce beast stood across from her, its nose wrinkled, its fangs bared. Ana grabbed a firebrand and thrust it toward her enemy, waving it and yelling. The creature retreated into the darkness. Ana panted as she fought to control her terror. If wolves could smell fear, she was rank with it.

Far away, a lone wolf bayed at the sky. The pack in the clearing responded with excited calls of their own. Soon the boisterous campsite grew silent. Ana no longer saw the shadowy forms pacing back and forth. She crept to the grotto's opening and held up her candle. No yellow eyes glowed from the trees. Relieved, she returned to her place next to the small pile of firewood, resolving to feed the flames until the sun came up. She drew her knees close and hunched into the bearskin cloak. Only her face and bare feet protruded into the night. On the ground next to her, the hunting spear lay close at hand.

The hours slipped by as the stars rolled through the heavens. Twig by twig, stick by stick, Ana kept the campfire going. Its coals glowed orange-white, seething in their innermost depths like worms writhing in the heat. The effect was mesmerizing as Ana stared at it. Her head drooped. She longed to close her eyelids.

No! Wake up!

Ana inhaled lungfuls of the cool night air, then slapped her face hard enough to sting. Though the wolves were gone, they might come back. She forced herself to remain alert.

A chill settled on the grotto. Ana's toes had grown cold, so she lowered herself against the boulder and stretched out her legs. Crossing her arms over her chest beneath the cloak, she extended her feet until they almost touched the flames. The warmth felt good as she wiggled her toes. Her chin nestled into the thick bearskin around her neck. Dawn was about an hour away.

It was the smell that awakened her—something wild and damp and reeking of carrion. Ana's eyes popped open. She froze. Across the firepit stood the black wolf, its lips curled in a snarl like an evil grin. Fresh blood stained its muzzle. The campfire had died to ashes.

The creature leaped across the grotto and slammed into Ana, its weight pinning her against the hard ground. She thrashed and fought as the wolf snapped at her neck. The bearskin cloak prevented the bites from finding their mark, offering mouthfuls of fur instead.

Ana reached for the spear, but her hand could find only a jagged stone, so she smashed it against the wolf's muzzle. The beast yowled and rolled away. Ana scrambled upright as the wolf regained its footing. Furious, it bared its bloody teeth, then sprang at its prey with unbelievable speed. Once again the bites found the loose fur cloak instead of flesh, but the creature was strong, and Ana felt herself being dragged down. She wriggled out of the cloak and hurled it over the wolf's head.

While the animal was entangled in the folds, Ana snatched the spear from the ground. She whirled to see her enemy rid itself of the encumbering cloak. Ana held the spear in two hands, feeling vulnerable in her thin chemise. She circled around the grotto as the wolf mirrored her every move. It lunged at her, but Ana's spear thrust forced it to dodge.

Before she could react, the beast came at her again, and this time its hungry bite found the flesh it sought. Strong jaws latched onto Ana's left hip. Searing agony exploded down her leg as the wolf's fangs ground into her pelvis. She started to fall. Off balance, she swung the spear as hard as she could, ramming the oaken shaft into the wolf's haunches. The animal let out a yelp and retreated.

Ana fell backward, landing on her rear with her legs splayed out. Her hip blazed, and her thigh was awash in blood.

The wolf rolled its malicious eyes, then bunched its muscles and pounced.

Ana saw the creature hurtling through the air—its black fur erect on its neck, its canines long and red, its paws stretching toward her. Screaming with a fury of her own, Ana stabbed the spear at the oncoming horror.

The blade took her enemy in the shoulder. Instead of receiving the impact of the charge, Ana collapsed backward, using the wolf's momentum to pitch it over her shoulder into the craggy wall of the grotto. She rolled onto her stomach. The spearhead had disappeared into the animal's thick ruff, but the shaft quivered as the wolf thrashed on the ground. Lying prone, Ana watched the fierce beast struggle and gnash as its life ebbed away. Its movements grew weaker. At last it lay still.

For a long time Anastasia rested on the ground, trying to recover her composure. The bite wound sent pain throbbing up her ribs and down her leg. She feared to look at it but finally realized that overcoming the wolf's attack was only the first step toward her survival. Wincing as she sat up, she lifted the hem of her shift and examined her injury in the morning twilight.

The wolf had latched onto the widest place in the curve of her left hip. Ana gasped as she saw the ragged laceration. Flesh was missing, and red muscle was visible in the wound. Her whole leg was smeared with sticky blood and bits of debris. Ana groaned and looked to the sky. *Help me, Deu!*

Swallowing and shaking her head, Ana cleared the despair from her mind and made a plan. *Fire. Water. Food. Clothing.* Her needs were reduced to the simplest elements of survival.

She wondered if she could stand up. Carefully she tried and found she could. Hobbling over to the dead wolf, she yanked the spear from its carcass, then leaned on it like a staff. As long as she kept her leg straight, she discovered she could limp around with a shuffling gait. Yet she knew her strength would not last. Time was running out.

Ana staggered out to the campsite, heading to the stream to fill a canteen and wash her wound. The water against the raw flesh was like a hot poker thrust into her side. She gasped and bit her lip hard, fighting off the dizziness that threatened to make her black out. Finally she caught her breath as the pain subsided. She pressed a wad of moss into the cut until the bleeding stopped.

Walking awkwardly, Ana went to the supply cache to collect the items she needed: a loaf of bread, more matches, and a spare soldier's jerkin to wear over her chemise. The outfit would look ridiculous, but it would protect her from the elements. The leather jerkin came to the middle of her thighs, which would allow her to raise it up to care for her injury. Ana shook her head with a rueful smile. The arrangement was immodest, but survival, not propriety, was her main concern right now.

Ana let out a long breath as she leaned on her spear shaft in the grotto. The exertion of the morning and the loss of blood had taken their toll. All she wanted to do was sit still, but she knew she needed one more thing. A campfire was essential in case the other wolves came back. Ana felt her leg beginning to stiffen. She dreaded the effort that would be required to obtain a sufficient amount of fuel, but the wood wasn't going to collect itself, so she struggled to her feet and limped to the forest.

The day had warmed. Sweat ran down her face as she hobbled around, gathering the easiest sticks. A soldier's belt enabled her to bind the wood so she could carry it over her shoulder. By the time she returned to her shelter and collapsed on the ground, she was exhausted. A warm, ticklish sensation on her leg told her the laceration had started oozing again, but she ignored it as she panted for breath. A fever was starting to cloud her mind, and a different kind of ache had begun to radiate from her hip. She gulped water from a canteen, then closed her eyes.

The sun was well past its zenith when Ana awoke. Feebly she reached for the loaf and chewed a few bites, then drank more water. She was incredibly thirsty. Her forehead felt hot, but at the same time her body was clammy. She labored to raise her garments to inspect her wound. The fair skin of her thigh was inflamed with angry red streaks. Ana knew of herbs that would draw out the infection, but she didn't have the strength to gather them.

For the next several hours she dozed off and on. As evening approached, Ana heard a distant sound that made her cringe: a wolf's howl, echoed by others in the pack. She crawled to the campfire and laid a few twigs in a pile, then lit a match with trembling hands on her fifth try. The twigs accepted the fire, and Ana nursed the flame until a few larger sticks could be added. Even in her semi-delirious state, she knew she didn't have enough fuel to last the night.

Ana slept again until a yipping among the trees woke her with a start. She shook her head and blinked, trying to clear the mental fog.

The fire had burned low. Shadows darted around the campsite. The wolves were back.

Please, Deu! Not another night of this!

Ana bent to the campfire and blew on it. A movement caught her eye, and she glanced up. A gray wolf stared at her from the opening of the grotto, its lips curled back from its teeth. Ana swallowed and held still. There was nothing else she could do.

Pounding hooves thundered into the clearing beyond the circle of rocks. The wolf squealed as a thick spear sent it tumbling across the ground. A man burst into the grotto and ran to the impaled wolf. Unexpectedly the creature's head flashed around, catching the man's shin in its teeth.

The man yanked his leg away and thrust his sword into the wolf's ribs, dispatching it without mercy. He turned and came to Ana's side.

"Ana, I'm here! It's Teo! Can you hear me?"

She nodded weakly.

"I'm going to take care of you, okay? I'm going to get you through this!"

He stroked her hair. Ana raised her hand and rested it on his shoulder.

"I knew you'd come, Teo."

She passed out.

CHAPTER

2

Lieutenant Celso, his two men-at-arms, and Teo stood outside the rock grotto considering their options. It was dawn. Ana was dozing after a fitful night, while Bard heated water to bathe her wound. He was better at that sort of thing than strategic planning.

"It doesn't look good," the lieutenant said. "I've seen strong young men die from an infection like this."

Teo winced.

"We could use herbs and stuff," one of the soldiers suggested.

"She's a fighter," the other added.

Teo frowned. He didn't like the idea of leaving Ana's fate to whatever weeds might be growing nearby. "Do you have any medicines in your supplies?"

"I know exactly what she needs for an infection like this, but unfortunately we don't have any with us," Lieutenant Celso said. "It's costly and hard to come by."

"What is it?"

"Bread-mold elixir."

"That doesn't sound like something that would do any good."

"I know it sounds strange, but believe me, it works. It's like a miracle. Our physicians make it with the help of the grappa distillers. They study the mold under special lenses and test it in dishes. It's difficult and expensive to make, and it doesn't keep long. But it has saved many a soldier's life. I'm afraid it's the only thing that can help Anastasia now."

"Deu is the one who will save Anastasia," Teo countered, "though he might use the elixir to do it. We're going to have to cut this mission short and return to your land. What's the quickest way back to Ulmbartia?"

Lieutenant Celso shot Teo a sharp look. "I'll give the orders around here, soldier."

Anger born out of deep concern for Ana flared in Teo's heart, but he remembered his place and swallowed the annoyed reply he wanted to make.

"I apologize, Lieutenant. Is it your intent to seek the medicine Anastasia needs?"

The other two men looked at Lieutenant Celso, and Teo could see they wanted him to say yes.

The expedition leader gazed into the distance as he considered his decision. At last he said, "Yes, it is my intent to get the medicine." The men breathed a collective sigh of relief. "But not in the way you might think," Celso added. "We cannot return over the pass by which we came— at least not in enough time to do Anastasia any good. There's only one way to help her. We must go forward."

Teo was startled. "Forward? Where?"

Lieutenant Celso caught the eyes of his men and silently called for courage. "Up the trail we found yesterday. It's a gamble, I know. We don't know what's beyond the new camp. There's a chance we're exploring a dead-end instead of the route we seek. However, if we're on the right track—and I think we are this time—then the pass into Ulmbartia should be a few leagues up the valley. The military outpost on the other side will have some medicine. It's the only place close enough to try."

"But, sir," one of the soldiers said, "we might wander around those high peaks for a long time while Anastasia weakens. By the time someone finds the pass, then rides down to the fort, then manages to get all the way back here, she'll be d—" He stopped and stared at his feet.

Teo looked at the faces of his new companions, so earnest and willing to help. He took charge again. "You're exactly right," he said, nodding. "She'll die if we leave her here. That's why we're taking her over the pass to the fort—and may Deu give us strength!"

Lieutenant Celso straightened his shoulders. "I concur. It's the only possible way. Pack up quickly, men. Don't take anything but food and necessities. Leave one horse unburdened. Teofil can ride double with our wounded friend, and they can switch horses along the way. Now move out."

The soldiers obeyed immediately, but Teo could sense their apprehension. They had ridden hard the day before, climbing high into the mountains to establish the forward camp. Now instead of enjoying a few days of rest, they were being asked to turn around and ascend the mountains again. Although no one complained, the atmosphere was tense. Only Bard seemed unbothered by the prospect of the arduous climb. The slender blond man bustled around, packing up food and discarding nonessentials. Although he carried himself in an effeminate way, Teo could see he was a capable soldier. Bard didn't deserve the constant teasing his comrades gave him.

In the rock grotto, Ana was quiet but alert. Teo knelt beside her. "What's happening?" she asked.

"We're taking you to an Ulmbartian fort to get some medicine for your wound. It won't be an easy ride, but I'll be with you the whole way. The sun is up, and it's time to go."

Ana nodded and started to stir, but Teo put his hand on her shoulder. He slid his arms under her back and knees, lifting her gently as she clung to his neck. He carried her to the horse and helped her up. Ana winced and held her leg straight but made no sound. Teo climbed into the saddle behind her, and she reclined against him.

"Been here before," she said wryly.

Teo chuckled, recalling the many times they had ridden together to escape danger. "Someday I'm going to get us a nice wagon that won't be so crowded." Ana laughed at the remark.

The expedition set out, following the big river that ran westward through the wild valley. On the right, across the mountains to the north, lay Chiveis. To the south was Ulmbartia—but it too was blocked by mountains, and only the undiscovered pass would give entrance to it.

The river valley was sunny and full of wild grapes, far more than could be grown in Chiveis. The vines clustered in large patches on sun-exposed slopes. Teo assumed the valley must have contained many vineyards in the time of the Ancients. The remains of those long-lost people were every-where: thick pillars that once supported elevated roads, crumbling houses peeking through the ivy, towers of metal lattice draped with limp wires, and occasionally a steel carriage rusting in the overgrowth. Teo studied a large building with the word *Migros* marked on it in orange letters. He didn't know what it meant.

Lieutenant Celso followed the landmarks until the party arrived at the tributary stream that signaled the turnoff to the south. The place had an odd feel to Teo, one he had often observed in the wilds. It seemed to be a blank spot where the remains of the Ancients were scarce or nonexistent. Teo pulled his horse alongside Lieutenant Celso. "Why do you suppose there are no ancient structures here?" he asked.

Lieutenant Celso's eyes remained fixed on the landscape. "Our lore tells us the Ancients knew how to make powerful fires that could destroy everything for many leagues around. I can't imagine such a thing."

Leaning against Teo, Ana whispered to him, "Astrebril's fire." The term referred to an evil powder dedicated to a Chiveisian god. Teo had learned the secret of making it. In fact, he had unintentionally brought a book of instructions with him into exile, stuffed into a pocket of his ruck-sack. He said nothing further about the deadly concoction.

Lieutenant Celso turned toward Ana. "I think we've pushed you hard enough today, Anastasia. It's late now. Let's get some rest. Tomorrow it'll be time to start climbing."

After making Ana comfortable on a bed of soft boughs, Teo helped her rinse her wound with water. The skin around the cut was a garish red. Teo applied a poultice of crushed garlic to draw out the infection, then read the Sacred Writing to Ana before she fell asleep.

By midafternoon the next day, the party reached the forward camp they had established three days earlier. The site was near the tree line, with bare, stony peaks reaching for the sky in every direction. A gray overcast had settled in, threatening rain. Though it was summertime, snow patches still clung to the highest summits. The soldiers knew they were at a very high elevation and were headed even higher. Their faces betrayed the sense of intimidation men feel when the scale of nature expands beyond them, reminding them of their fragility.

Lieutenant Celso gathered his party and pointed at the dim track leading toward the heights. "There it is, men! After six seasons of exploring, we've come down to this. We have to believe this is the pass we've been looking for. Today we're going to cross it and become Ulmbartian heroes! What do you say?"

The commander's pep talk was greeted by awkward silence. Although Teo was still struggling to catch all the words in Talyano, he understood enough to know the speech had been intended as motivational, but the men were too daunted right now to appreciate it.

Bard spoke up. "We'll do it for Anastasia!" he cried.

"For Anastasia!" the other men answered.

From her place in the saddle with Teo, she smiled weakly and raised her hand. "Thank you . . . brave men."

Lieutenant Celso turned his horse toward Teo. "I think a moment like this calls for prayer to a deity who reigns over everything. Ask your god for his favor, Teofil."

With the men circled around him and Ana in his arms, Teo raised his voice to the sky and invoked Deu's protection and healing. As soon as he finished praying, a light rain began to fall—not the answer he had hoped for. Teo kicked his heels against the horse's flank and led the way up the mountain slope.

The Ancients had built a road here. Its paving had long since been destroyed by the harsh elements, but Teo could barely pick out—often with the help of Bard's observant eye—a path that could still be followed. At one point they passed a metal sign whose letters were partially visible.

"Can you read it?" Lieutenant Celso asked.

"It's a lost language of the Ancients. In my homeland we called it the Fluid Tongue." He studied the sign until he could make out some of the letters: *COL DU GD ST*. Teo broke into a smile. "It says 'pass of' something," he announced. The men cheered.

Emboldened by the sign's encouragement, the expedition pushed upward through the constant wind and spitting rain. They reached the top just before nightfall. An oblong lake lay in the foreground, and more mountains stretched away to the south. Just beyond the lake was a gap in the peaks, leading down. Near the gap was a sturdy stone building that had survived from ancient times.

Teo whispered into Ana's ear, "We made it," but she was asleep in the saddle and did not reply. Her head lolled to the side. She was very pale. Teo held her close, his arms around her waist. The journey had taken a heavy toll on her. With sudden understanding, Teo realized that more travel would be her end.

Lightning flashed in the distant, ominous clouds. Teo turned to Lieutenant Celso. "She can go no farther."

"I think not," he answered gravely. "We will shelter in that stone building."

"I will descend to the outpost at first light. Send one of the soldiers with me."

Celso glanced toward the ground. Teo followed his eyes. Hoofprints were pressed into the mud. Rover tracks, less than two days old.

"If we're attacked, we can't defend the building with fewer than four men," Celso said.

"Ana will die if she doesn't get the medicine."

"And she will die if the Rovers take us."

"She has to have the elixir!"

Lieutenant Celso looked Teo in the eye. "I need four men to defend the building. I am responsible for this expedition. I will not risk my soldiers' lives by sending them into the wilds." He paused, then gave Teo a sly grin. "You, however, are a hired mercenary. In my commander's eyes you are dispensable, if you get my meaning."

Teo nodded to the lieutenant. "Thank you, sir." He turned his horse. Ana was like a rag doll in his arms. He tightened his grip on her. "I will leave at dawn. You can be certain I will return."

◆　◆　◆

Bard wrung out the cold compress and laid it on Anastasia's forehead. She moaned a little in her sleep but otherwise lay still.

The room was small and wood-paneled. Bard rose and peered out the window at the dreary, early-morning rain. The Ancients had built this squat, sturdy building of gray stone next to the lake to serve as an inn for travelers crossing the pass. The lower floors had a bar, restaurant, kitchen, and common room, while the upstairs rooms housed the guests. All the windows had been boarded shut. Of course, several hundred winters had taken their toll, so that today most of the boards were missing, and the once-comfortable inn was filled with rotted furniture and natural debris. Picking their way through the mess, the Ulmbartian soldiers had discovered one guest room that still had its door closed and its window-panes intact behind the boards. These had protected the room from the elements. While the pink-tiled bathroom attached to the chamber no longer supplied running water to the clever Ancients, Bard had decided that guest room 15 would still make a decent place to house a lovely guest from a much later era. He grimaced and turned to look at the feverish Anastasia. *A guest who is dying from an infected wolf bite*, he reminded himself. Bard returned to her bedside and wiped her cheeks with the wet cloth.

There was a knock at the door, then Lieutenant Celso entered. "How is the lady?"

"Not good," Bard answered. "Restless and running a fever."

"The wound?"

Bard folded back Teofil's bearskin cloak, which served as Anastasia's covering. A slit had been cut in her leather jerkin and linen shift to provide access to her wound while preserving modesty. Removing the bandage, he wiped away some pus from the inflamed gash. He had already numbed it with a tincture of poppies and closed it with stitches.

Lieutenant Celso winced. "Hmm. That's ugly."

"It's worse than it was," Bard agreed.

"Can she hear us?"

"I doubt it."

"I think she's going to die," Celso whispered.

Bard ignored the comment. Retrieving a fresh bandage, he smeared it with poultice and laid it against Anastasia's septic wound. She flinched, and her eyes fluttered open.

"Whe . . . where . . ." She closed her eyes again. "Teo?" she asked weakly.

Bard leaned close and spoke gently. "Just rest now, Anastasia. Teofil

47

is fine. He's gone to get you some medicine. It's not far, and it's quite safe, and he won't be much longer." Her expression relaxed as she slipped into a doze again. Bard looked up and met Celso's eyes. The men exchanged glances, then turned and left the room together.

"You know that's not true," Celso said in the hallway.

"Of course I know it, sir. But she needs hope. She's bound to Teofil. Everything now rests on him."

"Well then, I hope his god has the power to help him."

Bard frowned as he nodded. "I guess we'll find out."

◆　◆　◆

Teo's horse was tired. He had pushed it hard all day, covering close to forty leagues down the steep pass and along the wild river valley. Now, as night began to fall, the animal's head hung low with exhaustion. Water dripped from its flanks, and from Teo's cloak too, although for the moment the clouds were holding back their rain.

Ahead, on top of a rocky promontory, stood a castle. Teo had seen it from a distance and recognized it as the one Lieutenant Celso had described. It was the kind of fortress built by the Ancients long before their Great War of Destruction wiped them out. For centuries the castle had lain abandoned in the wilderness, but now it was no longer uninhabited. The thin line of smoke rising from a chimney indicated that a squad of Ulmbartian soldiers had claimed the castle as their own frontier outpost.

As Teo rode along, a dull ache throbbed in his shin where he had been bitten by the wolf that tried to attack Ana. It occurred to Teo that the wound might be getting infected like hers, but since he had no time for an infected leg on a mission of such urgency, he decided he would simply ignore it. Maybe it wasn't infected anyway. Maybe it just hurt a little as it was healing.

Teo knew he could have approached the castle unobserved. He had been well trained in woodland stealth. However, he rode in the open toward the castle, hoping to appear as a friend, not a threat. The sentries had no way of knowing he was a mercenary in their army. Teo turned his horse onto a grassy path that seemed to wind toward the castle.

"Halt where you are!"

The command rang out from the woods, accompanied by an arrow that lodged itself in the dirt in front of Teo's horse. If the archer had raised the bow a few degrees, he could have put the arrow through Teo's chest.

"I mean no harm," Teo called out in the Ulmbartian tongue. "I am an ally of your people, seeking aid." He hoped his accent was good enough that the sentry might actually believe him.

"Who are you?" The sentry sounded uncertain.

"A soldier of fortune employed by Ulmbartia. I've been sent on a mission from Lieutenant Celso. See here: I have his signet." Teo nudged his horse forward and held up the gold ring.

A second arrow hissed past Teo's head. "Do not come any closer! Perhaps you are a thief who took it from the lieutenant."

"How then would I know his name? Or that of his wife, Isotta? We have spoken of her often during the month I've served under his command. He gave me his ring as proof I have come from him."

The sentry stepped from the forest, a boyish soldier with a thin frame. Two other men emerged from the undergrowth behind him, while a fourth could be heard departing toward the castle through the brush.

The young leader gestured with his drawn sword. "You will throw your weapons to the ground, dismount, and follow us. Commander Duilo will see you."

Teo complied with the sentry's order and was led to the imposing fortress on the hill. Even in the waning light, he could see the place was strong and well built. It was constructed as a single building like a keep, not an enclosure with a courtyard. Only a few windows punctuated its massive walls. The castle had battlements on top and towers at its corners, some round, the others square.

Firelight flickered in a hearth as Teo entered. He was escorted to a room marked off by curtains. It was a well-appointed area with a desk, a bed, and a rug on the floor. Lanterns illuminated the space. A trim, battle-hardened commander rose from the desk to confront Teo.

"Give me the ring," he said gruffly.

Teo handed it to him.

"You are a friend of Lieutenant Celso's, you say?"

Teo nodded. "I was hired as a man-at-arms in exchange for food and shelter. Now I am on a mission of mercy from him."

"Your accent is terrible, and your grammar is jumbled, yet you speak our language well enough. How is this so?"

"I picked it up from the men. Languages come easy to me."

"If you are Celso's friend, he will no doubt have told you how he got the little scar above his eyebrow."

"He said a cowardly cadet at military school bit him in a fight."

Commander Duilo burst into laughter, standing for a long time with his hands on his hips and his head thrown back. Finally he shook his head in disbelief.

"Don't you believe it! That mangy old dog head-butted me in the teeth! Didn't help him, though. He lost that fight. We go way back, Celso and I. He's a good man." Commander Duilo waved the sentries out of the room, then pointed to a canvas chair. "Sit down, son, and tell me your name and why you're here."

Cold sausages and ale were brought as Teo recounted the story of the wolf attack. Soon the implications of Teo's presence at the castle began to dawn on Commander Duilo.

"Wait a minute," he said, holding up his hands. "You mean you've come from the wilderness? Over the pass? You actually found it?"

"We did. If you continue up this valley, then branch to the right at a certain point, there's a way over the mountains."

The news put Commander Duilo in good spirits. Clasping his hands behind his head and propping up his feet, he announced he was more than willing to provide the bread-mold elixir, along with a fresh horse and supplies for a return to the pass. "You can leave as soon it's light enough to see your way," he said. "But I can't send any men. The Rovers have my troops tied up, and it'll be four days before a new detachment arrives from headquarters."

After thanking the commander profusely, Teo was shown to a cot in a corner of the fort, where he removed his boots and settled in for a few hours of sleep. A headache pounded in his temples, and the bite on his shin hurt, but Teo was relieved to have already achieved so much in his mission to save Ana.

However, when the camp physician arrived with the medicine, Teo was disappointed at his news. The frontier outpost had only two bottles of the precious stuff, and one was of doubtful value because it was beyond its normal shelf life. The doctor explained that the other bottle was from a more recent batch and would likely be sufficient. He handed Teo a wooden case containing the good and the questionable medicine, describing the dosages before he left.

As Teo set the case under his cot, he found himself wishing he had something more reliable than a single bottle of the good medicine. *You do*, said a voice in his head. Teo chided himself for his lack of faith and prayed for Ana's safety until his weariness finally overcame him.

The next morning he left the fort an hour before sunrise with the vials of bread-mold elixir stowed in his saddlebag. Wisps of fog clung to the trees as Teo rode northwest. The overcast sky had lightened to a dull gray when he paused at a bend in the trail. Suddenly he heard a sound that sent ice water coursing through his veins.

A man's shout.

Teo looked up to see a party of eight Rovers in the distance, mounted on horseback. For the briefest moment, everyone remained frozen. Then, with fierce expressions etched on their faces, the men raised their weapons and charged.

To flee was useless. The Rovers would run him down. Teo knew he must use the element of surprise by standing and fighting. One thing was certain: he did not intend to die this day.

Unlike his enemies, Teo had been anticipating danger, so his bow was already strung. He whipped an arrow from his quiver and loosed it at the lead rider, who took the hit in the body and tumbled from his horse. The Rovers had not expected Teo to sit calmly and aim from the saddle, and they certainly had not expected such superb accuracy at this range. He took down a second rider before the war party closed upon him. Now his bow was useless. It was time for the bite of steel. Teo drew his ax and sword, then kicked his horse's flanks and leaped into the fray.

With the thunder of churning hooves and wild war cries ringing in his ears, Teo galloped toward the oncoming riders. The trail wasn't wide enough for them to fan out, so they had to follow each other in pairs. Two

Rovers rode at the front, wearing fur-trimmed garments and iron helmets. Instead of crashing directly into his enemies, Teo slid his mount between them, his arms spread wide. As he swept past at full speed, the ax in his left hand parried a thunderous blow, while the sword in his right slashed a rider's shoulder in a burst of crimson spray.

No sooner had the men passed than the second pair of riders was on him. Teo dodged sharply left so only one rider could attack. The enemy swung his sword in a vicious arc as Teo galloped by. Teo's weapons were out of position for a parry, so he leaned far out of his saddle. He felt the sword's tip whiz past his head.

The final two riders did not intend to let Teo escape. Their eyes were black and mean as they bore down on him. Before he could react or evade, the riders slammed into him. Teo felt the impact like a thousand clubs striking him at once. The horses screamed, and Teo was hurled from the saddle as his mount went down. His weapons were knocked from his hands as he cartwheeled across the rocky ground.

Rolling to his feet, Teo had no time to pause for breath. He snatched his sword and ax, knowing his enemies were turning their horses in the narrow trail to make another charge.

Though he would never have left the saddle intentionally, being unhorsed gave Teo one advantage: he could weave through the under-brush, making it difficult for a rider to follow. He sprinted toward the forest and ducked into a thicket.

Something flashed in Teo's peripheral vision. He leaped out of the way as a heavy weapon split the air beside him. Teo spun to confront an enraged Rover rushing at him. The burly man had an arrow shaft protruding from his left shoulder, but his right arm held a massive club, and his face bore a look of incredible malice.

Teo clicked a gemstone on the handle of his ax. The weapon was an ingenious gift from one of his former students back in Chiveis. The haft held cherry-sized metal balls that could be expelled into a cup at the ax's end. A strong flicking motion would send the balls flying toward an opponent with greater force than a human arm alone could achieve.

Growling, the Rover raised his club behind his head. Teo sent a ball flying toward his enemy. It bounced off a rib with a loud crack. The Rover's face blanched and contorted into a grimace. He dropped his club and clutched his side, moaning and writhing. Teo disappeared into the brush.

Mounted Rovers crashed through the forest as Teo dodged among the trees. He paused only to sheath his sword and tuck his ax into his belt before resuming his erratic course through the woods. Arriving at a river, he plunged into the water without stopping to catch his breath. He surfaced only once before reaching the far bank. His pursuers rode back and forth on the other side.

One of the men spotted him and shouted, but Teo knew crossing the river on horseback would take a lot of effort. The Rovers had little reason to pursue him now that they had captured his saddlebag with whatever loot they thought might be inside. They began to disperse.

Teo pounded his fist into his palm. Truth be told, there wasn't any loot. He was only carrying soldiers' rations and two bottles of the mysterious elixir that Ana desperately needed. She was dying at the top of a distant pass—and now he could do nothing to stop it.

The situation infuriated him. As he knelt dripping in the forest while the Rovers left the riverbank, a deep indignation rose in his soul. *Who do they think they are, attacking an innocent man without provocation and taking a sick woman's medicine!* Teo decided he would reclaim the medicine or die in the attempt. Death would be preferable to returning empty-handed, only to watch Ana's life ebb away. A future without Ana would be unbearable.

He recrossed the river and followed the Rovers' tracks. The smell of wood smoke told him they had set up camp nearby to tend their injuries. He had drawn blood from at least three of them, and now they were licking their wounds.

From the vantage point of an outcrop, Teo could see seven men around the campfire. One had removed his outer garment and was rubbing a salve into a deep slice on his right shoulder. Another applied cold water to his misshapen forearm, an injury no doubt sustained when his horse fell to the ground. The third wounded man, the big Rover whom Teo had met in the forest, was stanching the flow of blood from the arrow hole in his shoulder. An ugly red welt discolored his ribs. Four uninjured men were busy aiding their comrades, making a total of seven. It took Teo a moment to locate the eighth. He lay to the side of the camp with an arrow sticking out of his chest. A cloth was draped over his face.

A short distance away seven horses were tied to the trees. Two others stood with a foreleg off the ground, one of which was Teo's own mount. He spied his bow, quiver, and saddlebag lying with the rest of the men's gear. The saddlebag's buckles were still fastened, indicating nothing had been removed.

Teo considered approaching with stealth but quickly decided it would be impossible to reach the gear without being seen, much less untie a horse and escape. It was time to act boldly. He took a deep breath and broke into a run.

The Rovers shouted when they saw him, but Teo ignored them. He sprinted to his saddlebag and scooped it up, along with his bow and quiver. The uninjured men rose to give chase, but Teo was fast, and he soon outdistanced them. They were mounted fighters, not skilled woodsmen, and the forest was dense. Turning briefly, Teo loosed some arrows to force his pursuers to duck for cover, then resumed his sprint. When he paused to listen again, the sound of the Rovers had diminished. Evidently they had seen enough action for one day.

Slowing to a jog, Teo maintained a steady pace for about an hour. At last he stopped at a stream and drank deeply, then dug a hunk of dried beef from the saddlebag. He was gratified to see that the case of medicine was still there.

Teo slung the saddlebag over his shoulder and set off again. Though the high pass was thirty leagues away, he intended to go straight there. Teo resolved to run all day up the side of the mountain without stopping. It would be the longest, hardest run he had ever attempted, but he would do it. Ana needed him.

By the time he reached the landmarks that signaled the turnoff toward the pass, a light rain had started to fall. Teo's woolen cloak was rolled up with his bedding on his saddle, so he couldn't add an outer layer to shed the water. The rain began to fall harder. Soon he was drenched to the skin.

As the trail became steep, he began to feel the effects of the long-distance run. Though he was in good condition, the recent days had been arduous, and his body was reaching its outer limits. His thigh muscles burned, and his lungs seemed incapable of providing enough air. Teo's gait became less efficient, which only made matters worse. The wolf bite to his shin started to hurt with a stabbing pain instead of a dull ache. A few times his vision began to swim. He shook his head and squinted to clear the blur. Every part of him wanted to stop and rest, but Teo refused to listen to his body's demands. He had Ana's life-giving elixir in his bag. The thought of her lying in bed with her life slipping away kept him running even when his body cried out for relief.

A thunderstorm caught Teo as he emerged from the tree line. He knew it was dangerous to be in the high country with lightning flashing around, but there was no shelter nearby and he had no other choice. *Deu, protect me*, he prayed. *Help me make it to the top!* He glanced at the peaks far above, then immediately wished he hadn't. It seemed he had just as far to go as when he first began to climb.

Rain dripped from his hair and trickled beneath his jerkin. Water had long since soaked through the lacing of his boots, aggravating the blisters that had developed. At one point Teo stumbled and fell headlong in the muck. Dazed, he spat mud from his lips, then struggled to his feet and resumed his stride. Step-by-step he pressed upward.

The trail followed the ancient roadbed, snaking back and forth across the flanks of the barren mountains. It seemed to have no end. The hours of running made Teo delirious. His mind was a fog, his thoughts jumbled and confused. It took all his mental effort just to keep moving. His legs were like leaden weights. His chest heaved. Twice he vomited along the trail.

The rain ceased, and Teo stumbled on. The trail topped out. Bright light engulfed him, and he looked up. A brilliant sunbeam shone through a hole in the clouds. A stone cross illuminated by the sun's rays stood on a rocky knoll. Just beyond the cross was the ancient inn where Ana lay waiting. Teo collapsed in the doorway as Bard rushed to his side.

✦   ✦   ✦

Ana woke to the sounds of men moving around her room. She tried to lift her head but couldn't. Even her eyelids felt too heavy to lift. Her throat was parched. She swallowed, but it didn't help. Despite the bearskin cloak on her bed, she was chilled.

Ana was dying, and she knew it.

"Help me get his boots off," Lieutenant Celso barked.

"I'm—I'm okay."

Ana's heart skipped a beat. She knew that voice. Its familiar sound flooded her with relief and gave her the strength to open her eyes. Teo lay on the bed next to hers. He looked terrible. His clothes were filthy, and his face was pale. Even so, she was overjoyed to see him.

"We need to take off these wet clothes and get some food in him," Bard said.

"Go make hot broth. I'll take care of his clothing."

Bard left the room, and Ana rested on her pillow, listening to the sounds of Lieutenant Celso struggling with Teo's garments. Teo tried to speak, but his words were incoherent.

One of the other soldiers entered the room. "I found it, sir!" The man was holding a wooden case.

"Bring it here," Lieutenant Celso ordered. He opened the case and removed two bottles. Turning to Teo, he slapped him lightly on the chin. "Can you hear me, soldier? Wake up." He opened a canteen and splashed a little water on Teo's face.

"Huh? What? Huh?" Teo tried to sit up, but the lieutenant pressed him back into his bed.

"Easy there, Teofil. I just need to know what to do with this medicine. How much do I give her?"

Teo took a deep breath and lifted his head, staring the lieutenant in the eyes. "There's a spoon in the box. One dose, morning, noon, night, until the bottle is empty."

"Then she'll be well?"

Teo nodded and sank back on the mattress.

"It's a good thing they sent two bottles," Lieutenant Celso said. "That wolf bite of yours is infected too. You're both going to need the elixir."

Ana glanced at Teo's bare leg resting on the covers. An inflamed sore festered on his shin, with red streaks radiating from it. She remembered how he got that wound as he charged into the rock grotto to save her from the marauding wolves. *Like he always does*, she thought.

Lieutenant Celso started to stand up with the two bottles, but Teo gripped his sleeve.

"What is it, son?"

Teo pulled him close and gestured to the bottles. "See the notch?"

The lieutenant glanced at the bottles. "Carved into the cork?"

"Right. Now listen to me." Teo's tone grew serious. "That one is Ana's. Do you hear me? Give that one to her!"

"Okay, but why?"

"Swear to me!" Teo demanded with urgency in his voice.

"I swear it, Teofil. The bottle with the notched cork goes to the lady. What's the story?"

Teo closed his eyes and swallowed. "The other bottle probably won't work. It's too old."

As Ana listened to Teo utter these words, alarm seized her. *It won't work?* She was dumbfounded. *What does he mean, 'It won't work'?* Her clouded mind struggled to comprehend Teo's statement.

"You mean only one of these bottles is any good?" Lieutenant Celso frowned. "I have two sick patients here, and you both need the medicine!"

Teo's reply was emphatic. "You swore it, Celso. None of the good stuff goes to me. All to her. I'll take my chances."

The lieutenant's shoulders slumped. He set the two vials on an old barrel that served as a bedside table. "Then Deu be with you," he said. "Your god is the only one who can help you now." He exited the room. Teo sank into his bed, his eyes closed.

Ana extended a shaky hand and grasped one of the bottles—the one with the notched cork. *Give me strength*, she prayed.

◆　　◆　　◆

Sunshine sparkled on the breeze-ruffled lake at the high pass. It was a beautiful blue-sky day, but Teo didn't care. He was as depressed as he had ever been in his life.

Please, Deu! Have mercy on Ana!

She hadn't moved for days. The pallor of her sickness lay on her gaunt face like a death mask. Her normally curvy body was stick-thin and wasted. Her wrists were like twigs, her legs long and bony. No one knew what to do.

Teo put his face in his hands as he sat on a bench outside the inn. *Deu! Help her!*

The bread-mold elixir had worked wonders on Teo. Though the doctor at the Ulmbartian outpost had thought the batch was past its useful date, apparently the potion still had enough healing power to do its job. Within twenty-four hours, the redness in Teo's wound had subsided, and his fever had broken. The next day he was able to walk around a little bit, and his appetite returned with a vengeance. Now, on the third day, he was feeling like a new man.

But Ana had fared just the opposite. She continued to spiral down as the infection laid claim to her body. She couldn't eat anything; the thin broth offered to her just dribbled down her chin. She slept constantly. Day by day she grew weaker. It was only a matter of time until . . .

No!

Teo shook his head to clear away the horrific thoughts that plagued him. He stared at the sky and found himself frustrated with the Creator God's absolute silence. Holding up his palms, he supplicated the blue expanse. *Hear me, Deu! She has the good medicine! Why won't you make it work?*

Teo reached into the rucksack on the bench next to him and drew out his only source of comfort. He had spent the morning translating a new passage from the Sacred Writing. Deu had led him to the twenty-second Hymn. Its words were appropriate for a man in distress:

My Deu! My Deu!
Why have you abandoned me?
Why do you make yourself distant without helping me,
without hearing my groans?
My Deu!
I cry to you by day, and yet you do not respond.
I cry by night, and yet I have no rest at all.

Nevertheless, you are the Holy One.
You sit enthroned in the midst of Israël's praises.
Our fathers trusted in you;
they confided in you, and you delivered them.
To you they cried out, and were saved.
They put their trust in you;
and they were in no way wrong to do so.

The holy words comforted Teo, and he meditated on them, reminding himself of Deu's character. His journey with this God was still new, yet Teo had learned from the Sacred Writing and from direct personal experience that Deu could be trusted. Of course, it wasn't always easy. *But I am in no way wrong to do so,* Teo affirmed to himself.

Lieutenant Celso emerged from the stone building and sat down on the bench next to Teo. "Nice to see the sun again, eh, soldier?"

Teo nodded.

The lieutenant handed Teo his medicine bottle and spoon. "Here's your noontime dose," he said. Lieutenant Celso had taken it upon himself to guard the precious elixir and personally administer every spoonful. Teo knew the stalwart commander and his men were mystified at Ana's failure to recover. A sense of gloom pervaded the camp.

The other two Ulmbartian soldiers and Bard rounded the corner, carrying a field-dressed goat lashed to a pole. As they approached, Bard stumbled, and the carcass fell in the gravel.

"Watch out, Bardella!" one of the men yelled.

"You little weakling," the other man sneered. "You're like a woman."

"It's heavy," Bard protested. "I slipped."

As the men began to mock Bard, Lieutenant Celso rose and went back inside, shaking his head with a disgusted air.

"What good are you, Bardella?" shouted one of the soldiers as the other man cuffed him on the shoulder.

"Enough!"

Teo's tone was authoritative. The two men stopped their harassment and turned to stare at him.

"Bard is part of this mission just like the rest of us. Leave him alone."

"You're a man's man, Teofil. Why are you taking *his* side?" The taller of the two soldiers jerked his thumb toward Bard.

"Yeah," the other man agreed. "He's not like us."

Teo stood up and looked the two men in the eyes. "He *is* like us. He was made by Deu, the same as you and me. Bard has been at Anastasia's side the whole time she's been sick. In my book that makes him a friend."

The two soldiers frowned at the mention of Anastasia. Teo knew their tempers were short because of their concern for her. They were taking out their frustration on Bard like distressed children abusing the household dog.

The taller soldier swatted his hand. "Whatever," he huffed, turning to leave.

"Just make sure you wipe off any pebbles before you cook the meat," said the second man as he walked away. "I don't want to break a tooth."

Teo watched them go, then turned to Bard, who had a funny expression on his face.

"Thanks, Teofil," he said awkwardly. He gestured to the bench. "You should rest."

Bard and Teo sat on the bench in the sunshine and conversed for a while about trails and woodcraft and navigating through wild lands. It was the first time Teo had ever talked to Bard one on one. Though the Ulmbartian tracker was animated and emotive, Teo found Bard's mannerisms didn't bother him. Teo even caught himself laughing as he talked—something he hadn't done much of lately.

"Is this your medicine?" Bard picked up the bottle and held it to the sun.

"Yeah, that's the stuff. Mine wasn't supposed to work, but somehow it did. Lieutenant Celso has been a drill sergeant in administering it."

"What do all these marks mean?" Bard pointed to the label on the vial.

Teo glanced at Bard. "You can't read?"

"Few in Ulmbartia can," Bard answered defensively.

"Right. Well, those are words written in your language. Most of it is medical lore. These letters here tell what's in the bottle. See this?" Teo traced his finger along the words and sounded them out. "Bread . . . mold . . . elixir."

Bard did a double take. "What? Those marks right there? That says 'bread-mold elixir'?"

"Yeah. Why is that so surprising?"

Bard stared at Teo with his eyes wide and his mouth agape.

"What is it?" Teo held up his hands in bewilderment.

"Teofil!" Bard gripped Teo's sleeve. "I have a bottle with those exact marks among my cooking spices!"

"You *what?*"

"It's true! I have a bottle with those marks on it! I thought it was just some nasty seasoning that had turned sour. I was going to return the bottle to headquarters to be reused."

Teo jumped to his feet. "Show me!"

◆　◆　◆

"Ooh! It's so cold!"

"It's refreshing, though, isn't it?"

"Hmm. I don't know. You tell me." Ana kicked her toes, splashing lake water onto Teo.

He gasped. "You're right! It *is* cold!" He flicked water back at her with his foot, eliciting a squeal.

Ana laughed at the lighthearted moment. It was her first time out of the inn since Bard's elixir had been discovered almost a week ago, and she was in a good mood. Now she felt strong enough to lean on Teo's arm and take a short walk along the lakeshore. They had stopped to rest at the water's edge.

"What's on the bottom of your foot?" Ana asked.

Teo examined his sole. "It's a birthmark."

"Three little dots in a triangle? It looks too perfect to be a birthmark. More like a tattoo."

"No. I've had it ever since I was a baby."

"I wish I had known you when you were younger."

"Hey! You make it seem like I'm an old man now."

"Well, you are almost thirty," she said impishly, "whereas I'm just a mere twenty-five."

Teo smiled. "I can see the old Ana has returned—that feisty girl I brought over the mountains."

"You made me come," Ana reminded him, flopping back in the grass.

Teo lay beside her. For a while they watched the puffy clouds float through the sky. "Deu made us come," Teo said at last.

"Yeah, I know."

"I'm glad he healed you, Ana." Teo's voice cracked a little. Ana glanced at him but said nothing. "It's strange," he continued. "I put all my hopes in a little green bottle, but Deu caused it not to work. Then, just when I had almost given up, he supplied another bottle. It was completely unexpected—and yet we had it with us all the time!"

"Deu is like that," Ana said. "Full of twists and turns. He's an adventurous God."

"That's for sure." Teo rubbed his chin stubble and stared into the distance. "I wonder why he made the good medicine fail. That's really strange. I suppose we'll never know the answer."

Ana smiled and closed her eyes, letting the sun's warmth caress her cheeks. *Someday I'll tell him about that,* she thought to herself, *but not right now. Teo wouldn't understand why I switched the corks.*

CHAPTER

3

Teo burst into the common room at the inn. "Hey, Ana, I've been out exploring, and I've found some stuff I want you to see." He nodded over his shoulder to the door. "Come take a look."

Ana arched her eyebrows and set down the needle and thread with which she was mending a shirt. "Always exploring new horizons, aren't you, Captain?"

"Don't forget, I'm not a captain here. Just a lowly mercenary."

Teo's words weren't bitter, yet he couldn't escape the reminder that his exile from Chiveis had meant the complete loss of his social standing. Back home he was a high-ranking member of a renowned military regiment and also a respected professor. Now he was just an unknown foreigner with a blade for hire.

Even so, he didn't mind Ana calling him Captain. It was how she often referred to him, and he rather liked it. At first it had been a formal designation when she didn't know him well. Now she continued to use it in a playful way, almost like a term of endearment. "Come on," he said. "Follow your captain outside and see what I've found. It has to do with Deu."

Ana rose from her seat, immediately interested. "Is it related to the big cross?" Everyone had noticed the stone monument on a knoll behind the inn. Teo and Ana knew the cross was Deu's symbol, though they didn't know why.

"Yes, and there's something else too." Teo led Ana outside. Though

63

she walked stiffly, she had become much more mobile during the past week.

"Look here," he said, pointing to the ground.

"Look at what?"

"Right there. It's a corner. Cut stone."

"Oh, I see. It must have been a foundation for a building."

"Too small for that."

"What then?"

"It was a pedestal. A monument built by the Ancients used to stand here."

"Do you think it was another cross, like the one over there?" She pointed to the knoll a short distance away.

"I thought so at first. But when I looked more closely, I found something sticking out of the earth." Teo beckoned for Ana to follow him to an object partially excavated from the soil.

"A statue!" she exclaimed.

It was a figure of a man cast in bronze or a similar metal. The mud-encrusted face bore a stern expression as the man gazed into the distance. He raised a finger toward the heavens with one hand, while his other hand held a staff.

"I wonder who it's supposed to be," Ana said quietly.

Teo squatted next to the half-buried statue. "Check this out." He wiped away some dirt, revealing a sash hanging from the man's hand. There was a symbol on it: a cross. "Do you think this could be a depiction of Deu?"

Ana folded her arms at her breast and tapped her chin as she considered it. "I don't think so. I remember a line from one of the Hymns. It was either the ninety-sixth or ninety-seventh. It said something like, 'They are confused, all those who serve images, who give glory to idols.' I don't think idols belong to the faith of Deu."

"Maybe it's just art then," Teo agreed. "Remember the temple where we found the Sacred Writing? It had lots of statues and paintings."

Teo could see Ana going there in her mind. She had been captivated by that beautiful place. The temple was a soaring structure they had discovered in a faraway, lost city. Its massive pillars and buttresses had supported the highest roof Teo had ever seen. *I can't believe I lowered myself off that roof with Ana on my back!*

Ana's face wore a dreamy expression. "I can still picture those colorful windows. That's where I first experienced the beauty of Deu."

"Yeah . . . uh-huh . . . those were nice windows." Teo lowered his eyes and scraped a little mud off his fingers.

Ana awoke from her reverie. "They were stunning—and then you smashed one! I'll never forgive you for that!" Her tone was playfully accusing.

"I had a feeling you might bring that up. But if you recall, it was either smash the window or get shot full of arrows by the outsiders."

Ana approached him. Teo noticed how pretty she looked, especially now that she was wearing her gown again. Unexpectedly, she reached out and hugged him around the neck.

"I'm just kidding, you know," she said in his ear. "You came to me in the Beyond when I was all alone, and now you've come to me with healing medicine so I could get well. I'm so grateful for you, Teofil—especially in this lonely wilderness."

For a moment they stood together in an embrace, with Ana's arms around Teo's neck and his arms around her slender waist. Then, as the hug started to slip into something more than a friendly gesture, they quickly separated. Teo cleared his throat, and Ana's cheeks flushed pink.

"So . . . do you want to see what else I found?" Teo asked. Ana nodded vigorously.

He led her to the plain stone cross. It rose from a sturdy plinth, with rounded points at the tips of the crossbar and the upright beam. Teo pointed to an inscription on the cross. "I found these letters. Look."

Ana squinted as she tried to make out the inscription. Time had taken its toll, but after a moment she was able to read, *Deo optimo maximo.* The words were foreign to Chiveisian speech.

"*Deo* sounds like Deu," she remarked. "Can you translate it?"

"Not exactly. This isn't the Fluid Tongue of the Ancients, but the language is similar. I think it says something like, 'Deu, the best, the greatest.'"

"That makes sense. He's the one true God, and the cross is his symbol. We already knew that."

"Yes," Teo said, feeling the excitement of discovery rising within him, "but guess what? I found more writing. Look here. Somebody carved graffiti into the cross. It might be important."

Ana bent to look, but the words eluded her. "It's too faint to read," she said.

"I know. I spent the longest time staring at it, until finally I thought of this." Teo removed an ancient sheet of ledger paper and a piece of charcoal from inside his jerkin. "We can make a rubbing."

"Good idea! Let's see if it works."

Teo laid the fragile paper against the cross and lightly rubbed the charcoal across its surface. As the page darkened, the shapes of letters began to stand out. Teo's curiosity was thoroughly aroused. After blackening the entire page, he set down the piece of charcoal.

"What does it say?" Ana asked breathlessly.

Teo held the page to the light. "It seems to be the same language as the inscription. There are multiple linguistic cognates with the Fluid Tongue."

"Easy with the big words, Professor."

Teo grinned. "What I mean is, this language is close to the Fluid Tongue. Maybe one was a derivative of the other. I'll try to read it, though my pronunciation might be wrong." He sounded it out. "*O Iesu Christe, miserere mei.*"

"Any idea what that means?"

"Well, it's obviously a petition of some kind. It's addressed to Iesu Christe, whoever he is. *Mei* is probably the pronoun 'me.' The pronoun in the Fluid Tongue is similar." Teo paused. "But what's the verb? What exactly does the petitioner want Iesu Christe to do for him?" He bit his lip and racked his brain. "In the Fluid Tongue, there's a noun, *misère*, 'poverty.' But it doesn't make sense to pray, 'Please make me poor.'"

"Unless it's so he can depend on Deu's help," Ana suggested.

"Perhaps. But I'm thinking it might be related to another noun, *miséricorde*, 'mercy.'"

"I bet that's it! He's saying, 'Iesu Christe, be merciful to me.' A man living through the devastation the Ancients experienced would certainly need to pray something like that."

Teo folded the paper and tucked it into his jerkin. Excitement shone in Ana's eyes as she rested her hand on his arm. "This is important, Teo! We learned a new name today: Iesu Christe. The ancient believers addressed prayers to him. Maybe it's just another name for Deu, or maybe it's someone else, I don't know. But I'll tell you one thing—this is a mystery I want to solve."

Teo glanced at her. "For yourself?"

Ana's expression changed, and she looked wistfully into the distance. She was silent for a long time. Finally she answered, "Yes, for myself . . ."

"And?"

"And for my people. The people of Chiveis."

"You still hope to return and win them to Deu, don't you?"

Ana met Teo's gaze with a resolute look. "I do," she said.

He smiled. "Then I guess we'll have to see what Deu has in store for us. You're strong enough to travel now. Tomorrow we depart for Ulmbartia. Maybe that kingdom will have the answers we seek."

"I hope so," Ana said, her eyes bright and expectant. "I've been praying for this."

✦　✦　✦

Commander Duilo opened the camp storehouse and began preparing a feast in the castle when Lieutenant Celso's expedition party arrived. Teo appreciated that this time the sentries didn't confront him as a stranger but as a conquering hero.

Although everyone remained watchful for Rovers, the mood at the castle was as festive as it could be out on the frontier. A fire blazed in the hearth, and large tables had been set up in front of it. Lieutenant Celso was seated at the commander's right, while Teo, as the first man to cross the pass and reach the fort, was at Duilo's left. The Ulmbartians rejoiced to have discovered this second pass over the mountains. It was hoped that a military presence could be established to control both, preventing the Rovers from making incursions into the kingdom.

THE GIFT

The feasting hall fell silent as Commander Duilo stood from his chair. "Men, today we celebrate the presence of national heroes among us. The lords and ladies of Ulmbartia might look down their noses on the military profession, but they can't deny the great things we accomplish for our land!" Cheers of solidarity resounded from the gathered soldiers.

The commander turned to his right. "Lieutenant Celso, tomorrow I will be sending your expedition straight to Giuntra. A messenger has been dispatched already. For your outstanding achievements, you will be granted a royal audience!"

"Where's Giuntra?" Ana whispered to Teo.

He shrugged. "I don't know, but I guess we're about to find out."

Duilo raised his goblet, and all the men followed suit. "To my old friend Celso—the best brawler I've ever knocked down!" The toast drew a chorus of laughs as tin cups clinked around the room.

Turning to his left, Duilo continued the toast. "And to Teofil of Chiveis, who . . . who"—the tipsy commander searched for the right words—"who has brought to Ulmbartia the best-looking woman I've ever seen!" A raucous shout went up from the roomful of men. Teo laughed and nudged Ana with his elbow, but she only blushed and stared at her plate.

The feast continued late into the night. The wine was better than anything Teo had tasted in Chiveis, and the food was creamy and rich. Apparently even common soldiers ate like kings in Ulmbartia. At last Teo and Ana were escorted to a private chamber by the commander's personal aide. A bed had been set up in it, with a clean straw mattress and enough space for two. A candle on the bedside table cast a soft glow across the room.

"Commander Duilo apologizes for the lack of more comfortable accommodations to offer you on the frontier," the aide said. "He ordered his own bed moved here for you. It's the only thing better than a soldier's cot in this whole place." Teo thanked him, and the aide closed the door behind him as he left. The room was silent for a long moment.

"Everyone assumes we're . . ." Ana's voice trailed off.

"Lovers?"

"Right."

"But of course . . . we're not."

Ana shook her head. "No! Of course not."

Teo wasn't sure what to say next. He tried to think of some witty remark to relieve his discomfort, but no words came, so he and Ana just stared at the bed until the awkward silence became unbearable.

Finally Teo spoke up. "I guess I've slept in much worse places than on the floor of a room like this." He grabbed one of the blankets off the mattress. "You can have the bed."

"Okay, good idea." Ana hopped onto the bed and quickly blew out the candle.

The next morning the expedition party departed for Giuntra after a hearty breakfast of cured meat, cheese, and bread with jam. They rode alongside the river until it finally left the foothills and ran out onto a broad and fertile plain. By nightfall they had arrived at a fortified village that provided a safe home for the peasant farmers whose fields lay in a patchwork across the landscape.

"Welcome to Ulmbartia proper," Lieutenant Celso said. "It's a very good land."

The riverboat trip to the Ulmbartian capital took the better part of the next four days. Teo was impressed by the scale of the kingdom. It was much bigger than Chiveis, and most of it was rich bottomland that yielded excellent crops. Lieutenant Celso showed Teo a map that depicted the various towns and natural features of Ulmbartia. To the north and west lay the great arc of mountains from which the Rovers sometimes descended to raid the frontier villages. To the south was the coastal kingdom of the Likurians, a people whose luxurious territory stretched lengthwise along the Great Salt Sea. An area to the east was marked "The Forbidden Zone." When Teo inquired about it, Celso said it was a toxic wasteland from the time of the Ancients' great war.

The main river in Ulmbartia was called the Padu. It was a large waterway whose springs originated in the high mountains, flowing from west to east. The expedition would be traveling on the Padu toward its confluence with another river that ran from a freshwater sea in the north. At the two rivers' juncture lay the Ulmbartian capital, Giuntra.

"Giuntra is a splendid city," Lieutenant Celso said, "and we'll see it at its best. It's rare for commoners like us to get a royal audience. Only a historic contribution to the kingdom would merit it."

"I'll have to clean up first," Teo said, brushing dust from his jerkin.

"I should say so. We Ulmbartians are very conscious of our appearance. Style is important to us." The lieutenant shrugged. "But in the end it won't matter. A soldier is still a soldier, even if you dress him like a prince. We're no better than chimney sweeps in the aristocrats' eyes."

"Men in uniform aren't respected in your land?"

"Soldiers perform a service like any other craftsman or farmer. Some people make shoes, some people raise cabbages, some people weave silk. We beat back the Rovers. To those in the upper crust, we're all the same: commoners. The aristocrats like their lapdogs more than us. We count for nothing."

"Really? Even a man of rank like Commander Duilo?"

"Duilo got where he is because of his family connections. He's in the aristocrats' club because of his uncle. But believe me, unless somebody lets you in, that world is closed to people like us. If you're not admitted to their inner circle, you're always the object of their arrogance. Or worse—their pity."

"And yet they'll honor us for our discovery?"

"There's no reason not to. It makes them feel benevolent and patriotic. But don't think for a minute they consider you an equal."

Teo shook his head but didn't reply. He wasn't sure what to make of Ulmbartia.

When the riverboat rounded a curve on the afternoon of the fourth day, Teo discovered Lieutenant Celso wasn't exaggerating when he had bragged about the wonders of Giuntra. Even from a distance Teo could see the city was full of splendid palaces and impressive, monumental buildings. The high walls shone brilliant white, and flags fluttered from every possible spire or turret. Marble was present in abundance. The expedition disembarked at a pier amid the cheers of the onlookers.

A handsome man with gold loops in both ears strode out to meet them. "Welcome, brave adventurers," he said.

After greeting Lieutenant Celso, the man turned to Ana and bowed deeply. "You must be Anastasia of Chiveis. I received word that you are a woman of substance, and now I am pleased to discover those reports are true." He smiled warmly. "I am the king's steward. Tomorrow His Highness will meet with you. Until then we have prepared rooms for your comfort. Everything you need for your royal audience will be supplied." The steward glanced at Teo, looking him up and down, then turned back to Ana. "Your bodyguard will also be given a suitable outfit." He gestured with an open hand toward a waiting coach. "Shall we?"

As the party boarded the coach, Teo found himself irritated. *Bodyguard? What happened to "national hero"?*

✦　✦　✦

Ana had to admit: the gown was lovely. Gorgeous, in fact. It was made of a luxurious, burgundy-colored fabric the valet had called *taffeta*. The bodice was fitted to the waist and trimmed with an embroidered pattern of grape-vines. Long, loose-hanging sleeves adorned the arms, while the neckline was studded with red gemstones called garnets. The back was open and scooped low, a style to which Ana wasn't accustomed. She tried on the gown in front of the mirror. It was a stunning dress, no doubt about it.

The king's steward arrived and escorted Ana down the hallway. Lieutenant Celso and Teo awaited her around the corner. Like Ana, Teo had been given a fresh change of clothes. Ana had only seen him in his leather jerkin, rough breeches, and high soldier's boots; so to see him dressed in such a fashionable way startled her at first. He wore a close-fitting, navy-blue doublet with brass buttons, an upturned collar, and gold trim at the cuffs. His dark gray pants were made of fine wool, and his low black boots were polished to a shine. On his hip was his sword—the sword Ana's grandfather had once worn. With his dark hair combed and his chin freshly shaved, Teo had exchanged his usual wilderness look for something more sophisticated. *He looks so handsome*, Ana marveled. She glided forward to greet the waiting men.

"Can you believe this gown they gave me?" Ana smiled and twirled so the skirt would flare out.

Teo nodded. "They say Ulmbartia is a fashionable place. You certainly fit in."

"Really? You like how I look?"

"Sure. It's great."

Ana tsked. "Don't get too enthusiastic all at once."

Teo noticed the little edge in her voice. "I'm sorry, Ana. You do look nice." He shook his head. "My mind is just preoccupied with something Lieutenant Celso told me."

"What?"

Teo turned to Celso and asked him to explain.

"I told Teofil that the king will be making some decisions about your futures in Ulmbartia," the lieutenant said. "As foreigners, you're here by his permission. His Majesty will have some thoughts about where you should fit into our society."

"Indeed he shall," the steward agreed, "and it's time to go see him now. This way, please."

The palace steward led the group to the throne room. The doors opened onto a brilliantly lit hall with a thick red carpet on the floor. The king sat at the head of the room, while the royal courtiers, princes, and ladies-in-waiting lined the walls. As Ana was led down the carpet with Teo beside her, a murmur swept through the crowd. The steward and Lieutenant Celso knelt before the king. Ana and Teo knelt too. The king bade them to rise.

"Welcome home, Lieutenant Celso. Or should I say, 'Major Celso'? I ordered your promotion today because of your intrepid work on behalf of Ulmbartia."

"It will be my honor to serve you in this new rank, Sire."

The king turned to Ana, staring at her. She politely averted her eyes. "Anastasia of Chiveis, I greet you. The rumormongers told me you are a princess from a mysterious and exotic kingdom over the high mountains. Now that I have beheld your beauty, I believe those rumors."

"No, my lord. I am only a simple woman seeking a simple life in your land."

"Doing what, may I ask?"

"I can spin wool and sew, Your Highness."

When the king burst into laughter, the rest of the room followed suit. Ana didn't know what was so funny. Leaning forward on his throne, the king stared at her. "I do not think, my pretty, that sewing and spinning will do for you. Not at all. I don't know how things work in your land, but here in Ulmbartia we do not consign women like you to the tasks reserved for the ugly."

The remark startled Ana. She had no words for a reply.

The king smiled benignly. "Never let it be said that such a lovely foreigner came to our land, and we failed to treat her as her appearance deserves. You are welcome here in Ulmbartia, Anastasia of Chiveis. Even a rosebush as prolific as ours can make room for another glorious bloom."

"Thank you, my lord," Ana replied, more than a little bewildered.

The king scanned the crowd until his eyes fell on a pretty young aristocrat standing along the wall. He summoned her with his fingers. The woman walked forward, her blonde hair flowing behind her. Jewels dangled from her ears and draped across her ample bosom.

"Anastasia, meet Lady Vanita Labella. She is of noble birth from an ancient family. You will live at her palace." The king glanced around the room with an impish smile. "It's big enough for that, don't you think?" The question drew laughter and nods of affirmation. The king turned his attention back to Ana. "You will live in Vanita's little cottage and learn the ways of the Ulmbartian highborn. Does that suit you, Anastasia of Chiveis?"

Not knowing what other options were available, Ana nodded her assent. *Deu, may you go with me into this future*, she prayed.

Now the king fixed his eyes on Teo. "As for you, mercenary, I hear you were the first man over the pass. Commander Duilo speaks highly of your skills in the military arts. You will be commissioned into the Ulmbartian army as a private and will be deployed to the frontier."

Ana's blood turned cold. *What? I'll live in the heartland and Teo will be on the frontier?* She hadn't anticipated this turn of events.

"I'm not sure that's a good idea, Sire," Teo said. There was a sharp intake of breath from several of the courtiers. A hush descended on the room.

The king arched an eyebrow. "No?"

As Teo started to speak, Ana knew exactly what he was going to say. His protective instinct was at work. He was going to ask to be stationed somewhere close to her. Ana wanted the same thing, yet she understood the social dynamics well enough to see that Teo's request would be considered improper. She stepped forward and intervened. "Sire, if I may speak, Teofil is not only a good soldier, he is also a . . ." *What's that word again?* She desperately sought the right term in Talyano. "A chaser."

An uncomfortable titter arose from the watching courtiers.

"A *chaser?*" the king asked with a sly expression. "What does he chase? The skirts at the soldiers' brothel?" Everyone in the room burst into laughter.

Ana felt her face flush, but she gained control of herself. "Excuse me, Your Highness. I am only beginning to learn the Talyano speech. I meant to say 'teacher,' not 'chaser.' The words are similar, and I was confused. Teofil is a teacher."

Vanita Labella broke in. "I think I know what Anastasia is asking. She wishes to retain the services of her bodyguard and find useful employment for him somewhere nearby. Am I correct?" Ana nodded, and Vanita turned back to the king. "Your Highness, at my home we have a tutor called . . ." Her words trailed off as she tried to recall the man's name. "Well, never mind his name, but he's an overworked old geezer nearing retirement. He could use some help."

The king chuckled at Vanita's directness. "Very well, then. Mercenary Teofil will become Teacher Teofil. He can start training all those urchins your oversexed father keeps siring. And if they happen to be your mother's children too, so much the better!" The room exploded with laughter at the hilarious royal jest.

Vanita giggled, then stepped close to Ana and took her by the hand. "We're going to have a lot of fun, you and I," she whispered. "And now you owe me a favor for helping you keep your lover handy." She glanced at Teo. "He's cute. I think you might have to let me borrow him."

✦　✦　✦

"So you're from over the mountains, yet you're not a Rover, eh?" The scrawny teacher with long white hair grinned at Teo.

"Yes. I'm from a land called Chiveis."

The old man switched into a dialect of the Chiveisian speech. "I greet you with warmth. I am named Sol. Welcome to the Labella estate."

Teo was taken aback. "How do you know my language?"

"Am I not a teacher? Should I not have things to teach?"

"There are many things you might teach, but I wouldn't imagine the language of a distant people would be one of them."

Sol laughed, his eyes crinkling at the corners. "There are tribes among the Downstreamers who speak a language like yours. Long ago they migrated over the mountains from the north. I was among them for a time."

"Downstreamers?"

Sol fluttered his fingers in a flowing motion. "They live downstream from us. On the Padu. It goes all the way to the salty sea."

"Well, it's nice to hear my own language spoken. Only Anastasia and I use it here."

"And now there is a third! Yet I do not think it will be needed. Your command of Talyano is quite good already. I'll help you make it even better."

"Thank you." Teo offered his hand. "It's a pleasure to meet you, Sol. I'm Teofil." They shook hands, then Sol invited Teo to have a seat in his spartan living room.

The journey northwest to Vanita Labella's home had taken two days. The king had obviously been speaking with sarcasm when he expressed doubt that Vanita's house could accommodate any guests. It was an immense palace with more rooms than a man could use in a lifetime. The palace lay at the center of a vast estate of farmland and vineyards. Strangely, many of the fields were flooded.

Teo had been led to a stone cottage near a garden brimming with flowerbeds and fountains. The cottage's downstairs floor served as a schoolroom, while the upstairs contained living quarters for the teachers. There was an empty bedroom Teo could use.

"Lady Vanita's family must be very wealthy," he remarked.

Sol bent to a sack of grain and removed a tiny, light-brown seed. He placed it in Teo's palm. "The wealth you see around you is generated by this."

"What is it?"

"It's called rice. You'll be having a lot of it in the days to come."

Teo and Sol relaxed in the afternoon warmth, drinking cups of pale lager until the sun was low in the sky. Both men found their tongues loosened by the convivial atmosphere and the dry, crisp drink. The conversation ranged, as it often does among men of learning, across the great ideas of politics, art, philosophy, literature, and religion. Teo found himself drawn to the wizened scholar with the shoulder-length hair. Sol explained that Ulmbartian religion was superficial at best. The people tipped their hats to a variety of gods and observed many ancient superstitions, but they lacked a true sense of connection to the divine. Religion was employed mainly to enhance social standing and prestige.

As Teo listened to Sol talk, he decided to speak boldly on the matter of religion and see what would happen. When a lull arose in the conversation, he said, "I believe there is only one God, a single Creator."

Sol's face remained unreadable. "Is that so? And what if that view is uncommon in Ulmbartia?"

"I would hold to it nonetheless."

"Would you speak of it publicly?"

"Yes, to those who wish to hear."

"I see you are a man of conviction."

"I guess you could say that." Teo pressed ahead. "What about you, Sol? What are your beliefs?"

Sol eyed Teo for a long moment, then took a deep breath before speaking. "I tread on paths of ancient wisdom, my young friend. Unfortunately, they are paths whose origins are unknown and whose end is uncertain."

"That's a good way to get lost," Teo pointed out.

Sol uttered a cackling laugh. "Very true! But sometimes we have no other choice, so we decide that walking on the way to somewhere is better than wandering in the wilderness of nowhere. I have incomplete knowledge of the Creator, yet I find him superior to the thornbushes of the Ulmbartian cults."

"You believe in the Creator too?" Teo was excited to hear it.

"I do. His name is Deus. He is the one true God, and he existed before all time."

Teo sat up straight. "Did you just call him Deus?"

"Indeed I did," Sol answered quietly.

"How do you know about that God? I call him Deu. I'm one of his followers."

"You'd best keep that knowledge to yourself. It is opposed by the shamans."

"Who are they?"

"Many things could be said about the shamans. Do you wish to know what the people believe, or the secret I know to be true of them?"

"I suppose both, if you're willing to tell me."

Sol lowered his voice even more. "The shamans are officially called the Exterminati. Everyone thinks they exist to remove defective people from our midst—those who have a disfigurement of some kind. The shamans have obtained treaties granting them this right. All Ulmbartians fear being labeled defective. But there is more to this story."

"Tell me," Teo said, leaning toward Sol.

"The real purpose of the Exterminati is religious. They exist to suppress all knowledge of the Creator. If you speak of him openly, you will be certain to attract their attention. They are masters of assassination and abduction."

"So it's forbidden in Ulmbartia to believe in a single God?"

"No. I did not say it is forbidden. To forbid it would be to reveal the true purposes of the shamans. The Exterminati prefer to shroud themselves in secrecy. Proclaiming belief in one God has not been outlawed in Ulmbartia. Yet in reality there are none who do, for everyone who speaks of such things quickly disappears."

"Where did you learn all this?"

"Over the years I have met those who oppose the Exterminati and secretly follow Deus. They spoke of these things to me."

"And how did these people learn about Deus?" Teo sensed he was on the brink of an important discovery.

"There is an ancient book that speaks of him."

"The Sacred Writing! I have a partial copy of my own!"

It was Sol's turn to be surprised. "You do? Is it written in the Old Words?"

"Yes, they're old words. I am one of the few in my land who can read them." As Teo reached into his rucksack, Sol went to the window and glanced around, then walked to the door and shut it firmly before returning to his seat. Teo unwrapped a protective cloth and showed Sol the leather-bound copy of the Sacred Writing. The pages were brittle, and the final third of the book was destroyed, but much of it was still legible. Sol inspected it.

"These aren't the Old Words I just mentioned, though they are similar. The languages must be related. Can you read this book?"

"I can. The Ancients spoke it. In Chiveis we call it the Fluid Tongue because its sound is more melodious than our own speech."

"The book is not intact."

"I found it hidden in a lockbox after many centuries. Water had damaged it."

Sol went to the hearth and removed a book from behind a loose stone. The book was hand-copied, not printed. Although it looked very old, Teo didn't think it dated as far back as the time of the Ancients. It was probably an Ulmbartian copy of an earlier text.

"This is the book I spoke of," Sol said. "It is written in Talyano, translated directly from the Old Words. Few in Ulmbartia can read that tongue." He smiled at Teo. "Like you, I am one who preserves lost languages in my head."

Teo bent over the book. Scanning its table of contents, he could see from the headings that Sol's book was a complete copy of what the Ancients had called the Old Testament. There was no mention of the New.

"These are two versions of the same text," he told Sol. "But did you know the Sacred Writing has a second Testament?"

Sol glanced up. "Really? What does it say?"

"I don't know. That's the part that was water-damaged, so it's lost."

"The second Testament must be very important," Sol observed. "Perhaps another copy can be found."

"Anastasia and I intend to seek it."

Teo looked more closely at Sol's book in the Talyano speech. "You said this was translated from the Old Words. What do you know about that language?"

"The Ancients called it *Latin*. My knowledge of it goes back to my childhood."

Teo reached into the pocket of his doublet and removed the rubbing he had made from the stone cross. "I recently discovered an inscription in a lost language of the Ancients. See if you can tell me what it says." He handed it over.

Sol squinted at the smudged page. "This is indeed Latin. It reads, 'O Iesu Christe, have mercy on me.'"

"That's what I thought! Do you know who Iesu Christe is?"

"The proper form is *Iesus Christus* when it's not a direct address. As far as who he is, I cannot say."

"You must have some idea," Teo insisted.

Sol pursed his lips. "Long ago I heard this name used to describe a savior figure predicted in the Holy Book. Here, see for yourself." He thumbed through his copy of the Old Testament until he located the Second Book of Samuhel, the seventh chapter, then read aloud, "I will raise up your descendant after you, one who will go forth from your own body, and I will establish his reign. He will build a house for my name, and I will establish the throne of his kingdom forever." Sol looked up from the page. "This figure is known as the Promised King," he explained.

"Is Iesus Christus the Promised King?"

"Perhaps. But he might also be another man predicted by the Holy Book. Tradition says he helped the king."

"Who was he?"

"He is known as the Suffering Servant." Sol turned a few pages and showed Teo the fifty-third chapter of Isaias. It described the servant as a man who suffered many griefs and trials. He was truly "a man of sorrows" who ended his life in defeat.

"So which is it?" Teo asked. "Is Iesus Christus the victorious Promised King or the defeated Suffering Servant?"

Sol shrugged. "I don't know."

Out in the hall, a clay vessel shattered. Teo jumped up and flung open the door. A servant stood there, his eyes wide.

"I . . . I was bringing you water . . ."

"We didn't ask for water."

"I thought you might want some."

"Why didn't you knock?"

The man didn't have a ready answer.

"We don't need anything," Teo said, slamming the door in the man's face.

"The shamans have eyes in every head," Sol muttered. "Apparently they have ears too."

✦   ✦   ✦

Nikolo Borja stabbed the last dormouse with a meat fork and plunged the wriggling creature into a pot of boiling water, then yanked it out again. With the creature now dead and its fur loosened, Borja skinned and dressed it in a matter of seconds, then dropped it into a second pot of simmering meat stock. A chef could have done this for him, of course, but Borja enjoyed participating in the little drama of death.

While the dormice cooked, Borja walked onto the balcony of his palace and let his eyes rove over the city of Roma. It was the capital of a vibrant city-state—a kingdom whose politics Borja dominated by his great wealth. Soon he spotted something that excited him: a bird flew in a direct line to the palace roof. *News from afar*, he realized.

His ankles began to hurt, so he went back inside and reclined on a plush divan. Sitting down was the only way to alleviate the strain his immense weight put on his joints. Borja believed it was his spiritual duty to enjoy all the succulent delicacies the gods had lavished upon him. His obesity was proof of their heavenly beneficence to him.

A short time later, the messenger arrived from the rooftop pigeon roost. He held a pillow with a small gold box upon it.

"Read it to me," Borja said.

The messenger swallowed, then set the pillow on a table and removed a tiny slip of paper from the box. In a shaky voice he began to read:

The Chief Shaman of the Society of the Exterminati in Ulmbartia; to His Most Blessed and Abundant Corpulence, Nikolo Borja, at Roma; fair greetings and honor be thine.

An egregious and most unfortunate circumstance has brought evil tidings to this realm. From over the northern mountains, a stranger has come with his woman. The lords of men receive them with favor. The stranger speaks of the Creator and the Criminal, accursed be their names forever! The spirits are disturbed, and the underworld is all in unrest. As always, your bidding is a divine command. Life to you evermore.

When the messenger stopped reading, Borja stared into space, his jaw clenched against the rage seething within him. Roma, Likuria, Ulmbartia—these three kingdoms had been purged of the foul god of the Christiani. Or if not completely purged, the heresy was at least sufficiently contained. To hear that some foreigner had arrived in distant Ulmbartia, running free with news of the Creator and his executed son, made Borja feel like a man who discovers an unexpected stain on his white garment. *Ulmbartia must be cleansed of these interlopers!*

Though the situation had to be dealt with immediately, Borja knew a deft political hand would be required. A double assassination would be far too suspicious, attracting unwanted investigation from foreign authorities. If the Ulmbartian aristocracy had embraced the dangerous strangers, any move against them would have to be untraceable to the Exterminati. It was always better to pin the blame for one's actions on others. Fortunately, the Chief Shaman of Ulmbartia was clever. He could be relied on to devise a plan that would make the strangers' deaths appear to be the work of outside forces.

Struggling up from the divan, Borja lumbered across the room to the charcoal braziers with their cookpots, then signaled for the messenger to approach.

"Fill my plate," Borja commanded, his hands clasped behind his back.

The messenger looked at the pot of boiling stock and the empty plate. "Where is the meat fork, Your Corpulence?"

Borja slapped the messenger with the back of his hand. "Fill my plate," he repeated.

The messenger was distraught. He rolled up his sleeve and took a deep breath, then plunged his hand into the pot, his face twisting into a grimace. Beads of sweat popped out on his forehead as he dropped a handful of cooked dormice onto the plate. His hand and wrist were the color of a ripe tomato. The sight was relaxing to Borja. The pain of others always soothed him.

"I would have more," he said.

Again the messenger searched the bottom of the pot for a handful of rodents. He uttered a thin groan but did not speak. Three more dripping carcasses plopped onto the steaming plate. Blisters had appeared on the messenger's hand, and the skin sagged. He breathed rapidly through clenched teeth as he stood at attention.

Borja removed the meat fork from behind his back and speared one of the dormice. He soaked it in a bowl of vinegar for a moment, then rolled it in honey and spun the dripping tidbit toward his mouth. Its tiny bones made a delectable crunch as he bit into the meat. Finishing the dormouse in a second bite, he smacked his lips and spat a piece of bone to the floor.

"Go fetch a scribe," he said with his cheeks full. "I wish to send a message to Ulmbartia."

✦　✦　✦

The fragrant roses blooming on the palatial lakeside terrace normally brought joy to Count Federco Borromo, but on this day they were the last thing on his mind. He was trying to save his newborn son. The count pursed his lips, then turned to face his visitors.

"Our sources tell us a birthmarked child has been born to you," said the gravelly voice of the Chief Shaman of Ulmbartia.

The count regarded the shrouded figure standing a few paces away on the terrace. Two other shamans in dark, hooded robes stood behind their master. "Who told you this?" Federco asked.

"We have eyes in every head," the Chief Shaman replied. "Now bring us the boy."

Count Federco nodded toward the door, and a palace servant stepped onto the terrace with a portable bassinet. He laid it at the count's feet before scuttling back inside. The count glanced down at the sleeping baby, then abruptly spun away with his hands folded behind his back. He gazed at the placid lake for a long time.

At last he turned back to his visitors. "Take him if you must," he spat.

The Chief Shaman stalked over in his billowing robes and knelt beside the bassinet. He spat a glob of saliva on his two extended fingers, then rubbed the spittle on the infant's cheek. A pitiful cry arose from the bassinet. The count watched, horrified.

The shaman stood up. "Bring us the real child, Count Federco." The command was expressed in measured tones, but the threat was obvious.

"What are you talking about? That is the real child."

The Chief Shaman held up two moistened fingers, now stained pink. "Don't try to play me for a fool! The child's face is dyed!" The shaman's pointy chin and yellow teeth were the only part of his face visible beneath his hood. A pale, bony hand gestured at the lavish surroundings. "Do you think we cannot strip all this away from you? Do you wish to be despised as one who has spawned a Defective? Do you intend to live out your days in penury? Think hard on your actions now, Count. Our reprisals for non-compliance are severe."

The count swallowed. Though he made no audible reply, his head dropped. He beckoned toward the double doors of the palace. The servant reappeared on the terrace, carrying another bassinet. He laid it on the ground between Count Federco and the Chief Shaman. The baby's face was blemished by a port-wine stain.

"Now you are being reasonable," the Chief Shaman said. He picked up the bassinet by the handle.

Count Federco stifled a cry of frustration and grief. The baby was his last link to Countess Benita, who had died in childbirth.

The shaman paused. "What? Do you have some affection for this Defective?" The count did not answer, but the shaman stepped close to him. The hooded man's breath was foul. "Perhaps we could make an arrangement."

A surge of hope arose in Count Federco's soul. "What arrangement?"

"It's simple enough. You may raise this boy as a slave in your house, never to be seen by the eyes of society at large. In return you need only do one thing—a thing at which you already excel."

"What do you seek?" the count asked, hardly daring to breathe.

"You must throw a party."

"A party? What kind of party? Speak plainly! What do you intend?"

"You will offer a party for your aristocratic friends. We will supply the guest list. I believe you have a remote chateau on the northern lakeshore, yes? Was it not the custom when you were young to host parties for the rich and beautiful on the island with the ruined castle?"

"That is true," the count acknowledged. "But it is too dangerous now. The Rovers have infiltrated those wild lands and have been known to stage raids. Though my chateau is fortified, it could not withstand an attack. As for the island, it's undefended and vulnerable."

"The thrill of danger is appealing to the young," the Chief Shaman said, his eyes narrowing. "And so, Count Federco, you will revive the practice of throwing parties on the castle isle." The shaman's hand flashed into the bassinet. He yanked the infant by his ankle and held him up, wailing and thrashing. "Or you will never see this accursed monstrosity again!"

❖   ❖   ❖

In the week since arriving at Vanita's house, Ana had come to learn one thing about Ulmbartian female social life: hair was very important. The aristocratic girls talked about their hair constantly, and when they weren't talking about it, they were jealously eyeing the hairstyles of others. Ana had been told more than once, "Your hair is so beautiful!" only to sense envy rather than admiration from the girl giving the compliment.

Vanita Labella, however, was different. She was the acknowledged ringleader of her social bunch, and that gave her the freedom not to be so catty. It also helped that Vanita was gorgeous, so she had no need to be jealous of anyone. With her lustrous hair, flawless skin, long sensual legs, and curves in all the right places, Vanita knew how to stop a man in his tracks. Yet she was no empty-headed socialite. She was smart and witty and had a sweet disposition. If she was a little callous at times, it was because she didn't know better, not because she was mean. Ana had taken a liking to Vanita.

"Oh, it's *so* hot today! Anastasia, do you want something cool to drink?" Vanita fanned herself with her hand.

"Yes, thanks. That would be great."

Vanita spun from where she was sitting with two other girls on the rim of a marble fountain. They had all taken off their shoes and were dipping their bare feet in the water. Vanita padded over to a nearby table, leaving dainty wet footprints on the flagstones. She picked up a bell and rang it, but the servant did not appear, so she rang it again more insistently. Finally a middle-aged woman with red-rimmed eyes arrived.

"You rang, m'lady?"

"Matilde, cold drinks for all four of us, and hurry up. We're sweltering here!"

"Right away, m'lady." Matilde disappeared through a door.

"She's so slow lately," one of the girls observed.

"She's been like this ever since the accident," Vanita said, returning to her seat.

Ana joined the others on the edge of the fountain. "Accident?"

"She lost her husband when he became a Defective," Vanita explained.

"I'm not sure I know that word."

"You know—*Defective*." Vanita contorted her face into a weird grimace with her eyes crossed and her tongue lolling out. She held her hands like claws in front of her face. "People who have something wrong with them."

"I still don't understand."

A dark-haired girl with tan skin chimed in. "We're an advanced society here in Ulmbartia. We don't like flawed people in our midst. That's what the shamans are for: they remove the Defectives and take them to a better place."

Ana was repulsed. "What happened to Matilde's husband?"

"He was a woodcutter, I think. Lost a foot. You can't have stump-legged people hobbling around in public, you know. The shamans took him away." The dark-haired girl tossed her hair and wiggled her toes in the fountain.

"Where did he go?"

Vanita smiled sweetly and held up her hands. "No one knows. But don't worry about him. His life here was ruined anyway, so he's better off somewhere else. The shamans have a beautiful palace in a distant valley. They take care of the Defectives so they can live with others of their kind."

"Their *kind?*"

"Yes," Vanita insisted, as if speaking to a child, "their *kind*. Other Defectives, like I just said." She made the same gruesome face as before.

"So who has to go live in the shamans' palace? Anyone who's injured? What counts as 'defective' around here?"

Vanita sighed. "The lame, the blind, the maimed, the half-witted, the disfigured. Anyone you wouldn't want in a civilized society."

"And deformed babies," the dark-haired girl added. "I once saw one with a sixth toe on its foot. It was disgusting."

"*Babies?*" Ana demanded.

Vanita shrugged. "That's life."

Matilde returned with the cold drinks. Ana couldn't meet the servant's eyes as she took a cup of apple cider from the tray.

As Vanita was served, Matilde handed her an envelope of embossed linen. "The courier just arrived, m'lady," she said.

"Look, girls! A message!" Vanita opened the envelope and scanned it for a few seconds. Her eyes lit up, and a smile spread across her face. "You'll never believe it! This is like the old days, when partying was classy and sophisticated!"

The other two girls begged to hear the news, and Ana was more than a little intrigued too. Vanita waved the letter in the air.

"Count Federco Borromo is throwing a two-day party at his lakeside chateau. Imagine the ambience an old place like that will have! Lots of mystery and danger and romance. All the richest men will be there. You should see this guest list! It reads like a register of Ulmbartian high society."

"I can hardly bear to ask," the dark-haired girl said, covering her eyes with her hand, "but am I on the list?"

"Hmm. Let's see." Vanita mischievously scanned the letter longer than seemed necessary, then finally looked up at her two aristocratic friends. "Yes, you two made the cut." Both girls squealed and clapped their hands. "However," Vanita continued, "Anastasia's name isn't here."

Ana dropped her eyes to the ground. Though she was an unknown foreigner with no reason to expect an invitation to such an elegant event, she had gotten caught up in the excitement and now felt deflated.

Vanita winked at Ana and held up a slip of paper. "Your name isn't on the list because you're not a highborn Ulmbartian. But Count Federco has written you a personal note. Listen to this: 'Dear Anastasia of Chiveis: As a gesture of courtesy to a visitor in our midst, please accept my warm-est invitation to join Lady Vanita Labella at the party at my chateau four days hence. Considering that the location is remote and the route is formidable, provision will be made for your bodyguard to accompany you during the journey. I look forward to meeting you in person. All finest wishes, Count Federco Borromo.'"

Though Ana wasn't sure what to say, Vanita was ecstatic. She scram-bled to her feet and stood on the edge of the fountain. "Can you believe it? This party is going to be a dream! You'll love it, Anastasia, I promise you. It'll be the perfect prelude to the Harvest Ball!" Vanita began unbuttoning the front of her high-priced gown.

"What are you doing?" the dark-haired girl asked.

Vanita grinned expansively. "It's hot. I'm going to celebrate this happy news with a swim." She dropped her gown to her ankles and stepped out of it. The red satin chemise she wore underneath glistened in the sunlight. Vanita spread her arms and threw back her head, letting her blonde hair dangle behind her.

"Life is good, girls." She closed her eyes and toppled backward into the fountain with a tremendous splash.

CHAPTER

4

Ana sat with Teo on a shaded bench in the gardens outside the schoolhouse. Since it was still summer, the demands of education had not yet called the estate's children away from their swimming holes and ball games. Ana knew Teo wasn't busy, so it was her fault she had hardly seen him in the nine days since they had moved to Vanita's fabulous home. She felt glad to see him again.

"Teo, guess what?" Before he could start to guess, Ana answered her query. "I've been invited to a fancy party of Ulmbartian aristocrats!"

He smiled. "It seems partying is what they do best. When is it?"

"Three days from now. It's an overnight party at a chateau on the big lake up north."

Teo's expression changed to a look of concern. "Wait a second," he said, holding up his hand. "That lake is in the mountains where the Rovers are. Is the party near the southern tip of the lake? That's the only safe part."

Ana tsked. "Don't be such a worrier! I think the party is happening up the shore a ways. Vanita says it's remote, but that's part of the fun. I'm sure it's perfectly safe."

"No, it's *not* perfectly safe. I've seen the maps, and I've discussed the frontiers with Lieutenant Celso. The lake you're talking about is called Greater Lake. It's actually more of an inland sea that extends deep into the mountains. The southern part is fairly civilized, but it becomes wild the farther north you go. The pass that Lieutenant Celso's expedition

89

used to enter the wilderness isn't far from there. If he can go over it to leave Ulmbartia, the Rovers can also use it to come in. The passes aren't secured yet."

"So what are you saying? Do you think I shouldn't go?"

"That's right, I think you shouldn't go. There's no need to put yourself at risk. Danger seems to find you easily enough already."

"But, Teo, it would mean so much to me."

He shrugged with his palms up. "Why? I don't get it."

Ana put her hand on his arm. "I know you don't get it, but let me explain. You're a man; I'm a woman." The obvious statement made Teo chuckle. Ana smiled in return as she continued, "You and I are very different, Teo. Back in Chiveis you were an independent soldier with nothing to tie you down. You lived in the wilderness for months at a time and loved it. But think about me. I had security, a home, a family—" Emotion caught in her throat, and her words faltered.

Teo slipped his arm around Ana's shoulder. "Okay, I do understand that. But are you sure the Ulmbartian aristocrats are the best substitute for what you used to have?"

"No," she said, staring at her feet, "but right now that's all I have."

"Ana, you have something far better."

She glanced up at Teo. Leaning her head on his shoulder, she said, "You're right. Deu is my strength. But maybe Deu will use my new friends to provide a community I can become a part of."

"I want that for you. I really do. I just don't like you taking unnecessary risks to achieve it."

Ana lifted her head from Teo's shoulder and looked him in the face, smiling. "There might be some danger," she acknowledged, "but I won't be alone. My 'bodyguard' is allowed to come along."

"Oh, I'm allowed to stand in their presence, am I?"

Ana felt a little embarrassed. "Actually, no. Not at the party. Just to get me there."

Teo rolled his eyes and flicked his hand dismissively.

A melodious voice called from behind the manicured hedges. "Yoo-hoo! Are you two decent? If not, grab a cover-up! I'm sorry to interrupt your little tryst, but I need to talk to you."

Vanita appeared on the gravel pathway in the garden. "Oh . . . you really are decent," she said with apparent surprise. "That's too bad. I've been lusting for Teofil since I first saw him." She threw him a saucy wink, then turned her attention to Ana. "A bunch of us are traveling to the party in a caravan. We'll have our servants with us, and we'll take things easy, so that means we need to leave tomorrow. I assume you'll be going with us. There's a lot to do to get ready." Vanita put her hands on her hips and looked at Teo again. "So, you big stallion, give her what she needs, then send her straight to me!"

Ana shifted uncomfortably on the bench, taken aback by Vanita's salacious assumptions. She was beginning to understand Ulmbartian culture well enough to know what Teo represented in Vanita's mind: an extremely handsome but low-status man with whom Ana could sate her desires until a man of proper rank came along. Vanita had stated in no uncertain terms that Ana's future in Ulmbartia depended on contracting the right marriage to a well-placed aristocrat. All of Vanita's assumptions were untrue, but Ana hadn't figured out how to explain that to her. She took a deep breath. "Actually, Vanita, I was thinking I'd leave the day after next. Teofil can escort me on horseback. I'm quite used to that."

"Really? How come you don't want to come with us?"

The question made Ana uneasy. She didn't want to insult her hostess, yet she didn't like the idea of traveling with Teo in a band of the young Ulmbartian elite. She had a feeling that if Teo were put in proximity to the local aristocrats, the social dynamic would become awkward. Torn between the man sitting next to her on the bench and the challenges of the new world she was trying to navigate, Ana offered the first excuse that popped into her head. "Teofil is uncomfortable in that setting," she said apologetically.

Teo made a sound of protest, but Ana ignored it.

"Suit yourself then," Vanita replied. "But you're going to miss out on some fun along the way. I guess I'll see you at the count's chateau." She turned and headed back to the palace.

"What was *that* about?" Teo demanded after Vanita left. "I'm not uncomfortable among that crowd. I don't respect them enough for them to have that effect on me!"

"I know. I'm sorry," Ana pleaded. "I just didn't know what else to say."

"So you pinned the blame on me?"

"Well, it's sort of true, isn't it? You don't exactly fit in with those aristocrats!"

Teo's face fell, and Ana immediately regretted her words. *I've hurt him,* she thought. She tried to salvage the situation. "What I mean is . . . your place here in Ulmbartia is uncertain—"

Teo stopped her with an upraised palm. "Enough. My place in life might be uncertain to you, but it's not to me. And it didn't used to be to you either."

He got up and left.

Ana didn't talk to him all the next day. Early on the morning of their scheduled departure for the chateau, she saw him standing in the palace courtyard with two fine palfreys, the kind whose ambling gait would quickly eat up the leagues. The horses were saddled and ready to go. Ana bit her lip, wondering if the journey would begin with another confrontation or just simmer with tense but submerged feelings.

The first thing Ana did when she entered the courtyard was apologize. Teo nodded and put his hand on her shoulder. "Listen, I know it's hard for you to make your way in this new kingdom," he said warmly. "I'll give you a lot of space to figure things out, okay? And I'll be here for you whenever you need me." Ana felt a burden lift from her shoulders at Teo's sweet words.

They left Vanita's estate, traveling easily on the well-marked road. The last portion of their journey hugged the southern tip of Greater Lake, a turquoise sea dotted with quaint fishing communities and the ruins of old villas.

The sun had already slipped behind the rugged foothills on their left when Teo and Ana arrived at a lakeside village. Some of the buildings along the waterfront had been reclaimed from the Ancients, their architecture a telltale mix of old-world grandeur and Ulmbartian ingenuity. The air was pleasantly warm, and the lake breezes carried the fragrance of honeysuckle. During spring the region would be awash with flowers, but even now, late in the eighth month, Ana could see why Vanita had called the lake district "the most beautiful part of Ulmbartia." A gorgeous place like this would be an inevitable resort area, in present times or in ancient.

"Look at those strange trees," Teo said.

Ana regarded the pole-like trees with bushy fronds on top. "Vanita told me about those," she said. "They're called palms."

They halted at an upscale inn. Teo entered, then quickly returned. "There aren't any rooms for the night because of all the travelers headed to the party. The barkeep says the only place with vacancies is a little island used by the fishermen." He pointed across the water to a pair of islands a short distance offshore. "We can leave our horses here at the stable and catch a ferry at the pier. How about if we have a drink and rest for a bit, then head out to the island for the night?"

"Anything is fine by me as long as I don't have to ride anymore," Ana said. "My hip is pretty sore."

The interior of the inn was pleasantly cool, with dark cherrywood paneling and a flagstone floor. From the many bottles behind the bar, Ana knew this was an establishment where any wine she might order would be a good one. The tables were occupied by travelers of various social positions, from immaculately dressed courtiers to simple peasants. Apparently the fruit of the vine was a universal pleasure for rich and poor alike.

Teo and Ana ordered at the bar, then found a table for two in the corner. As Ana had expected, her straw-colored spumante was exquisite. Teo, on the other hand, had ordered an ale, to the bartender's obvious displeasure.

They chatted for a while and sipped their drinks, then Teo excused himself. As Ana sat alone at the table, three men in expensive clothes approached.

"A woman as beautiful as you should never have an empty glass when courteous men are nearby," said a good-looking young man with even teeth and a light beard. He winked at Ana and held up a bottle of the exact wine she was drinking. "May I?" Without waiting for an answer, he refilled Ana's glass.

"We couldn't help but notice you're traveling alone," said another man. "We thought perhaps you'd like to join us. No doubt you're headed to Count Federco's chateau."

"Thank you. That's very kind of you," Ana replied. "But I'm not alone."

The men exchanged confused glances. "We saw no others with you," one said.

"I'm traveling with the man who was seated at the table."

"Oh, him!" The three young aristocrats chuckled among themselves. "We meant a man of your own station, not your groom. We thought you might want some genteel company along the way."

"Again I thank you, but my escort is all the company I need."

"The roads aren't safe as you go north," said the man with the beard who had spoken first. "We *insist* you travel with us." Ana sensed an aggressive undertone in his voice.

Teo walked up to the table. "Is there a problem here, friends?"

"We're making arrangements. Your opinions aren't needed."

Teo laughed and shook his head. "How about if you three move along and leave us alone?"

The bearded man turned and faced Teo with an angry glint in his eye. "How dare you speak to me like that!"

"I've done a lot of daring things in my life. Speaking to you isn't one of them."

The other two men closed around their leader. "You're going to be sorry you said that," one of them snarled.

"Where I'm from, a man has to back up his threats with action." Teo's tone was firm.

The leader drew a dagger from his belt and held it in front of him. "Maybe this will back up my words," he said. The other two men drew their blades as well.

Teo glanced down at the dagger, then grinned broadly as he met the leader's eyes. "Not if you're going to hold it like a little boy."

Teo's hand flashed out so quickly, Ana scarcely saw it move. It was as if she had blinked, then Teo was holding his opponent's knife. The leader's eyes were wide, and his mouth gaped in his close-cropped beard.

"Now it's two knives to one," Teo said, holding up the blade. His other hand shot out and disarmed a second man with the same wrist-twisting motion. Once again, the move was incredibly fast.

"Well, what do you know?" Teo asked good-naturedly. "Now I have two fine knives. It sort of changes the odds, doesn't it?"

The three men were unsure of themselves. "Give me back my dagger," the leader said. "It's a family heirloom."

Teo nodded with a knowing smile. "I didn't think it got much every-day use."

He spun the daggers in his hands, the blades whirling and causing the men to step back. Abruptly Teo flipped them up and caught them by the sharp tips above his head. In a single motion, he hurled them toward the leader. The man shrieked as the two daggers whizzed past his head and implanted themselves in a wine cask across the room.

Teo reached into his pocket and tossed the man a coin. "Buy your-selves a stout ale, gentlemen." He looked down at Ana. "Are you ready?"

"Definitely."

Ana couldn't help but smile as she slipped her arm into Teo's and let him escort her outside.

✦　✦　✦

For a few pennies, the boatman rowed Teo and Ana to the islands. The nearer one was covered in shrubbery and uninhabited. Though in the time of the Ancients it had housed a magnificent palace and botanical garden, the island had long since been scavenged for valuables; then nature took its course.

The second island, however, contained a thriving hamlet of fisher-men. After Teo and Ana were dropped at the quay, they entered a maze of quaint cobblestone alleys with hidden nooks and secret restaurants. Cozy plazas gave periodic glimpses of the dark blue evening sky. Every window seemed to be lit with an oil lamp, and strings of candle lanterns in bright colors were strung from building to building.

Ana wore a delighted smile on her face. "This island is so charming!"

"What do you think of spending the night at this place?" Teo gestured toward an inn with a clean and well-kept appearance tucked into a corner of the island. The patio faced the lake, whose waters caught the sheen of the newly risen moon. A pergola supported by carved stone pillars overflowed with climbing roses. The inn's proprietor had placed a single red blossom on each candlelit table.

"I couldn't imagine a better place," Ana said. "Let's check into our rooms first. I'll meet you at the restaurant in a few minutes."

Teo carried Ana's bag to her bedchamber, then located his own room. He found it to be exactly what he had expected: a simple yet comfortable space with a mirror, a bowl and ewer, and a bed overlaid by a thick duvet. He freshened up and straightened his clothes, then went down to the restaurant to wait.

Drumming his fingers on the table, Teo scanned the menu. The fare centered on the popular Ulmbartian specialty called pasta, which was served with creamy sauces and various kinds of fish. *I guess that's what I should expect at a place called Fisherman's Isle. I wonder—*

Teo's jaw dropped as Ana entered the restaurant.

She had put on makeup and changed into the same red dress in which she had appeared before the king. Her honey-blonde hair was done up around her head in an elegant style. Sparkling gemstones adorned her ears, and her neckline was trimmed with garnets. She had paused to smell one of the rose blossoms on the pergola, so she was turned away from Teo at an angle. The low scoop at the back of her dress revealed her pale skin and lovely female form. It occurred to Teo that perhaps he should look away, but it was impossible. He could only stare at her, transfixed by her beauty. Ana turned toward him, smiling as she caught his eye. He gulped. She was dazzling.

"I thought I should change into a gown for our nice dinner," she said as she approached the table. Teo stood up and held her chair. The action surprised Ana. "Why thank you, Captain," she said sweetly as she took her seat. "Isn't this a gorgeous place?"

He didn't answer right away. Instead he just sat across from her, gazing at her face. *Could any woman be more beautiful?* Ana's eyes were a stunning blue-green, surrounded by long eyelashes and delicate eyebrows in perfect little arches. Her cheekbones were impossibly high, and her skin was so smooth Teo had to fight the urge to trace his finger along her cheek. His eyes moved to her mouth. Those full, pink lips with just a hint of gloss made Teo's heartbeat accelerate. Ana's upper lip was dimpled, giving her mouth a heart-shaped appearance. She had a dainty chin . . . a creamy, caramel-colored throat . . . rounded, feminine shoulders.

Teo forced himself to arrest his gaze.

"What is it?" Ana asked. "What's the matter?"

Teo shook himself back to reality. "What?"

"You had a funny look on your face."

"Oh. Just hungry, I guess."

Ana motioned toward her surroundings. "I was just saying what a gorgeous place this is."

Teo leaned toward Ana, resting his elbows on the table. "You know how Vanita's house has that grand painting in the entry hall?"

"The one with the wild horses at sunset? I love that painting."

"Have you ever noticed the frame?"

"Sure. It's gilded and ornate. Such a magnificent painting deserves a frame like that."

Teo smiled and nodded. "Exactly." He gestured around the restaurant. "That's what this amazing place is tonight—merely a frame for a woman of exquisite beauty."

Ana inhaled sharply, and color rose to her cheeks. "That was nice, Teo," she said, unable to suppress the smile that played at the corners of her lips. She fiddled with her menu, then looked up at Teo from underneath her eyelashes. Their eyes met. Blushing some more, she glanced away with a little laugh.

The waiter arrived with a plate of sliced meat and artichoke hearts, then took their orders. Teo and Ana relaxed in the nearly empty restaurant as they talked in the soft glow of the candle. The wine was plentiful, and each course of the meal was a delight. As the moon rose higher in the sky, the stars came out one by one over the lake. The conversation turned to spiritual matters, and Teo told Ana about his theological discussions with Sol. Such topics had to be closely guarded, Teo warned, because of the evil shamans. Despite that grim reminder, Ana was pleased to hear that Sol was a believer in Deu and had his own copy of the Sacred Writing.

"So he has the entire Old Testament?" she asked with excitement. "All this time we've been missing the last few books. Maybe that's where we can learn about, um . . . what was that name carved on the cross?"

"It was Iesus Christus, but Sol told me that name isn't mentioned in the Old Testament. He thinks it's the name of a predicted savior—either the Promised King or the Suffering Servant."

"I would think the savior sent by Deu would rule as a king, wouldn't you?"

"Yes, that's my theory too. The Suffering Servant was his helper in some way."

Ana pounded her fist lightly on the table. "The key to all this is the New Testament. That must be where the predictions are fulfilled. Teo, you have to find the rest of the Sacred Writing."

"Why me? Why not both of us?"

Ana hesitated for a moment, biting her lip. Teo sensed she was experiencing profound uncertainty about what she wished to say. Finally she gathered her courage and spoke. "There's something I've been wanting to tell you, but I'm not sure how you'll react."

"Go ahead. I won't judge you."

Ana nodded gratefully and took a deep breath. "When we were on the pass and I was sick, I did something you don't know about. You'll think it strange when I tell you, but I want you to know why I did it." Teo offered encouragement, so she continued. "I switched the corks in the bottles so you would get the good medicine."

The news struck Teo like a physical blow. He shook his head, trying to understand what he was hearing. *She intentionally took the bad medicine? That explains why she didn't get better! But it also means . . .*

"Why would you do that?" Teo asked. "You almost died!"

"It's simple. I knew I wouldn't be able to discover the story of Deu without you. That's the kind of mystery only you can solve. Maybe I can be at your side when it happens, but I'm not an explorer. I can't go investigating old libraries and ancient ruins. I don't know what to look for, and even if I did, I can't read old languages. That's your world, Teo. You're the only one who can uncover the truth about Deu and his savior. And also . . . you're the only one who could find the way back to Chiveis."

"But the medicine . . . even though you were dying, you secretly gave the good bottle to me. In essence, you gave—" Teo was reduced to stunned silence as the enormity of Ana's self-sacrifice crystallized in his mind.

Her blue-green eyes grew deadly serious. "Swear something to me, Teo. Swear right now that you'll find the New Testament and learn the message of Deu. Swear that nothing will deter you until you've found it—nothing at all! And then swear you will return to Chiveis with the message of salvation."

She reached out for him. Teo grasped her hand in his, deeply moved by what Ana had done, and what it meant, and what she was now asking.

"I swear these things to you, Ana," he said. "I will do them as you have asked. May Deu be the witness of my oath."

"Thank you, Teo. I can't tell you what that means to me."

Ana relaxed, and Teo released her hand. It took a few seconds for the intensity of the moment to pass.

The waiter's arrival broke the spell. With the second course now finished, he brought a dessert of sweet chestnut parfait and glasses of amaretto. At last, when Teo felt he could eat no more, he suggested a stroll around the island. Ana was happy to oblige.

Under the multicolored glow of twinkling lamps, Teo and Ana browsed the few shops that were still open. Ulmbartians typically ate dinner very late, so they were just now putting away their wares and heading out for a meal. Ana stopped at a jewelry shop and bent close to the case. "Teo, come here!" She beckoned him with her hand while staring at the jewelry. "Look at this!"

He joined her. The case was filled with necklaces and bracelets of various styles. Teo's eyes fell on the pendant Ana was inspecting: a gold cross with a man nailed upon it. The man's side was wounded, and on his head he wore a crown of thorns. An inscription on the cross read *Passio Iesu Christi*.

"The cross is Deu's symbol," Ana said, "but I didn't know it was a place of death."

"And look, it mentions Iesus Christus. That must be him on the cross."

"What do you suppose *passio* means?"

"I'm not sure. I'll ask Sol when we get home." Teo caught the attention of the store's owner, an attractive, middle-aged woman. "How much for this piece?" he asked.

The woman glanced at the cross pendant on the gold chain. "It's an antique. It was dug out of the ground somewhere around here. The art dealers have no idea what it is, but anything made by the Ancients is costly." She held up one hand, her fingers spread. "Five scudi."

Teo reached into his pocket. "I'll take it." He handed over the money.

"Teo, that's way too much," Ana whispered. "You can't afford it."

"On this night, I can."

Teo laid the pendant in Ana's palm. She stared at it, caressing it with her finger. "The man's face is so sad. But his eyes are full of love."

Ana looked up at Teo. "Put it on me." She spun around so he could fasten it behind her neck, then turned to face him again. "Thank you, Teofil," she said with a tremor in her voice.

"You're welcome. I wanted you to have it as a symbol."

"Of what?"

"Tonight you made me swear to seek the meaning of this mystery. I admire how you're so committed to proclaiming Deu's message in Chiveis. You had that desire even before we left home. Your refusal to deny him is why you're standing here now. Only Deu knows how long we'll wander in exile. But if he allows it, we'll discover the whole truth and take the message back to our people."

Ana nodded with her eyes closed. "Yes. Come to our people, O mighty Deu."

Teo reached out and touched the pendant with his finger. "Let this gift be a reminder of Deu's presence, and let it symbolize our goal of discovering his teachings."

"So be it," Ana agreed.

The hour had grown late, so Teo and Ana circled the island and made their way back to the inn. They paused at the water's edge to enjoy the breeze for a few moments before going inside. An alley cat howled in the distance, while at their feet the water lapped against the cobblestone pavement.

Ana inhaled deeply. "This island is magical," she said. "Everything about it is romantic and charming. It's the kind of place every girl wants to go with the man in her life."

Teo glanced over at Ana. Her eyes were fixed on some distant point across the lake. "Do you wish you had a man in your life?" he asked.

She nodded. "More than ever before."

Teo didn't answer right away. He stood in the moonlight, turning Ana's statement over in his mind. No doubt it was prompted by her trauma at being yanked from her homeland. *Women seek security*, Teo thought. *She's feeling the need for that right now. So what does she want from me?*

The answer struck him with clarity: My *presence.*

Okay. But does that mean romance?

Teo started to speak, then held back, recalling Ana's comment that he wouldn't fit in with the aristocrats. Although he didn't think Ana wanted to marry some rich prince, he wasn't sure she wanted to make her way in Ulmbartia on the bottom of the social ladder either. That wouldn't be much of a life for her. It certainly wouldn't provide any security. Teo tried to think of the best way to care for Ana. *You said you'd give her space to figure things out*, he reasoned. *Don't take advantage of her just because you shared a night of rosebushes and candlelight!*

He let his voice take on a casual, joking tone. "Right now the man in your life is worn out from a day's riding." He stretched and yawned. "What do you say we turn in for the night?"

Ana nodded, then turned and walked inside. When Teo followed a few moments later, she had already retired to her room.

✦   ✦   ✦

Vanita Labella had been right about one thing: Count Federco's lakeside chateau was remote. As Ana rode up to it with Teo beside her, she had the feeling of being in the wilderness again.

After departing Fisherman's Isle in the morning Teo and Ana had ridden hard so as not to arrive too late. Now it was only midafternoon, leaving plenty of time for Ana to get changed before the evening feast. The elegant meal was a precursor to the main event: the vintage gala on the island the next day.

Ana could see the island a short distance offshore jutting out of the lake. Unlike Fisherman's Isle, this one was just a tiny rock with nothing on it but the abandoned fortress. It looked as if the ruined castle rose straight out of the water. *Spooky and atmospheric,* Ana thought. *The perfect place for a mysterious soirée.*

A page greeted Teo and Ana at the chateau's grand entrance. He asked for their names and checked his list. "I'll gladly show you to Lady Vanita's rooms," he said to Ana, then looked at Teo and pointed over his shoulder. "The stables are that way."

Teo bowed to Ana and gave her a salute. "I believe this is where your bodyguard takes his leave, m'lady."

Ana smiled uncertainly. "Alright. So, uh . . . thanks for getting me here. I guess I'll see you around."

She was led to the opulent staterooms of the chateau's living quarters. The page knocked on a door, and Vanita answered. "Anastasia! I'm glad you made it! Come in."

Vanita threw her arms around Ana in an effusive hug, then led her into a room full of pretty young women. "We're all trying on our gowns for the feast tonight. This is going to be like the old days when Ulmbartians threw parties that rivaled those of the Likurians! Let's see if we can find you something special, okay? I'm thinking you need a low-cut number to catch a few eyes. You certainly have the body to pull it off!" Vanita winked at Ana in a conspiratorial way.

As the girls chatted, the topic shifted from hairstyles to that other inevitable subject: men. Vanita suggested the names of a few courtiers Ana should get to know. The idea repelled her.

"What would be so wrong with a teacher?" Ana asked. "Like Teofil, for instance?"

Vanita gave her a blank look. "You can't be serious."

"Why not?"

"First of all, a teacher has no money. He has to earn *wages* of all things! And even worse, nobody of our station would ever speak to you again. All this"—Vanita waved her hand around the room—"would just disappear. *Poof!*"

Ana wouldn't have minded doing without the luxuries, but the thought of starting over with a new social group was daunting. Though the aristocratic girls could be vain and superficial at times, they provided a sense of belonging that Ana cherished. Vanita came to her side, putting an arm around her shoulder.

"I really like you, Anastasia," she said. "I don't want you to disappear into some commoner's hovel. Teofil isn't husband material. He's for physical enjoyment only."

Ana had finally had enough of that sort of talk. "Listen, Vanita, we're not involved like that. We don't sleep together. In fact, I've never even been with—" She stopped, not wanting to say too much, though she feared she already had.

Vanita stared at Ana, then a slow smile crept across her face. She leaned close. "So . . . you're one of those proper girls, are you? Well, don't worry, your secret is safe with me." Ana didn't consider it a "secret" to be ashamed of, but she wasn't sure what to say next, so Vanita continued. "That's all the more reason not to waste your time with Teofil. He's of no use to you whatsoever."

"He's my friend," Ana protested. "We have a—a *bond*."

"A bond? What makes you think he has a bond with you? In my experience men aren't bonded until you've gotten a ring from them—and even then it's iffy."

"Teo isn't like that. He has—" Ana sought the right word. "He has strong feelings for me."

"Has he ever said so?"

Ana thought it over. One time, back in Chiveis, Teo had made a pass at her, but she had found it inappropriate. Pushing him away, he had toppled into a fountain. Ana shook that unpleasant memory out of her head and recalled a different instance—the time they stood together on a balcony, holding hands in the moonlight. She believed something profound had passed between them then, forged by their shared adversity in the wilderness when Teo rescued her from her abductors.

Yet despite their seeming bond, they had never actually discussed whether their relationship included romantic feelings. Ana's thoughts went to the previous night, when she and Teo had enjoyed such an idyllic evening on Fisherman's Isle. True, he had complimented her looks, but why hadn't he expressed interest in a more serious relationship? Last night would have been the perfect opportunity. She had dressed up just for him.

She had expressed her desire for a man in her life. But in the end he had yawned in her face.

An unbidden thought entered Ana's mind: *I bet Teo spoke sweetly to Sucula! He whispered tender things to her in the secret warmth of her bed!* Ana recoiled at the memory of the beautiful Chiveisian housewife with whom Teo had almost committed adultery. *If he's capable of that*, whispered the voice in her head, *could he truly have feelings for you?*

Vanita broke into Ana's turbulent thoughts. "Anastasia, sweetie—I can see I've upset you. Tonight isn't a night for sadness. Let's get you dressed in something slinky and go have some fun."

Ana let Vanita lead her by the hand toward the other girls. *Maybe I would like to try something slinky for once*, she said to herself.

◆　◆　◆

After parting with Ana at the gatehouse, Teo decided a little reconnaissance was in order. He knelt in the forest, inspecting the tracks on the ground. Rovers had passed by here. A large group of them. Recently.

Teo returned to the lakeshore chateau, examining its defenses as he approached. The building had been constructed for an idealized appearance more than for fighting off real enemies. Its battlements and towers were ill-positioned for actual defense, and vines clung to its walls, giving any invader the opportunity to climb to the second floor. The place had the charming and archaic look of a stronghold but lacked the fortifications a true stronghold would require.

The guard at the gate was dozing, his chair leaned back against the wall. Teo kicked it out from under him. The man cried out and scrambled from the ground, sputtering in confusion. Before he could speak, Teo challenged him. "Does your commander know Rovers have been within a league of this place in the last two days?"

"Huh? There aren't any Rovers here! Who are you?"

"The only person who understands the danger we're in, apparently," Teo said in disgust. He brushed past the guard, ignoring the man's indignant protests, and entered the chateau's central courtyard.

Lords in fine tailcoats and ladies in elegant gowns were making their way to the ballroom, where tables had been set for the evening feast. Teo could sense the excited buzz that had fallen on the place. Everyone seemed oblivious to the threat of a raid. Either they were ignorant of it or they deliberately chose to ignore it. Teo resolved that even if the pompous aristocrats were willing to flirt with danger, no harm would came to Ana because of it.

Although Teo was well-dressed, he knew his navy blue doublet and gray pants weren't suitable for such an upscale event. Unable to mingle unnoticed, he decided to find a vantage point from which to keep an eye on the ballroom, while at the same time watching for any disturbance outside.

After a few twists and turns in the chateau's labyrinth of corridors, Teo came to a staircase. It led to a hallway lined with the doors of numerous guest rooms, but another door opened onto a mezzanine that encircled the ballroom. Empty suits of armor stood at attention around the room, holding staffs with heraldic banners that dangled over the railing. Down on the parquet floor, the aristocrats in their finery sat at cloth-covered tables or mingled in witty conversation. Teo didn't see Ana.

As he crept toward a part of the mezzanine with exterior windows, a sudden movement in the shadows caught his attention. He glimpsed two figures in black hooded robes make a quick exit. Though he had no idea who they were, he made a mental note of their appearance.

The windows looked out on the forest. From this position, Teo could see the expanse of grass in front of the chateau's entrance. Everything was quiet outside, so he turned toward the ballroom. He hadn't scanned the floor long when he spotted Ana making conversation with a gaggle of handsome men of varying ages. One of Ana's conversation partners, a distinguished gentleman with a gray mustache, wore a medallion around his neck and a purple sash across his body. No doubt it was Count Federco Borromo himself.

Ana was dressed in a shimmering gown of silver sequins, with a plunging neckline and a slitted skirt that revealed her slender legs. Even from a distance Teo could see the gown was formfitting and very appealing. He frowned and shook his head, annoyed by what he knew was running through the minds of the eager young men surrounding her.

As the party wore on and the evening dusk faded into darkness, Teo kept watch at the window for any sign of trouble. Every time he turned to look down at the ballroom, he grew more irritated, but he tried not to let the stream of men mobbing Ana bother him. *This distraction is exactly what she needs,* he reminded himself. *She's been through enough, being displaced from her home and family. Let her make some new friends in Ulmbartia. You don't own her, Teo. Give her some space.*

Teo did notice, however, that throughout the evening Ana had little to eat but a lot to drink. One man in particular, a pale fellow with slicked-back hair, was particularly attentive to her thirst. He kept returning from the punch bowl with a new glass for her. Teo watched the man closely as he paused in a corner with Ana's drink. The man's body was turned away so his actions couldn't be seen, but Teo had been to enough parties to realize what was happening. When Ana put her hand to her forehead a few minutes later and the man reached out to steady her, Teo rose from his hiding place. The man began to steer Ana toward the door with his arm around her waist. It was time to move.

As Teo was turning to go, a flickering orange light in the darkness outside caught his eye. He pressed his face to the windowpane. The light flared up the way a match will do, then settled to a smaller flame that pulsed a few times, then went out. Someone was in the forest, smoking. Teo watched for several seconds. Once he felt certain an attack wasn't imminent, he turned back to the ballroom. Ana was gone.

Teo left the mezzanine and ran downstairs to the main floor. Forcing himself to walk at a reasonable pace, he circled the ballroom. Ana was nowhere to be seen in the foyers outside each of the doors. He pounded his fist in his hand. *Where would that guy have taken her?* The obvious answer hit him. He dashed back upstairs to the corridor lined with guest rooms. Rounding a corner, he crashed into Ana's devious escort, knocking the man flat on his back.

"Ach! What is the meaning of this?" the man exclaimed. He struggled to rise from the floor, his slick hair now standing up wildly.

"The meaning is, *Nice try.*" Teo grabbed an ornamental sword from a suit of armor and planted its tip through the man's pant cuff deep into the hardwood floor. Grabbing Ana by the arm, he steered her around the corner.

"T-Teo! What's . . . goin' . . . on?" Ana staggered, and her breath reeked of alcohol.

"Your punch was spiked, and you're drunk. I'm putting you to bed. What's your room number?"

"Twen' two," Ana said dizzily.

Teo was standing outside Ana's chamber fumbling with her key when she began to groan. He looked at her ashen face. Beads of sweat stood out on her forehead.

"Don't worry, Ana, I'll—"

She gagged, then vomited explosively down the front of his doublet. "Ohh . . ." she moaned, swaying on her feet. He wiped her mouth with his sleeve and unlocked her bedroom door.

A voice rang out from down the corridor. "Look! It's that uppity groom again!"

"Get your paws off her, you dirty commoner!" cried someone else. Teo recognized the voice: the bearded courtier from the confrontation at the tavern. The group of young aristocrats began to hurry down the hallway.

Ana's eyes widened. Though she was inebriated, Teo could see she recognized the embarrassment of the situation. She would be the butt of jokes in Ulmbartian social circles for years to come: the peasant girl who tried to become a lady had revealed her true colors at her first ball. Ana would become a laughingstock.

He could not let that happen to her.

Teo spun away from Ana and stumbled toward the approaching men. He put a drunken slur in his voice. "Whada you guys want?" he demanded, staring at them with his eyelids half-closed and his jaw slack.

"Oh, gods! You're covered in *filth*." The bearded courtier gagged and shielded his nose with a kerchief. The other men shrank back as well.

"Yup! Stole me a bottle." Teo mimicked a stupefied chuckle.

The leader with the manicured beard called out over Teo's shoulder, "Miss, are you alright? Is this man bothering you?"

"I'm fine," Ana managed to say.

"Allow me to help you to your room." He made a move toward her.

Teo stepped into his path. "Uh-uh." He shook his head. "Stay back."

"Out of my way or you'll be sorry." The man wrapped his kerchief around his knuckles and cocked his arm.

Teo laughed to himself. *This guy's too dainty to touch me with his bare hand.*

"Move now, groom, or I'll take you down."

Teo shook his head again.

The lace-covered fist started to move.

How did I get myself into this? Teo wondered.

The man hit him square on the jaw.

"Nicely done, lord!" cried one of the courtiers.

Teo took a dive, stumbling back so he would knock a vase from its stand. It crashed to the floor and shattered. Ana squealed and ducked into her room, latching the door behind her. The bearded aristocrat walked over to Teo, lying on his back among the porcelain shards.

"You disgust me," the man said, spitting in Teo's face. He turned abruptly and walked down the hallway with his retinue behind him.

✦   ✦   ✦

Hrath the Almighty tightened the strap on his iron helmet as he sat in the prow of the boat. Though the vessel was crowded with warriors, it was well made and slipped easily through the murky waters. Even so, the Rover chieftain wanted to get his feet on dry land as soon as possible. His wandering tribesmen were not used to boats.

"Quietly, men," he grunted over his shoulder, gesturing for silence.

From up ahead, the sound of genteel music wafted across the water. A few lights twinkled on the island. Hrath glanced at the sky. The moon was hidden behind a thick overcast—an auspicious omen.

When the emissaries from the shaman brotherhood had approached him a week ago with a proposal, Hrath had thought the deal was too good to be true. For a long time he had wanted to pillage the Ulmbartian chateau on the lakeshore but had held off because the consequences outweighed the benefits. Hrath knew he could capture the poorly defended chateau—but what would the payoff be? Carved furniture and massive tapestries were of no use to him. As a wandering man, Hrath traded in a currency of a more mobile sort: treasure and slaves. An attack on the chateau would put the Ulmbartian army hot on his trail, and for what? A few old gardeners to cart into slavery? The rich aristocrat who owned the place wasn't foolish enough to keep anything of value there. A raid wasn't worth the effort.

The arrival of the shamans in Hrath's camp had changed matters entirely. The hooded priests announced they could provide slaves in abundance—beautiful young women draped with jewels of the most expensive sort. A hot hunger stirred in Hrath's belly as he considered the violence he would soon enjoy. And to think, the price for all this was something he could easily provide. The only payment the shamans had demanded was the annihilation of every living person who wasn't carried off as a slave.

As the island began to draw near, Hrath mentally rehearsed his battle plan one more time. The guests had enjoyed their feast yesterday without disturbance. Now their guard was down, so a quick strike at the island would take them by surprise. Hrath's boats would surround the place, while a contingent of men with axes would scuttle the barge by which the revelers had been ferried to the lonely island. With the victims having no chance for escape, Hrath and his raiders could slaughter the defenseless men at leisure and round up the females. A squadron on the shore would encircle the chateau and prevent anyone from fleeing. Once the island was secure, the main bulk of Hrath's forces would close on the chateau and kill whomever they found inside. Hrath smirked as he considered how the chateau's fancy featherbeds would be used tonight.

The castle loomed large up ahead. Hrath raised his fist, and the leaders in the boats to his right and left repeated the signal for absolute silence. A hush fell upon the war party. The only sound on the lake was the gentle drip of water from the paddles as the boats moved into position.

Hrath glided toward a cobblestone landing that gave entrance to the castle's central keep. In a moment he would be ashore with his sword in hand, while his men surrounded the island and attacked from all angles. Hrath could feel his heart thumping as the battle neared.

From high above, a war horn shattered the darkness. The startled raiders cried out, their surprise echoed by fearful shouts from inside the castle ruins.

A streak of fire shot to the surface of the lake, and a flame sprang up where the arrow landed. The attackers were illuminated in a flickering glow as three more fire arrows followed in rapid succession, setting ablaze an oily film that clung to the water.

Hrath had no time to consider the mysterious oil upon the lake. Though the flames now blocked any progress around the fortress, a channel of undisturbed water provided access to the main gateway at the head of the cobblestone landing. Enraged, Hrath lifted his sword and pointed toward the opening.

"Press the attack, brothers! Straight ahead! We can still take them! Follow me!"

He hit the cobblestones on the run and dashed underneath the ancient portcullis into the keep. Having scouted the island earlier, he knew the way through the decrepit building to the exit on the other side. His new plan was to burst upon the terrified partygoers in a flood of mayhem and steel, slaughtering them as if things had gone according to his original design.

Hrath rushed into the final room at the head of his ravenous war party and threw his shoulder against the door to the castle's courtyard.

It didn't budge.

Furious, he kicked the door with the sole of his boot, but it remained firm even though it had no latch. Someone had obviously barred it with a stout beam. The room filled with angry warriors, all of them shouting murderous threats and clamoring to be released. More men pressed from behind.

"Retreat, brothers!" Hrath shouted. "We'll find another way in!" He tried to push his men back, but the general confusion and tight quarters prevented his order from being obeyed.

A screeching sound assaulted the men's ears. "It's a demon!" one of the raiders yelled, and a ripple of terror coursed through the room. The men cowered and stopped their ears as the screech intensified, culminating in a tremendous crash.

"It's not a demon, you fools! It's the portcullis! It's been dropped! We're trapped!"

Hrath shoved aside the flustered men and clawed his way to a fireplace. He scaled the stone face until he could stand on the mantel and stretch to look out a high window. The warrior with the horn was now in the courtyard, ordering gentlemen in their formal coats to pull on thick ropes. Hrath's eyes followed the ropes to where they were attached. Fear gripped him for the first time as he realized they were tied to the timbers that buttressed the wall of the keep.

A squad of Hrath's tribesmen burst into the courtyard from a different door. Their axes identified them as the men who had been sent to scuttle the barge. Hrath's heart swelled as he saw them rampage among the terrified aristocrats. In a moment the men pulling the ropes would be scattered by the axmen, and then the threat of a collapse would be over. His brave comrades would unbar the door and secure their victory. "Over here, brothers!" Hrath shouted, but he couldn't be heard over the din.

The lone warrior spun to face the oncoming raiders. He was tall and lean and built like a fighting man. A long sword and a battle ax were in his hands.

"Taste our steel," Hrath snarled.

The invading axmen rushed to attack, but it was they who tasted the mortal bite of the blade. The dark-haired warrior was like a demigod, a fighter of such skill that Hrath couldn't believe his eyes. His movements were impossibly quick, each calculated to waste no effort in delivering a devastating blow. He dodged among Hrath's raiders as if they were children playing war games with a grown man. Every time the warrior's sword slashed down, a raider fell to the earth. Every time his ax descended, a raider's helmet was split open in a shower of blood.

With a loud scraping noise, one of the timber buttresses snapped free from the wall. The aristocrats tugging the rope toppled backward at the sudden release of tension. A cascade of dust and mortar fell on Hrath's shoulders. He winced as a heavy rock glanced off his ear.

Another buttress was pulled away from the wall outside. The explosive thunder of stone breaking apart reverberated in the crowded room.

Huge chunks of masonry slammed to the floor, crushing those below like insects underfoot.

Outside, the lone warrior turned his stare upon the keep. The bodies of his defeated foes lay about him.

CRACK!

A gaping fissure opened in the keep's exterior wall. The trapped raiders screamed as the massive stone ceiling began to tumble.

I've been outdone, Hrath realized. His men cried for mercy from the gods.

The last thing Hrath the Almighty knew before the world went black was the warm trickle of his bladder letting go.

CHAPTER

5

Nikolo Borja turned his head on the pillow. "Not so hard, you incompetent fool," he barked to the masseur. The fingers rubbing Borja's fleshy back lessened their pressure. A splash of olive oil trickled down his spine, and the strokes became more soothing.

"Mmm . . ." he murmured. "That's more like it."

There was a knock at the door, then it opened. Borja struggled to lift his jowls from the massage table. Squinting, he discerned the silhouette of his personal bodyguard and most trusted lieutenant standing in the doorway of the dimly lit room.

Known to all as the Iron Shield, the man towered head and shoulders over Borja, yet he moved like a cat. His crushing mace hung from his belt, and a chain-mail hauberk protected him even though an attack did not seem imminent, for the Iron Shield lived by the principle that violence was a way of life. Borja had seen the man fight: he was a maelstrom of aggression and speed, a giant against whom few opponents could stand.

"You summoned me, my lord?" The dark warrior spread his hands and bowed at the waist.

"Two strangers have arrived in Ulmbartia," Borja said gruffly. "A man and a woman. They have knowledge of the Creator and the Criminal."

The Iron Shield uttered a curse. "Ulmbartia has been purged of that religion," he said. "It must not be allowed to reemerge there."

"Indeed not." Borja let out a grunt as the masseur began to knead his hamstrings. "I ordered the Chief Shaman of Ulmbartia to devise a plan. The death of the man and woman was to be blamed on the barbarians that infest the northern mountains. Unfortunately, that plan was thwarted by the man."

"How, my lord?"

"It turns out he is no wandering prophet with a shaggy beard. He's a proficient warrior who outfoxed a horde of barbarians."

"Interesting. A worthy foe perhaps."

"Yes. And one we must pay closer attention to. Such a man could gain a following. I would not wish to see him galvanize the masses around his religion and spark a rebellion."

"What then is your command?"

"A new approach. The strangers must be apprehended and interrogated. I wish to know as much as possible about them. Who sent them to Ulmbartia? Are others in league with them? What do they know about the Enemy? Do they have his writings? Only after we have learned these things can the strangers be dispatched."

"I will accomplish this as you command, my lord."

"Good. And I am certain you will not fail me as the Chief Shaman of Ulmbartia did." Borja blinked sweat out of his eyes. "What course of action would you advise?"

The Iron Shield folded his arms across his chest. "It would be unwise for me to appear in Ulmbartia. It would arouse suspicion against the brotherhood. Instead we should lure the strangers to the Likurian coast. There I could deal with them personally, without intermediaries to fail us this time."

Borja stared at his lieutenant. "Do we now tremble in fear of the people's suspicions, shield of my life?"

The Iron Shield met Borja's gaze without flinching. "We do not fear, Your Abundance. I merely counsel a strategic approach. In Likuria I would be free to deal with the strangers as I please. The dominion of our brotherhood is greater there."

Borja allowed a smile to creep across his face. "Many men are blessed by the gods with the strength of brutes, but few are like you—both strong and crafty! Very well, we will lure the strangers to Likuria so you can apprehend them. How can we achieve this?"

"Perhaps we can use the Likurian dohj? He is youthful and fears us."

Borja turned the idea over in his mind. Several years ago he had traveled up the coast from Roma and met the Likurian prince named Cristof. Borja could tell by the way the dohj carried himself that the man was cowardly and stupid—useful traits in a foreign ruler.

The masseur slapped Borja on the hip. He rolled over, wheezing with the effort, and lay on his back. Sweat ran in ticklish streams into the folds of his great belly. The masseur began to work on Borja's right thigh with firm, squeezing motions. Since he could no longer see the Iron Shield, Borja spoke into the air, which was thick with menthol. "The strangers, it seems, have taken up residence with a rice baron, Duke Labella of Novarre. I believe we can turn the local politics to our advantage. The Likurians and Ulmbartians have concluded a trade agreement pertaining to rice and olives. In such instances the exchange of hospitality is considered normal. Dohj Cristof likes nothing better than to cavort on the beach with the glittering aristocracy of the neighboring realms." Borja chuckled and licked sweat from his upper lip. "Duke Labella's household would be a logical choice to be invited to Likuria for a pleasant winter on the coast, don't you think? Perhaps you could travel to Likuria and convince the dohj of this."

"Consider it done," said the Iron Shield.

Borja hawked mucus and spat a wad on the floor. "I will send you with enough gold to ease the way, in the event that fear is not a sufficient motivator."

"Fear and gold can accomplish any desire."

"Indeed it—ow!" Borja flinched as a cramp seized his calf. The muscle felt like it had been tied in a painful knot. The masseur gasped and tried to rub it out, but Borja shook his leg free of the man's grasp and craned his neck until he could see his bodyguard. "Shield of my life, apply a harsh punishment to this clumsy slave!"

The Iron Shield exploded across the room, his mace flashing in a wide arc. With a sound like a butcher tenderizing beef, the masseur took the impact of the mace on his left shoulder. The blow lifted the man from his feet and hurled his body across the room. He lay crumpled in a corner, making a gurgling sound.

Borja massaged his calf and stretched his foot until the cramp finally subsided. He squirmed off the massage table, wiped the top of his bald head with a towel, then waddled to the masseur in the corner. The man's tunic bore a spreading red stain. Borja looked down at him and cackled.

"Quick! Fetch a slave from the spa! I think this poor fellow could use a rubdown!" He laughed until his belly shook, delighting in the irony of his clever joke.

The Iron Shield disappeared, then returned a few moments later. "Your every word is a divine command to me, my lord," he said as he gestured to a figure behind him.

Another masseur stood in the doorway, his eyes wide.

❖   ❖   ❖

An evening coolness had descended on the teachers' cottage at the Labella estate. Teo accepted a glass of grappa from Sol's hand. "Cheers," Teo said, lifting his drink and putting it to his lips.

Sol winked and drained his glass in a single slug, then grimaced and set it on the table next to the empty dinner dishes. "That's hard stuff we Ulmbartians make! It'll help the risotto go down. Do you have anything like it in your land?"

"We have many spirits, but not from grapes. We distill a lot of other fruits though."

"Sometime I'll have to try some Chiveisian brandy."

"Sometime," Teo agreed with a nod.

Sol handed Teo a bowl of nuts, then took a seat by the window of his little apartment. "So continue with your tale, young Teofil. It seems your relationship with Anastasia is like a bird's flight—erratic and hard to predict."

"Yeah, that's for sure. Where was I?"

"You had shared the lovely dinner, then parted ways at Count Federco's chateau."

"Oh, right." Teo resumed the story of his recent escapades in the north, describing the grand feast and Ana's accidental drunkenness, then the battle on the following night at the island castle. Sol listened in amazement.

"You mean you single-handedly defeated a war party of Rovers? I've never heard anything like it!"

"It wasn't as hard as you might think. All it took was an eye for tactics and a little planning. I tied a couple of ropes to a rickety wall, barred the door, then funneled the attackers into the castle with some casks of lantern oil that I broke open in the lake. That stuff is really flammable."

Sol nodded. "There are places in Ulmbartia where black fluid oozes from the ground. Our oil is prized not only for lighting but for naval combat. It burns on water and sticks to hulls."

"Well, it worked perfectly this time. The invaders charged into the keep, then I cut the rope to the gate. Once they were trapped, all I had to do was bring down the ceiling on their heads. Count Federco was extremely grateful. I think I made a friend that night."

"It's good to have at least one friend among the Ulmbartian aristocrats," Sol said. "It sounds like you've made enemies of others."

Teo tsked. "Do I care?"

"Probably not, but perhaps you should, at least a little."

"I'll watch myself. Thanks."

"How do things stand with Anastasia?"

"Exactly the same as before: confused."

"She's listening to bad voices."

"I know. Those rich girls."

"And perhaps something even worse."

Teo sighed. "I haven't talked to Ana since we got back. In fact, I didn't speak with her the whole time I was at the chateau, except when she was, you know—"

"Intoxicated?"

"Yeah." Teo frowned. "I didn't like seeing her like that. I wish I could get my hands on that guy who—"

"Revenge never satisfies," Sol said, holding up his hand. "Deus does not call us to be his vigilantes."

"You're right." Teo shook his head to clear away the negative thoughts. "Hey, speaking of Deus, I wanted to ask you about something I found on the island where we had dinner. It was a gold pendant with words engraved on it. The Old Words, I believe."

"Latin?"

"I think so. It said *Passio Iesu Christi*. I assume that's another form of the name Iesus Christus?"

"Yes. The phrase means 'the suffering of Iesus Christus.'"

"Suffering! That explains a lot. The man on the pendant was suffering alright. He was nailed to a cross."

Sol's head jerked around. "Nailed to a cross?" He rose from his seat and approached Teo's bench. "Describe it," he whispered.

Teo assumed a hushed voice as well. "He had a crown of thorns, and a wound in his side. His hands and feet bled too. And yet his face was peaceful."

"The Pierced One!" Sol said as he exhaled.

Teo arched his eyebrows but didn't know how to reply.

"It's a lost religion," Sol went on. "I'm sure if the shamans found out I know of it, I would be taken away to their 'pleasant valley.'"

"Where's that?"

"No one knows. But I can guarantee you, it's not pleasant."

"What do you know about the Pierced One?"

Instead of answering, Sol went to his desk and brought out a slate and chalk. "Let's do some serious thinking. I want you to write down every fact you know about Deus." He handed the slate to Teo. "Write it in Talyano," he added.

"I'll try. I can speak Talyano well enough, but I'm not sure how well I can write it yet."

"You're doing fine, Teofil. This is how you learn. Begin."

Teo thought for a moment, then scrawled his list on the piece of black slate. He could think of ten things:

1. Creator of all
2. Only true God, no idols
3. Good, benevolent
4. Hates sin, requires sacrifice
5. Land is called Israël
6. King David wrote hymns

7. Promised King predicted
8. Suffering Servant predicted
9. Book has Old, New Testaments
10. Iesus Christus = Pierced One on cross

"How's this?" Teo showed the slate to Sol, who inspected it for a long time.

"Good. Most of these things you've learned from the Holy Book, and so have I." Sol looked up from the slate and met Teo's eyes. "Except for the last two. These are new to me since you've arrived."

"Really? It sounded like you already knew about the religion of the Pierced One."

"I'd heard of it, but the pendant you found has added something new. I had no idea Iesus Christus is the Pierced One. I had never connected those two figures before. Until you came to this land, I only knew the name Iesus as a savior promised in Deu's book—either the king or the servant. Now I think I know which one he was."

Teo waited for Sol to finish. When he didn't speak, Teo motioned for him to go on.

"The Suffering Servant obviously."

Teo slapped his forehead as the facts slipped into place. "Of course! Passio means 'suffering'! Iesus Christus suffered on the cross. Maybe he even died for Deu's cause. Somehow that helped the king establish his reign."

"I think you could be right. But we need to find out more." Sol ran his fingers through his long white hair, then went to a cabinet against the wall. Returning with the bottle of grappa, he refilled the two glasses with the clear spirit, then proposed a toast. "To a journey of discovery!"

The two men clinked glasses and drank. Teo coughed a little at the strong liquor. The corners of Sol's eyes crinkled as he smiled. "Pure Ulmbartian firewater. Fifty percent alcohol," he bragged.

Teo winced and pounded his chest with his fist. "So tell me—what exactly did I just drink to?"

"As I said, a journey of discovery."

"An intellectual journey?"

Sol came to Teo and sat beside him on the bench. "Yes. And a physical one too." He leaned over mysteriously. "If Iesus Christus is the Pierced One on the cross, we have to go where we can get more information about him."

"And where is that?" Teo was open to anything.

"Have you ever noticed a place on Ulmbartian maps called the Forbidden Zone?"

"Yes. It's a blank spot between you and the Downstreamers. My commanding officer told me it's a disease-ridden wasteland."

"It was once disease-ridden, young Teofil. During the Ancients' War of Destruction they infected it with a powerful plague. Everyone fell down dead. Ulmbartians believe the disease lingers there still, so they won't go near the place. But guess what? All plagues eventually pass."

"Maybe Ulmbartia could reclaim the land?"

"Pfft! We have no interest in such a thing. A race of deranged outlaws lives there now. The local peasants set out food for them so they'll stay in the Zone and leave the farmsteads alone."

"The Forbidden Zone is a large area. Why can't the outlaws grow their own crops?"

Sol laughed in his strange, cackling way. "Grow their own crops! Ha! No, Teofil, you can't grow crops there. The Zone has no fields. It's a massive city—a metropolis of the Ancients filled with towering buildings and crumbling pavestones. I should know. I went there once as a young man."

"Is that where you learned of the Pierced One?"

"Yes. And that's where we're going tomorrow. The boundary is a day's journey away. The next day we will go inside."

"What will we find there?"

Sol cleared his throat but did not reply. Instead he went to a table and moistened a cloth in a bowl, then tossed it to Teo.

"What's this for?" Teo asked.

Sol pointed to the slate lying on the bench. "Wipe it clean, Teofil. A text is a dangerous thing."

◆　◆　◆

The swift waters of the Farm River sparkled in the afternoon sunshine. Ana speared a wriggly earthworm on a split-shank fishhook and pitched it into the river, then leaned back on the sandy bank with her skirt hiked up to her knees and a straw bonnet pulled low on her head. She dug her toes into the wet sand and waited for a bite.

The man with the gray-specked beard lying next to her on the sand noticed her line moving before she did. He nudged her with his elbow. "You've got one, Little Sweet! Haul it in!"

Ana scrambled to her feet and began to wrestle the splashing fish to shore. The man wrapped his strong arms around her, helping her manage the ash-wood pole until the trout had been landed.

A beautiful woman was there too, watching the events on the river-bank. Ana held up her fish. The blonde-haired woman said, "I'll cook it for dinner. Let's go home." The threesome stood on the sand for a moment, then started up the bank into the forest.

Something grabbed Ana's bare foot. She looked down to see a thick brown snake encircling her ankle. The creature spiraled around her calf, then yanked her into the river.

"Help me!" Ana cried.

The man and woman turned to look but did not move. Ana reached out to them, repeating her cry. The couple remained motionless.

Ana was dragged deeper into the water, her feet sinking into the squishy sand. The snake slid higher, wrapping itself around her thigh, pulling her down. She tried to pry it off with her hands, then thrashed furiously in an attempt to break free, but her movements only sucked her deeper into the miry clay.

"Please! I need help!" Desperation began to set in. Ana was now chest-deep in the water and still sinking.

"Let's go home. Come home," said the woman in a flat voice. She held out her hand, though her face displayed no emotion.

"You have to want to come," the man intoned.

"I want to! Help me!"

Ana threw out both hands as the water reached her neck. The snake had encircled her torso, pressing hard, constricting her body in rhythmic pulses. Only its brown head poked out of the water.

"You're never going back," it said in its whispery voice. "Never . . . never . . . never . . ."

"Good-bye, Little Sweet," said the man. He took his wife's hand and turned to go.

"Never going home," hissed the snake.

The water was up to Ana's chin now. She tried to keep herself afloat, but it was no use. The tightness around her chest stifled her breath. Ana threw her head back to keep her mouth above the water.

"No! Please! I want to go with you! Help me!"

The man and woman disappeared into the forest. Murky water closed over Ana's head.

She shrieked with all her strength.

It was dark. Every sense was alive, yet Ana understood nothing. She panted with quick, shallow breaths. Her heart raced. She clutched cloths in her hands.

Where am I?

Slowly awareness of her surroundings returned. She was sitting up in bed. The sheets were twisted around her ankles.

The door burst open. "Anastasia! Are you okay?" It was Vanita.

"I'm—I'm—" Ana wasn't sure what she was.

"Oh, honey, you had a terrible nightmare!" Vanita lit a candle and sat down on the bed. "Look at you! You're drenched in sweat!" She used the edge of a blanket to wipe Ana's forehead.

"I dreamed . . . I dreamed of my parents. Of my home."

"You poor thing. Do you want to tell me about it?" Vanita waited quietly on the edge of the bed in her silky chemise, a look of concern on her face.

Ana shook her head. Tears came then—big, hot tears that welled up from deep inside her soul and overflowed from her eyes and ran down her cheeks. She didn't sob but covered her mouth and let her shoulders tremble as she mourned the loss of her parents and her home. Vanita patted Ana's hand on the bed but didn't speak.

At last Ana's tears were spent. She shuddered deeply. "Am I a fool?" she asked.

"You're not a fool," Vanita said. "It's part of the grieving process. You have to put that part of your life behind you. It hurts, but you have to let it go."

"I hope to go back someday."

Vanita's voice was tender. "Anastasia, don't cling to that hope. Release it so you can build a good life here in Ulmbartia."

Ana sniffled, then reached for a handkerchief on the bedside table.

"Hey, what's that?" Vanita gestured toward Ana's neck.

Ana glanced down at the cross pendant that had slipped from where it had been tucked into her nightgown. "Oh, it's just a . . . a little necklace Teofil gave me."

Vanita rolled her eyes. "Teofil gave it to you?" She leaned close and inspected it. "That's the tackiest thing I've ever seen."

"It means a lot to me."

"Anastasia, don't you see that Teofil is like a chain around your leg? He's a symbol of your old life. He's holding you back from building a future of your own. You need to break free of him and everything he stands for."

"I can't do that, Vanita."

"Why not? I'm telling you what's best, sweetie. You should ditch him and find a good Ulmbartian lord. We have plenty, and you're so pretty you can have your pick of them."

"I don't want an Ulmbartian lord. I want—"

"You want what? *Teofil?* Well, he sure doesn't seem to want you!"

Ana didn't answer.

"Think about it," Vanita continued. "He's never expressed any interest in you. If he liked you, don't you think he would have said so? He goes to an upscale party with you, and what does he do? Instead of treating you like a lady, he gets smashed and pukes on himself like the town drunk. I heard all about it."

The memory of that night was embarrassing. Ana didn't try to correct Vanita's mistaken understanding of what had happened at the chateau, but neither did she wish to hear Teo being mocked. "Teofil is nice to me," she insisted.

Vanita scoffed. "Niceness won't provide you a good living. Look, the best gift he can afford is that grotesque pendant of a tormented man. I'm telling you, this guy's not worthy of a woman like you."

"Vanita, stop. If you knew him, you'd see. The truth is, I'm not worthy of him."

Vanita threw her hands in the air. "Come on, Anastasia, snap out of it! Stop looking backward! Your future is to make a good match with an Ulmbartian aristocrat—not a woodsman from over the mountains." Vanita stared into a dark corner of the room, then swung her head back to Ana. "The fact is, I saw Teofil take one of the servant girls up to his room."

"What? I don't believe that."

"It's true! I saw it with my own eyes. A hot little thing, too. Probably ten years younger than him."

"Who was it?"

"Bianca, the scullery maid," Vanita answered promptly.

"Bianca! She's not even out of her teens!"

"I know. But that's the way single men are. They latch onto any little sweetheart who wiggles her hips at them. You have to get a man locked up—*legally*, I mean. Then no matter what they might do, you're in the money." Vanita stroked Ana's forearm. "Listen to me—stop all this foolishness with Teofil. I think it's because of him that you're having these bad dreams. You're not going to be able to move on until you cut your ties with him."

"I'm not going to cut my ties with Teofil. Never."

Vanita frowned and fiddled with the bedsheets. Suddenly she glanced up at Ana with a twinkle in her eye. "I know a man who's been asking about you," she said.

Ana tsked and looked away.

"Not just any man. The most coveted man any Ulmbartian girl could ever dream of. He's from Likuria. In fact, he's the ruler of that land."

"Is that supposed to make me change my mind?" Ana kept her face turned away from Vanita.

"His name is Cristof di Sanjorjo. He's the dohj—that's their name for their king. The Likurians are very classy, and filthy rich. Dohj Cristof also happens to be extremely handsome."

Ana threw Vanita a skeptical glance. "Are you trying to say he's been asking about *me*? I'm barely known in Ulmbartian social circles, much less in Likuria."

"I know. But somehow he's heard of you. He's coming here in four days to mark the signing of a treaty that my father is involved in. Our rice for their olives. Dohj Cristof specifically mentioned to my father that he'd heard a beautiful foreigner had come to stay with us. He said he hopes to meet you at the Harvest Ball."

"The Harvest Ball? I was planning to go with T—"

Vanita arched an eyebrow, then lunged at Ana and pushed her flat on the bed. Startled, Ana stared at Vanita as she loomed over her, pressing her shoulders into the sheets. Vanita's blonde hair dangled so close, Ana could feel it brushing her cheeks. Vanita spoke deliberately: "You . . . are . . . not . . . going . . . home. Do you understand? It's time to start thinking realistically. Your future is *here*. I'm your friend, Anastasia. I'm the only one speaking truth into all your jumbled emotions. Teofil is nothing to you, okay? But Dohj Cristof? He's—" Vanita pursed her lips as she considered her words.

"He's what?"

Vanita released Ana's shoulders and stood, a big grin on her face. "He's mine," she said with a wink, then bent to the candle and blew it out. "But there are plenty more for you." Vanita giggled in the darkness and closed the bedroom door behind her.

✦   ✦   ✦

"There's something I haven't told you," Sol said as he reined up next to Teo.

The two riders sat side by side in front of an earthen wall protected by a ditch with wooden spikes along its length. The forest here was tangled, making passage difficult. A faint trail ran past a tree stump to a narrow gate in the Forbidden Zone's wall.

"If there's something I need to know, it seems like now's the time," Teo said.

Sol's horse shifted its feet. "The people in there are—"

Teo glanced at Sol, whose eyes stared at the earthwork ahead. He waited for Sol to continue.

"They're Defectives."

Teo nodded at the announcement, though he wasn't as shocked as Sol evidently thought he should be. The Ulmbartian abhorrence of physical deformity was a quirk Teo considered odd, but he didn't share Sol's revulsion toward the so-called Defectives. In Teo's experience most people were defective in one way or another. It was just more obvious in some than it was in others.

"Come on," he said, goading his horse. "Let's go meet some Defectives."

Teo led the way past the stump where the local farmers left their bribes of food at each full moon to keep the Defectives inside. A sharp blow from Teo's ax broke the lock on the gate. He swung it open. The earthen wall wasn't much of a barrier. It didn't have to be. It only had to mark a mutually agreed-upon boundary.

"The ground slopes away here a little," Teo called over his shoulder as he rode through the gate. "Come take a look." Sol hesitated before trotting his horse into the Zone as well.

Teo gazed across the flat expanse of the Forbidden Zone. Although vegetation had ensnarled the ancient city, Teo could see numerous buildings and other large structures poking from the forest. Apparently the destructive fires of the Ancients had never consumed this region. The city's inhabitants had simply abandoned it—if they had remained alive long enough to do so.

Sol shook his head as he stared at the mysterious ruins. "There's nowhere like this on earth," he said.

"I saw a place like it once," Teo remarked. "Anastasia and I found the Sacred Writing in a lost city like this, left to decay over the centuries."

"Does she know you're here?"

"I didn't tell her. She probably believes what everyone else does, that we're visiting a library for our teaching."

Sol cackled. "I suppose you could call it a library. The Forbidden Zone is a place where knowledge is kept by a few, lest it be forgotten altogether. That's the only reason I'd return to such a fearsome place."

"Fearsome? Should I be afraid?"

"Hmm." Sol tapped his chin, his eyes narrowing. "You may find that knowledge demands its price, young Teofil."

Teo's horse pricked its ears, and it whinnied as its head came up. Teo snatched an arrow from his quiver and nocked it, scanning the undergrowth. Sol crowded close behind him.

126

"I know you're there!" Teo shouted in Talyano. "Show yourself!"

They did.

A crowd of them, all Defectives.

They materialized out of the bushes, warped and twisted forms of human life. Many had hunched backs or missing limbs or disfiguring scars or misshapen skulls. Some walked with an awkward, jerky gait, while others shuffled along with dull expressions. They emitted a cacophony of vague noises and grunts and moans. All were dressed in rags, and not one looked well fed.

A man with a commanding presence rode forward on an old nag. The left side of his face was an eruption of bulbous red tumors, yet his eyes shone with lively intelligence. He held a spiked club. "What brings strangers into the Zone? Do you seek asylum? I see no defects upon you. Speak!"

Teo released the tension on his bowstring and returned the arrow to his quiver. "We are not here for asylum. We wish to befriend the people of this territory." The statement brought grunts and screeches from the watching crowd.

"Defectives are not befriended by the Whole," said the leader. "What trick is this?"

Dismounting, Teo approached the rider and held out his hand. "I am Teofil of Chiveis," he said. "I befriend all children of the Creator."

For a long moment the forest was absolutely still. Then, as if on a signal, the Defectives burst into an excited babble. Sol squirmed in his saddle, though he remained silent.

The mounted leader swung to the ground and stared at Teo's outstretched hand, then glanced from it into Teo's eyes. Though the man's disfigurement was startling, Teo did not flinch but held his gaze steady. Slowly the man reached out and grasped Teo's hand in a firm grip.

"You see with the vision of the Creator, Teofil of Chiveis. Such a thing is rare among the Whole."

"Yet it is fitting for those who know the Creator's goodness. I am a follower of the one true God"—Teo hesitated, then plunged ahead—"and his Pierced One."

The leader of the Defectives was visibly surprised. "The Pierced One? We believed him to be unknown in Ulmbartia."

"He is unknown. Would you have him be known to those who seek him?"

The man did not reply. Instead he spun around and mounted the nag again. Looking down at Teo from his horse's back, he said, "You will come with me. I will take you to the Domo."

Teo returned to his horse. "Who's the Domo?" he whispered to Sol as he put his foot in the stirrup and swung up.

"It's not a *who*, it's a *what*. The Domo is a great temple of the Ancients."

The man with the tumorous face led Teo and Sol through the decayed ruins of the lost city. The farther they went, the more urban their surroundings became. The trees thinned out, and the landscape began to be dominated by cracked pavement and large buildings instead of forest. Many of the buildings were ten or twelve stories high, with empty windows and gaping doorways. Shrubs grew from the roofs. Steel carriages of the Ancients lay scattered about, rusted and decayed.

The rough trail the riders had been following became a winding pathway through a maze of city streets. They rode in silence for the better part of the morning. The only signs of life were pigeons and an occasional hawk.

At last the man in front held up his fist. He dismounted and walked around the corner of a city block. When he returned, he was accompanied by a thin man whose hair was shaved in a ring around his head.

"This is Brother Toni," said the man with the tumors, gesturing at the other man. "He will take you from here."

Brother Toni folded his hands into the sleeves of his robe. "L-l-leave your w-weapons behind," he said as he began to walk around the corner. "F-f-f-follow me." Brother Toni had no obvious physical ailment, so Teo guessed his stutter was what made him a Defective. Not sure what else to do, he disarmed and followed the monkish figure around the corner. Sol trailed close behind.

They entered a spacious plaza that had been cleared of foliage and debris. At the far end, an immense building rose into the sky. Teo discerned immediately from its architecture that it was a temple of Deu. The intricate pinnacles and carved statues reminded him of the ancient temple in the lost city where he and Ana had discovered the Sacred Writing. The main facade of that temple had contained three doors, but the building in front of Teo had five great doors that towered several times the height of a man and were recessed into decorated portals. The building's white stone seemed to glow in the midday sun. It was shaped like a letter A whose apex reached into the clouds. Spire-topped columns rose along its stone face, and numerous windows punctuated its walls.

This beautiful structure is truly worthy of Deu, Teo thought.

Brother Toni beckoned with his hand. "The Overs-s-s-seer awaits." He marched toward the temple's central door.

As Teo followed him, the carvings on the building's facade became more discernible, though time had certainly worn them down. Teo noticed a depiction of a youth holding an oversized sword. The boy smiled as he displayed the severed head of a giant whose forehead was broken by a stone. The neck of the giant's corpse spilled forth gore. Teo resolved to look through the Sacred Writing to see if he could find the account.

Entering the Domo, Teo found himself stunned by its massive scale. It was even larger than the temple he had discovered with Ana. The ceiling disappeared into the darkness far above, while five great aisles divided the cavernous space. The aisles were defined by pillars so large they would dwarf even the greatest trees. It seemed that such mighty pillars could support the sky itself.

Brother Toni's footsteps echoed on the marble floor, which was decorated in a geometric floral pattern. He walked toward the far end of the temple, where windows covered the rear wall. Some of the panes were broken and admitted shafts of sunlight, but others retained their scintillating glass. A large stone table stood upon a dais. Numerous candelabras illuminated it, along with specks of color from the rays shining through the windows. Behind the table stood a lone man wearing a white robe with a gold sash.

Brother Toni approached the dais and bowed at the waist, sweeping both hands away from his body. Sol glanced at Teo and indicated they should do the same. After they had bowed, the man in the white robe beckoned Teo toward the table.

"I am the Overseer," he said. The hood of his plain robe hung loosely over his forehead and draped around his neck. The Overseer's beard was snow-white, though he carried himself with an erect posture that proved he had not yet succumbed to old age. Staring at Teo with his stark blue eyes, he asked, "What brings the Whole to our land?" Teo could not tell if the voice was stern or welcoming—or somehow both.

"We come as friends," Teo said. "We would learn of the Pierced One."

The Overseer frowned. "For what purpose, O Seeker?"

Teo took a deep breath. "I worship the Creator, known to me as Deu. I have learned he had a servant named Iesus Christus, who suffered on a cross. I believe you call him the Pierced One. I wish to understand the mysteries of my God."

"Approach."

Teo climbed the steps of the dais until he stood directly across the table from the Overseer. Two lampstands flanked the table, while a bowl, a hammer, a nail, and a leather pad lay on its surface. The Overseer dipped the nail in the bowl of clear liquid, then lifted it to a lamp. A blaze flared up as the liquid burned off. The Overseer picked up the hammer.

"To perceive the truth, you cannot be whole," he said in a solemn voice. "Only the broken can truly see." He pushed the leather pad across the tabletop. "Place your hand here."

What?

Teo stared at the thick pad, then looked up at the Overseer.

The man waited quietly, holding the hammer and nail. Teo swallowed. "Sir, if I do this, will you tell me what you know of the Pierced One?"

The Overseer nodded. "Yes, if you are worthy."

Teo laid his left palm on the pad. Sweat broke out on his forehead. He reminded himself of his oath to Ana. He had sworn to discover the truth of Deu, no matter what the cost. *You can do this, Teo! Men sometimes have their limbs amputated; they endure arrowheads being dug from infected wounds. Grit your teeth and take the pain. The wound will heal in time. You have to do this to find out more about Iesus Christus.*

The Overseer pressed the tip of the nail, still hot, into the fleshy place between Teo's thumb and forefinger. Teo clenched his jaw but held his hand still.

Everything was silent in the spacious hall as the hammer was raised.

Teo looked up from his hand to the Overseer's bearded face. The man stared back at Teo with an intense gaze.

"I am willing to join you," Teo said.

The hammer swept down.

A metallic bang resounded as the nail was struck. Pain flooded Teo's hand. He squinted and grimaced as stars exploded before his eyes. A gasp escaped his lips. After shaking his head to let his vision clear, he glanced down.

The nail protruded from his hand. However, its tip had been moved at the last second. Instead of going through the thick flesh, it had only pierced the web of skin at the base of his thumb. As the initial burst of pain subsided, the Overseer yanked out the nail.

"It is enough," he said. "You have passed the test." He came around to Teo's side of the table. "Come now. We will climb to the roof and espy the land. There I will speak truth to you."

Brother Toni brought ointment and a bandage. Still somewhat shaken, Teo allowed him to bind the wound, then followed the Overseer toward the exit. Sol's face was pale as he walked silently at Teo's side.

An exterior door led to a staircase. Teo climbed the twisting stairs until his thigh muscles burned. It seemed the steps would never end, but at last he reached a roof with delicately carved pinnacles sprouting everywhere. Saints and gargoyles and lovely angels adorned every available surface. Following the Overseer, Teo traversed the roof's length by walking under the buttresses that supported the temple's mighty columns.

More stairs brought him to the main peak of the roof, which was lined along both sides with slender spires. A breeze cooled Teo in the afternoon sun. The ruined metropolis of the Ancients lay spread before him. Farther from the temple, the urban core of the Forbidden Zone gave way to a dark ring of forest that receded into the distance.

Sol joined Teo on the roof, panting with his hands on his knees. "This is amazing," he said between gasps. "I've never seen anything like it!"

The Overseer approached and removed his hood. A jagged scar stretched across his forehead. He smiled as he saw Teo's eyes go to it.

"You notice my crown, do you? It was put there by my own hand so that I might become one with the flock Deus has given me."

"You're a Defective by choice?"

"Yes. And in this way I am truly whole." He touched his fingertips together and gazed into the distance. "Do you know what is done with those whom the Ulmbartians call Defectives?"

"It's said they are taken by the shamans to a pleasant valley."

"It is enslavement, make no mistake," said the Overseer. "They are worked to death in frightful conditions, mainly in quarries. The Ulmbartians' desire for marble is outstripped only by the insatiable appetite of the Likurians."

"I don't doubt it. I sensed evil in the practice of banishing the Defectives."

"Some flee here to the Forbidden Zone for refuge when they receive their defect from the hand of Deus. I am here to welcome the weak." The Overseer turned and faced Teo. "I believe you may one day understand the nature of weakness, Teofil of Chiveis."

Teo was startled. "What do you mean?"

"Deus favors the weak and the downtrodden. He hides his strength in them. Sometimes they will surprise you."

"I will look for that," Teo said, nodding.

Evidently it was the right thing to say. A broad smile crossed the Overseer's face. "Well spoken, O Seeker. And now, if you would learn of the Pierced One, listen to these words."

The Overseer removed a book from his sleeve and began to read. "So says the prophet Zacharias: *Aspicient ad me quem confixerunt et plangent eum planctu quasi super unigenitum et dolebunt super eum ut doleri solet in morte primogeniti.*"

"The Old Words," Sol whispered to Teo.

When the Overseer finished reading, he translated the text. It described a man who was pierced, a man who would be looked upon with grief. His death would be mourned like that of a firstborn son. The Overseer explained that the text was a prophecy of Iesus Christus, the servant who suffered.

"What about the Promised King?" Teo asked. "How did the death of Iesus help him?"

The Overseer looked at Teo sadly. "While we know the servant was pierced on a cross and suffered for his beliefs, we do not know what became of the king who was prophesied. It is said he followed in David's mighty footsteps and established a kingdom for a time. Beyond that his story is forgotten."

Teo was dumbfounded. "What then are your beliefs? Tell me everything you can."

The Overseer folded his hands into his sleeves. "Much has been lost through the ages, and what remains is only dimly remembered. Traditions and rituals have come down to us, and we observe them, though we do not know their full meaning. Nevertheless, I will give you what knowledge I have. The brothers and sisters here belong to the Universal Communion of the Christiani. Twenty of us are in holy orders, and none but I have ever set foot outside this forgotten city. Each week we celebrate a meal of bread and wine in memory of the Pierced One's death. In this sacrifice we feed upon him. In our brokenness we find the way forward. In our suffering we bind ourselves to Deus. In love we serve the abandoned, until the day of victory comes. More than this cannot be known in the Forbidden Zone."

"What? Surely you have a complete version of the Sacred Writing? What does the New Testament say about all this? I thought you'd be able to answer my questions!" Teo could feel disappointment rising within him, though he tried to keep the edge out of his voice.

"The Testament of which you speak is lost among us. It is lost in Ulmbartia, and it is lost in Likuria as well. It has nearly been wiped from the face of the earth. The Exterminati have made sure of that—those whom you call the shamans. Yet we believe a secret copy of it still exists. There is but one man alive today who can recover that book: the leader of the Christiani. His servants scour the earth even now, always looking, looking, looking . . ."

"Then I must go to him," Teo declared. "I am sworn to it. I will help him find the sacred book, so that we might know the whole truth."

The Overseer looked at Teo with a strange expression in his blue eyes. "Perhaps you will, O Seeker of wisdom. Yes, indeed, perhaps you will. My prayers and my dreams and my thoughts have been visited of late by a man like you. I think it is time for you to play a role in the great and mysterious saga of Deus."

"I'm willing, sir. Where can I find the man of whom you speak?"

The Overseer went to the edge of the roof and spread his arms to the distant horizon. "Far to the south, across both land and sea, lies a great city. It is the home of the Universal Communion, though evil holds sway there now. You must go there, Teofil the Wisdom Seeker. You must go to Roma, and there you will find the Papa."

✦　✦　✦

Exhilarated, Ana swept around the ballroom in her flowing silk gown. The steps to the waltz were much like the folk dances she had enjoyed in Chiveis, but the setting at the Harvest Ball was infinitely more elegant.

"You are as graceful at dancing as you are in conversation, Lady Anastasia," Dohj Cristof said as the music came to an end. He bowed, and Ana returned the compliment with a curtsy.

The night was magical. Vanita had loaned Ana a gown of the finest silk in a delicate ivory color, with bare shoulders and gloves that came to her elbow. The triple strand of pearls around her neck added a lovely finishing touch. Ana felt like a princess.

Vanita floated up to Ana and Cristof, her diamond jewelry glittering in the bright light of the chandeliers. "Anastasia, are you going to monopolize our Likurian guest all night? Other men would like to dance with you as well—and there's a certain lady who'd like the dohj to lead her around the room at least once tonight."

Cristof nodded politely. "It would be an honor to dance with the daughter of a gentleman as noble as Duke Labella." He took Vanita by the hand and led her out to the ballroom floor. Ana used the moment to slip outside to collect her thoughts.

She stood for a long time at the railing of a broad terrace, enjoying the cool air of the early autumn evening. The grape harvest had begun, and all of Ulmbartia was in a festive mood. A sliver of pale moon shone in the sky as Ana gazed out on the splendid city of Giuntra. Her thoughts went to Teo. *I wonder where is he right now.* He had said something about visiting a distant library with his new teacher friend, though that didn't seem like a good reason to be gone during the Harvest Ball. Ana found herself wishing she could have danced with Teo on a night like this. In fact, she wished she could have been his escort at the ball. She sighed and shook her head. *Would he have wanted that?* She didn't know. Ever since the embarrassing events at the count's chateau on the lake, she had felt confused about Teo.

"There you are. I've been looking for you," said a voice from behind.

Ana turned to see Dohj Cristof walking toward her. He was a remarkably handsome man, about thirty years old with sandy blond hair and a strong jaw. He wasn't rugged like Teo, but he had a certain polish about him that was attractive. Ana felt more than a little flattered by the attention the esteemed prince had shown her all evening. She wasn't sure what to make of that.

"I'm just enjoying the gorgeous view out here on the terrace," she said as the dohj approached.

"As am I," Cristof replied.

From his tone and the look in his eye, Ana knew the dohj's words were intended as flirtatious, but she didn't rise to his bait. Instead she made polite conversation for a while, then offered an excuse about needing a drink and hurried back inside.

For the rest of the evening Ana danced with anyone who asked her, enjoying the fine music, the glamorous atmosphere, and the magnificent architecture of the grand ballroom. She had forgotten how much she enjoyed dancing. As she was whisked around by her partners, she experienced the same exuberance she often felt at the barn dances back home, though her elation was more intense in such enchanted surroundings. Everyone was nice to her—the men so complimentary, the women so lighthearted and congenial. The Ulmbartian aristocrats genuinely seemed to want her in their midst.

As the evening drew to a close and the guests began to leave, Ana found Vanita, and the pair made their way to the Labellas' waiting carriage. A tall man in commoner's attire stood next to the tailcoated coachman.

Someone approached Ana unseen, startling her by slipping his arm around her body in a familiar way. She turned to see the smiling face of Dohj Cristof. "Did you think you could leave without saying good-bye?" he asked.

"I looked for you, Your Highness, but I missed you in the crowd."

"That's because I was waiting out here to be sure to catch you."

Vanita laughed melodiously and put her hand on the dohj's shoulder. "It's certainly hard to escape your watchful eye, Dohj Cristof."

The Likurian prince faced the two women. "If I may," he said in a more formal tone, "I wish to extend you an invitation. I've already cleared it with your father, Lady Vanita, but I would ask you in person as well."

Vanita's eyes shone. "Do tell," she giggled.

"As you are perhaps aware, the Likurians and Ulmbartians have recently concluded a commercial pact. It seems appropriate to celebrate this event with an exchange of hospitality. In that vein I have invited the Labella household to join some other noble families in spending a few months in the pleasant confines of the Likurian seashore. All guests of your home would be welcome to stay at my palace at Nuo Genov"—Cristof fixed his eyes upon Ana—"and that would of course include you, Lady Anastasia."

Ana was taken aback. Before she could answer, a voice spoke from over her shoulder. "Good evening, Ana."

She recognized the voice at once. *Teo!*

Ana whirled to greet him, suddenly realizing he was the man who had been standing by the carriage. He was dirty from his travels to the distant library. His hair was unkempt, and his chin sported a few days' worth of stubble. Nevertheless, the comforting feeling she always experienced in his presence flooded her heart in a rush.

I've missed him so much!

She started forward to embrace him, then hesitated, uncertain about what was appropriate.

"Oh, gods," Vanita muttered. "What's he doing here?"

"Lady Anastasia, do you know this man?" Dohj Cristof asked.

"Yes, he's . . . a friend of mine."

Vanita rolled her eyes, and Cristof uttered a dismissive grunt.

Teo laid his hand on Ana's upper arm. "Listen," he said quietly, leaning close, "there's something—"

"Get your dirty hands off her!"

Dohj Cristof smacked Teo's arm away from Ana's shoulder. Teo drew back with an annoyed expression, staring at the dohj.

"A noble lady doesn't want to be manhandled by the likes of you," Cristof said.

"I'm pretty sure she doesn't mind," Teo retorted.

Cristof stepped to Ana's side, placing his arm protectively around her waist. "The lady is in my care now, young man. She is to be a guest in my home for the next few months." He waved Teo away with the back of his hand. "Be off with you, before I have you tossed into an alley on your ear."

Teo shot Ana a questioning glance. She sensed anger in his expression, or perhaps disappointment.

He's drifting away from me, Ana realized with a panicky feeling.

"Is that true?" Teo asked. His tone was sharp.

"Well, yes, I've been invited to the coast. And I was . . . um . . . yes, I was considering it."

"Are you going?"

"Why shouldn't I?"

Ana kicked herself as soon as she said it. Her words sounded like a challenge, though that was the last thing she intended. She desperately wanted Teo to give her a reason to stay.

Teo folded his arms across his chest and looked away. He exhaled a deep breath through his nose. Ana couldn't read his emotions, though she knew irritation was certainly one of them. Teo grimaced and shook his head but said nothing.

"What, Teo? Do you want me not to go?"

As Ana stood waiting for Teo's answer, a powerful emotion swept over her. She felt alone and anxious and afraid. *Please, Teo! Just say it! Say you want me to stay with you and I'll do it in a heartbeat!*

Teo stared at the ground. The moment was poised on the edge of a knife. Ana felt herself starting to tremble. Her knees sagged, and Dohj Cristof instinctively tightened his grip around her waist. With sudden clarity Ana knew she had reached a turning point in her life.

At last Teo looked up and met Ana's eyes. "This isn't a decision I can make for you, Anastasia."

Ana's breath caught. *Teo just called me Anastasia!*

Darkness invaded Ana's soul. She felt as if her heart had been crushed like a flower under a boot heel. Everyone else called her Anastasia, but Teo always called her Ana. It was her familiar name, her intimate name, her special name that she had invited him to use as one whom she loved. Long ago, in another land, they had stood together on a balcony in the moonlight. On that night Ana sensed she had become inextricably bound to Teo. From that time on, through all their many adventures, he had never addressed her as anything but Ana. For Teo to call her by her formal name—now, in this vital moment—conveyed more to her than anything else he could have said. Not only had Teo refused to claim her, he had symbolically rejected the bond they shared.

Ana's heart fell. For a long moment she stared at her feet. A queasy feeling roiled in her stomach. Tears rimmed her eyes, but she blinked them away before they could be noticed. She lifted her chin and turned toward Dohj Cristof.

"I'd be delighted to come visit you, Your Highness," she said.

PART TWO

EXTRAVAGANCY

CHAPTER

6

Around noon on her third day of travel, Ana arrived at the most beautiful city she had ever seen. Giuntra was lovely, but Nuo Genov—the artistic though not the political capital of Likuria—was even more stupendous, a gleaming city of milky marble palaces and sun-drenched vistas. Everything was clean and pure and grand beyond imagination. No building was without domes or arches or colonnades or balconies. Innumerable statues of muscular men and voluptuous women celebrated the human form in the many spacious plazas. The city clung to the steep coastal hillside in terraces that descended to a bustling commercial port. From the harbor the great ocean at Nuo Genov stretched toward a horizon so distant Ana could scarcely comprehend it. On the journey down from Ulmbartia, Dohj Cristof had described the infinite salt sea of the Likurians. Still, when Ana saw it with her own eyes, it took her breath away.

"The Ancients destroyed this city, but now we've made it even more superb than it was before," Cristof had bragged. *It truly is superb*, Ana decided.

The dohj's palace was as elegant as the man himself. All the visiting Ulmbartian aristocrats were shown to private rooms with balconies overlooking the ocean. Ana threw open her glass doors and walked outside, inhaling the foreign smells of the seashore. Though it was now the ninth month of the year, a warm sun still shone down on this southern locale. Ana felt she had arrived in paradise.

The first evening was spent at a sumptuous casino. Ana didn't know the rules of the games, so she merely stood at Dohj Cristof's table and watched him lose huge sums of money as he placed bets and moved his chips around. The losses seemed to bother him no more than if a penny had fallen from a hole in his pocket. Ana wondered if he even knew how much wealth he possessed. Cristof laughed and bantered with a crowd of gorgeous girls in sequined gowns as the house took his money again and again. The dohj was oblivious to his bad luck.

Breakfast was scheduled suitably late the next day. In fact, in most places it would have been called lunch. Ana awoke three or four times with bright rays of sunshine slanting across her bed from the shutters, but each time she managed to fight off morning's arrival and slip into a doze again.

At last she put her bare feet to the floor and stumbled into the bathroom. Although a bowl of cold water and a bar of soap were all she was accustomed to back home, here in Likuria morning ablutions were done differently. An iron stove was set into the wall, tended by servants on the other side. The stove heated a tank of water, which could be released from a spout to trickle over one's shoulders. Ana had always enjoyed soaking in a tub, but the unusual feeling of warm water running down her back was a new and decidedly pleasant sensation.

Clean and refreshed, Ana went down to the breakfast salon and took a seat next to Vanita. A uniformed servant brought a dish of eggs over ham slices and muffins, all smothered in creamy sauce. Ana tried it and found it to be delightful. She and Vanita had started making plans for the day when Dohj Cristof approached. Vanita glanced up and smiled at him.

"Welcome, Your Highness," she said, saucily pushing out a chair with her foot. "Would you care to join us?"

The dohj seemed happy to comply. "Did you sleep well, ladies?" he asked as his eggs were served.

"I certainly slept later than I normally do," Ana said with a laugh.

"How did you enjoy our hot-water spouts? An ingenious invention, no?"

"Oh, it was wonderful," Ana agreed.

"I trust there was sufficient water for you? Were you were able to linger there as long as you wished, with that warm water trickling all over your body?" Cristof arched his eyebrows.

"Mm-hmm," Ana said, taking a bite of her eggs.

Vanita changed the subject. "Anastasia and I were just discussing our agenda for the day. What do you recommend we do in your fair city?"

The dohj pursed his lips for a moment. "Nuo Genov presents an infinity of things to see, so don't try to do it all at once. Perhaps we could make a visit to the Museum of Ancient Artifacts? I'd be happy to show you around."

"Lovely!" Vanita said, clapping her hands.

Ana was intrigued as well. "What kinds of things will we see?"

"Oh, the archaeologists have discovered many items in the earth around here. The Ancients destroyed their buildings with great fires, but some of their objects remained in the soil. Let's see . . ." The dohj looked into the distance as he tried to recall the museum's holdings. "There are lots of paintings, damaged but still exquisite." He tapped his chin. "Pieces of their steel carriages, everyday items, quite a few statues. There are two stone lions from the ancient temple of Sanlorentso. And you should see the priceless treasure that was found there! It's a gold cross studded with jewels."

Ana's heart skipped a beat. *A cross?*

A flood of memories broke free from the mental compartment she had put them in, surging into her consciousness. Unbidden thoughts tumbled through her mind: thoughts of Teo . . . the Sacred Writing . . . Chiveis . . . Deu.

Ana sipped her hot tea. "What kind of cross?" she asked nonchalantly.

"It's a religious artifact, I believe. Some relic of an ancient superstition."

"Do you—do you follow a religion, Your Highness?"

Ana wasn't sure the question was appropriate, yet she had the sudden urge to clarify the spiritual situation she was facing. Teo had warned her that talking about Deu would attract the attention of the Exterminati, but surely those eavesdropping ears were far away now. It occurred to Ana that if religious tolerance was the policy among the aristocrats, she could tell her friends about Deu without fear of reprisals. *In fact,* Ana thought, *Dohj Cristof might even come to believe in him! Wouldn't that be something?* She

143

resolved to build a close relationship with the Likurian prince in order to testify about her God.

Cristof swatted his hand. "Religion doesn't interest me," he said.

"Waste of time," Vanita agreed.

Ana swallowed, then decided to be bold. "It matters to me. I'm . . . I'm a person of faith, I guess you'd say."

The dohj glanced up. "Really? Tell me about that."

Ana's heart began to race. She tried to calm the butterflies in her stomach, hoping her voice wouldn't shake as she spoke. "I believe in the Creator God. I call him Deu. He's loving and powerful and very holy."

"That explains a lot, sweetie," Vanita said with a smile on her lips.

Dohj Cristof's eyes were fixed on Ana's face. She looked back at him, trying to read his expression.

"Your viewpoint is uncommon in my realm, Lady Anastasia," he said. "But I must confess, you've intrigued me. I would love to discuss these matters further. Of course, it's an unpopular idea, so it should be just the two of us. Do you think we could find some time alone to discuss—what was the god's name again?" He waved his hand around.

"Deu."

"Yes, let's meet privately to discuss Deu." The dohj stroked his sandy beard. "Tell you what. I have to go to Manacho to conduct some government business. I'll be back in a week. I was thinking of taking my guests for a sea trip when I return. My yacht is delightful for that sort of thing. Sometime during our excursion, how about if you and I slip away to a private place for a little while?"

"Great!" Ana nodded her agreement to the dohj's proposal.

Vanita stared out the window. She wiped her mouth with a napkin and made a sucking noise as she cleared her teeth with her tongue, then turned toward Ana and Cristof. "I'm sure that will be just lovely for you two," she said.

✦   ✦   ✦

Teo kicked a pebble with the toe of his boot. *This stinks*, he thought to himself.

He stood outside one of Giuntra's grand hotels, watching the lords and ladies ride off in their carriages with their ridiculously large entourages. It seemed the Ulmbartian aristocrats could do nothing for themselves. They needed servants for every task.

Teo watched the busy exodus with a feeling of uncertainty. For once he wasn't sure of his next move. His ostensible plan was to leave Giuntra and return to the Labellas' palace. Ana would eventually return from Likuria, and Teo could decide then what he ought to do. In the meantime he would join Sol in instructing the children of the estate.

As Teo considered his options, it occurred to him that it wouldn't matter if he didn't show up for his academic duties. He would send a message to Sol, of course. No doubt everyone at the palace would quickly forget about the missing schoolteacher. *Then I would be free*, Teo realized. *Free to go to where I'm being called. Free to go to . . .*

Roma.

The name of the ancient city slipped into Teo's mind like a wisp of fog. He refused to blow it away, letting the word linger in his thoughts. *Yes*, he said to himself. *I'll find my way to Roma, begging if I have to. Then Ana and I can find the Papa, and we'll help him discover the New Testament, and everything will be . . .*

Teo arrested his train of thought, shaking his head to quash his futile daydream. Bitterness rose in his heart as he watched the aristocratic caravans rolling away from the hotel. Everything was changed now. When the Overseer had told him about the Universal Communion in Roma, Teo imagined a scenario in which he and Ana would somehow make their way to that distant city and discover the truth of Deu together. He had rushed to the Harvest Ball at Giuntra to tell her about it. Now that dream was broken. Dohj Cristof had made sure of that. Teo pounded his fist in his palm and turned his back on the luxurious carriages.

As he walked across the hotel's courtyard, a man in groom's livery emerged from a stable and waved him over. After looking around to see if the man was summoning someone else, Teo decided the groom wanted to speak to him, so he ambled toward the low building.

"Morning," said the groom. "You look like a man who could use a job."

"I don't think so, but I'll hear you out. What did you have in mind?"

145

"I'm the stablemaster for one of the lords who's heading down to Likuria for the winter. We lost a stableboy to cholera, so now I need to make a quick hire."

Teo was amused. He started to say he wasn't interested, but then closed his mouth and paused. *Did he just say they're going to Likuria?* Teo considered the idea some more. "Just a minute, let me think about it," he said.

Walking a few steps away, Teo stared at the sky. The job would take him in the right direction, and it would certainly be better than begging his way to the coast. At least he would have food and a means of transportation. Once he was in Likuria, he could inquire around the seafront to see if any mariners were headed to distant Roma.

But what about Ana?

Teo exhaled a long breath. He felt more confused about her than about any woman he had ever known. Even so, despite his confusion he sensed their recent parting of ways wasn't the end of their story. Teo knew the adventures he had shared with Ana bonded them with an affection so intimate only a colossal disaster could sever it. Together they had faced common enemies with united resolve; they had revealed private thoughts over lonely campfires; they had stepped hand in hand into the vast Beyond, relying on each other in the grace of Deu. Teo had laid down his life for Ana, and she for him. On more than one night she had slept nestled against his side—and yet, strangely, he had never even kissed her cheek. Whatever else might be said about his relationship with the beautiful woman from Edgeton, one thing was certain: their intertwined lives would not be easily untangled.

However, now that Ana had gone to Likuria with Dohj Cristof, Teo didn't know what to think. He didn't believe she was romantically attracted to the prince, though that notion had occurred to him. *Well, why shouldn't she be?* Teo asked himself. *And why should you care? She's your friend, not your lover. You have no right to tell her what to do.*

Yet as these thoughts crossed Teo's mind, he admitted he wasn't being honest. Though he didn't intend to "tell her what to do," he knew he cared for Ana very much. She had started down a bad path, and that meant he would have to follow. Teo believed she wouldn't intentionally forsake

Deu, yet in her weakness because of being displaced from her home, she might be lured away from her God. Teo would help her if he could.

Wrestling with his emotions, Teo tried to discern his true motive for going to Likuria—to find passage to Roma or to protect Ana? The memory of his promise to her on Fisherman's Isle forced its way into his consciousness. He had sworn to find the New Testament no matter what. It was an oath he could not break. *But you swore a different oath to Ana long before that!* Teo's thoughts drifted back to the rainy night they had taken shelter in a faraway castle. Shivering in her bedroll, Ana had thanked him for rescuing her from her abductors. "Thank you for coming for me," she had said. Without thinking, Teo had answered, "I always will." He believed that spontaneous promise bound him still.

"Hey, buddy, do you want the job or not?" The stablemaster's voice was impatient.

Teo's attention snapped back to the present. "What does it involve?"

The groom led him into the stable and picked up a shovel. "Standard stableboy labor. Mucking out mostly."

"I'll take it."

"Then you'll have to give me those," the stablemaster said, pointing to Teo's weapons. "I'll keep them safe, but you can't wear them around. In fact, you'll have to give me those clothes too. We're a uniformed staff."

Teo emptied himself of his ax and knife. His sword was even harder to give up, but Teo released his grasp on it too. The stablemaster went to a trunk and returned with a groom's livery. It consisted of cream-colored riding pants, a mauve shirt, and high leather boots sporting jaunty brass buckles.

"We had a kid who was nearly as tall as you, though he wasn't as wide in the shoulders," the stablemaster said. "But don't worry, it'll stretch." Teo sighed and took the items.

After putting on his new clothing, he offered the stablemaster his hand. "I appreciate the job," he said. "Thanks for asking me."

"Don't thank me. The lord of the manor told me to offer it to you. He said he owed you far more than this, but at least it's something. And he said to pay you well too."

"Really? That's strange. I don't know any lords. Who is my new master, anyway?"

"You don't know?"

Teo shook his head and shrugged.

"He's one of the richest noblemen in Ulmbartia. You're now in the employ of Count Federco Borromo."

✦   ✦   ✦

The Iron Shield stared at the three shamans gathered around him in the inner sanctum of the chapter house at Nuo Genov. The robed men wore red bands on their arms, signaling they were high-ranking brothers in the Society of the Exterminati. A shaman reached that rank only by gaining intimate knowledge of the brotherhood's lore—not only arcane secrets of the occult religion, but a practical knowledge of things like stealth, lock-picking, poisons, and garrotes. The expertise of an assassin.

"These are the targets," said the Iron Shield, laying three charcoal portraits on the altar in the musty room. The shamans crowded close, their hoods drooping as they bent to inspect the drawings by the flickering light of the torches on the wall.

The Iron Shield spoke to the shaman on his right. "The old man you see there is a teacher in Ulmbartia called Sol. The brotherhood has been watching him for a long time. Until recently his actions were merely suspicious, not enough to act upon. Now, however, he has joined with the strangers from over the mountains. He even made a trip into the Forbidden Zone. We believe he is trying to learn more about the Creator and the Criminal."

The three shamans hissed and drew back. One of them began to rub an amulet at his neck, while the other two muttered protective charms.

"You know this for certain?" asked the shaman on the right.

"We have eyes in every head, do we not?"

"What then would you have me do, my master?"

"You will depart this day for Ulmbartia. There you will contact the brothers and form a plan. The old man must be tortured in secret until he has revealed all he knows. The pain must be severe enough to wring everything from him. Remember, the man himself is no threat to us. It is his knowledge that poses a danger. We must find out how much of this ancient heresy has crept back into Ulmbartia—and from what source."

"After he has divulged all he knows, what then?"

"He is decrepit and not worth dragging to the quarries. Kill him in his bed with poison, but make it look natural. Leave no mark of torture on him to disturb the local barons."

The shaman chuckled darkly. "Many painful things can be done inside the body where no eye can see."

The Iron Shield pointed to the next drawing. "This warrior is Teofil of Chiveis. He too entered the Forbidden Zone. We believe he is actively seeking knowledge of the Enemy. The Lord Borja wishes to know the full scope of his understanding and the extent of his designs."

The shaman on the left spoke up. "It will be my pleasure to crack him open," he said.

The Iron Shield crossed his arms at his chest, feeling irritation rise within him. "Unfortunately, this one has disappeared. He did not come south with the Labella clan. We lost him in Giuntra."

"I will find him, my lord."

"Yes, you will. But you will not put him to torture. I reserve that pleasure for myself. You will leave today for Ulmbartia as well. Once you have located Teofil of Chiveis, apprehend him and bring him to me. No one must know of your doings."

"He will be yours to interrogate within a fortnight," vowed the shaman on the left.

"Excellent. He will spill all he knows, and if he lives through the ordeal, he will provide much good labor in the quarries."

"And what of the woman?" asked the shaman who stood in the middle of the trio.

The Iron Shield frowned as he leaned on the altar to inspect the sketch of Anastasia. "I will handle her, and you will assist me. This target will require finesse, for she has been drawn deep into the protection of the royal house of Likuria. Stealth will be essential in this matter. As you know, the Lord Borja likes his dealings with the aristocrats to be . . . clean."

"You have a plan?"

"My sources within the palace tell me Anastasia of Chiveis will soon make a sea voyage with the local dohj." The Iron Shield's voice took on a sly tone. "Have you seen that yacht of his? The staterooms overlook the water. I will enter the woman's chamber and strangle her into submission, then remove her in a boat under cover of darkness. No one will suspect an abduction. Drunken guests have been known to fall from a window and drown. Dohj Cristof will mourn her for a day, then move on to his next delectable young fancy."

The third shaman nodded his agreement. "A well-conceived plan. And she is young. After we force her to reveal what she knows about the Enemy, she will have many years left for the marble quarries."

"No. She will fetch a higher price elsewhere. The woman will be coveted by the pimps. They will pay us well."

"Even better."

The Iron Shield stepped back from the altar and rose to his full height. "The task before us is clear. You each have your orders. Let us now draw holy power from an act of domination."

He removed a garrote from his belt. Holding the strangling wire by its wooden handles, he went to a hutch and reached inside, withdrawing a rabbit by the ears. It kicked and struggled in the Iron Shield's gauntleted fist.

"*Crudelitas vis est*," he intoned as he set the rabbit on the altar with the wire encircling its neck.

The three shamans repeated the brotherhood's motto. "Cruelty is strength!" they declared in unison.

The Iron Shield began to tighten the garrote.

✦　✦　✦

Teo had always wanted to see the ocean. Now, having seen it at last, he had to agree it was as impressive as the books had said.

He stood on a pier in the harbor at Nuo Genov, looking out over the vast blue expanse. The midday sunshine beat down on his shoulders. Seabirds called to each other as they circled overhead, and the smell of brine was in the air. Ships of all types came and went, some of them great vessels, others just little fishing boats. The busy port bustled with commerce and energy.

A row of taverns lined the seafront, so Teo made his way there. He entered the first one he came to, La Lanterna. The establishment was dark yet clean. Seafarers sat at tables or in booths by the windows. Teo found a place at the bar and ordered a beer.

"Don't see too many stablemen in here," the bartender said.

"Shoveling out the stalls is thirsty work," Teo answered as he received his foamy glass.

He drank for a while and casually surveyed the room. The young sailors kept to themselves, laughing uproariously as they exchanged tales of the sea over their brews. A few old salts sat in the corners, drinking harder, laughing less.

A wiry mariner with white stubble on his cheeks approached the bar. His hands trembled, not from drunkenness but perhaps from age or some unknown malady. When the bartender poured him a shot of whiskey, the sailor accidentally dropped the glass, which shattered on the floor.

"I got to charge you for that, Bosun," the bartender said.

"Aw, c'mon now! You know I ain't been paid yet," the sailor protested.

"Here you go." Teo slid a coin across the counter. "And you can leave the bottle with us."

Shrugging, the bartender picked up the coin. He set two shot glasses next to the whiskey bottle and left the men alone.

Teo extended his hand. "Name's Teofil."

"They call me Bosun." The lean seafarer smiled and returned the handshake. His black eyes were like slits in a piece of tanned leather. "You don't look like a sailor."

"I'm not. Never saw the sea until a few days ago. I envy you."

"She can be a hard mistress at times, but she'll make you love her too. Where you from? Your accent is strange."

"I used to live in the far north. I'm still learning your speech, so forgive me if I'm a little off."

"It won't be the worst sin that's ever been forgiven."

"Tell me about it." Teo pulled the cork from the bottle and poured two shots. He didn't normally chase his beer with whiskey, but this morning

151

he would make an exception. "To your health," he said, then drained the glass and set it down. Bosun did the same.

Teo leaned his elbows on the bar. "So, I'm looking for passage to a foreign city. You know a place called Roma?"

"Heard of it, but never been there. It's far-off, and I only do short jumps along our coast. You need to talk to one of the long-distance merchants. The sea's closing up, though. Another few weeks and the winter storms will have set in."

"Are there any long-distance ships in port right now?"

Bosun poured himself another shot. "There's one, but you don't want to talk to those people."

"I'll talk to anyone."

Bosun gave Teo a funny look and shook his head. "Not this lot. Did you see the caravel out there with the black sails?"

"I noticed it. It stands out."

"Belongs to the shamans. One of their chiefs is in town—up from Roma, actually. Giant man, always wears armor. A killer, they say. Few have ever seen him, but we know when he's here. He's called the Iron Shield." Bosun shuddered.

"I didn't know the shamans were sailors."

"Some of them are. They got to be able to move their, you know, *cargo*." Bosun put a strange emphasis on the last word.

"What kind of cargo?"

Bosun took a swallow of whiskey. "Ya see, the shamans are like maggots or vultures. They ain't creatures you want to be around, but you're mighty glad they're there. They get rid of the rotten stuff no one else wants to touch."

"You're talking about the Defectives."

"Right. You can't have those types running loose. Someone has to cart them away. The shamans do the dirty work for us, so we let them be." Bosun leaned close. "People who complain about the shamans have been known to disappear too. It's best to steer clear of them altogether."

"What's the Iron Shield here for?"

Bosun shrugged. "No idea. His ship's getting ready to leave. The word on the dock is he's heading over to Camoly."

Teo was surprised. "Camoly? The dohj's yacht just left to go there on a pleasure cruise. Some of the aristocrats I work for went with him." *And no doubt Ana went too*, Teo thought.

"Oh yeah? That's strange."

"What is?"

"It's strange for two big ships to go there at once. There ain't much in Camoly. It's just a fishin' village. The dohj likes to swim at the little cove down the coast. I don't know why the Iron Shield would go there, unless it's just a stopping point on his way to somewhere else."

"Hmm. Must be a coincidence." Teo kept his tone casual. "Can you get to Camoly by land?"

"It's difficult, but there's a rough trail along the shore. I got a chart in my duffle if you want to see it."

"I think I would," Teo said.

✦　✦　✦

The dohj's yacht weighed anchor off Camoly and set its sails to catch a stiff breeze. The large vessel—a galleon, Cristof had called it—had three masts and two decks of cabins, plus staterooms in the sterncastle. Though such ships could be used for war or commerce, this particular one had been outfitted solely for pleasure. No luxury had been spared.

Ana stood on the main deck with the other Likurian and Ulmbartian glitterati, holding a fruity drink in her hand. The midday sunshine beat down on her bare shoulders. The warmth on her skin felt unusual, for she wasn't used to wearing the skimpy swimming attire that the sophisticated Likurian women wore. The outfit consisted of a band around the chest and a brief cloth on the hips. Although the women also wore wraparound skirts to cover their legs, their only garment from the waist up was the chest band. Ana had been apprehensive about wearing such revealing clothing, but when she realized all the other women thought nothing of it, she decided to adapt.

Vanita came and stood by Ana as she leaned against the bulwark. Together they watched the sleepy village of Camoly recede in the ship's wake. All the buildings were painted in pastel colors that stood out against the green Likurian hills. When they had gone ashore earlier that morning, Ana had marveled at the way in which architectural details had been painted onto the walls. They were made to look three-dimensional through shadowing and perspective. "Trick the eye," the dohj had called it.

"We'll be at the cove in a few minutes," Vanita said, sipping her drink. "The ruins there are very old. I think it was a monastery of the Ancients or something like that. It's charming in an archaic sort of way."

"Have you been there before?"

"Once, as a young girl. I've always wanted to go back. It's a sheltered little place with a pebbly beach. Makes you feel secluded."

Ana fiddled with her hair, then leaned close to Vanita. "What do you think of these Likurian swimming outfits?" she whispered.

Vanita arched her back and stretched in the sun, reveling in her sensuality. "They're great, aren't they? I wish Ulmbartia wasn't so straitlaced. We could learn a lot from Likuria."

Ana blew out a breath of air. "I don't know. Back in Chiveis, women didn't go around like this. Do you think when we swim it's required to take off the long skirts?"

Vanita regarded Ana with a bemused expression. "What's wrong? Is the religious girl having second thoughts about going to the beach? Of course you should take off the skirt! Or you could play sick and stay in your cabin if you're too much of a prude."

"I'm not a prude," Ana protested. "It's just that—"

"What?"

"Well, um—"

"Go ahead, say it."

Ana looked around, then took Vanita by the hand. "Come with me." She led Vanita below deck to her stateroom and closed the door. "You remember how I told you a wolf bit me on the leg?"

Vanita nodded.

"I got better after I took the bread-mold medicine, but the scar is still there. I've been putting olive oil on it every day. I think it's been getting lighter, but it's still visible. Just a little though."

Vanita glanced at Ana's hip. "Let me see."

Ana untied the knot at her waist and opened her sarong. Vanita recoiled. "Ew! It's huge and disgusting!"

Ana quickly closed the skirt again. "Is it really that bad?"

"It's bad," Vanita said. "But stick with me. I'll help you."

The yacht had come to a stop, so Vanita and Ana went topside. Tenders were lowered, and all the aristocrats went ashore, taking only the most necessary servants. The cove was just as Vanita had described it: secluded and quaint, exuding an Old World charm. The monastery of the Ancients was draped in vines, and a domed tower protruded from the foliage. Reclining canvas chairs had been set up on the beach. Ana had never seen such crystalline blue water. Some of the lords and ladies had already entered the sea for a swim.

Vanita and Ana found two chairs off to the side. As they were sitting down, Vanita untied her skirt and let it fall. Ana removed hers as well, grateful that no one seemed to notice her scar before she slid into the seat. Ana let her arm fall casually over the blemish on her hip. The sun felt good as she lay back in the warmth. After a few moments, she turned her head to speak to Vanita, then gasped in surprise. Vanita had taken off her chest band as she reclined in the chair.

"Vanita!" Ana whispered. "What are you doing?"

"Look around," Vanita answered, remaining perfectly calm as she relaxed in the sunshine with her eyes closed. "It's the way things are done here."

Ana glanced at the beach. All the younger women had removed the tops of their swimming outfits. The women walked around like that, and no one seemed shocked about it.

Vanita rotated her head and shaded her eyes as she looked at Ana. "You'd better do the same or you're going to be noticed. I told you I'd help you. Believe me, no one's going to be paying attention to your hips."

Flustered, Ana sat in the lounge chair, torn about what to do. She hadn't been raised in such an indulgent culture as Likuria. The rules of modesty were very different in Chiveis. *But you're not in Chiveis anymore,* Ana reminded herself. *Like it or not, you're in Likuria now!*

"Just take it off," Vanita said. "Stop dithering."

Ana swallowed. The chest band was tied at her back. She reached around and undid the knot. *Just because it feels wrong doesn't mean it is,* she reasoned. *That's just the way you were brought up. Here in Likuria it's perfectly normal.*

Timidly, she dropped the band on the pebbles next to her chair.

◆　　◆　　◆

When Teo first laid eyes on the impossibly tall warrior in the chain-mail hauberk, he knew at once it was the Iron Shield. It wasn't just the man's height that told Teo this; it was the agile way he moved. The Iron Shield walked with the confidence of a man who has absolute mastery of his body and his surroundings.

Teo had ridden straight to Camoly after his conversation with Bosun at La Lanterna. The estate of Count Federco Borromo owned excellent horses, and Teo had borrowed one of the best, though that was not the normal prerogative of stableboys. He knew the stablemaster would have some choice words for him upon his return, but Teo was far more concerned about the sneaky activities of the shamans than a tongue-lashing from his boss.

Since speaking with Bosun earlier that day, Teo had felt a nagging apprehension about the Iron Shield's presence in Camoly. The more he learned about the Exterminati, the more he wanted to make sure they were nowhere near Ana. He thought back to the Rovers' attack at the island castle. Though he didn't understand all the ins and outs, he suspected it was no coincidence that the dark-robed shamans had been lurking around the count's chateau when the attack came. Whatever was afoot, Teo intended to make sure the events at the northern lake didn't reoccur in Likuria. He would watch how things unfolded, taking action only if necessary. Teo felt it was his responsibility to have Ana's back. His relational difficulties with her would never change that fact.

It was early evening now. Teo had wandered the streets of the seaside fishing village for more than an hour. On a different day he might have been charmed by Camoly's pastel buildings and sparkling waterfront, but today he had other things on his mind. The Iron Shield's dark caravel floated offshore like a stain upon the clear blue sea.

After trailing a pair of shamans to the outskirts of town, Teo had finally discovered their local outpost. It wasn't much of a shrine—just a run-down hovel, really—but it served well enough as a rendezvous point for the Iron Shield. Two black horses had been made ready. Teo watched from the bushes as the Iron Shield swung into the saddle along with a shaman who wore a red armband. When they departed into the forest, Teo moved off a short distance and retrieved his horse, confident the riders' trail wouldn't be hard to follow.

The Iron Shield and his companion headed south along the seashore. The area was remote, and the men's tracks led down what was little more than a deer path. Because the hills around here dropped sharply into the sea, it wasn't a good place for farming, or even olive growing. This part of Likuria was a stretch of dense wilderness punctuated by isolated fishing villages whose primary means of access was by sea, not road.

The orange orb of the sun had touched the ocean's distant horizon when Teo spotted the Iron Shield standing at the water's edge in a sheltered inlet. The shaman with the red armband sat in a rowboat, which had been painted black. As Teo watched, the Iron Shield removed his hauberk, belt, and heavy boots. When he took off his gambeson and waded shirtless into the sea, Teo was stunned by the man's incredible physique. The Iron Shield's shoulders were corded with bands of sinew; his biceps and chest muscles bulged; his body rippled in the evening sun like a glossy horse galloping across a field. *No wonder the man is so feared*, Teo thought.

Dismounting, Teo worked his way toward a vantage point that would allow him to watch the Iron Shield's actions. The dark warrior had swum out into the ocean, becoming almost invisible in the fading daylight. Teo would not have been able to see him if he hadn't known where to look. Raising his eyes along the line the Iron Shield was taking, Teo's heart jumped. Dohj Cristof's massive yacht was anchored there, and the Iron Shield was swimming straight to it.

It was time to act.

Sliding down a steep incline to the water's edge, Teo threw off his boots and shirt, then slipped into the water. He chose a course that would keep him directly behind the Iron Shield, staying submerged as much as possible.

As Teo neared the dohj's galleon he noticed sailors busy with the rigging. The ship was being readied to leave. Tenders moved toward the beach to retrieve the last of the aristocratic lords and ladies after their relaxing day in the sun. The aroma of cooked meat wafted to Teo's nostrils. No doubt a great feast was being prepared for the cruise home.

A shadowy figure rose from the water at the yacht's stern. The high sterncastle, decorated with intricate carvings, contained many windows for the vessel's staterooms. As Teo swam closer he watched the Iron Shield stealthily ascend the exterior of the ship. The warrior reached a window from which a white kerchief had been hung, then crept inside.

The dark waters lapped against the ship's rudder. Teo reached for a handhold and worked his way up the hull, finding the climb more difficult than the Iron Shield had made it look. The wood was slick with algae, and the sun had now set, making secure footing hard to see. Teo managed to pull himself up to the cabin with the white kerchief, whose window remained open. By balancing on a carved mermaid and craning his neck, he was able to peek inside the room.

The first thing he saw confirmed his worst fear: one of Ana's gowns hung on a peg, and the luggage on the bedspread was hers. Although no one was in the luxurious cabin, wet footprints on the floorboards proved the Iron Shield had been there.

No sooner had Teo spotted the footprints than the dark warrior appeared from the attached bathroom, holding a towel. Teo shrank back so he could watch the man's movements through a gap between the window's curtain and its frame.

The Iron Shield, dripping and shirtless, appeared even more formidable up close. A knife, a garrote, and a pair of manacles dangled from his belt. He dried himself with the towel, then knelt and wiped away the footprints. Next he went to a liquor cabinet and removed a bottle of brandy, which he sprinkled liberally on the furniture around the room until the bottle was empty. He pitched it on the bed and rumpled the covers. Stooping, he began to slide under the bed—and then Teo's foot slipped.

As Teo lurched in front of the window to catch himself, the Iron Shield glanced up, startled. He scrambled to his feet and drew his knife, dashing to the window with a savage snarl. Teo was completely off-balance. As the Iron Shield's blade came slashing down, Teo realized that in his awkward position he could not deflect his enemy's thrust. The only way to dodge the stabbing attack was to leap into empty space.

Teo jumped clear of the ship as the knife flashed toward him. Twisting in midair, he grabbed the Iron Shield's rock-hard forearm and did not let go. The weight of Teo's falling body yanked the dark warrior out of the stateroom window. The two men hit the water hard and plunged beneath the surface of the Likurian sea.

Entangled with his enemy, Teo refused to relinquish his hold on the Iron Shield's knife hand. He knew if the blade were free, only a split second would pass before he felt its sharp point slide between his ribs. As the combatants thrashed and tumbled end over end, they sank into the depths. Their fierce struggle was all the more intense because neither man could see the other.

Teo had managed to grab a breath before he fell in, but his lungs were beginning to demand more air. The Iron Shield's strength only seemed to increase as he pressed the knife toward Teo's bare skin. The two men fought each other in the cold water, kicking, punching, wrestling, and churning, until finally Teo had lost any sense of which way was up. His lungs ached. Fear seized him as he realized that if he let go of his enemy's wrist to seek more air, he would be stabbed, but if he remained entangled with his foe, he would drown.

The Iron Shield seized Teo's neck and began to squeeze. Teo clawed at the hand encircling his throat, trying to release the man's grip. In an unexpected move, the Iron Shield brought his arm across Teo's body in a vicious slash. The edge of the knife sliced a hot burn along his chest. Only Teo's grip on the Iron Shield's wrist prevented the cut from splitting him wide open.

Dizzy blackness threatened to engulf Teo's mind, but with an animalistic urge to survive he fought off unconsciousness and continued to battle. The Iron Shield strained to bury his blade in Teo's flesh. Teo pressed the Iron Shield's forehead with his palm, forcing his enemy's head backward. With his other hand he maintained his vise-grip on the Iron Shield's wrist. No air was left in Teo's lungs. He longed to open his mouth and inhale, but he knew it would be his end. *Deu! Help me!*

As Teo pushed against his enemy's face, he felt something give way to the press of his thumb. The Iron Shield abruptly ceased the attack and pulled back. Teo let him go, hanging suspended in the murky ocean. Everything was black except for a pale white glow, very far above.

Teo kicked his legs and shot toward the light, swimming with the desperation of a dying man. Agony seared his lungs. He could hold his breath no longer. After all his striving to protect Ana, it had come down to this. *Was this how it was going to end?*

Sadness and despair overtook him. His throat went into spasms. His mouth opened involuntarily. He choked . . . retched . . . gagged . . .

And could breathe.

Yes! He had reached the surface and could breathe again. Teo sucked in great lungfuls of air, making heaving sounds as his body sought to resupply its oxygen-starved cells. He bobbed in the sea with his head thrown back, gasping and gulping through an open mouth like a fish tossed on the grass. The white light of a full moon reflected off the water's surface as Teo floated on his back, utterly spent.

A stinging sensation on his chest snapped him back to reality. When he touched the injured place and held up his hand, his fingers glistened black in the moonlight. The sight of the blood and the burning pain of the cut triggered a memory. Long ago, while he was chained in a prison cell, the High Priestess of Chiveis had slashed his chest with the tip of his own sword. Now a twin scar from another evil hand would mark his body forever.

Teo became aware that his left fist was clenched. He opened his hand and inspected the object in his palm, unable to comprehend what it was. Suddenly he recognized it: *a human eyeball.* Horrified, Teo threw away the grisly reminder of his life-or-death battle and furiously rinsed his hand. Cognizant of danger again, he glanced around, but the Iron Shield was nowhere to be seen. The assassin's severe injury would probably force him to return home. *By the time he recovers the sea will be closed to sailing,* Teo thought with no small relief.

The dark bulk of Dohj Cristof's galleon loomed a short distance away. The anchor had been weighed, and the ship had set sail, but Teo could still see its main deck decorated with colored lanterns. Most of the yacht's windows were illumined by a warm yellow glow. Lords and ladies gathered on the deck, blithe and carefree, oblivious to the struggle that had just unfolded in the sea below them.

Teo sighed. He longed for a cold drink to wash the salt from his mouth. The yacht had caught a breeze and was moving quickly now. Teo could do nothing more at the moment, so he turned and began to swim toward shore. All was quiet except for the gentle splashes of his strokes and the sound of flirtatious laughter floating across the water.

◆　　◆　　◆

When Ana opened the door of her cabin, it reeked of alcohol, and everything was in disarray. An empty bottle of brandy lay on the rumpled bed. Evidently some of the servants had chosen her room to have a little party while their masters went onshore. Ana decided to speak to the cabin steward about it the next time she saw him.

Entering the bathroom attached to her cabin, she was pleased to see that her porcelain bathtub had been filled with hot water. Though the water-spout contraptions used in the dohj's palace couldn't be installed on a ship, the servants had been busy heating water in cauldrons, then taking kettles around to the staterooms. Steam rose from Ana's tub, and an extra kettle wrapped in a cozy sat nearby, ready to top off the bath when she decided to get in.

As she was undressing, Ana caught a glimpse of herself in the mirror. She was shocked at what she saw. Though she could already feel that her body was radiating heat and was sensitive to the touch, she couldn't believe how red she had gotten from the sun's rays. She had only been on the beach a few hours, but her fair skin was badly burned. Ana pressed her finger to the skin below her collarbone. A white dot was visible when she removed her finger, but it gradually returned to the same garish red as the rest of her body.

Ana sighed. *I'm a mess! I've never looked so bad!*

No sooner had that thought sprung to her mind than a competing voice said, *But did you notice how attracted Dohj Cristof was to you?* It gave Ana a strange sensation to recall the look on the dohj's face when he had approached her chair on the beach as she sat next to Vanita. The handsome dohj had stayed for a long time, standing against the backdrop of the turquoise lagoon as he conversed with the two sunbathers. Ana had wondered if he would want to discuss religion, but Cristof had been more interested in making suggestive remarks about her looks. Although Ana didn't return his comments with coquetry of her own, she had found the attention rather exciting.

Now, though, as Ana gazed in the mirror, she felt disgusted. She consoled herself with the thought that she certainly had no intention of pursuing a romantic relationship with Cristof. He was, after all, the most powerful man in the kingdom of Likuria—a prince whose blood was bluer than the waters of his beloved ocean. Ana reminded herself that her true purpose in spending time with the dohj was to tell him about Deu.

How's that going? Ana shook the question from her mind, deciding there would be ample time for such matters in the days ahead. She would no doubt have an opportunity during the next several months to pursue spiritual conversations with Vanita and Cristof. And then, after the visit to the coast was over, she would return to Ulmbartia. Teo was still there, and maybe she could patch things up with him . . .

Teo.

I miss him so much.

Tears sprang to Ana's eyes. She let them fall as she stared with increasing horror at her reflection in the mirror. How had she gotten here, all sunburned and ruined on the lavish yacht of a rich playboy? Ana's fair skin had never seen the light of day, and now she had exposed herself like . . . what?

Like a common harlot!

Ana whirled away from the mirror, pressing the heels of her hands to her eyes. In her anguish and shame she felt an overwhelming desire to talk with her mother, but that voice of wisdom was lost to her. All voices were lost. Chiveis was lost. Teo was lost. He would never want her back.

Ana wiped away her tears. There was only one way to go forward. As it turned out, Vanita had been right all along. Ana decided she needed to make a home for herself in the real world, the actual world, the rough-and-tumble world in which she found herself—not the elusive world of vague hopes and empty dreams. *If I don't provide for my future, who will?*

Ana emptied the kettle into the porcelain bathtub. Stepping over the tub's edge, she sank into the steaming water. Though the intense heat stung her skin, Ana clenched her fists and ignored her pain.

CHAPTER

7

The dungeons at Nikolo Borja's palace were buried deep beneath the earth. It was better that way, for then no one outside could hear the constant screaming of the damned.

Borja faced his loyal servant, the Iron Shield, who stood across a pit in the dungeon floor. The warrior looked the same as always. Though his shoulders were broad, his body tapered to a narrow waist, for rigorous daily exercise prevented the accumulation of fat on his chiseled physique. The elegantly wrought links of his hauberk were the work of a master metalsmith. The Iron Shield's boots were thick-soled and rugged. At his side hung his fearsome mace. His black hair glistened with oil. Only one thing was different about the Iron Shield since Borja had seen him last: the dark warrior now wore a patch over his right eye.

The sound of wailing cats echoed off the arched roof of the underground chamber. It was an annoying sound, and Borja let himself feel hatred for the disgusting animals whose screeches emanated from the pit in the flagstone floor. He stepped to the edge of the pit and looked down. Though the room was lit only by torches, Borja thought he could see shadows moving around in the narrow well into which the cats had been dumped. Perhaps the ones on the bottom of the pile had already suffocated? He hoped they still lived—for a little while longer.

Borja looked up from the pit and met his bodyguard's eye. "Have you healed from your injury, shield of my life?"

"It has been four weeks since I confronted Teofil of Chiveis, my lord.

Though the wound grew infected, I am strong, and I have regained my vigor already."

"And yet you were not strong enough to overcome your adversary." Borja put a note of derision in his voice, testing his servant's response.

The Iron Shield remained silent. Borja noticed movement at the corners of his jaw—a twitch that wasn't caused by the flickering torchlight. The warrior could barely contain his rage. Borja could feel his anger wafting across the pit like a tangible force. *Yes . . . good . . . let it come! It will make you strong.*

Borja provoked his servant further. "You have nothing to say for yourself? Are you then defeated by this foreign interloper?"

"No, my lord, I am not defeated. I await my revenge. And when I gain it, my enemy's torment will be beyond that of any man who has ever lived."

Smiling at this, Borja said, "Delight me with the details."

The Iron Shield balled his fists and approached the edge of the pit, staring into Borja's face. "I will crush him with my own hands. I will open him wide. I will burn him . . . break him . . . rip him . . . devour him! The death of my enemy will be prolonged over many days. He will beg for the pain to stop, but I will only make it worse, until at last he is no longer human, but an animal driven insane by agony. And then, when every bone is broken, and his body is smeared with gore, and redness oozes from him like butchered meat—then, at the end of it all, the last thing he will see is my smiling face as I snuff out his life."

The Iron Shield's vivid description gave Borja deep satisfaction. His fleshly lips curled into a smile he could not suppress. Swallowing the great quantity of saliva that had gathered in his mouth, he spoke to his favorite lieutenant. "You are worthy to receive the spirits of cruel sacrifice," he said in an ominous voice.

"Thank you, my lord."

"Has the loss of your eye affected your skill in combat? A man with one eye cannot gauge distance."

"What has been lost can be overcome with effort and training."

"Yes, it can, though it will take time. Since the sea is now closed to sailing I want you to use the winter to regain your former skills. I will provide as many slaves as you need to practice upon."

The Iron Shield hesitated, then spoke his mind. "My lord, I am not afraid of the turbulent seas. I wish to return immediately."

"No! Absolutely not!" Borja knew his servant was driven by lust for revenge—a worthy motivation, but one that needed to be tempered by common sense. The Iron Shield was an unparalleled warrior, an asset far too valuable to risk losing to some unexpected winter storm. "I will put watchers on the targets," Borja said. "In the meantime you must learn to compensate for the loss of your eye."

The Iron Shield persisted, though his tone remained respectful. "We must deal with the heretics quickly, Your Abundance."

"Enough! I have spoken. Our spies can watch the heretics until we are prepared to deal with them. I am far more concerned that your fighting capacity is now diminished. I need you at full strength, shield of my life. Regain your former power, and when spring comes and the seas grow calm, you may set sail for Likuria to exact your revenge. I only hope you will make it as painful as you have promised."

"Do not fear, my lord. You can be certain Teofil of Chiveis will die the excruciating death he deserves."

"If he was able to survive your attack and even do injury to you, he must be a worthy opponent. Strength will be needed for your task. It is time for you to receive the spirits."

Borja snapped his fingers. A slave materialized from the shadows, pushing a large cauldron on wheels. As the cauldron was tipped, its contents emptied into the pit. The cats confined below began to screech even louder as gooey oil poured over them.

Borja walked to the wall and removed a torch, handing it to the Iron Shield. "Begin when you are ready. The walls and ceiling are made of thick stone lined with silver. The spirits cannot get out. There is only one place for them to go. What say you, my servant?"

"*Crudelitas vis est*," replied the Iron Shield.

"Indeed it is."

Borja exited, making sure the slave closed the door behind him. A moment later an unearthly caterwauling erupted from the room. Even through the thick door, the commotion was raucous and intense. Borja could only imagine the horror of the sounds that were reverberating off the walls inside the dark chamber.

Finally the plaintive cries of the sixty-six cats died out. There was a knock on the door. When Borja opened it, a stinking cloud billowed from the room. The Iron Shield stood in the doorway, ripe with the stench of singed fur and burnt flesh.

Borja placed his hand on his servant's forehead. "May these familiar spirits invigorate you with their life force," he intoned.

"I can feel their presence, my lord."

"Yessss . . . I feel it too. It is very good."

Reaching to a pouch at his waist, Borja removed an object and held it in his fist. "I have a gift for you, shield of my life."

The Iron Shield knelt and bowed his head. "The grace of Your Abundance is beyond measure."

Borja removed the Iron Shield's eye patch. The dark warrior looked up at Borja from his kneeling stance, waiting silently. The gaping socket of his right eye was like the entrance to a cave—repulsive and forbidding.

"See what I had made for you," Borja said, opening his fist. A rounded lump of glass lay in his palm, fashioned by an expert lens grinder. It was a sickly yellow color, pierced by a single black slit.

"The eye of a cat," said the Iron Shield.

"A legion of spirits now indwells you, mighty warrior. From this day forward you shall be even more fearsome than you were before."

Borja held the glass orb in his fingers. It glinted in the torchlight. With grave solemnity he pressed it into the waiting eye socket of the most dangerous man on earth.

◆　◆　◆

Teo's boots were caked with manure. Pitchfork in hand, he mucked out one of the stalls in the stable assigned to Count Federco Borromo on the outskirts of Nuo Genov. A beautiful autumn sun shone down on the gleaming city. Teo rolled a wheelbarrow to the compost pile in the yard and dumped it out. Shirtless and covered in grime, he wiped sweat from his forehead with the back of his gloved hand. At least the sweat no longer stung the slash across his chest. The cut had healed up nicely in the four weeks since his battle with the Iron Shield.

In the distance a few boats bobbed on the ocean. Soon they would be brought into winter storage, for it was the middle of the tenth month, and the season of unpredictable storms was at hand. Today, however, the sky was clear and the sun still had some warmth. Teo chuckled and shook his head. Though it would be nice to be out on the water with a breeze on his face, he realized it was not his destiny to enjoy a leisurely day at sea. Eight more stalls remained to be cleaned.

Teo returned to the stable and was about to start forking soiled hay into the wheelbarrow when something caught his eye: a partial footprint pressed into the mud. Years of training as a wilderness scout had accustomed him to observe details that would escape most people's notice. Teo knew the footprint wasn't his, yet it was fresh, which meant someone had slipped into the stable while he was outside. Since the horses had been turned out to pasture and no one was likely to be in the stable right now, the footprint was more than a little suspicious.

Glancing at the stalls he had already cleaned, Teo noticed the door to one of them was ajar. He eased toward it, pitchfork in hand, then swung it open with the toe of his boot. An elderly man with long, white hair crouched in the shadows. Seeing he was discovered, he stood erect and stepped into the light.

"Sol!" Teo exclaimed. The Ulmbartian schoolteacher was the last person Teo had expected. "What are you doing here? I'm so glad to see you!"

"And I'm glad to see you, Teofil! Much has happened to me, and we need to talk." Sol looked around. "In private."

"This place is as private as any, I suppose. Sit down. I'll be right back." Teo went to the trough outside and cleaned up, then put on his shirt and returned with his lunch pail. It contained sandwiches of a Likurian flatbread called *fokatcha*, layered with slices of white cheese and a spread made from pine nuts and basil.

Sol was ravenous when Teo brought him the food. Looking at him more closely, Teo realized how gaunt his friend's face had become. Sol's

169

clothes were ragged from hard use, and his hair was unkempt. Teo let him eat his fill before trying to start a conversation.

Finally Sol's appetite appeared to be sated. He reclined against the wall of the horse stall and reached for a flask of wine. After guzzling a long draft he looked at Teo and said, "The shamans came after me."

"What? Tell me exactly what happened."

Sol wiped his mouth on his sleeve and recounted the entire story. A barnyard cat at the Labella estate had saved his life. Sol had been awakened one night when the cat yowled from the stairs outside. Realizing someone was ascending toward his apartment above the schoolhouse, Sol listened until he heard his lock being picked, then dashed to his bedroom wall and opened a panel leading to a hollow place in the eaves. The panel blended into the wood, and Sol had just pulled it shut behind him when he heard his door open. He watched through a knothole as a tall shaman with an armband crept to the bed. Sol had fallen asleep in a chair that night, so his bed was still made. Whispering a curse, the shaman turned and left the apartment, relocking the door and leaving the place just as he had found it.

"My only choice was to leave," Sol explained, "because I sure wouldn't get a second chance. I knew I couldn't keep hiding and dodging those killers. One day or the next they'd get me. So that very night I stuffed a blanket and a bunch of food in my pack and left before dawn."

"Where did you go?"

"I just hit the road. I don't think the shamans were expecting that. They didn't know I was onto them. I slipped through their fingers and became invisible. Joined up with a bunch of vagabonds. Good folk, those people. They're quick to share a stew with you around the campfire. Of course, they'll rob you too. I had my pack rifled more than once. Ha! Those hobos had no idea what I was carrying in my tunic!"

Teo arched his eyebrows. "What was it?"

Sol crawled to the stall's door and peeked out, then turned back to Teo. He used a pocketknife to slice open the hem of his garment. Four iridescent gems, pale blue, spilled into his hand. "My life's savings," Sol said proudly. "They're moonstones."

"Those gems could keep a man comfortable for a long time."

"I was thinking of two men."

Teo gave Sol a quizzical glance but did not speak.

"Alright, let me explain," Sol said. "I came here to Likuria for a reason. When I got your message that you had taken the stable job with Count Federco, I was disappointed. I had grown to like you quite a bit." Sol smiled affably, and Teo nodded to show the feeling was mutual.

"But there was something else," Sol continued. "I felt *safe* with you. You have a way of making people feel you have things under control—or could get them under control if something came up. Do you know what I mean?"

"I guess so. Anastasia has said that sort of thing to me before."

"She's right. You take good care of her."

Teo tsked, shaking his head. "Not lately. I haven't talked to her in over a month. She's in deep with Lady Vanita, and now the dohj too. Those aristocrats have a way of putting up walls."

"Unfortunately, Anastasia isn't trying to climb out."

Teo was glum. "I know." He looked up at Sol. "I did drive an assassin away from her though. A leader of the shamans."

"She was attacked by them too?"

"Yeah. And I barely survived."

"What happened?"

Sol listened, astounded, as Teo described his battle in the sea with the Iron Shield. "I think his eye injury forced him away from Likuria," Teo said. "His caravel hasn't been seen since our fight."

"Have the local Exterminati been up to any trouble?"

"I've been keeping tabs on them. As far as I can tell, they're lying low."

"So what are you going to do?"

"I can't let the shamans get near Ana. But since I don't have access to her, I can only look for anything suspicious and be ready to act immediately. Believe me, I'll be watching those rats like a hawk in the sky."

"Okay then, listen to my idea. Since you're cut off from your woman but you want to stay close and keep an eye on her, let me make you a proposal. I need the kind of protection you can provide. You have the ability to sniff out those killers, see what they're up to, fight them off if necessary.

The safest place I can be right now is near you. Otherwise I'm going to wake up with a knife in my chest."

"I won't let that happen, Sol. You're welcome to stay with me. I rented a cottage on the property of a farmer's widow."

"Good. That'll be perfect for the project I have in mind." Sol rummaged in his rucksack and pulled out his version of the Old Testament. "Remember this? It's written in Talyano. You want a version in the Chiveisian speech, right?"

"Definitely. I've only translated bits and pieces of it, and most of those scrolls were left back in Chiveis. There are large portions of the Old Testament I've never even read because I haven't had time to translate them."

"I assume you have your original copy of the Sacred Writing? The book you found in the lost city?"

"Sure. It's in my pack right now. I try to keep it with me so thieves don't get it while I'm gone. That happened to me once, and it wasn't a good feeling."

"And didn't you tell me you have a dictionary too?"

Teo laughed as he recalled his unintentional theft. "Yeah. I found a lexicon in a Chiveisian temple that I intended to take to my university. One thing led to another, and I never got to do that. The lexicon stayed in my pack until I discovered it again."

"Excellent! Then we have everything we need to make a new translation. My moonstones will keep food on the table for the time being. You can quit this dirty job and get back to doing what you really love. With nothing else to do, we can knock out a version of the Old Testament in the Chiveisian tongue in just a few months!"

The idea excited Teo. The more he thought about it, the more sense it made. He grinned at his friend. "It might be possible," he admitted.

"Of course it is!" Instead of speaking Talyano, Sol answered Teo in the guttural speech of the Chiveisi.

"Hey!" Teo exclaimed. "I forgot you know my language."

"A dialect of it anyway. That should speed things up for us. And my penmanship is decent too. If you'll do the bulk of the translating, I'll make a nice, clean copy. All I ask is that you keep the shamans off my back."

Teo considered the proposal. His previous translations of the Sacred Writing for a community of believers in Chiveis had been slow—partly because he was being meticulous and partly because his other responsibilities had demanded much of his time. *But if I devote myself to translation full-time, and I have Sol's help, and I don't linger over each verse . . .* The possibilities were intriguing. By the time the translation was finished, the seas would have opened up again, and the long-distance sailors would be back in Nuo Genov. Then perhaps he could find a ship to take him to Roma. Teo figured if he could help the Papa locate the New Testament to complement the Old, he would be well on his way toward a recovery of Deu's religion.

"Alright, I'm in," Teo said, holding up his pitchfork. "I'll trade this for a quill any day."

◆　　◆　　◆

The winter months slipped by, sometimes sunny, sometimes rainy, but never truly cold. As the vernal equinox approached, a spell of unusually warm weather set in. Ana decided seaside Likuria was a much better place to spend the winter than the frigid mountains of the north. Back in Chiveis, snow would still be falling, but here in Likuria it was time to get out and enjoy the sun even though it was only the third month. *I could get used to this,* Ana thought.

She and Vanita strolled arm in arm through the grand aquarium near Nuo Genov's harbor. Sea creatures of all kinds had been given new homes in glass tanks to amuse the spectators. Fish swirled around the two women in every direction, some in large schools of flashing silver, others in proud displays of multihued color. The aquarium even had tanks with the large, playful fish called *delphini*. Ana had seen them jumping and frolicking around ships in the ocean, but seeing them up close with their bottle-shaped noses and permanent grins made her appreciate them even more. She had never known there were so many kinds of fish in the seas of the world.

"Oh, look at that!" Ana pointed to a sea turtle drifting by with lazy flaps of its fins.

Vanita grinned. "It would be fun to sit on its back and ride it."

"Cristof said the turtles live as long as a man. Eighty years or more."

For a moment Vanita was silent, then she turned toward Ana with an inquisitive glance. "So it's just 'Cristof' now, is it? Apparently you've grown quite friendly with the sovereign of the realm."

Ana felt her cheeks flush. "Oh, he, uh—he told me to call him that. Because we're close, he said."

"Sounds like you two have really hit it off over the past few months. Lots of face time with the dohj for Anastasia."

"Not really. Just here and there."

"It seems like more than that."

"It's not."

"Are you sure?"

Vanita's remarks embarrassed Ana. She had told herself many times she wasn't romantically interested in Dohj Cristof. However, she couldn't escape the nagging thought, *Then why do I enjoy being in his inner circle so much?*

"It's nothing!" Ana insisted. "And even if it were, I'd only be taking your advice. Aren't you the one who told me to set myself up for life by finding a man?"

"Not that man."

"Well, don't worry. I'm not after him like that."

"Then why do you spend so much time together?"

"I don't know," Ana blurted out. "Somehow he just makes me feel secure."

"He makes you feel secure?"

"Yes—I guess that's what you'd call it. Cristof gives me a feeling of safety, like he would take care of me if things got bad. He's rich, he'd pay for what I need."

"Every girl's dream, huh?"

"That's not fair! You told me to go after this. You said men have all the power in the world, so we have to attach ourselves to them. Perhaps I finally realized you were right and decided to take matters into my own hands."

"Are you intimate with the dohj?"

"Intimate? You mean . . . ?" Ana glanced at the fish tanks, knowing her face had grown red. "No, Vanita! Of course not!"

"Why is that such a crazy idea? Everybody has heard about his insatiable appetite for women."

"Maybe so, but you know I'm not like that. I told you already—my feelings for Cr—for Dohj Cristof aren't romantic. I'm spending time with him because he's interested in my faith. I have to keep a good relationship with him so I can bear witness to Deu." Even as Ana said it, she knew it wasn't the whole truth. Although she had spoken to Cristof about Deu, she was aware that evangelism wasn't her only motivation to be in his company. The realization was painful to her, and she brushed it away.

"There you go again, talking about your god," Vanita said. "You're obsessed with religion. You'd be a lot better off if you had never even found that ancient book."

Ana put her hand to her forehead, feeling confused and upset. "You don't understand. The words of Deu used to comfort me so much. When I was in the wilderness with Teofil, he would read to me every night. But now . . ." Ana's voice faltered. She turned away from Vanita.

"I thought you had forgotten about that soldier. Don't start up with him again."

Ana didn't respond. Over the winter months she had written letters to Teofil at the Labella estate in Ulmbartia. Though she had waited anxiously for a reply, the letters had gone unanswered. Ana felt hot tears rise up. She squeezed her eyes and covered her mouth, but her sniffle gave her away.

"Are you crying?" Vanita demanded. "Anastasia, are you crying?"

Ana shook her head as Vanita came around and stood in front of her. "Listen to me—what you need isn't Dohj Cristof, and it isn't some working-class soldier boy. We're going to find you a handsome lord when we return to Ulmbartia. No more fooling around! As soon as we get back, I'm going to make some arrangements."

"I might not even be going back," Ana said bitterly.

"What are you talking about?"

Ana waved her hand. "Nothing, probably. It's just that a few days ago Cristof asked if I would stay down here with him."

Vanita did a double take. "He asked you *what?*"

"I know it's crazy. He asked if I would stay in Likuria at the palace. He said—oh, never mind."

"What did he say?"

"He said he liked being around me. He called me 'regal,' though I wasn't sure what he meant by that."

"Oh, so now you're *regal*?" Vanita folded her arms across her chest and narrowed her eyes. "Are you aware that the di Sanjorjo house has been exploring plans with the Labella clan for an alliance?"

"What does that mean?"

"It means I'm supposed to marry the dohj, you stupid girl!"

Ana was shocked at her friend's venomous tone. "I told you, Vanita . . . I'm not trying . . ."

"Right, of course not! You're not *trying* to do anything!" Vanita's voice assumed a high-pitched, breathy tone. "I'm sweet, innocent Anastasia," she mocked, fluttering her eyelids. "How can I help it if the dohj falls for my angelic face and perfect little figure?" She pointed her finger at Ana. "Don't think I can't see what you're up to!"

"Vanita, stop!"

"No, *you* stop, Anastasia! You're the one who's conniving here. I'm warning you—keep your hands off Dohj Cristof! I'm going to be the Queen of Likuria someday, and when that day comes, you'd better find yourself on my side!"

Ana didn't know what to say. Vanita stared at her a moment longer, then whirled and marched off. "Find your own way home," she spat over her shoulder. "I don't want your company right now."

✦　✦　✦

Sol sat at a table, hunched over an open book. "How about this: 'Behold, I will send you Élie the prophet before the great and horrible day of the Lord happens; and he will turn the hearts of the fathers to the children, and the hearts of the children to their fathers, lest I come and strike the earth with a curse.' What do you think?"

Teo considered Sol's translation of the last two verses of the Old

Testament into the Chiveisian speech. "It's fine, except we would probably say, 'before the great and horrible day of the Lord *arrives*.'"

"Alright," Sol agreed, "we'll do it that way." He wrote it out, then set his quill on the table.

"I guess we're done then," Teo said, pumping his fist triumphantly.

Sol returned Teo's broad smile. "I guess we are."

The translation had required five months of intensive work on the part of the two linguistic scholars. Throughout the Likurian winter, they had sat together day after day with their texts and parchments and dictionary spread before them. Toward the end of the book of Habacuc, Teo's water-damaged copy of the Sacred Writing had become illegible, but Sol had urged him to continue the translation by using the Talyano version. "It's a literal rendering of the Old Words," Sol said. "Let's finish the job." Teo had been happy to comply, so the two men pressed on with the task.

Sol was indeed a good copyist. He wrote with a fine, clear hand, easy to read and beautiful in appearance. Teo had fashioned a leather cover for the book, and the men had bound the pages inside it, using the best vellum they could obtain. Though a professional bookbinder would have done it better, all in all the first Chiveisian copy of the Old Testament was a work of art.

"I have a name for it," Sol said, holding up the book. "We'll call it the *Versio Prima Chiveisorum*. The First Version of the Chiveisi."

"Great! Maybe we can call it the Prima for short." As Teo looked at the brand-new volume, the fruit of so much hard labor, a sense of accomplishment filled him. He rose and went to a cabinet. "I think it's time to celebrate," he said, uncorking a bottle of good wine and filling two cups. Sol's emphatic nod signaled his wholehearted agreement with Teo's suggestion.

The two men went outside to enjoy the spring sunshine by reclining against the trunk of a gnarled cork oak. The widow on whose property Teo was living liked to boast that the tree had been producing cork for a century. "Many a bottle has been stopped with the bark of that tree," the old woman had said, but the only bottle Teo cared about right now was the one in his hand.

Sol held the Prima in his lap, gently thumbing the pages. "I imagine this has been quite an interesting journey for you. Now that you've read the entire Old Testament, what do you think of it?"

It wasn't an easy question. Teo stared at the puffy clouds in the sky, sipping his wine and turning his thoughts over in his head. It seemed a thousand new characters had been introduced to him since he first encountered the sacred book: Adam and Eve, the original human pair; Noé and his boat of animals; Abraham the patriarch; Isaac, his nearly sacrificed son; tricky Jacob, who wrestled with Deu; faithful Joseph, sold into slavery; the great lawgiver Moses, who led the people of Israël out of Égypte; heroic and brave King David; wise but tragic Salomon; and many others too: kings and queens, prophets and priests, warriors and shepherds, prostitutes and widows, people of every age and personality and walk of life. It was a lot to take in. Teo felt overwhelmed. At last he gathered his thoughts and spoke. "I think what impresses me most is the faithful loyalty of the God in this book. I knew Deu is the All-Creator and that he has high demands for his followers. But what I noticed throughout the book was that even when his people failed him, he always sent a deliverer."

"Like Moses?"

"Moses is one good example, but there are others. Joseph and Néhémie were deliverers, and so were the magistrates. And the kings were supposed to be deliverers too, though not many of them lived up to it."

Sol smiled but didn't say anything. Teo looked over at the old man. "What are you thinking?"

"I'm thinking you just put your finger on something important," Sol replied. "The kings didn't live up to expectations. That's why the prophets kept pointing ahead to someone else—the Promised King."

"Right, I noticed that too. Deu promised to send a mighty deliverer who would defeat the wicked and bless the righteous. That's consistent with everything Deu has revealed about himself in the Old Testament. He's a saving God who overcomes evil."

"So the question is, who was this Promised King, and how can we receive his strength?"

"I'm sure the New Testament must explain all this," Teo said. "We know Iesus Christus was involved somehow. Even though he died, the Promised King was able to win. But how? That's what we've got to figure out. How did the king tap into Deu's power? If we learn the secret, maybe we could have that power too."

"I'll drink to that," Sol said, draining his glass.

The two men sat in contemplative silence for a time, allowing the breezes and the birdsong to quiet their souls. The little cottage under the oak tree had become their place of refuge for the past five months. Laboring in obscurity during the winter, they had been free from the malicious attention of the shamans. The Iron Shield's caravel had never reappeared in Likuria, which Teo viewed as a welcome respite. Yet while Teo had enjoyed these months of sabbatical, he could feel the wheels of human events starting to turn again with the coming of spring. A sense of urgency was beginning to gather in his soul. He knew some hard decisions had to be made.

"I think it's time for me to go to Roma," Teo said at last. "I can't avoid it anymore."

"What about Anastasia?"

Teo sighed. "I guess she'll return to Ulmbartia with Vanita."

"Will she be safe there?"

"I'm not sure, and that's my biggest problem. I feel the need to stay and watch out for her, yet I have to go to Roma. I can't be in two places at once! What am I supposed to do?"

"You have to follow your calling, Teofil. Deus has a role ordained for you. You're a man of action. You remind me of the Old Testament heroes like David or Samson or Josué. Few men in the world have the abilities you have. Don't squander that gift."

"I consider it a compliment to be compared to David," Teo acknowledged. "He was a brave fighter surrounded by mighty men. Remember when he wanted a drink of water and his soldiers ran into the enemy's camp to get it for him? Now that's courage."

Sol nodded. "And he showed that same kind of courage when he faced the giant with a couple of stones and a sling."

"What a story that was! I remember seeing that scene carved on the Overseer's temple in the Forbidden Zone. I didn't recognize it at the time." Teo sipped his wine and stared into the distance. "But the truth is, I don't feel adequate to follow in the footsteps of heroes like that. What if I fail?"

"I've noticed that Deus often turns our failures into his victories."

"So you're saying I should take a risk."

"Deus can be trusted, can he not?"

"Yes. I believe that with all my heart. But that doesn't mean there won't be pain along the way."

"Can you handle that?"

"There are things I could handle and things I couldn't." Teo exhaled a heavy sigh. "Alright, I'll make some inquiries around the dock. Maybe I can find passage to Roma. I promised Anastasia I'd find the New Testament, so I have to try. But I'm bound by another oath as well."

"An oath to protect?"

"Yes—an oath to protect something I'm not prepared to give up. I can only pray I'm never asked to."

✦ ✦ ✦

Lustful thoughts filled the mind of Dohj Cristof, and he had no interest in chasing them away. Instead he reveled in them, letting his imagination run wild. His fantasies were extravagant in their sensuality and detailed in their lewdness. One woman was the focus of Cristof's obsessive desire: the exotic beauty from over the northern mountains, Anastasia of Chiveis. His need for her was irrational, stoked by many hours of mental indulgence and aggravated by her inaccessibility to him. As the guest of a powerful and respected Ulmbartian duke, Anastasia could not be had for the taking like a housemaid or courtesan. She had to be treated with the deference due to the highborn. Cristof found that maddening.

The dohj stood at the window in his briefing room, his hands clasped behind his back. He shifted his feet uncomfortably, feeling inflamed with lust, yet unable to do anything about it at the moment. A knock sounded on the door, and Cristof hurried to take a seat at the large cherrywood table in the center of the room. "Come in," he barked, knowing the irritation in his voice was unwarranted. The director of intelligence was only doing his job.

A tall, spare man with graying temples strode into the room along with two younger aides. All were elegantly dressed. "Greetings, Your

Highness," said the director, laying a satchel on the table as he sat down. "We have some disturbing matters to discuss with you."

"Not so disturbing that you can't handle them, I trust."

The director glanced up and stared at the dohj from underneath his eyebrows. "Some matters are more complicated than others," he said ominously.

"Let's get on with it then." Cristof was in no mood for stalling.

The director took a deep breath. "Your Highness, we have reason to believe the Exterminati have issued a death mark on certain persons within our borders. Or perhaps they intend kidnapping and torture. Either way it's illegal."

The announcement made Cristof wince. The black-robed shamans gave him a shiver of revulsion every time he noticed them creeping around the streets. He understood they were necessary to rid Likuria of defective people, yet he preferred to have no direct dealings with them. Their blend of secrecy and occult power scared him.

Cristof mustered the will to appear kingly. "Turning a blind eye to murder and secret abductions are not part of our agreement with Lord Borja," he said.

The mention of Borja's name prompted a memory of the obese man's visit to Likuria. Several years ago he had arrived unexpectedly from distant Roma, exuding evil spirits like sweat from his pores. Cristof knew the dark arts of the Exterminati gave them access to powers that were not of this world. The dohj had been only too willing to grant the shamans the legal right to remove Defectives from Likuria—anything to get Borja to leave the realm. The official policy toward the Exterminati had been one of tolerance and avoidance ever since. However, if they started overstepping their limits with unauthorized killings of non-Defectives, Cristof would have to take action. If he dared.

Opening his satchel, the director removed two crumpled documents that looked like charcoal drawings. "Our intelligence suggests three individuals have been targeted by the Exterminati. Portraits like these have been distributed among the shamans to help them locate the targets. These persons are slated to be killed, or possibly tortured and sold into slavery."

"How do you know all this?"

"The shamans pride themselves on having eyes everywhere, but they aren't the only ones with informants. We have our own sources. Many a household slave can be bought off. They have nothing to lose."

"So who are the targets?" the dohj demanded. "Quit playing games and explain yourself."

"One of them is an unknown Ulmbartian who is not important to us. The other two are currently living in our realm. I have their portraits here. The female will be of concern to you, I believe." The director of intelligence handed the two wrinkled drawings to an aide, who brought them to the dohj and laid them on the table. They were smudged and torn, yet the faint images of a man and woman remained. Cristof bent over the picture of the woman and let his gaze focus on it.

His eyes widened. He sucked in his breath and gripped the edge of the table with both hands. *What's going on here?* Cristof wanted to speak, to ask lucid questions and receive easy answers, but he couldn't think coherently enough to put his thoughts into sequence, much less utter any words. All he knew for certain was that Anastasia was in mortal peril.

"We do not know why Anastasia and Teofil of Chiveis have been targeted," the director said, filling the awkward silence. "If it were a matter of their being defective, they would be subject to legal removal. However, since they have been singled out for kidnapping or assassination, we suspect there is something else at work here."

"I think I know what it is," Cristof said quietly.

The director signaled to the aide on his left, who brought out a quill and a blank piece of parchment for note taking. "Go on, Your Highness," the director said.

"Anastasia believes in a single god. When I first heard about it, I feigned interest and played along because . . ." The dohj paused. "Never mind that—it's beside the point. The pertinent facts are that Anastasia and her peasant friend have brought a new religion to our land from over the mountains."

"He is the other target," the director observed, pointing toward the second charcoal drawing. "He has taken up residence here since last summer."

"I met him once. An arrogant boy, that one."

The director pursed his lips, waiting a moment before speaking. "Your Highness, there are numerous gods in the world. Many of our citizens express devotion to one superstition or another, and the Exterminati do not get exercised about that. With all due respect, I'm not sure your hypothesis about Anastasia's religion is correct."

Cristof grimaced. "At first I thought it was harmless too. But the more I learned about what she believes, the more concerned I became. I tried to hush her up, but she wouldn't be quiet."

"A deity hardly seems a sufficient reason for a death mark."

"Trust me, this god of hers is plenty sufficient. He's not some petty inhabitant of a vast pantheon. This god—Deu, she calls him—claims to be the Creator of all. His religion is presented as the only true one, and he allows no competitors. Anastasia says all other gods must be cast aside."

"Hmm. Very interesting." The director made sure the aide had recorded the information, then turned back to the dohj. "Rest assured, we will investigate the matter fully. It is all the more important in light of the naval report I received yesterday."

"What did you find out?"

"A foreign ship was spotted entering our waters. A black caravel. Lord Borja's lieutenant—the so-called Iron Shield—is heading our way again."

Cristof spat an expletive. The news made him feel panicky. "Is he coming here for Anastasia?"

"Possibly. We believe he attempted an abduction already. His ship was near Camoly at the same time as your yacht, and several eyewitnesses saw Teofil of Chiveis there as well. One of your cabin maids reported seeing two men climbing the hull. The physical description of the intruder in Anastasia's room would match a large man like the Iron Shield. Later that night a local doctor treated a knife wound to Teofil's chest. The evidence suggests he may have thwarted an attack on Anastasia. Both of them appear to be in grave danger."

Cristof leaned on the table, holding his forehead in his hands. "I don't care what happens to the soldier," he muttered, "but we have to find a way to protect Anastasia. She needs me! She's so delicate, and . . . and . . . innocent!" He banged his fist on the table. "By the gods, that makes her enticing! I'll go mad if I don't get to . . ." The dohj's words trailed off into an inarticulate groan.

The director kept his tone professional. "Protecting the woman will be difficult, Your Highness. The Exterminati are experts when it comes to such matters. Only the kind of continuous protection afforded to the royal family by bodyguards would be sufficient."

The room was silent for a long time. Then, slowly, Dohj Cristof raised his head, gazing into the distance with a blank stare.

"Yes," he whispered. "Yes, that's the answer."

"What is, Your Highness?"

Cristof did not respond as a plan began to crystallize in his mind. A slight smile came to him, and he moistened his lips with his tongue as he thought it over. At last he focused his gaze on the man seated across the table from him.

"She must join the royal family," Cristof said.

✦　　✦　　✦

The day the shamans came was rainy and cold.

Sol was returning to the cottage from the covered market at Nuo Genov, carrying his groceries in a basket. Since it was late in the third month, a few sailors had begun to trickle into port again, and Teofil had gone to the waterfront to see what he could learn from them about Roma. Sol was looking forward to a cup of hot tea and a quiet afternoon alone. But it was not to be.

They came in a fury, four men in black robes with garrotes in their hands. Sol tried to flee into the forest, but the attackers quickly overtook him. Though he kicked and struggled as they grabbed him, they were too strong to resist. He felt a wire close around his neck, cutting off his ability to breathe. Sol clawed at it, but the wire dug into his flesh, and he could not pry it away.

A shaman with a red armband approached him. "You made it easy for us, old man," he said in a friendly tone that obscured his evil intent. "By coming here where you are unknown, you made secrecy less needful for us. It will give us a wider array of choices when we torture you."

Sol's need to breathe was overwhelming. He thrashed against his attackers, but the man with the garrote did not release his grip. Sol had played breath-holding games as a boy, which always ended when the awful feeling of having no air in the lungs became unbearable and was followed by a grateful gasp. Now that urgent moment had long since passed, and still there was no air. Sol felt himself grow dizzy. His desperate pain dissolved into a peaceful acquiescence. His body went limp, and then the world went black.

Consciousness did not return easily to Sol. For a long time he remained in a delirious state, only dimly aware of what was happening around him. Some periods were blacker than others, but at no time did Sol completely wake up. At last he managed to shake the fog from his brain and claw his way back to reality. He moaned and tried to push himself up but found that his hands were tied behind his back. A sharp toe kicked him in the ribs. He lay still.

After a while Sol realized he was lying in the bottom of a boat. The slap of the oars on the water told him he was being rowed out to sea. A gentle rain continued to fall, pattering softly onto his back. The boat stopped, and a thick rope was slipped under his armpits. Sol was hoisted into the air and dumped on the deck of a large ship. Thick-soled boots stood before his nose as he lay on his belly with his hands bound. Sol craned his neck and glanced up. It was the shaman with the red armband.

"Follower of the Enemy," the shaman cried, "you belong to me now. Relinquish all hope that your false god will save you."

"Where am I?" Sol asked weakly.

"You are being exterminated, Sol of Ulmbartia. The days ahead will be filled with torment. We will find a quiet place to go ashore, where you will be interrogated until you have told us the full extent of your heretical activities. Until then, I will have that pleasure to look forward to, and you will have that agony to dread." The remark elicited snickers from the other shamans standing around the deck.

"If I tell you what you want to know, will I be allowed to live?"

Everyone on the deck broke into uproarious laughter. Sol's face burned with shame.

"You will live a few years more," said the leader of the shamans. "The

185

question is, will you want to? By fleeing to Likuria, you unintentionally extended your life. Had I taken you at Duke Labella's estate as I intended, you would not have been worth the effort to transport, and you would be dead already. But since you have come here on your own, I can toss you in the hold with the rest of the cargo and perhaps get a few coins for you. And so your life will go on, until day after day of backbreaking labor in the quarries finally claims what I did not. Before that end arrives, you will come to regret this extension of your miserable life."

"The quarries, is it?" Sol summoned his last remnants of courage. "Let it be known to all that I don't fear your quarries, shaman, and I don't fear death! You may kill my body, but I know the God who will claim my soul on the other side. Your threats of death have no power over me."

Sol felt a heavy boot step on the back of his head, grinding his face into the slick boards of the deck.

"You are mistaken," the shaman hissed. "There is nothing beyond this world but suffering and despair."

The shaman's oppressive words were spoken with such venom, they seemed undeniable. Sol's strength collapsed before an onslaught of hopelessness.

The boot released its pressure, and the shaman barked a command to his men. "Throw this wretch into the hold with the rest of those pathetic mistakes!"

Sol was picked up and tossed into the seething darkness below.

CHAPTER

8

High on the white roof of the Domo, the Overseer beheld the face of Deus. The Almighty was truly beautiful—a God worthy of worship.

The Overseer had observed a sleepless vigil through the night. Praying on his knees in the darkness of the ancient cathedral, the Overseer had approached his God with increasing intimacy. He spent the first two hours confessing his sins, allowing the ache in his knees from the hard stone floor to remind him of what sin does to the body of a man. Then he rose stiffly from his kneeling position and seated himself on a stool before a large window whose glass had broken out long ago. Moonlight poured into the church, illuminating him in a beam of white translucence. Like a mouse crouching on the forest floor, the Overseer was reduced to a tiny speck inside the cavernous cathedral with its immense pillars of stone. From his seat he chanted his way through the entire psalter:

> *Beatus vir qui non abiit in consilio impiorum*
> *et in via peccatorum non stetit*
> *in cathedra derisorum non sedit*
> *sed in lege Domini voluntas eius*
> *et in lege eius meditabitur die ac nocte. . . .*

The Overseer's sonorous tones had lulled him into a state of rapture—not sleep, but something infinitely sweeter. The law of the Lord was like a honeycomb in his mouth.

†HE GİF†

In the latest part of the night, candles were lit inside the Domo. The nineteen other brothers and sisters of the Universal Communion had arrived from all corners of the Forbidden Zone, dragging their warped bodies to the place that made them whole. There, around the holy table, the Overseer had shared the Sacred Meal with them. Through bread and wine, each believer bound himself anew to the Pierced One. It was a pledge of community and service. Whatever else it was beyond that, the Christiani did not know.

After the meal, the Overseer began to climb the stairs. He carried a silver crucifix, which he kissed with each upward step out of love for Iesus Christus. The deep spiritual longing of all the Christiani became his urgent prayer: *Lead us into truth, O Deus! Show us the fullness of all that is thine! We believe, yet we wish to understand—reveal it to us!*

As he ascended the staircase, the Overseer prayed that the holy Papa might discover the lost Testament and so enlighten the Christiani with the wisdom that had almost died out. It was a bitter loss. Truths had been forgotten that should not have been. During the brutal and chaotic decades following the Ancients' great war, few believers remained to preserve sound doctrine, and many evil forces worked against it. Now the truth was difficult to find, and to declare it among men was impossible. Only Deus could bring about its return. It was for precisely this grace that the Overseer now prayed.

He reached the roof just before dawn. The night was clear and cold, and the Overseer tucked his arms into the sleeves of his robe against the chill. The morning star gleamed brightly in the dark blue sky, oppressing the Overseer, for it was not a holy star. The Evil One who inhabited it fought against the man on the Domo's roof. For what seemed like an eternity, the devilish star clawed at the Overseer's mind. "*Quomodo cecidisti de caelo Lucifer, qui mane oriebaris!*" the Overseer shouted in defense. "*Quomodo corruisti in terram, qui vulnerabas gentes!*" The words of Isaias's fourteenth chapter, the twelfth verse, served as the Overseer's only protection against the wicked impostor—that Bringer of Light whose ways were actually darkness.

At last the dawn came, and the morning star was banished. The

Overseer stood with his face to the east, letting the warmth of the rising sun shine on him and enliven his bones.

And then, unexpectedly, Deus Omnipotens visited him.

There was no audible voice, no angelic appearance, no dazzling beams from heaven. The coming of God was entirely inward, yet it was no less real to the man on the roof of the ancient cathedral. An aura of beauty surrounded him; a peace beyond understanding entered his soul. The Overseer knew without a doubt that Deus was on the move. Times were changing. Truth was being reborn.

As had happened often over the past few months, the image of a lone man appeared in his mind's eye. Though the man's face wasn't distinguishable, the Overseer knew he was a brave warrior with a noble heart and a deepening love for Deus. The man lifted his hand. It was a strong hand, the kind accustomed to the sword, but now the man laid it on an altar with his fingers splayed out. The hand remained there, absolutely still, waiting for Deus to do his will.

It is the hand of Teofil of Chiveis, the Overseer realized.

With that, the vision broke.

The Overseer found himself aware of his surroundings again. He was standing alone in the early morning light. The sun, still low in the sky, cast its rays across the ruins of the Forbidden Zone. Shivering, the Overseer turned toward the stairs and made his way back to earth.

Brother Toni met him in the plaza outside the Domo. "Did the Alm-m-m-m-mighty visit you?" he asked.

"Yes, my son. He has given me insights upon which I must act. I have two tasks for you regarding these matters." Brother Toni nodded his willingness to obey, so the Overseer continued. "First I want you to compose a message to the brethren in Roma. Inform them that Teofil of Chiveis will visit them soon. You should describe his appearance in detail, especially the scar he bears between his left thumb and forefinger. Tell the brethren Teofil is a friend of the Christiani, so they should aid him in every way. Is that clear?"

"Y-y-yes," said Brother Toni, bowing deeply. "And w-what else?"

"Prepare a horse with provisions. I intend to go on a journey."

Brother Toni's head came up sharply. He stared at the Overseer with a startled expression, his mouth open. Though he tried to speak, his stutter kept him from pronouncing his question. Finally he was able to vocalize a single word. "Outside?"

The Overseer nodded and put his hand on his disciple's shoulder. "Yes, I am going outside. Do not be afraid, Brother Toni. I am certain Deus wishes me to leave the Zone and make contact with one of our allies. He is an old friend of mine, though I have not seen him in many years."

"W-w-who is it, my lord?"

The Overseer turned away from Brother Toni and looked toward the west. "He is a Knight of the Cross, one of very few left in that renowned order. Of course, no one in Ulmbartia knows that about him. To them he's just a rich and powerful count by the name of Federco Borromo."

◆　◆　◆

The harbor at Nuo Genov wasn't exactly bustling, but it was more lively than it had been through the winter months. Each day a few ships came and went whenever the weather looked fair. Though none yet risked a journey to faraway locations, Teo could sense the sailors' urge to be out on the open seas again. It wouldn't be long before the port would be busy once more.

Teo had left the cottage earlier that morning after Sol went to buy groceries at the covered market. Arriving at the waterfront, Teo spent the day wandering along the docks, conversing with anyone who was willing. No one knew how to sail to Roma, but he didn't let that dampen his spirits. Just to be doing something other than translation work was a welcome change. He also stopped in a tailor's shop and purchased new clothing: a dark leather jerkin with a high collar, a linen shirt, gray wool trousers, and black boots of an excellent make. As he meandered around the harbor in his new garments, Teo felt optimistic and hopeful, as if something good was bound to happen.

Around dinnertime Teo made his way to La Lanterna in hopes of finding the old sailor Bosun. He was not disappointed, for the man soon walked in. It seemed Bosun was something of a regular at the tavern.

Though Bosun didn't know the way to Roma, he gave Teo a helpful hint over drinks. "The people you need to talk to are the long-distance merchants, but they don't use this bar. Theirs is off by itself at the edge of the port. The Rusty Anchor, it's called. Watch yourself there—it's a rough place." Teo thanked the leather-skinned seafarer for his advice and went outside into the gathering darkness.

The Rusty Anchor was a rundown tavern surrounded by youths smoking pipes of the imported weed called *tabako*. Gray smoke swirled around them in a pungent fog. They eyed Teo suspiciously as he went inside.

The atmosphere at The Rusty Anchor was very different from La Lanterna. Instead of old salts relaxing with an ale, the tavern was dominated by rough-looking sailors drinking hard liquor in shot glasses. Busty women in short skirts caroused with the men in the corners. The air was rank with raw language and body odor. Apparently the long-distance sailors were cut from a different sort of cloth than the local fisherman and merchants who hopped up and down the Likurian coast.

Teo elbowed his way to the bar, knowing this wasn't the kind of establishment where a polite request would do the trick. The bartender glared at him, but Teo returned the stare and demanded, "Good whiskey, and hurry up." He thumped a coin onto the counter and held it in place with his forefinger until he got his drink.

The two men on Teo's left were engaged in a heated argument. Swear words and spittle flew between them in even proportions. One man shoved the other, knocking him into Teo, who had raised his glass to his lips. The jostling caused whiskey to dribble onto the man's glossy boots. He stared down at his feet, then looked up at Teo and cursed him to the depths of hell.

Teo wasn't looking for trouble. He had come to the tavern to make friends and obtain information. "Sorry about that," he said to the furious sailor. "Let me buy you a drink."

"I don't want your drink!" the man roared. Instantly a tense silence descended upon the barroom as everyone turned to see what would happen.

The other man, who a moment earlier had been cussing his comrade in the foulest way, now jabbed his finger toward Teo. "Hey, you! Get down there and lick up that spill," he demanded.

Teo wasn't about to lick anybody's boots. He faced the men, wearing a friendly grin, yet wishing he had his knife with him. Though he had reclaimed his weapons when he quit his job at the stable, he had left them at the cottage because it wasn't legal to go around Nuo Genov armed like a soldier. Nevertheless, there was a good chance one or the other of the sailors had a blade hidden on his body. Teo hoped his congenial demeanor would keep it that way—hidden.

"Look, fellas," he said, "that spill was an accident. Let's just forget it, and I'll buy you both a stiff shot." To let the ruffians save face, Teo grabbed a barkeep's towel and dropped it on the man's foot. The cloth would soak up the spilled whiskey, and the gesture would show everyone that Teo had more or less complied with the men's request.

Unfortunately, the sailors had no interest in defusing the situation. Kicking away the towel with a flick of his toe, the man with the glossy boots stepped toward Teo and growled, "Lick my foot right now, stranger."

Realizing a fight was inevitable, Teo claimed the element of surprise. He bunched his fist and hit the man square in the jaw.

The barroom exploded with raucous shouts as Teo sent his opponent sprawling. The other man leaped past his fallen partner and barreled at Teo with his fists flying. He was strong, and the fighting was intense, but Teo held his own. For every blow he took, he gave one in return. Teo's nose was bloody and his ears were ringing, but the other guy didn't look so good either.

Suddenly the man threw his knee into Teo's stomach, knocking out his wind. As Teo gasped and stumbled, the sailor grabbed him from behind and choked him with an arm around his neck. Teo lurched backward and slammed the man into the bar, but he couldn't dislodge the elbow at his throat. The onlookers screamed encouragement to their fellow seafarer. The whole place was in an uproar.

A few paces away, the man who had been hit in the jaw was getting to his feet. He blinked his eyes and shook his head, then turned a fierce gaze toward Teo.

"I got him pinned," shouted the man choking Teo from behind. "Finish him off!"

The first man drew a knife from inside his vest and sneered. Teo wres-

tled with the assailant holding him in place, but because they were standing by the bar, he couldn't get his feet in the right position to break free.

The man with the knife raised it behind his head as he prepared to
throw it. Teo's entire torso was exposed, and the assailant was too close
to miss. Teo felt his stomach muscles clench as he saw the attacker's arm
start to move.

As the knife was leaving the man's hand, a new combatant entered
the fray. He smashed the knife-thrower over the head with a bottle, which
shattered in a spray of glass and liquor. The blow caused the man's knees
to buckle and, more importantly, diverted his knife onto a harmless tra-
jectory.

Everyone was stunned by the intervention, including the man at Teo's
back. The split-second of surprise allowed Teo to lower his stance and gain
a leverage advantage. He thrust his elbow into his assailant's abdomen,
hurling him backward to the floor. The ruffian's head glanced off the bar
on the way down, and he remained still.

All the patrons of The Rusty Anchor gaped in silence. The stranger
holding the broken bottle looked at Teo with a mischievous grin. Realizing
the show was over, the onlookers turned back to whatever they had been
doing, and a hubbub of conversation trickled through the crowd. Teo
breathed a sigh of relief.

"Let's get out of here," said the man with the bottle.

Teo had no idea who he was, but the man seemed friendly enough,
and right now Teo's friends were in short supply. He nodded and followed
the sailor outside.

"I owe you one," Teo said as the pair stepped into the cool air of the
waterfront.

"You have no idea how much you owe me," the stranger answered.
"That was an expensive bottle of gin."

The remark elicited laughter from both men, and Teo decided he
liked his newfound acquaintance. He studied the man by the light of the
moon. Though he wasn't quite as tall as Teo, he had the same kind of lean,
athletic build. His hair was jet black, and he wore a mustache that blended
into the goatee on his chin. He was a handsome man, though scruffy in a
way that suggested he was too preoccupied with other matters to bother

with his good looks. His clothes were those of a seaman: navy blue pea-coat, scarf around his neck, buff-colored pants, and bucket-top boots.

"My name is Marco," the man said, extending his hand.

"I'm Teofil. Pleased to meet you." Teo returned Marco's firm handshake.

"The word on the docks is you're looking for passage to a distant city."

"That's right, to Roma. Do you know where it is?"

"A few of the merchants around here make trips to some pretty far ports," Marco answered evasively.

"And are you one of those?"

"I'm no merchant, but my business requires me to go where they go. That's how I acquire my cargoes for such low prices, if you know what I mean."

Teo glanced at Marco. "I'm afraid I don't."

"*Extremely* low prices," Marco said with a sly wink. "Like the price of a few grappling hooks."

"Oh, you're a pirate."

"I suppose you could say that. But unlike the Clan, I don't stop every ship I come across, just those of the racketeers and swindlers. Then when I sell my spoils in port, the people get a better price than they would have gotten otherwise, and my men are well paid. Only the crooks are out of luck. It's not exactly legal, but I consider it a good business."

"And does your 'business' take you to Roma? I need to get there as soon as possible."

"I know. Why do you think I bailed you out at the tavern? Carrying passengers from one port to another is easy money for me, especially if I'm headed that way already. I couldn't let those thugs kill a paying customer, could I?"

Teo grinned at Marco's audacity. The man was a rascal, but a likable one. "So you can take me to Roma?"

"If you have the money, we leave in two days."

"I'm in."

After coming to terms and making departure arrangements, Marco offered Teo accommodation aboard his clipper for the night. Since Teo was bleeding and bruised, and his cottage was an hour's walk uphill from the harbor, he gratefully accepted Marco's offer.

Teo's bed was a hammock below deck. Exhausted, he turned in for the night, but sleep eluded him. He lay awake in the darkness, swaying restlessly, plagued by worrisome thoughts. Now that he had made concrete plans to go to Roma, the idea of leaving Ana unprotected seemed intolerable. Although the Iron Shield hadn't been seen in Likuria for several months, he might return, and Teo didn't know enough about the shamans' intentions to feel good about leaving Ana vulnerable to their evil designs. Yet it was obvious Deu was calling Teo to Roma—and he knew Ana would want that too. In a distant part of his mind, Teo believed he would someday patch things up with her and restore their broken relationship. Now as he lay in his hammock and considered the matter, he realized he was counting on the discovery of the New Testament in Roma to be a part of that reconciliation. Teo knew how much Ana wanted the book. *O Deu,* he prayed into the darkness, *help me find your book! And help me . . .*

A wave of sorrow washed over Teo, bordering on grief in its intensity. He swallowed the lump in his throat and squinted against the moisture that had gathered in his eyes. With an ache in his heart, he finished his prayer: *Help me find my way back to Ana!*

✦　✦　✦

Vanita Labella had prepared herself to do a necessary evil. Now as she stood before the door of the shamans' shrine at Nuo Genov, she took a deep breath and knocked.

People did not often visit the shrines of the Exterminati, especially not at such a late hour, so it took several minutes for anyone to respond. Finally the door creaked open, and a hooded shaman appeared. A gravelly voice spoke from inside his cowl: "What business have you here in the dark of night?"

"I am the daughter of an Ulmbartian duke, and I wish to speak privately with your leader," Vanita said with as much authority as she could muster.

The shaman's only response was to open the door wider and disappear into the shadows. Vanita waited for a moment, then peeked inside. The man was gone. She went a few steps into the shrine, unsure if she was supposed to follow or wait outside. In the distance lightning flashed and thunder rumbled, then everything was quiet again. A cool mustiness pervaded the air of the vestibule.

"This way!" said the rough voice. Vanita almost jumped out of her skin.

Take it easy, girl, she warned herself. *They won't hurt you.*

Or will they?

Vanita followed the shaman through an arched corridor to a room with two chairs. Each chair faced the other, with a rug on the floor in between. The room was lit by candle sconces on the walls.

"Wait here in the receiving room," the shaman instructed. "I will see whether the Lord Necromancer of Likuria will speak to the likes of you." He left.

As Vanita sat in the smaller of the two chairs, she steeled herself for the mission that had brought her to such a fearsome place at night. Dredging up memories from the day before, she let herself relive the anger, the shock, the hurt she had felt when her father showed her the letter from Dohj Cristof di Sanjorjo. Vanita could tell immediately from the look on her father's face that the letter did not bear good news. "The dohj has broken off negotiations with us," he had said. "It is not to be."

It is not to be.

The words were burning red-hot in Vanita's heart when a door opened across the room. The Lord Necromancer of Likuria floated in like a wraith.

He was clothed in robes of a different sort than the other shamans. His garment was made of very fine cloth, black as ink and trimmed with sable. He wore a hood that drooped from his forehead, yet it did not overhang his face enough to obscure it. Vanita discerned the aquiline features of an aristocrat in the man who seated himself in the chair opposite her.

"Speak," he commanded. "Speak now, or leave and never return."

Vanita steeled her nerves and shoved Ana from her mind. "My name is Vanita Labella of Ulmbartia. I have come to report the grievous news that Dohj Cristof di Sanjorjo is consorting with a secret Defective—a woman with a hideous disfigurement beneath her clothes."

The Lord Necromancer hissed and drew back as if the uncleanness of the Defectives could be transmitted to him like a disease. "Is the woman within his family?" he asked. "We have agreed to extend immunity to the dohj's nearest kin."

"She is not related to him. In fact she is not even a citizen of Likuria, nor of Ulmbartia. The woman is a foreigner whose leg is mutilated from an attack by a wild beast."

"Ach! Such defilement is like mold on bread. No prosperous society can allow such corruption in its midst. Who is this contaminated woman of which you speak?"

"Her name is Anastasia of Chiveis," Vanita answered.

It's done, she realized. *No turning back.*

At the mention of Anastasia's name, the Lord Necromancer rose without a word and exited the room. He was gone for a long time while Vanita fidgeted in her chair. At last the man returned and sat down again, his black robes blending with the burnished wood of his throne. He offered an oily smile and spoke a word of praise. "Vanita Labella of Ulmbartia, you dignify your realm with your commitment to social cleansing."

Ignoring the compliment, Vanita asked, "What happens next?"

The Lord Necromancer shrugged. "We will send a letter at dawn, of course."

"What kind of letter?"

"To the dohj. If he is in fact harboring the defective woman as you claim, he must hand her over for immediate removal."

Vanita licked her lips. "It is my understanding that your brotherhood takes the Defectives to a quiet valley where they can live peacefully among their kind for the rest of their lives. I assume this will be the case for Anastasia of Chiveis?"

The Lord Necromancer laughed darkly as he rose from his throne and began to walk toward Vanita. She remained seated and kept her head still, watching him from the corners of her eyes until he slipped past her and was lost from view. Although she did not dare turn around, his ominous presence behind her chair was nearly unbearable. Vanita's heart pounded as she waited for the Lord Necromancer to break the silence.

Clothing rustled. Above and behind her, Vanita sensed two hands descending slowly on either side of her head. Her body trembled, but she gripped the skirt of her gown with clenched fists and forced herself to remain still.

The Lord Necromancer's hands passed in front of her. Something cool and ticklish touched Vanita's neck. She screamed.

"A gift," said the Lord Necromancer, undisturbed by the outburst, "because you understand that some life is unworthy of life."

Vanita put her hand to her throat. A delicate silver necklace had been draped there, left unfastened. She snatched it away. "Tell me what will happen to Anastasia!"

"Rest assured, Vanita Labella. The woman of whom you speak will receive everything she deserves."

A nauseous feeling rose in Vanita's gut. The silver necklace shamed her; she hurled it to the ground. "Keep your gift!" she cried. Scrambling to her feet, Vanita dashed out of the room and ran from the shrine into the moonless Likurian night.

◆ ◆ ◆

It was raining. Everything was dark. Teo's mind was shrouded in the dim twilight between sleeping and waking. He couldn't tell if the mental images that flashed before him were dreams or actual memories. Maybe they were somehow both.

Ana was there. Teo knew this because lightning suddenly illuminated a stone-vaulted chamber, and he could see her lying under blankets with her eyes closed. Her hair was wet, and her cheeks were pale. The chamber returned to shadow, then lightning flashed once more. This time Ana stared at Teo with large, round eyes. Was she pleading? Waiting? What?

Teo reached out his hand to her, but nothing met his fingers.

Ana spoke into the blackness. The sound of her voice was familiar and comforting, yet she seemed to speak from a great distance. "Thank you, Teofil," she said.

Thank you for what? Teo responded inside his dream.

"I think you know."

No, I don't.

"Of course you do," came the sweet reply.

I don't. Tell me!

Ana paused before answering. "Thank you for coming to me, Captain."

Brilliant light flashed all around, and thunder exploded in Teo's head like Astrebril's Curse. The strike was so loud that Teo was yanked from sleep into instant awareness. He cried out and bolted upright, his heart racing. The thunderclap shattered his dream, but reality rushed to take its place.

As Teo swayed in his hammock in the hold of Marco's ship, a serene confidence flooded his heart. At last he knew what to do. He had known it all along. Tomorrow, when the day was fresh and new, he would go to the dohj's palace. He would find a way inside its forbidding walls. He would come to Ana, reclaim her, cover her, and take her to where she should be.

To Roma.

At his side.

And I will do this because I promised to.

Always.

◆　　◆　　◆

Ana was sitting in a lovely courtyard reading a book and listening to bird-song when she heard footsteps behind her. A deep masculine voice asked, "May I speak to you, Anastasia?"

Ana smiled as she turned. "Of course, Cristof."

She scooted over on the stone bench and made a place for the dohj. He circled around some masons' tools from the repair work being done on the walls, joining Ana on the bench.

They made small talk for a while, until Cristof's expression became more serious. "Anastasia, there's, uh—there's something I want to talk to you about." He gazed at his feet and ran his fingers through his blond hair, making it shimmer in the afternoon sun. Ana had never seen the dohj nervous like this. He was usually so confident and suave.

"Okay," she said, unsure of the situation.

"You see, it's like this. I received a letter this morning that changes everything. Well, not everything. I had already decided what I have to do." He shook his head. "Not that I 'have to'! I *want to*, of course. You have no idea how bad I want to—" He sighed in frustration.

199

"Cristof, slow down. What are you trying to say?"

The dohj raised his eyes and stared at Ana. The expression on his face was one she had seen before in men—a wild, primal urge that made her uncomfortable. She recoiled from the man seated next to her. He noticed it and moved toward her, gripping her by the forearm.

"Anastasia, you're in danger! Deadly danger! They're after you!"

Ana wriggled out of Cristof's grasp and sat at the far end of the bench. "Who's after me? What are you talking about? What's going on?"

"Those cursed shamans! They've put a removal order on you!"

"On me? Why?" Ana was shocked.

"Because of your stupid god! You blabbed about him too much, and the shamans have caught wind of it."

"Since when is it a crime to talk about my God?"

"It's not a crime to talk about *a* god, but *your* god is a problem. You keep saying he's the only true one."

"That's what I believe. Is it wrong to say so?"

"The Exterminati don't want to hear that! Most people don't know what religious fanatics they are, but I've seen them up close. Before all else, they're a *cult*. Now they're after you, Anastasia, and they're not going to stop until they take you down. You were such a fool to talk about your god. I should have known better. I never should have allowed it."

"Allowed it?" Ana felt anger rise within her. "How would you have stopped me, Cristof?"

"That's beside the point now."

Cristof moved toward Ana on the bench, exuding the same randy mixture of desperation and desire he'd displayed before. Ana had originally been flattered by the way the handsome dohj had treated her, but now she was frightened by the fierceness of his attraction.

Attraction? Who am I kidding? Let's call it what it really is: lust of the most bestial kind!

Ana stood up from the bench and backed away. She felt an urge to flee from the courtyard, but before she could move, Cristof lunged at her and snatched her into his arms.

"Anastasia, I want you!" He pressed his body close, rubbing against her. "Don't you feel the same? Tell me you do!"

"Let go of me!"

The dohj knelt in front of Ana, gripping her by the hips. His fingers were not where she wanted them to be. Cristof looked up at her, and she met his eyes.

"Marry me," he said. "I want you as my wife."

Marry him?

Ana's head spun. *He's asking me to marry him! What's going on here?*

She wrenched herself from his grasp and dodged around a ladder resting against the wall. He circled toward her, holding up his palms in a placating gesture.

"Just listen to me," he implored. "Listen to the voice of reason. I received a letter today from the Lord Necromancer. The shamans say you have a disfigurement on your leg. They want to declare you a Defective and remove you from the land."

"Me, a *Defective?* That's wrong! I do have a scar, but it's not so bad. It's not even visible! They can't take me away for that!"

"They certainly can. The people of Likuria hate anything imperfect. We chase deformity from our midst. Several years ago I granted the shamans the authority to remove disfigured people from the realm. They're legally allowed to remove you."

"Then cancel the law! You're the dohj!"

Cristof approached Ana, pleading with his eyes. "I can't cancel it, Anastasia. The law is binding. That's why I want you to marry me. The royal family is exempt from extermination."

"I don't see why I'd have to marry you to be protected. I'm deep inside your palace. They can't get me in here. I'm safe."

Cristof's face turned dark. He picked up a hammer and hurled it against a wall, its iron head clanging as it ricocheted in an explosion of stone chips and dust. The dohj glared at Ana with his fists clenched and his neck veins bulging. "You're not safe at all, you foolish woman! You don't know how dangerous these shamans are. The spirits empower them to do whatever they want. They tried to get you once already! While you were on my yacht last fall, one of their assassins entered your room. The only reason you're still alive is because that bodyguard of yours fought him off!"

Ana's heart skipped a beat at the mention of Teo. She shook her head, confused by what Cristof had just told her. *I was targeted by the shamans? They got into my cabin in the yacht? And then Teofil stopped them?* Her mind couldn't take it all in. "I thought—I thought he was in Ulmbartia."

"Who? The bodyguard?" Cristof waved his hand. "No, he moved here last summer. Apparently he thinks his mission in life is to follow you around. He may have gotten lucky once, but don't think you'll be so fortunate next time. You can't stop these people once they target you." Cristof's voice assumed a gentle tone. "Don't you see, Anastasia? They have you under a double threat. If they can remove you by law as a Defective, they'll do it. If that doesn't work, they'll send another assassin. Either way you're doomed. There's only one way out of this. If you marry me you'll have legal immunity from removal, as well as full-time bodyguard service. It's your only option."

"But, Cristof, I don't—I can't—"

"You can't what? Be a queen?" He smiled, lifting his hands as he glanced around the beautiful palace. "Think what it would mean for you. All this would be yours. All the wealth and status and luxury of Likuria. You'd be the toast of society. Everyone would love you, and you'd never have to worry about anything. Your future would be secure."

Ana stepped around the masonry tools and faced Cristof. She held her back straight and her head high. "Your Highness, your offer is gracious, but I decline."

Cristof recoiled as if he'd been slapped. He blinked his eyes and held his body stiff. Ana could see the dohj struggling to collect his thoughts. Her heart pounded at the gravity of the moment. The intense emotions swirling in the courtyard seemed more than she could bear.

Licking his lips, the dohj moved forward a step. "I see," he said formally. "May I know the reason for your refusal?"

"Yes. It is because I am not in love with you."

The dohj didn't move. Ana turned away and edged toward the courtyard door. Reaching it, she paused and looked back. Cristof remained motionless, a blank look on his face. He was standing in the exact position where Ana had left him. She entered the palace and ran to her bedroom, locking the door behind her.

The two glass doors in Ana's room opened onto a balcony facing the sea, but another window looked down on the courtyard. Ana peeked out, afraid the dohj would still be there, but he was gone. She collapsed onto her bed, emotionally drained by all that had transpired. Her tears came in great, heaving sobs. Ana had never felt so alone.

She cried for what seemed like hours, until her bedcovers were wet and her nose ran and her eyes felt swollen and hot. Though she wanted to pray, she felt she had forgotten how, or even to whom. *When was the last time I spoke to Deu?* It had been far too long. *I abandoned my God, and he is right to abandon me. I deserve no favors, no deliverance from him.* She breathed in shuddery gasps as the torment of overwhelming grief raked her soul.

Ana considered the stunning news that Teo had been in Likuria all this time. She thought back to that strange night when she had entered her cabin on the yacht and discovered it in disarray. To think that Teo had been so close, watching over her unseen, yet protecting her from a threat she couldn't even discern. *He always does that . . . he comes for me . . . but now . . .*

More tears erupted as Ana's sadness swamped her in a sea of bitter regret. She clenched the bedcovers and curled into a ball with her knees at her chest. Spasms of despair wracked her body. Ana longed to speak to Teo once more—just once, just to tell him she was sorry for all she had done. Though she knew things could never be the same between them again, she wanted a chance to tell him how sorry she was. Everything had turned out wrong. *If only I could go back to the way things were! How did I get here? How did it all come to this? Oh, Teofil, I miss you! I want to be back in our tent in the wilderness when you read Scripture to me at night! I want to be at dinner with you on Fisherman's Isle when I was beautiful in your eyes! I want to ride with your arms around me as we gallop to safety! Oh Deu, my God, I cry out to you!*

A key jiggled in the lock. Ana sat up on the rumpled bed, not wanting any attention from the servants right now. "Go away!" she cried. "I don't need anything!"

The door opened. Dohj Cristof was there, and the look in his eyes was evil. Behind him was a priest. He held a ribbon, an olive branch, and a bowl. Horrified, Ana recognized what it meant.

"Leave me alone!" she screamed.

Cristof locked the door behind him and advanced toward Ana on the bed. She darted away, trying to dodge around a table, but he was too fast. He snatched her and held her tight as she wrestled with him in front of the window. His fingers hurt as they dug into her shoulders.

"You'll do things my way from now on," he snarled.

"No! Let go of me!" Ana squirmed in Cristof's grip, trying to break free. And then he hit her.

Ana had been struck before, but never had she taken a blow like this one. It wasn't an openhanded slap across the face but a rock-hard fist to the chin. Stars exploded in her head, and a gush of warm blood filled her mouth. She sagged in the dohj's arms, her knees watery and weak. The pain of the smashing blow reverberated through her skull. Darkness threatened to engulf her. Ana was dizzy and disoriented.

"Maybe now you'll learn to submit to your new husband!" Cristof turned to the priest and motioned him forward. "Begin the hand-fasting."

As Ana struggled to keep herself upright, she watched the Likurian priest bind her hand to Cristof's with a green silk ribbon. The dohj's other hand curled around her waist, holding her against his side. Ana spat blood on the floor. "I won't say any vows," she said through swollen lips.

Cristof laughed. "You don't have to. The woman is only property. It's the man's vows that count in this ritual. Once my ring is on your finger, you're mine for life."

Ana tried to move away, but her steps were unsteady, and her head throbbed. Cristof grabbed a handful of her hair and jerked her back to himself. Ana squealed. Nodding to the priest, Cristof yelled, "Get on with the ceremony! Hurry it up!"

The priest began to recite the words of the nuptial sacrament. Periodically he would dip the olive branch in his bowl and sprinkle the couple with holy water. Every time Ana fought to escape, Cristof would cruelly pull her back. Finally he drew a serrated knife and held it to her throat, warning her not to move.

"Do you, Cristof di Sanjorjo, take Anastasia of Chiveis in her body and soul as your lawful possession, both in this life and the next?" the priest asked.

"I do."

"What token of ownership do you supply?"

"This ring." Cristof held up a golden band with the insignia of the di Sanjorjo house.

"May the gods bless you. Place the ring on the finger of the bride and seal the union."

A feeling of revulsion washed over Ana. The thought of being legally wed to Cristof made her sick. She knew it was a sham, yet the marriage was binding under Likurian law, and the dohj would indeed be her husband. Disgusted, Ana realized she was about to become the wife of a repulsive man—and there was nothing she could do about it.

The priest untied the hand-fasting ribbon. Cristof tucked his giant knife into his belt and gripped Ana's left hand, reaching toward her with the gold ring. "The consummation will be rough," he whispered in her ear.

"Never!"

Ana slapped the ring away. It bounced off the windowpane and rolled across the floor. Cristof shoved Ana onto the bed and knelt to pick up the ring.

"Get out!" he yelled to the priest. "Lock the door behind you! No matter how much she screams, don't open it again!" The befuddled priest nodded and scurried out of the room. The latch clicked, and then Cristof turned his wicked grin on Ana.

"Time for some love, my sweetheart."

He approached her with the ring in his hand. Ana lunged toward the door, but Cristof thrust her back to the bed and pinned her under his knees. He grabbed her left hand and isolated the third finger. Ana struggled fiercely, clawing at the dohj's face with her free hand, but it was no use. The ring touched her fingertip.

"I don't want to marry you!" she cried.

"You don't have to," said a strong voice across the room.

❖   ❖   ❖

Dohj Cristof was on top of Ana, holding her down. As soon as Teo spoke, both faces turned toward him. Ana's eyes conveyed the desperation she felt at the hands of the lascivious prince, but that wasn't what angered Teo most. It was her swollen, bloody lip. The sight of it filled Teo with cold fury.

He had entered the room by means of the masons' ladder. It hadn't been difficult to sneak into the palace and bribe a slave to point him toward Ana's quarters. When he looked up from the courtyard and saw the dohj shove her across the room, Teo had leaped into action. Now he was infuriated by the scene before him.

"What are you doing here?" Cristof growled. "How dare you barge in on a man and his wife!"

"I am not your wife!"

Ana pushed Cristof away and rolled from the bed. Throwing open the doors to the balcony, she hurled an object outside with all her strength.

"You little whore!"

Cristof's face bore the twisted expression of a madman. He started to move toward Ana, then realized he would have to deal with Teo first. Gnashing his teeth, he turned and charged his adversary at full speed.

Teo was too angry to stand back and wait. He barreled toward the dohj with a savagery of his own. The two men collided in the middle of the room and caromed off a decorative table. A porcelain vase tumbled to the floor and shattered. Ana shrieked as mayhem filled the room.

"Guards!" Cristof yelled. "Come to me! Hurry!"

The two combatants were locked in each other's grip. Cristof forced Teo to the window and pushed him backward over the sill, trying to cast him to the hard stones below. In the struggle the ladder was knocked away and banged against the ground.

Teo hooked Cristof's foot and tripped him. Both men hit the floor, thrashing like wildcats. As Cristof scrambled to his feet, he drew a knife from his belt. The massive blade tapered to a wicked point—a fighting knife if ever there was one.

Ana ran toward the dohj, but he cuffed her with the back of his hand and sent her sprawling. Rage took hold of Teo as he saw Ana go down. Cristof advanced toward Teo, knife in hand.

"I'm going to kill you, peasant," he snarled.

"Try it," Teo muttered through gritted teeth.

The dohj had obviously received training in the art of combat, for he didn't flail around but held the blade close and slashed with surprising quickness. Teo stepped back to avoid the vicious thrusts. Any one of them would have laid him wide open.

"Now you die," Cristof vowed. He rushed at Teo and stabbed low.

Teo saw his chance. Deflecting Cristof's arm with a sweeping motion, he collapsed his opponent's elbow and forced him into submission. Teo's fingers closed on Cristof's clenched fist, which still grasped the knife but now had little control. It was a standard combat move whose coup de grâce was to turn the blade toward the assailant and finish him off.

"Teo, don't!"

In the heat of battle Teo paid no attention to Ana's shout. Years of training took over. He finished the move by plunging the blade into the dohj's throat at the base of his neck. Cristof gagged, then coughed up a spray of bright red blood. His eyes rolled, and his body went limp. He hit the floor with a thump, his lifeblood draining away.

Teo stared at the dohj's back, breathing hard as he tried to comprehend what had happened. The awful reality began to sink in: he had just killed the sovereign of the realm. Teo turned toward Ana, whose eyes were wide and afraid.

"Open up immediately!"

Fists pounded on the door. There was a pause, then the door rattled on its hinges as a foot kicked it from the other side.

"We have to get out of here!" Ana's voice was thick from her swollen lip.

Teo ran to the balcony and looked down. Far below, waves broke against the sheer palace wall, and jagged rocks protruded from the frothy sea. *Suicide*, Teo realized.

He dashed to the window overlooking the courtyard. The ladder he had used to enter the bedroom lay useless on the ground. He swung his leg over the sill and began to lower himself.

"Wait!" Ana's plea was urgent. "You can't jump from here! It's too high!"

"The wall is rough. I can climb down and get the ladder."

"Please, no! You'll fall!"

Ana held on to Teo's jerkin, but he pulled away from her and dangled his legs until he found a foothold. The wall was old and crumbly. *Maybe this wasn't such a good idea*, he thought. The pounding on the door to Ana's room reminded him he had no other choice. The guards would be inside in a moment.

"Be careful, Teo! Oh, be careful!" Ana was watching the precarious descent from her position at the window.

With his fingers straining to find purchase, Teo clambered down the wall. A chunk of masonry broke away under his foot. He heard Ana scream as he plunged. His feet hit the ground first, rattling his teeth at the impact. He fell backward and conked his skull on the flagstones.

Teo squinted and shook away the dizziness. "I'm okay," he called as he got to his feet and went to the ladder.

He was about to raise it to Ana's window when he looked up and saw her standing at the opening with her back to the courtyard. Teo could tell from her movements she was wrestling with men who were trying to subdue her. He ducked into a shadowed niche and crouched behind a fountain.

When Teo glanced at the window again, Ana was gone. A man in the livery of the palace guard surveyed the courtyard with a stern expression. He reached out and grabbed the two casement windows, banging them shut. Then curtains were yanked across the glass.

Teo closed his eyes and hung his head. "She's in your hands now," he whispered to his God.

9

I t was a pleasant spring morning. Count Federco Borromo sat on the terrace of his lakeside palace, nibbling figs from a bowl. Of course, every day at Greater Lake was pleasant. The climate here was mild in both summer and winter, and the variety of plant life provided a lush environment that was excellent for gardening. The count's lavish estate boasted a diverse array of flowers, shrubs, and trees, all of which thrived in the temperate setting. On this sunny morning the winds flowed off the northern peaks and ruffled the water's surface. Later they would switch directions and blow from the plains in the south. It always happened like that. Having attained a state of near perfection, everything in this paradise was notoriously reluctant to change.

Count Federco had arrived at his palace only a week earlier. Though he had enjoyed his extended wintertime visit to Likuria with all its glitz and glamour, he felt glad to be home. The servants who stayed behind had taken good care of the place under the watchful eye of the majordomo. Still, having the lord of the manor back on the premises would tighten up operations even more.

The voice of a servant girl interrupted the count's thoughts. "Good morning, m'lord," she said with a submissive nod of her head. She was a heavyset lass of childbearing years, no doubt nursing an infant of her own in addition to the baby she held on her hip. "I've brought the boy as you instructed. He just ate. Quite an eater, that one."

"Very good. Give him to me and leave us."

Count Federco took the squirming child in his arms, cuddling him awkwardly until he realized what the little fellow really wanted was to be set down. As soon as Count Federco released him, the baby scooted across the terrace and began to investigate the base of a large urn. The boy's hair was a shock of black curls that Count Federco knew hadn't come from him. The boy had received that hair from his mother, Benita, who had died almost a year ago after a long and arduous childbirth. Though the silky curls were his mother's gift, the other trait with which Federco's son had been born was a curse: the blotchy port-wine stain that covered the left side of his face. Because of this blemish, the boy would be raised as a slave—never to leave the estate, never to inherit, never to be acknowledged as the beloved son he was. Though a few palace servants knew the truth, everyone else would assume the little Defective running around in their midst was just a deformed slave. Only the boy's name might have suggested otherwise to those who gave it some thought. Count Federco had named his son Benito after his cherished wife, who was now in the arms of Deus.

The count stroked his mustache as he watched the inquisitive Benito explore the vast universe of the patio. The baby crawled around the flagstones, reveling in his newfound freedom. At length a servant approached and announced the arrival of Federco's expected guest. Although none of the household staff would recognize the visitor, Federco knew him as the one man who would not turn away in disgust at Benito's marred face: his old friend Ambrosius, the Overseer of the Christiani in the Forbidden Zone.

Count Federco rose to greet the saintly old man as he was ushered onto the terrace. "Welcome, brother," he said, shaking hands. "It has been many years."

"They fly by, do they not?" The Overseer smiled warmly. He wore a rough-spun white tunic with a rope belt knotted at the waist. Underneath his hood, a black skullcap was pulled low on his forehead. Federco knew it concealed the disfigurement that lay underneath: a scar put there by the Overseer himself as an act of solidarity with the Defectives.

A loud crash across the terrace caught both men's attention. Benito had pulled a potted plant from a table, and the container shattered upon hitting the ground. Frightened, he began to cry, so the Overseer went to him and picked him up. Soon the baby was his usual laughing self again. The Overseer handed him to his father.

"An excellent child," Ambrosius said. "Full of boyish mischief."

The count grinned, then leaned close so no one else could hear. "Just like his father."

"By his presence here, I assumed as much. Do you wish me to give him shelter?"

"No. I cut a deal with the shamans. The boy can stay on the grounds as a slave. He's the only connection I have . . ." The count faltered and lowered his eyes.

"Your Benita was blessed in life," the Overseer said gently. "Now the blessings of the Almighty rest upon her."

Federco swallowed. "I know. My faith comforts me, simple though it may be."

"Even those with simple faith can be used by Deus. And in fact it is to discuss the implications of our faith that I have come to you."

The count did not respond at first but strode to a table and rang a handbell. Benito's nurse arrived and took him away, leaving the two men alone on the patio. They strolled out onto a dock that jutted into the lake.

"Have you discovered more about Deus?" Federco asked.

"Such discovery is difficult in this evil world of ours. Nevertheless, I believe we are on the cusp of a breakthrough."

"Tell me more, my brother."

The Overseer clasped his hands behind his back and stared at the luxuriant hills across the lake. "A man has come to me. First he came in my dreams, then in body. He knew the Creator and had heard of the Pierced One. He was a seeker of truth."

"A Defective?"

"No, he was whole. Yet he had the spirit of one who sees the broken as Deus does."

"A brother of ours then?"

"I believe so."

"What is his role in the mysterious plans of Deus?"

The Overseer sighed. "I cannot say what the outcome will be. Yet I discerned that this man is capable—a warrior, but much more than that. Intelligent. Wise. A divine hand rests upon him, of this I am certain. I sent him to Roma to meet the Papa."

"For what end?"

"It remains to be seen."

Count Federco nodded. He had learned enough about the secret religion of the Christiani to know that unresolved mystery was a necessary part of the spiritual life. The count glanced at his longtime friend standing beside him on the dock. Many years ago Ambrosius had begun to testify about the Pierced One—the one who gives instead of takes, who heals instead of injures, who sacrifices instead of abuses. "The purpose of life is to expend it for the sake of the weak and the downtrodden," Ambrosius had said. "This is the way of the true God. His prophets cried out for justice, and the Pierced One gave us an example to follow. What few legends survive tell us he loved the poor and joined them. For this great love he was killed by wicked men."

Though the details about the ancient religion had been lost through the centuries, Count Federco recognized these fundamental truths when Ambrosius spoke of them. He had asked to join the faith in a formal way. Because the count wasn't called to live among the Defectives like his friend, Ambrosius had offered him an alternative: join the Order of the Cross.

The secret society of knights was fiercely suppressed in Ulmbartia by the shamans. To Federco's knowledge, he was the only such knight in the realms of Ulmbartia and Likuria. Periodically delegates would sail up the coast to Likuria from the distant city called Roma. They would then journey overland to communicate with him privately, leaving behind carrier pigeons by which messages could be exchanged with the Christiani leadership. Count Federco considered membership in the Order of the Cross his best opportunity to establish a connection with the faith of Deus. Of course, it meant living with partial knowledge of the truth, since many teachings had been lost over time. Yet what remained was good and wise.

The Overseer turned and faced the count, gesturing at the beautiful surroundings. "Your estate is lovely, Federco. You have clearly prospered over the years. Everything you have touched has been blessed from above."

"It's true. Deus has given me more wealth than I know what to do with. I only wish I could give something back to him in gratitude."

"What makes you think you can't?"

Federco arched his eyebrows, inviting his friend to say more. The Overseer smiled and continued, "The enemies of the faith have great resources at their disposal, and they aren't afraid to use their riches for wicked designs. Is it wrong, then, for those who stand against evil to marshal their resources as well? Deus gives us wealth so we might do good with it."

"What do you need? Do your brothers require food for distribution? I would be honored to provide charity for the broken ones in the Zone."

"I am thinking of something far more costly than that."

"Is that so? Go on. I'm listening."

"Federco, the wealth of your entire estate could fund a sizable army."

"An army!" The count was shocked. "Do you know how expensive it is to hire mercenaries? To supply them over time? To move men and maté-riel around the realm? Raising an army is a task for the state, not private individuals. No man is rich enough for that!"

"You could do it, my friend, though it would come at great personal sacrifice."

"I would have to sacrifice everything."

"At what point would that become worthwhile to you?"

The count stared across the lake with his hands on his hips, gazing at the horizon without really seeing it. "I guess if we knew we could defeat the Exterminati once and for all, I'd consider it," he said.

"I believe the man of whom I just spoke is going to be a catalyst for something exactly like this. Things are coming to a head. The spiritual world is in unrest, and it is beginning to manifest itself in the physical realm. I can feel a storm gathering."

"I don't know," the count said, shaking his head. "This is a lot for me to take in. Who is this man anyway? What's he like?"

"He is a foreigner from over the mountains. His name is Teofil."

"Teofil of Chiveis? I know that man!" Count Federco's mouth hung open as he stared at the Overseer. "He's the most impressive warrior I've ever seen. He single-handedly defeated a band of Rovers and saved the lives of everyone at my castle—including me. I'd be dead if not for him."

"It doesn't surprise me. As I said, the mighty hand of Deus rests upon him."

The count turned away from his guest and gazed toward his palatial house. He studied it for a long time, taking in its grand marble columns, its ornate facade, its manicured gardens. At last he sighed and faced the Overseer again.

"Alright," Federco said, "if the opportunity presents itself to crush evil underfoot with a final destruction, I will give whatever Deus asks of me."

"You are wise, my friend. Yet be prepared. It may be that Deus will ask for everything."

✦   ✦   ✦

The dungeon reeked of urine and excrement. It was a dank, dark chamber buried under the monumental courthouse at Likuria's capital city of Manacho. Ana had been taken there aboard a ship. Now she was all alone.

She shifted her position on the floor, but what she really wanted was to free her wrists from the shackles that bound them. The two chains, attached to the wall at eye level, were just long enough so she could lower herself to sit on the cold ground. Yet it was awkward and numbing to keep her arms suspended above her head. Having been in the cell for many hours, Ana was worn down by the unrelenting discomfort.

Something furry brushed her ankle. "Get away!" she cried, kicking her foot. A rat skittered into the shadows, then paused and regarded her with beady eyes. Ana wanted to throw something at the disgusting creature, but her restrained arms would not allow it.

Her feet were bare, and the cheap tunic she had been forced to wear was made of sackcloth that itched against her body. She was certain the garment hadn't been washed in many years. The thought made her skin crawl. She hoped the ticklish sensation was only her imagination, not an infestation of body lice.

Voices sounded in the hallway, then the door creaked open. Two men with torches entered the gloomy cell.

"Get up," the leader grunted.

Ana gathered her feet under herself and rose. With her arms chained to the wall, she felt completely helpless as she stood there with the two surly guards staring at her.

"You're gonna die, you know," the second man said. He had tiny eyes and an upturned nose like a pig. "Everyone knows what you did."

"Yeah," the leader chimed in. "The priest will testify against you. You were the only one in the bedroom, and the murder weapon was in the dohj's neck. You're a *killer*." He shoved Ana and knocked her off balance. She could tell from the badge on his chest and his arrogant demeanor that he considered himself quite the big man around the jail.

"You're going to the quarries for sure, you dog," said Pig-Nose.

The leader turned to his partner with a smirk. "No, she ain't. She'll get much worse than that. She's goin' down the hole. Buried alive—that's the penalty for murdering the dohj."

Buried alive . . .

The words made Ana's knees go slack. She wanted to fight back, to argue, to resist the dire prediction. But she had no strength.

"Turn her around," the leader said.

The pig-nosed man sneered and grabbed hold of Ana, spinning her toward the wall with her face pressed against the clammy stones. Though she squirmed, he held her in place with a firm grip on the backs of her arms. She couldn't see what the men were preparing to do.

The sound of a blade being drawn from its sheath made Ana's heart leap in her chest. *What's happening? What's going on?* Desperation rose within her as she realized she had no rights at all. Down here in this secret place, the cruel men could do anything they wished. Ana tried to steel herself against whatever pain might be about to come.

A hand seized her hair and yanked it roughly. From the corner of her eye, she saw the leader raise his knife toward her head.

"No!" she cried.

The man began to slice the blade back and forth.

Sadness engulfed Ana as she realized her hair was being shorn. The blade was dull, and it felt like the jailer was ripping her hair from her scalp rather than cutting it. Ana's tresses fell away in large chunks. She had always taken pride in her thick, honey-colored hair. Now it lay in piles on the floor.

"That should do it," the leader said. The other man released his hold.

Ana put her hands to the back of her head. Instead of the long hair that used to hang over her shoulders, she felt only uneven tufts. Though she was glad her head hadn't been shaved bald, she knew the rough haircut made her look disheveled and freakish. Tears rose to her eyes as the men guffawed at her distress.

Pig-Nose pointed and grinned. "Look at her cry like a baby!"

"She ain't so pretty with all her hair chopped off, huh? And guess what else? She's a Defective."

What? Ana was startled by the leader's assertion. *How could he know about my scar?* She straightened her shoulders and met the man's gaze. "You don't know what you're talking about," she said.

"Oh yeah? You think I don't know what's happening in my own jail? I run this place! I had your charges read to me. You killed the dohj, and you'll be executed for that. But if not, the shamans will cart you away for that mark on your hip. The daughter of some rich Ulmbartian told them you're scarred. Face it, little girl, you're twice condemned."

A sick feeling seized Ana. "What was the daughter's name?"

"Vatina Labello, or somethin' like that."

No! That can't be! Vanita is my friend! Why would she . . . ?

Ana stared at the floor as the awful truth sank in. *The dohj. Vanita betrayed me!*

The thought made Ana reel. It was all too much. First Cristof's savage attack, then the harsh imprisonment, then the ridicule and mockery, and now this backstabbing from a supposed friend. Though Ana tried to keep her voice firm, she felt shaky and weak. She faced her two tormentors. "No matter what people may say, I am not a murderer. And I am not defective."

The jailer lunged at Ana and grabbed her arm. With his other hand he hiked up the hem of her sackcloth tunic.

"Leave me alone!" Ana cried, wrestling with the cruel man. Pig-Nose urged him on with lusty cheers.

"Look at that!" the jailer shouted as he exposed Ana's hip. "It's disgusting!"

Ana wrenched herself free and stepped back from the men as far as she could. "No," she said evenly. "What's disgusting is your inability to look past imperfection."

The two men exchanged glances. Each hoped the other would have a swift comeback, but neither could produce one.

"Stupid girl," the leader finally muttered, swatting his hand.

Ana remained silent as she stared at the brutes. They turned and left the cell, locking the door behind them. Ana slumped to the floor with her arms above her head.

Vanita, how could you?

She began to weep. For a long time she sat in the stinking cell and let tears spill down her cheeks. Her shoulders heaved as the agony in her soul came pouring out. Ana reflected on the months she had spent in Ulmbartia and Likuria. All the amusements she had viewed as enjoyable now seemed frivolous and tawdry. She regretted her extravagant lifestyle, her immodesty, her prideful and sensual perspective. She had listened to lies and made unwise choices. The end of it all wasn't peace but emptiness and despair.

Deu, I'm sorry! I'm so sorry!

Ana's weeping intensified as she lamented the state of her spiritual life. Though she had never rejected Deu outright, she had excluded him from her day-to-day activities. Many months earlier she had come over the mountains to seek the truth of Deu so the people of Chiveis could know about him. But somehow she had forgotten that goal amid the sunshine and luxuries and fancy parties. Ana realized she had lost her focus . . . lost her way . . . lost her true identity. Instead of worshiping the true God, she had become captivated by idols.

O merciful Deu, she prayed at last, her fingers clenching and unclenching, *I need you so much! Please, please, please don't reject me! Oh, forgive my sinful ways. I admit it all!* Ana shivered, and she turned her face to wipe her eyes against the dirty sackcloth on her shoulders. *My God, I don't see any way out. I know I don't deserve to ask you for any favors, but there's one thing I would beg of your grace. Don't let my life be wasted! You know I want Chiveis to hear your truth. In whatever way you see fit, use me to bring your name to the homeland I love. Please, Deu! Come to my people, and somehow let me be your servant again in that holy task.*

I miss you, Deu.

Ana's chin fell to her chest. Though her tears were spent, grief had not released its hold. Dry shudders wracked her body, and there was no one at her side to share her pain.

✦   ✦   ✦

The city of Manacho lay spread before Teo, crowning a rocky promontory whose cliffs plunged into the sea. The city's buildings were constructed of marble in imposing proportions, for while Nuo Genov used marble to decorate, Manacho used it to dominate. Somewhere beneath one of those haughty buildings, Anastasia languished in her chains, alone and afraid.

Teo stood on the deck of Marco's clipper ship, the *Midnight Glider*—a name Teo considered appropriate for a pirate vessel. Convincing Marco to make the voyage to Likuria's capital had required some arm-twisting. Nevertheless, despite Marco's complaints about the navy ships that always lurked around the port, he had seemed eager to combat the injustice being perpetrated on Ana. Something told Teo the pirate wasn't the scoundrel he pretended to be.

"There it is," Marco said, pointing to a white building perched on the edge of the cliff. "That's the courthouse."

Teo eyed the building from the deck's bulwark. It pained him to think that Ana was enduring hardship right now, locked up in some harsh dungeon. It pained him even more to think of the mode of execution planned for her. Marco had explained that the worst offenders in Likuria were dropped into an oubliette, a narrow shaft in the courthouse floor. Often the condemned were forced to drink seawater to exacerbate their thirst before suffering a claustrophobic death in a deep, dark well. The sensation of being trapped in a tight space beneath the earth, unable to move as one's muscles cramped in the utter darkness, was enough to drive a person insane.

"One time they hauled up a guy after only two days in the hole," Marco had told Teo during the trip to Manacho. "His hair had turned white all over, and he could no longer speak. He just stared into space and babbled. When they were about to lower him again, he got loose before they could rope him up."

"What happened to him?" Teo asked.

"Dived headfirst down the hole."

Teo grimaced as he stared at the courthouse. *I will never let Anastasia die in torment like that!*

He turned toward Marco. "What do you know about the courthouse's defenses? Is the place heavily guarded?"

"It'll be crawling with troops on the day of the trial. You can't see it from this side, but there's a garrison across the plaza from the front door."

Teo analyzed the building from a tactical perspective. Though it sat on the cliff, it didn't face the sea. Apparently it fronted onto a plaza, while its rear wall dropped straight to the churning water below. There was no space to walk behind the courthouse because the wall aligned with the edge of the cliff, meaning no guards would ever be back there. It would provide a stealthy approach—if one could find a way to scale the massive rock face.

"Can you row me to the base of that cliff?" Teo asked.

Marco shook his head. "The waves would smash a boat against the rocks. The best I could do would be to get you within a short swimming distance."

"Do it," Teo said. He began to unbutton his leather jerkin.

The waves were rough and the sea was cold when Teo dived from the boat after being rowed out. He made for the cliff face with the strong strokes of an experienced swimmer. No other ships were nearby because the winds weren't favorable for sailing. *That's to my advantage*, Teo thought as he cut through the water.

At the base of the cliff he hauled himself out of the sea by a couple of slippery handholds. Craning his neck, he glanced up. The rock face seemed much higher from here than when he had surveyed it from the deck of the *Midnight Glider*. The blue sky beyond the cliff-top seemed impossibly far away. Teo looked around at the choppy water, realizing that to fall from more than halfway up the cliff would mean certain death. Jagged rocks thrust from the sea, and the pounding waves foamed them up like the fangs of a rabid dog. Yet despite the danger, Teo resolved to ascend a short distance and test his options. If this was the best way to save Anastasia, it was worth a try.

Teo put his foot on a mossy protuberance, but as he did, he was startled to notice an object wedged into a crevice in the cliff. He released his handholds and dropped into the water, then swam over to the thing that had caught his eye. Closer examination confirmed his initial suspicion: the object was a human skull.

Floating in the water, Teo considered what this turn of events might mean. It seemed important, though at first he couldn't figure out why. *There's no reason for a skull to be here*, he realized. *No one would be likely to fall from this place on the cliff. The sea currents wouldn't have brought it this way. So what is it doing here then?* The significance of the skull's presence eluded Teo, until suddenly everything clicked into place. Excited about the unexpected discovery, he pushed himself away from the wall and began studying the rock face.

The Likurians had been executing convicts at the courthouse for decades. Their oubliette was deep but not bottomless. Over time the mortal remains would pile up. That meant the hole would have to be emptied from time to time. But how? Would the putrid bones of the condemned be hauled into the elegant courthouse of Manacho? Or would a better solution be . . . a clean-out shaft that opened to the sea?

Teo stared at the cliff, looking for two things in particular. He inclined his head and swam around to different vantage points until he found what he was looking for. About three-quarters of the way up the cliff, Teo discerned what looked like the dark mouth of a narrow opening. Below it a thin line traced its way down the rock face. When a gust of wind stirred the line and moved it slightly, Teo knew it was what he had supposed it to be: a dangling rope. Evidently some agile servant was sent periodically to access the bottom of the oubliette and dump its grisly contents into the ocean.

Cautiously, Teo scaled the cliff until he reached the end of the rope. The opening that was his destination was still far above him, but the rope was knotted, and he was able to climb it. At last he reached the place where the rope was fastened to a piton pounded into the stone. Next to it was a hole in the wall. Teo crawled inside.

The clean-out shaft was inclined at a very steep angle, and the rocks were slick with seepage. Only a series of notches carved into the slope allowed Teo to ascend without sliding down. Feeling his way forward, he crept deeper into the heart of the earth. At every moment he maintained at least three contact points with the notches. He had removed his shirt for the swim from the ship's boat to the cliff, and now the rock felt clammy against his chest. With painstaking deliberation he inched up the shaft until the entrance was a dot of light far below, and the tunnel ahead was pitch-black oblivion.

Finally Teo's probing hands touched a wooden door overhead. The shaft became vertical, and Teo realized he had reached the underside of the oubliette's floor. This would indeed be a terrifying place to live out one's final, pain-wracked hours. With a clenched jaw and gritted teeth, Teo swore anew he would never let Ana perish in such horrific torment.

Knowing the trapdoor must have a brace to support it, Teo stretched upward with his tiptoes in the climbing notches until his hand closed on a thick piece of iron. He tried to twist it in his fingers, but the brace was stiff. Grabbing it with two hands, he gave it a hard yank, then instantly realized his mistake.

The heavy trapdoor dropped open and smacked Teo on the head. The blow was hard enough to stun him, but worse, it knocked him from his footholds. He tumbled down the shaft in an awkward position, unable to arrest his fall. Twisting around, Teo careened off a wall until he was sliding on his back instead of his stomach. The bright hole at the end of the tunnel sped toward him as he looked down between his feet. In a matter of seconds he would plummet into the sea. Teo frantically sought a handhold, but there was nothing to grab.

Just as he was about to be ejected from the cliff, Teo managed to spread his legs wide enough to create friction against the walls with his feet. The tactic slowed his descent, though not enough to stop his fall completely. He shot feetfirst from the hole into open space. As he did, he made his grab, knowing he would have only one chance.

Teo's left hand seized the rope that dangled next to the opening. He clenched his fist and determined to hang on no matter what. The rope went taut at the end of Teo's outstretched arm, yanking him out of his free fall. The sudden deceleration wrenched his shoulder socket and sent pain shooting down his arm. He swung toward the rock wall and slammed into its unyielding face. Despite the teeth-rattling blow, Teo managed to keep his grip on the rope, then quickly grabbed it with his other hand as well. Wrapping his legs around the line, he stood on a knot and groaned as he let the pain dissipate from his body. At last he dared to look down. The sea's toothy maw would have to wait for another day to claim a fallen victim.

While Teo clutched the rope and caught his breath, he reworked his original plan. He had imagined he could climb up the shaft and wait until Ana was sentenced to death, as she surely would be. When everyone had left her for dead in the oubliette, he would open the shaft from below and make good their escape. But now Teo realized his plan was far too dangerous. In the cramped and precarious conditions of the clean-out tunnel, the chances were ten to one that either he or Ana or both would slip at some point and go tumbling into the sea.

"There has to be a way to make this work," Teo muttered as he dangled on the line. The discovery of the secret shaft was his best chance at a rescue, but how could he pull it off?

The wheels turned furiously in Teo's head. A new plan began to take shape, one that was complex, yet perfectly workable if a person knew what to do and followed the steps with precision. Instead of closing the trapdoor with the iron brace, the door could be wedged shut with a chunk of wood. If that stopper were pulled out, the door would fall, sending the unfortunate prisoner speeding down the shaft to a violent death. However, if a rope were threaded through the trapdoor's gap into the oubliette, then tied off to a sturdy anchor point, the prisoner could hold onto the rope before removing the stopper. The trapdoor would drop, but the person could cling to the rope for safety. Then the prisoner could ease toward the exit, descending hand over hand until reaching the outside. After climbing down to a waiting boat, the prisoner would escape, and no one would be the wiser. Teo grew excited as he considered his plan. *This could work! All I need is a length of rope from the ship and a wooden wedge!*

Teo began to make his way down the cliff. As he reached the water, however, he realized his plan was riskier than he had first imagined.

Perhaps if he could somehow draw it up or explain it to Ana, she could pull it off. But he would have no chance to speak with her prior to the trial. Even if he had such an opportunity, when the actual day came she would be terrified by the oppressive oubliette and physically and mentally weakened, and in no state for such a demanding task in a dangerous place. One mistake would send her plunging to her death.

Teo started swimming to the waiting rowboat, frustrated to have come so close to a solution, yet to have fallen short. He pondered the problem while slicing through the waves. As he neared the boat, the answer hit him.

Ana cannot be the one to go down the shaft.

❖   ❖   ❖

Ana had spent a hellish week in the cell. She was filthy and cold and weary. Her food had been meager. Her water was brackish. Her toilet was a bucket. Her sleep was fitful. Her chains were unyielding.

And yet, unbelievably, Ana was at peace.

As the hardships of her incarceration became worse, the renewed presence of Deu had become all the more sweet. Ana's heart was soft again, and she could feel her God's mercies once more. She finally had real prayers to say to him—not desperate pleas, but heartfelt words of intimate communion. Snippets of Deu's holy book came to her mind, such as the promise of the twenty-third Hymn: "When I walk in the valley of death's shadow, I won't fear any evil, because you are with me." Ana meditated on those powerful words, recalling how they had comforted her long ago when she still lived in Chiveis and Teofil had been captured by the forces of wickedness. All that seemed like a different world now.

As Ana's thoughts went to Teo, a flood of memories rushed through her mind. She imagined herself galloping away from danger with her arms around his chest . . . talking late into the night by the glow of a campfire . . . reading the Sacred Writing together . . . quickening his heartbeat over a candlelight dinner the way only a woman can. Teo had snatched her out of the Beyond after her abduction. Hauled her from a glacier's crevasse. Walked by her side when she was exiled from her homeland. Thrust his spear into a ferocious wolf. Run himself to exhaustion to bring her the bread-mold elixir. He had even let himself be shamed lest she be seen drunk by her friends. *To think that I once vomited on him!* Ana cringed at the thought. Teo had always been there to protect her, to fight for her, to shield her from enemies—whether they were unscrupulous womanizers with spiked drinks or predatory Rovers or deadly shamans or the carnal Dohj Cristof himself. *In all these ways*, Ana realized in the lonely prison cell, *Teo has spread his wing over me.*

And I've thrown it all away.

What a fool I am! He's the only man in my life who truly loves me!

Ana shifted her position on the floor, emotionally drained and exhausted. Her arms had grown numb, so she pulled herself up to a standing position to let the circulation return. Soon the tingling in her hands was maddening. At that moment she heard footsteps in the hall.

The head jailer and his assistant, Pig-Nose, entered the dungeon. The men tied a rope around her neck. Ana was unchained from the wall and led up a stairway that emerged into a plain, stone room. Though the windows were high, sunlight streamed through. Ana squinted as she gazed at the sky.

"Take a good look at it, woman," Pig-Nose said. "This is the last day you'll ever see the sun."

"I do not fear death. I am in Deu's hands."

Ana's defiant words caused her to remember the object she had hidden under her clothes when she was arrested. Knowing it would have been taken from her, she had kept it out of sight by attaching it to a strap of her undergarment. Now, with her hands free of her chains, she reached beneath her itchy tunic and brought it out: the costly gold necklace Teofil had given her. The face of Iesus Christus was peaceful as he hung on his cross. *I will wear it proudly in the sight of all*, Ana told herself as she slipped it on.

A crowd had gathered around the courthouse. It sounded as if the capital city of Likuria was in turmoil over the dohj's death. Ana could hear one man giving a speech about Cristof's greatness. Women wailed and men bellowed as the populist orator stoked their fires. A roar of approval went up when the speech concluded with the line, "Today, my people, we must have blood for this heinous murder!" Ana winced at the crowd's vehement ovation. The jailer noticed her expression.

"The whole kingdom hates you," he said. "Everyone wants to see you die. Your trial was delayed so people could travel here." Ana turned away from the vile man.

A bailiff arrived and removed the rope from Ana's neck, then gave her a pair of shoes. He escorted her through a maze of passageways to an ornate door. When he opened it and pushed her forward, Ana found herself facing a sea of hostile faces. The wood-paneled courtroom was filled to capacity. Everywhere she looked, steely eyes gazed at her with malice. Ana's heart lurched as she realized that any hopes she might have had of pleading self-defense were futile. These people were out for death and nothing less. An awful realization crystallized in Ana's mind: *There will be no deliverance*.

She closed her eyes.

If this is the end you have for me, Deu, then give me the courage to accept it!

Emboldened by her prayer, Ana strode forward with her head held high. Though the Likurians might dress her in sackcloth and cut off her hair, Ana decided she would conduct herself with a dignity that would put them to shame.

Jeers and boos erupted as she entered the courtroom and stepped onto a dais before the judge's high bench. The judge pounded his gavel to quiet the commotion. When a measure of silence had been achieved, he fixed his gaze on Ana and stared down at her. The top of the man's head was bald, but a corona of wild hair encircled the back of it. He pointed a gnarled finger in her direction. "Anastasia of Chiveis, you have been condemned. Do you have any last words?"

Condemned? I haven't even had a chance to speak yet!

Ana met the judge's eyes. "Your Honor, is it the custom in Likuria to sentence a person without a trial? Is this what passes for law and human decency in your land?"

The courtroom burst into an uproar. The judge's face crumpled like a prune. "You impudent little cur! How dare you lecture me!"

Ana felt tempted to wilt under all the shouts and hostility, but she forced herself to stand firm on the dais and not flinch.

The judge turned to his prosecutor. "Read aloud the findings in this woman's case. She who questions our legal procedures must bear the weight of the evidence arrayed against her!"

A man with a white wig and black robe stepped forward with a scroll. Unrolling it, he began to read: "Fact! Anastasia of Chiveis was alone with our most glorious dohj. Fact! She was angry at him and resisted his sovereign will. Fact! She threatened him with death. Fact! Dohj Cristof was found dead with a knife in his throat. Fact! This woman was discovered in the locked room with her hand on the knife. Fact! Anastasia of Chiveis is guilty of regicide!" The crowd groaned at each accusation. When the prosecutor issued his final charge and rolled up his scroll, the tumult rose to a crescendo. Everyone clamored for Ana's death. The charges weren't even true, yet this miscarriage of justice would make them seem so. Ana bowed her head, overcome at last by the hatred directed toward her.

And then everything changed.

The double doors at the rear of the courtroom banged open. A lone man walked down the center aisle, though Ana could not see who he was.

"I have come to testify on behalf of Anastasia of Chiveis!" the man proclaimed.

Teo!

Once again he has come!

He made his way toward the dais where Ana stood waiting. With his broad shoulders, handsome face, and confident demeanor, he cut an impressive figure. Ana could sense the crowd's awe at this unexpected development. Yet it was not awe that she felt, but a human emotion far more beautiful than that.

As Teo stepped onto the dais and took his place at Ana's side, he slipped his arm around her waist. "Don't worry," he whispered to her in Chiveisian speech. "I know what I'm doing."

The judge glared at Teo with disapproving eyes. "Who are you, young man? What business do you have with this court? Speak!"

"My name is Teofil of Chiveis. I have come to declare before you and all Likuria that the woman you have condemned today is innocent of her charges." A murmur of surprise rippled through the crowd.

"Is that so?" the judge sneered. "And how do you know this?"

"Because I am the one who killed Dohj Cristof!"

Teo's shout threw the courtroom into chaos. The place exploded with cries, protests, and arguments. Nobody knew what was happening, but everybody had an opinion.

"Silence! Silence!" The judge banged his gavel on his bench, then ordered his bailiff to remove the defendant while he got to the bottom of the matter. As the bailiff grabbed Ana's arm, she turned to Teo, imploring him with her eyes. "Teo, you can't do this! They'll bury you alive!"

He nodded. "I know. Just let me do what I have to do. Trust me!"

The bailiff hauled Ana out of the raucous courtroom.

✦ ✦ ✦

"Young man, if this is some kind of joke, I'll have you whipped so hard you'll wish you were thrown down the hole instead." The judge motioned for the prosecutor to approach Teo. "Take his statement. Get the facts straight."

"It's no joke, Your Honor. I'm confessing to a capital crime. I entered Anastasia's bedroom through a window and killed the dohj with his own knife."

Teo's bombshell announcement had created a massive disturbance in the courtroom. Everyone was in a state of shock, from the judge all the way to the back-row spectators who had come to the trial out of morbid curiosity.

The prosecutor grilled Teo for the better part of an hour. The man knew how to ask penetrating questions, and Teo cooperated by laying out the facts, holding nothing back.

At last the prosecutor was satisfied. He read the charges aloud to the stunned courtroom. Teo could feel outrage rise in the room as the fury that had been directed toward Ana was turned on him instead. He became the object of the people's scorn as they poured out their wrath on a new victim.

"So you couldn't stand the burden of your guilt, eh?" The judge seemed delighted that his prosecutor had obtained a confession, despite the fact that Teo had offered himself freely to the court. "It seems what we have here is a classic case of a burning conscience. Well, do not suppose your confession will earn any leniency from me! Regicide is regicide, no matter how it is discovered."

The judge raised his eyes from Teo's face and looked at the ravenous crowd. "Good people of Likuria, what should be done with the man who has killed your king?"

"Death!" they shouted. "Kill him! Send him down the hole!" The threats and accusations filled the courtroom with venomous hate. Though Teo had prepared himself for this moment, the weight of the people's contempt oppressed him nonetheless. It was a difficult burden to carry, even though he had sought it out.

The charges against Teo were written up as an affidavit, which he signed in large, bold letters. An affidavit of innocence was prepared for Ana to sign, and the bailiff was sent to fetch her.

As the climactic moment drew near, the spectators' mood evolved from anger to bloodlust. They were ready to wreak vengeance upon the guilty. Teo's wrists were locked into manacles, and he was led to an open space in the flagstone floor. A burly man lifted an iron hatch, revealing a hole no wider than Teo's shoulders. The musty smell of death wafted up from the abyss.

The man turned a winch and hauled a chain out of the oubliette. A small plank on the chain was shoved between Teo's legs so his weight would rest on it like the seat of a childhood swing. In this way prisoners could be lowered down the shaft to ensure a slow death. Teo swallowed as he stared at the mouth of the fearsome oubliette. The thought of being dropped into that tight space made his heart thud in his chest. *Deu, help me go all the way*, he prayed as he faced the blackness that waited to swallow him whole.

A door opened across the courtroom. Ana was led in by the bailiff. Teo noticed she was wearing the necklace he had given her. He caught her attention, nodding confidently, but she shook her head at him. Grief was etched upon her face.

The judge rapped his gavel until the courtroom quieted. "Anastasia of Chiveis, earlier today this court found you guilty of murder. Now that the true facts are known, the penalty owed by you has fallen on this man instead. Affirm your innocence, and you will be a free woman." He slid the affidavit across the bench, and the prosecutor brought it to Ana along with a quill.

She gripped the affidavit, her head bowed. For a long moment the courtroom held absolutely still. Teo stared at Ana as she stood illumined in a ray of afternoon sunlight. Though she was dressed in sackcloth and her hair was ragged about her head, Teo found himself transfixed by her beauty. Anastasia's incredible radiance overpowered the room physically, morally, and spiritually.

I love her, Teo realized. *I will do this deed for her gladly!*

Ana raised her head and held up the affidavit. "Your Honor," she said, "I refuse to sign."

She ripped the paper in two.

◆　　◆　　◆

The judge scowled as he pounded his gavel, trying to settle a courtroom that had been thrown into confusion again. Ana stood on the dais while the tumult swirled around her, remaining unmoved like the placid eye of a terrible hurricane. She knew what she had to do, and she intended to see it through.

Teo's magnificent act of self-sacrifice had touched Ana to the core. How many times had he put himself in harm's way for her sake? How many times had he offered himself on her behalf? *Too many times to count!* Now he had even proven himself willing to die in her place. While Ana waited in the anteroom for Teo to be arraigned, she had been awestruck by the love this man had demonstrated for her again and again. Such deep and precious love had awakened an extravagant love of her own. Ana had arrived at a single, irrefutable conclusion: *Though Teo would gladly lay down his life for me, in truth it is I who must lay down mine for him.*

The events in the courthouse had served to clarify a fact Ana already knew in her heart. The person whom Deu would use to recover the New Testament and bring salvation to Chiveis was Teo. Yet the Likurians were going to insist on executing someone today for the murder of their king. Ana could see her death was required so that Teo—and Chiveis—might live.

As she faced this stark truth, Ana experienced a peace she hadn't thought possible. Amazed, she realized, *I truly want to do this! I rejoice to die in this way!* She wasn't afraid of the oubliette. She wasn't afraid of death. The suffering would be temporary, and then Deu would welcome her into his arms. Like so many other martyrs in the annals of history, Ana found herself a willing victim in her moment of destiny. Deu had answered her prayers. He had given her one last chance to serve his purposes. For that Ana was grateful beyond words.

"You brazen woman!" the judge yelled. "Do you think you can make a mockery of my courtroom? I'm not afraid to send you to your doom right now! I swear by all that's holy, someone is going to pay for the dohj's death, and I don't care which of you it is! Now sign that affidavit or the judgment that rests on you will remain!"

Ana lifted her chin. "Your courtroom is already a mockery. Your justice is a sham. I will never sign."

The judge went berserk. Through gnashing teeth he screamed, "Then I sentence you to death and condemn you to hell!" His unruly hair stood up like the mane of some crazed monster.

Ana stepped off the dais and followed the bailiff to the place where Teo was standing.

"Ana, no!" he pleaded. "Listen to me! Stop! It has to be me!" He waved his hands wildly, chains clanking at his wrists. Though he tried to approach her, the bailiff intervened and restrained him.

"Guards, subdue that man!" the judge roared.

Three deputies hurried forward and grabbed Teo by the shoulders. One of them threw his arm around Teo's neck in a choke hold. Although Teo fought back, they forced him to his knees. He kept trying to speak, but his voice was suppressed by the deputy's grip on his throat.

Immense sorrow rushed upon Ana as she looked at Teo's face. She pushed aside her sadness and gathered her resolve. No matter the cost, she would not waver from the path Deu had assigned to her.

Manacles were brought by a young deputy. His hands trembled as he attempted to bind Ana's wrist, but she clasped his hand in hers and snapped the cuff in place. Her other hand was bound, then the wooden seat on the chain was placed between her legs.

The crowd leaned forward as Ana teetered at the lip of the oubliette. All the onlookers held their collective breath. Only Teo uttered any sound as he fought against his captors.

Ana didn't want to make Teo's anguished face her final image of him, yet she had something important to say. She caught his attention. He stopped thrashing and looked at her.

"I love you," she mouthed to him.

She saw Teo gasp. Tears flooded his eyes and rolled down his cheeks. *Deu, help me go all the way*, she prayed.

Ana was forced to drink a cup of seawater. Its saltiness made her gag.

Then, before anyone could push her, she grasped the chain and stepped into the dark mouth of her grave.

CHAPTER

10

As the lid of the oubliette clanged shut, the spectators in the courtroom moaned, their hunger for sacrifice satisfied. The echo of iron against stone was a death knell that signaled their gratification was complete. The deed was done. Vengeance was achieved, and its taste was sweet and delicious.

Nevertheless, on the back row of the crowded courtroom, a lone woman cringed at the day's proceedings. In contrast to the mob's surfeit, the woman felt nothing but emptiness inside. Vanita Labella despised herself.

O god, what have I done? She bowed her head and stared at her feet. *Who are you, Vanita?*

You're a murderer!

Though Vanita told herself she hadn't intended things to turn out like this, she knew the sequence of events that had just culminated in the courtroom had been initiated by her own traitorous deed. By approaching the shamans, she had set the wheels in motion. Although Anastasia had ended up being punished for the crime of murder instead of for the defect on her hip, the awful fact remained that Vanita had sold her friend into enemy hands. For what? *For a man! For a brainless prince and his accursed money!* The whole affair made Vanita feel defiled. "It wasn't supposed to end this way," she whispered to herself. She had imagined Anastasia would live out her days in a distant, peaceful valley. *Peaceful valley? Who am I kidding? There will be no peace for Anastasia now—just the slow and agonizing death of an innocent woman!*

Vanita gripped her gown in her fists, scrunching her eyes shut. The idea of being forced into that tight underground hole terrified her. The press of its walls . . . the inability to move . . . the cold darkness . . . the thirsty minutes that stretched into hours, then days until Anastasia finally met her end, all parched and shriveled like a skeleton . . .

Oh god oh god what have I done oh god!

The tormented woman bolted from her seat and ran from the courtroom to the plaza. The crowds were beginning to disperse, but Vanita didn't wait for a lane to open among the pedestrians. Elbowing her way past the rabble, she hurried to the grand hotel where she had taken a room. Her father didn't know she had come to Manacho, but so what? He cared more about his ledger books than his daughter, except when he wanted to show off her beauty to his lecherous friends. Vanita grunted, suppressing the dirty memories. She entered her room and stuffed a few items into a bag, then locked the door and went back outside.

The stable behind the hotel wasn't a place Vanita would normally visit, but she made her way there now. A man in high boots greeted her as she approached.

"Good afternoon, m'lady," the stablemaster said with a courteous nod. "How can I be of service?"

"Your best palfrey, and make it quick," Vanita snapped.

"You ride alone?" The stablemaster arched his eyebrows.

"Just shut your—"

Vanita stopped, exhaling slowly. *Girl, you have a lot of flaws.*

She continued more kindly, "Yes, I will be riding alone today." The stablemaster shrugged and brought the horse. Vanita mounted like the experienced equestrienne she was and ambled into the main street.

An hour later she was well outside Manacho, having departed through the northern gate that faced away from the sea. Like all of Likuria, Manacho's city limits stretched west and east in a coastal strip. The mountainous region to the north was primarily agricultural, dotted with quaint farming villages. Past the olive plantations, vineyards, cork groves, and orchards, the land became rougher and more wild. The forests were infested with homeless vagabonds. Vanita wondered if she would run into any bandits.

Steep hills rose on either side of the road. Vanita turned her horse into a thicket and dismounted. The ride had done little to lift her spirits. Every time she noticed the pleasant warmth on her shoulders or the fresh spring air, the thought of Anastasia suffering in the oubliette caused the accusing voices to return. Unbearable guilt pressed down on Vanita, forcing her to consider things she had never thought about before, things like morality and evil and the virtuous life. Anastasia of Chiveis—an excellent woman if ever there was one—had demonstrated a different way to live. It was attractive. For the first time ever, Vanita was asking questions about the state of her soul.

Is there really just one God? she wondered. Anastasia had believed so. She had called him Deu. Vanita's mind returned to the breakfast the two women had shared with Dohj Cristof at his palace. Anastasia had described Deu as "loving and powerful and very holy." *Great! Just what I need! A God who's holy enough to hate me for what I've done and powerful enough to get me for it!*

"No, he loves you, Vanita."

It was Anastasia's voice that uttered the words. Vanita heard it inside her head as clearly as if her friend were standing next to her. She knew it was exactly what Anastasia would have said.

Could it be true? Could that God love me?

A stream ran through the place where Vanita had stopped. She went over to it and knelt at the water's edge, drinking from a deep pool. The water lay quiet and still as Vanita stared at her reflection. The face that gazed back was unquestionably beautiful. The men of the world were mesmerized by it, while the women were insanely jealous. An unbidden thought sprang to Vanita's mind: *I am desirable . . .*

No! I'm detestable!

She smacked the water with her palm, splashing droplets on her gown and making her reflection disappear in the turbulence. Vanita got to her feet as anguish gripped her like a vise. Scenes from the courtroom played themselves out in her mind. She remembered Teofil standing on the dais, so handsome and self-assured as he made the deadly confession that would set Anastasia free. And then Anastasia had refused to accept it! Her radiant beauty as she relinquished her life was more than Vanita could comprehend. Such resplendent joy was not of this world. Clearly Anastasia loved Teofil beyond measure, and he loved her like that in return. *What kind of love suffers death for a beloved?* Stunned, Vanita realized she had never demonstrated anything close to such an act of self-giving. She wondered if she was even capable of it.

The palfrey grazed on the lush grass. Vanita walked over to the animal and removed a saddle valise from its back. When she left the hotel an hour ago, she had intended to flee the crowded city and take refuge in some plush country inn. Now, however, that plan seemed utterly self-centered. Vanita realized bigger issues were at stake than numbing her guilty conscience. An idea began to coalesce in her mind—not something selfish or escapist, but noble and redemptive. *Is there a chance Anastasia might still be saved? Could she survive in that horrible place until . . . until . . . what? How could this be done?*

Vanita racked her brain for a solution. The answer struck her with sudden clarity. *Of all the people in the world, the one most capable of finding a way is Teofil! What if I sought his help? Maybe Deu would lead me to him?*

No! That good God wouldn't have anything to do with filth like me!

Vanita's soul felt as unclean as the pile of droppings at the horse's feet. She let out a desperate cry, wanting to show the Creator she was sorry for her treachery, yet not knowing how. At last she shook her head and blinked away the tears. She marched over to the brook again. After lighting a small fire, she removed an ivory-handled razor and some soap from her valise. The razor's steel edge glinted in the sun. Its purpose had always been to make her body appealing. Now she had a different use in mind.

Kneeling beside the stream, Vanita lathered her hair. Without stopping to question herself, she lifted the razor to her head and shaved it clean to the scalp. Her long, blonde hair fell into the stream and floated away amidst the suds. When the job was done, Vanita reached toward the remains of her little fire and rubbed ashes upon her shorn head.

"Mighty Deu, this is the sign of my repentance," she whispered with her chin upon her chest. "I don't know anything about you, but Anastasia says you're forgiving. I know I need forgiveness—I'm covered in *sin*! I can't stand it anymore. I want to make this right. Help me find Teofil. And help us get Anastasia out of that hole!"

Vanita collected her things and buckled the valise behind the palfrey's saddle. Though she wasn't sure where Teofil was right now, she had heard the judge sentence him to exile from Likuria forever. That meant he would soon be led away in chains, and the roads leading north were few. It might be possible to locate him. Vanita grabbed the reins and a tuft of her horse's mane, then put her foot in the stirrup as she prepared to swing into the saddle.

A man's rough voice suddenly spoke from the forest: "Don't move!"

But Vanita did move. Dropping her foot, she collected her wits in an instant. She turned around with a confident expression on her face. The fat man emerging from the forest didn't know what to make of that. He had obviously expected her to cower.

"I suppose you think you're going to rob me?"

"How you gonna stop me?" the man demanded, brandishing an ax.

Vanita put her hands on her hips and flashed the man a cocky smile. "I'm going to stop you by suggesting an even better idea."

❖   ❖   ❖

Every step along the road was torment to Teo. Every minute that passed was an intolerable delay. Every league journeyed north took him in the wrong direction. An entire day had passed since Ana had been dropped into the oubliette, and the thought of her suffering in that claustrophobic hole was more than Teo could stand. She was trapped underground enduring extreme agony while he—the one who had promised to take care of her always—could do nothing about it.

Deu, keep her alive until I can get there!

The detachment of six Likurian soldiers had departed on horseback with their prisoner soon after the trial. They had camped in the woods and resumed their northward journey in the morning. Teo would have fought to escape, but there was no chance. His wrists were in chains. He had no weapon. All he could do was hope to reach the boundary of Likuria soon. The judge had exiled him from the realm, though Teo had no intention of leaving as he had been commanded. As soon as he was turned loose, he would sneak back to Manacho to rescue Ana. *I have to get her out of that hole!* Teo ground his teeth at the maddening delay.

Around midday a thunderstorm rolled in. Teo's cloak had been left in his cottage at Nuo Genov, so he was soon soaked to the skin. When the rain finally let up, the commander of the Likurian detachment ordered a halt. After conferring with his pathfinder, he signaled for Teo to dismount and step forward.

"This is the boundary of Likuria," the commander said gruffly. "The road runs through wilderness, but if you keep going north and pass through the mountains, you'll reach the open plains of Ulmbartia. Do not ever return to our land, on pain of death."

Teo held out his wrists. "At least remove my chains. Show a bit of the human decency your kingdom claims to have."

The commander's eyes narrowed. He turned to two of his men and jerked his thumb. "Throw this guy off the road and let's go."

The pair of soldiers seized Teo by the wrists and ankles. With a tremendous heave, they launched him over an embankment. Teo hit the ground with a thud that knocked his wind out. He went rolling down the hill through the undergrowth until he came to rest in a small clearing. Spitting out debris, he sat up. He looked around for something with which to tap out the pins that held the manacles shut. As he picked up a rock to do so, a menacing voice startled him, sending a chill down his spine.

"So, Teofil of Chiveis, did you think I had forgotten you?"

Teo glanced around, unable to identify the speaker. He scrambled to his feet with the rock in his hand—his only weapon. "Show yourself!"

The shrubbery parted, and a tall, broad-shouldered man stepped into the clearing. He wore a black chain-mail hauberk. His right eye glowed yellow like a cat's. Teo felt his mouth go dry.

"What do you want with me?" Teo put an aggressive edge in his voice, but he knew he was in deep trouble.

The Iron Shield laughed as he stared at Teo with his hands on his hips. Somehow the man's laughter seemed to echo within his chest, as if many voices were contributing to the sound. "What do I want? Let me tell you, Teofil. Over the next few days I intend to get to know you very well." The Iron Shield's face darkened into a scowl. "From the inside out."

The tall man beckoned over his shoulder toward the forest. A gaggle of six or seven shamans erupted from the underbrush and grabbed Teo. The shamans lifted Teo's body and suspended him from a stubby tree branch by the chain linking his wrists.

The Iron Shield clasped his hands behind his back and stared into the distance as if musing on some perplexing thought. "The oubliette is indeed a horror," he said at length. "What do you know of it, Teofil?"

Teo remained silent, so the dark warrior continued. "It prolongs death over many hours, even days. There is no terror like being enclosed in that tight space. Soon the victim's muscles begin to cramp, and the body longs for a change of position, yet there is no relief of the pain. Thirst is enormous. Fear is intense. The victim wallows in his own filth. A more gruesome death could not be devised."

At these taunting words, fury rose within Teo. He grunted and thrashed, but it was no use. The Iron Shield nodded as he saw Teo's distress. "I know what you're thinking, my friend, and you are correct. All of this is happening right now to Anastasia. She has been in torment for a day already, and her sorrows will not let up any time soon. The oubliette will draw out her suffering to the very end. Perhaps you can keep her agony in mind as I take you apart over the coming days."

"You're a fiend. A monster."

"Oh, yes," the Iron Shield replied in a deep, reverberant voice. "Yes indeed we are."

The dark warrior slowly approached. He was tall, so despite Teo's suspension from the branch, their faces were even. The Iron Shield stared at Teo and leaned close, his cat's eye giving him an evil aura. His expression was deviant and malicious. Suddenly the man kneed Teo in the groin. Though Teo didn't wish it, the pain caused him to cry out. Nausea overwhelmed him. He gasped and spat bile from his mouth.

The Iron Shield laughed again. This time there was no false pleasantry in his voice, but only the sinister gloating of a sadist who relished his work. He motioned toward one of his henchmen. "Go get the instruments," he said, "and let us see what Teofil of Chiveis is made of."

The shaman returned with a set of knives, claws, hammers, and even a pair of pliers that could be worked with two hands. The Iron Shield placed a stick in the pliers and crushed it. "*Crudelitas vis est*," he said, then started forward with a sneer on his face.

Teo set his jaw and steeled his resolve. A bead of sweat rolled down his forehead. He would endure the torture as long as he could without giving his enemy the pleasure of breaking his spirit. One thing was certain: the pain was going to be extreme. Teo's heart raced as the Iron Shield opened his instrument of evil.

Thock!

An arrow glanced off the Iron Shield's helmet, while another snagged in his hauberk. The warrior whirled and drew his mace, but the attackers did not show themselves. Several shamans lay on the ground, their bodies bristling with feathered shafts. Teo watched, stunned, as a barrage of arrows filled the clearing with a whizzing sound.

"Retreat!" the Iron Shield shouted, dashing to the forest with his few remaining men. Judging by the number of arrows being loosed, the shamans were sorely outnumbered.

Teo waited for an arrow to come flying toward him, but none did. Though he listened for the sounds of battle in the woods, he heard nothing. Evidently whoever was loosing the arrows had no intention of engaging in hand-to-hand combat. They were content to shower the Exterminati with deadly missiles from their hiding places. Hoofbeats retreated into the distance, and then all was silent. Teo hung helplessly from the tree.

A ragtag band of men crept into the clearing with their longbows, perhaps thirty in all. The leader was a fat man with a scraggly beard. He walked up to Teo with a two-handed battle ax in his meaty fists. The man braced his legs and raised the ax above his head, then brought it down hard. The blow severed the branch from which Teo was suspended. He dropped to the ground, relieved to ease the severe ache in his wrists.

"You're free to go," the leader said, tapping out the pins in Teo's manacles.

Teo was dumbfounded. "Who are you?"

The fat man grinned through his whiskers. "We're what some call outlaws, though we like to think we have a law of our own." His hearty chuckle revealed a row of brownish teeth.

Teo glanced from the leader's face to the other men standing around. He felt grateful for their intervention, though he was also confused by the turn of events. "Why did you help me?" he asked.

The man held up a coin. "Money talks. A stranger offered us a ridiculous sum to spring you from those shamans on your tail. As soon as you show up in Manacho, we'll get paid the rest of our reward."

"Did the stranger say why he wanted to help me?"

"Funniest thing," the bandit answered. "It wasn't a man. It was a woman with a shaven head, covered in ashes."

◆　◆　◆

Darkness.

All was black, and cold, and tight.

No space to move. Barely enough room to breathe. The air was foul, and it stank of the crypt.

Ana was terrified. She had chosen this path freely, but now, having chosen it, she wanted it finished. She was ready to die.

Take me to you, Deu! Please hurry . . . I beg you . . . make it stop . . .

The panic of claustrophobia rose up for the hundredth time as Ana stood in the cramped space. She clawed at the walls that pressed all around. Her heart beat wildly, and her breath came in desperate pants. Sweat streamed down her face. *Take me, Deu! Let it end!*

Ana longed to lie down. Though she was exhausted, she could find no sleep, no respite from the horror. There was only one way to escape her plight. She prayed for death's sweet release.

Her throat was parched. The saltiness in her mouth drove her mad. Her stomach rebelled at its load of seawater. She felt dizzy and hoped she would faint.

Help me, my God, help me!

Ana's thighs ached from standing upright for so long. Her calf muscles began to seize up. She shifted her feet, and a rough piece of rope brushed her ankle, but nothing alleviated the torment in her legs.

Fleeting images raced through Ana's brain. A smiling man with a gray-specked beard. A beautiful middle-aged woman cooking supper in a familiar kitchen. Snowcapped mountains. A handsome young man reading from a book by the glow of a candle. His hair was thick and dark. His expression was tender. *Oh, Teo, I will miss you!*

Ana lost consciousness.

Something cool and wet against her face jerked her awake. *Where am I? What is that? Water!*

Ana pressed her lips to the wall of the oubliette. A trickle had seeped through the rock, and she lapped it up greedily. Its taste was cold and earthy, but it was satisfying. She kept drinking until she had sucked all the moisture from the wall. The water eased her thirst. *Thank you, Deu.* She remembered him and was glad.

Her legs were in agony. *I want to lie down. If only I could lie down . . .*

Will it ever end? How long before I go? I want to go. Take me, Deu! Take me to you . . .

The throbbing in Ana's legs ceased. The exhaustion of her body slipped away as a warm light washed over her. She saw a gateway open up, and beyond the gate lay grassy hills. She stepped forward. A man stood there in a linen robe with a golden sash—a powerful man, full of love and glory. His eyes were ablaze, and upon his head were many crowns. The music of infinite worship surrounded him. He smiled. His hair and beard were white like lamb's wool.

"You are beloved to me, Anastasia," he said in a resonant voice.

The man held out his hand. It was scarred.

Ana reached for it, and the world of pain was no more.

❖   ❖   ❖

The horse's hooves pounded on the granite pavestones under a pale moonlight. The creature's breath made wisps of fog in the cool night air. Its rider was pushing it hard along the road, for he was a desperate man.

Teo had set out for Manacho while the bandits stayed behind to harass the Iron Shield. Upon reaching the city, the borrowed horse would be returned to the bandit who guarded the stranger until she paid the promised reward. Teo didn't know why the unknown woman was helping him, and he didn't care. All his thoughts were focused on getting to the oubliette as quickly as possible to free Anastasia.

If she's still alive . . .

Ana had been trapped underground for . . . how long now? More than thirty-six hours, Teo realized. By the time he arrived it would be the morning of Ana's third day in the hole. Her thirst would be agonizing. Her body would be wasted. Teo winced and cried out. The thought of Ana's suffering was more than he could bear. *Please, Deu, just let her live!*

As Teo rode south toward the capital of Likuria, he couldn't escape the fears that attacked him. Though he worried Ana might have died from thirst or exposure, he knew those weren't the only dangers. If she somehow removed the stopper he'd placed in the trapdoor, she would plunge down the clean-out shaft into the sea. Ana's body would be broken on the jagged rocks that thrust from the foamy waves.

Teo had intended to knock out the stopper himself while holding onto a rope for safety. However, when he went back to the oubliette to set it up, he found no secure anchor point for the rope. Changing his original plan, he decided that once he was in the oubliette, he would affix the rope to the chain that lowered the prisoners. The chain was securely attached to a winch above, and the new solution would have worked nicely—except Anastasia had gone down the hole instead of him. Teo berated himself for letting that happen.

It should have been me! Why did you do it, Ana?

The twisting course of events had thrown Teo into confusion. His mind felt jumbled. All he could do was rush to Manacho as fast as possible. He knew severe anguish might be in store for him, yet as he rode along he reminded himself to trust Deu. Deep inside Teo believed things would turn out well. Ana would be found, weakened but alive, in the oubliette. Then he would whisk her away from Likuria forever.

Dawn had just started to break when Teo arrived at Manacho's northern gate. No one was awake yet as he rode through the quiet streets toward the waterfront. The bandits had told him to leave the horse at a certain tavern, and Teo didn't bother to tie it up when he arrived. Somebody would attend to the spent animal. He left the tavern yard and crept to the marina. Untying a rowboat, he pushed it away from the wharf. The stolen craft had the insignia of the coast guard on it. Teo figured the Kingdom of Likuria owed him a whole lot more than a leaky boat.

As Teo approached the seaside cliffs, his heart began beating rapidly, and not from the exertion of pulling the oars. He realized the moment of truth had arrived: would Anastasia be alive up there in the oubliette? He prayed for the thousandth time he'd find her clinging to life in the oppressive hole. Drawing near the foot of the cliff beneath the courthouse, he glanced at the rocks but saw no corpse floating among them. *Thank you, Deu!*

Teo dropped anchor and dived into the chilly waters. The sheer stone face loomed above him as he swam to the place where the climbing rope had been fixed to the wall. And then Teo spotted something he didn't want to see.

A knotted cord floated in the water, tangled in some boulders. It was the safety rope he had left in the oubliette to be tied off to the chain. If it had been used for escape, it should still be fastened above. Yet there it was, floating among the rocks like a deadly snake.

No.

This isn't happening.

There has to be another explanation!

With dangerous abandon Teo scrambled to the climbing rope that dangled a short distance above his head. He ascended to the entrance of the clean-out shaft in the rock wall. Slipping inside the tunnel, he wormed his way upward, leaving the morning light behind.

"Ana! Are you there? Can you hear me?" His shouts echoed off the walls but received no response. Using the notches carved in the floor, he crawled up the shaft until it became vertical. Everything was dark. "Ana!" he yelled again. He was at the bottom of the oubliette. If Ana was alive, she should be able to hear him. Perhaps she was too weak to respond.

Teo stretched upward and groped around with his hand. Nothing. He reached even higher, feeling for the trapdoor, but encountered only empty space. Agonized, he extended his hand toward the wall on his left.

His fingertips touched wood.

It was the trapdoor, hanging down.

Ana had opened it. With no safety rope.

Teo's mind recoiled, and he uttered a groan he could not suppress. As he inched back down the tunnel, he recalled his own precarious descent when he had been knocked loose and went sliding down the incline. Only a quick grab of the climbing rope outside had prevented a smashing impact on the rocks below.

Maybe Ana did the same?

Teo tried to convince himself it was true, though subconsciously he knew she couldn't have managed the feat in her fragile state. She didn't even know the rope was there. The cold, hard facts were beginning to force Teo toward an unthinkable conclusion. Like an oubliette of his own, he was trapped by a logic he could not escape.

Down in the water again, Teo looked at the shaft's entrance far above. *Too far? Maybe not! Maybe Ana fell in just the right place . . . clung to a rock to rest . . . swam away to the shore. Even though she was weakened and chained up, she could do that!*

It's possible! Yes, entirely possible!

Aghast, Teo stared at the rocky fangs in the ocean's gaping mouth. He shook his head. *No, it isn't possible at all.* The realization hit him like a blow to his gut.

"Ana, where are you? It's Teo! I've come for you!"

He shouted the words and began to swim around, his movements growing frantic as he felt his mind lose touch with reality. Everything seemed like a dream. At any moment he imagined Ana would rise from behind a boulder and reach out to him. He called her name over and over, becoming more hysterical with each shout.

Finally, exhausted from the all-night ride and the frigid waters, he hauled himself onto a rock and sprawled there like a dead man. The wind chilled his body, but he didn't care. Nothing mattered. Nothing mattered at all.

Teo's gaze fell on an object floating nearby. The wave action at the base of the cliff didn't carry things away but pressed them close to the face, often wedging them into a crevice. Teo slipped into the water and retrieved the object. It was a peasant's shoe—the kind Ana had been made to wear in the courtroom. The sight of it made Teo's stomach lurch and at the same time triggered a memory.

"Ooh, that water's cold," Ana said, giggling as she dipped her toes.
"But isn't it refreshing?"
"You tell me." She spritzed lake water onto him with her bare foot.

The reminiscence of that day at the inn on the mountain pass rushed into Teo's mind as he contemplated the empty shoe. He and Ana had reclined side by side in the warm sun, laughing and rejoicing that her infected hip had finally healed.

But that day was a distant memory now. Ana was gone.

Forever and always, she was gone.

✦　✦　✦

The days that followed the discovery of the empty oubliette were as dark and dreadful as the hole itself. A cold rain settled onto Likuria, matching Teo's dreary mood. He had often feared for Ana's safety when she encountered mortal danger, yet in those cases he never doubted that by some daring action he could find her, rescue her, shield her, defend her. Now, with the awful realization that she was dead, Teo was forced to embark on a new journey—a journey not of finding, but of letting go. It was the hardest thing he had ever done in his life.

At first Teo defiantly refused to give up hope. He clung to it like a castaway sailor grasping a piece of flotsam during a storm at sea. For a week he lurked around the shoreline, staying out of sight with the hood of an old cloak pulled over his head. Most nights he slept on the beach. Once he dreamed Ana climbed out of the water like a mermaid in a seaman's tale. It was a glorious dream, and it soothed his pain—until, while still asleep, he became aware that he was dreaming and the illusion dissolved. Teo had awakened then, and only the bottle of cheap liquor on the sand beside him enabled him to find any rest.

After seven days Teo finally stopped denying what he knew to be true. He had heard no news in the taverns about the notorious female criminal being washed ashore, bedraggled but alive. No sailors were gossiping about a forlorn woman they had plucked from the sea. Could she have made it to safety on her own? Even a fit person would have found it difficult to swim from the base of the cliffs to the nearest beach, much less a person with severe injuries caused by falling against the rocks. The conclusion was unavoidable: Ana had plunged to her death in a watery grave.

As Teo's denial gave way to anger, he balled his fists and shook them at Deu, knowing it was wrong, yet unable to refrain. "What purpose could you have in taking her from me?" he screamed. "You're cruel! You're weak! I hate you!" Though Teo shouted and raged and spat out curses, the mute sky gave no response to his appalling blasphemies.

On the morning of the eighth day, the *Midnight Glider* appeared offshore. Teo dragged his stolen rowboat from under some torn fishing nets and miscellaneous debris. It didn't take him long to launch the boat and draw near the clipper ship.

"Cease rowing and show yourself!" The voice from the deck was stern and commanding. Teo saw a row of crossbowmen pointing their weapons at him. He raised his hands and held them up, palms outward.

"I seek passage," he called.

"We're taking no one aboard. Be off!"

"What about a passenger who's already paid?"

The question seemed to confuse the men on the ship. Some lowered their crossbows, and the speaker hesitated before replying, "Who are you then?"

"Tell your captain I'm his friend from the fight at the Rusty Anchor."

A man was sent, and soon Marco appeared at the rail. "Teofil? Is that you?"

Teo removed his hood and stood up in the boat. "So you thought you could sail away with my fare, eh, pirate?"

Marco laughed, his white teeth bright against his black goatee. "Throw him a rope," he said to one of his men.

In Marco's stateroom, Teo relaxed on a padded window seat with a glass of gin. Alcohol in its many forms had become his best friend of late.

"You look terrible," Marco said.

Teo shrugged.

"You want me to take you to Nuo Genov?"

"I suppose. A friend of mine is looking after my stuff there. My sword, my ax, my cloak. And some books," he added.

"You can get it all tomorrow."

Teo grunted, then knocked back his gin in a single swallow.

The city of Nuo Genov sparkled in all its marbled glory as the ship approached late the next day, but its beauty left a bitter taste in Teo's mouth. He went ashore with his hood pulled low, an alien sojourner in a land not his own. A series of winding alleys and staircases brought him up the city's flanks to its outskirts away from the seafront. After another quarter hour of walking, Teo reached the property of the widow whose cottage he had rented. He wondered how much Sol knew about all that had happened. The urgent circumstances of Ana's arrest had not allowed Teo to return to the cottage, but news of the king's death and the subsequent trial was on everyone's lips. Surely Sol had heard about it.

As Teo approached the cottage, he found himself disturbed by its unkempt appearance. Sol always liked to keep the porch swept and the bird feeders filled with seed, but now the place had the conspicuous look of an abandoned building. When Teo drew close and found Sol's basket lying overturned in the dirt, he rushed to the house and threw open the door.

"Sol? It's Teofil! Are you here?" The place was small. Teo realized right away it was empty and had been for many days. He ran back outside.

Teo's training as an army scout enabled him to read a story from tracks in the earth. Though this particular story was over two weeks old and obscured now, Teo could piece it together nonetheless. Sol had dropped his basket to flee an attack. He had broken several branches in his haste to escape into the underbrush. A scuffle had taken place, then men had departed on horses. The most logical conclusion was that the Exterminati had caught up with Sol. His body wasn't lying nearby, which meant he hadn't been murdered by thieves or attacked by wild animals. He had been carried away as a captive, and only the shamans were in the business of abduction.

Teo hung his head and pounded a fist against a tree. *First Ana . . . now Sol!* Both had looked to him for protection, and he had promised to provide it, yet failed. Teo felt utterly defeated. The Exterminati had won.

Despondent, he entered the cottage and plopped into a chair. Everything was still in its place, a sure sign the attackers weren't petty criminals. Teo reached over to his sword and slid it from its sheath. The blade glittered as it caught the evening sunlight. The sword was legendary in Chiveis, having belonged to Ana's grandfather, Armand. What would that heroic and noble warrior think of the man who now bore the weapon—a man so powerless he couldn't even protect two people entrusted to his care? Teo shoved the sword back into its scabbard in disgrace.

Deu, are you still there? My spirit is broken. I'm at the end of everything. What should I do? Teo didn't have an answer, and none was forthcoming, so he let himself fall into a restless doze.

The sound of an approaching horse woke him. Teo bolted from the chair and scooped up his sword in a single motion. Stepping lightly to the window, he peeked out. A woman in a long, elegant cloak dismounted and went to the front of the cottage. Though it wasn't raining or cold, she wore her hood over her head. Teo crossed to the door and heard a knock just as he reached for the handle. He opened the door.

A woman's beautiful face stared back at him. Her beauty wasn't glamorous, for she wore no makeup, and in fact her face was dirty. Yet the perfection of her classic features couldn't be missed even without adornment. She gazed at Teo with mournful eyes, her face framed by the emerald-green hood that draped along her cheeks. Slowly she put her hands to the hood and laid it back on her shoulders. Teo did a double take. The woman's head had been shaved close to her scalp, though it now sprouted a short blonde fuzz. In the same moment that Teo realized she was the stranger who had paid the bandits to help him, he also recognized who she was: Vanita Labella, the highborn daughter of an Ulmbartian duke.

"Hello, Vanita. I wasn't expecting you."

"The pirate who gave you passage said I'd find you here. Do you have a moment? There are some things I need to say."

Teo backed away from the door. "Sure. Come in." He shut the door behind Vanita and took her cloak, hanging it on a peg. When he turned around, he was surprised to see the woman kneeling in front of him.

"I must beg your forgiveness, Teofil." Vanita's head was bowed. "I have sinned against you, and I'm truly sorry."

"Vanita . . . I . . . um . . ." Teo broke off, not sure what to say.

She looked up at him. "I dismissed you. Scorned you. Tried to separate you from Anastasia. I thought you weren't good enough for her. Now I see it was I who lacked goodness."

Teo sighed. "Whatever you did doesn't matter anymore. Anastasia is gone, so in the end we're separated regardless."

As he stared at Vanita's face, Teo was startled to see tears well up. The sight of those tears made moisture gather in Teo's own eyes, but he scrunched his face in resistance to his emotions. Quickly he turned away with a fist pressed against his lips. "I forgive you, Vanita, if that's what you want," he said after he regained control of himself.

Vanita rose and approached Teo, laying her hand on his arm with a gentle touch. He faced her, unsure if she wanted to cry on his shoulder, or seduce him, or beg further absolution from him like a priest. Vanita did none of those things but simply asked a question. "What now, Teofil?"

He swore bitterly, staring at his feet. "I have no idea."

"I know what to do."

Teo raised his head. "What?"

"Honor Anastasia."

"What does that mean?"

"Since this great woman is lost, and you and I both realize her worth, we owe it to her memory to honor her."

"How?"

Vanita gripped Teo's sleeve and locked her eyes on his. "If anyone knows the answer to that, it's you."

Teo spun away, his thoughts suddenly clear for the first time in days. He gazed out the window at the distant ocean. *Of course you know what Ana would want! You sat across the table from her at Fisherman's Isle! You swore an oath to her, an oath to find the New Testament and bring salvation to the Chiveisi. Why are you moping around like a petulant little boy? Is this how Ana would act? Is your behavior worthy of the dignity and courage she displayed when she laid down her life? She did that because she understood Deu had called you to this task! Ana saw it and loved you for it. Honor her memory by fulfilling her heart's desire!*

Turning back to Vanita, Teo regarded the penitent woman with a mixture of anguish and hope—anguish because his grief was still raw and hope because he had finally found a way to overcome his grief with a noble task. He felt grateful to Vanita for her bold exhortation. She had snapped him out of his despondency and had given him an overriding purpose.

"You're right, Vanita," he said. "Thank you."

"What will you do?"

"Honoring Anastasia will take me to a city far away. The place is called Roma, and Deu's book can be found only there."

"Then pack up your things," Vanita answered, "because I'm going with you. This is the beginning of my new life as well as yours."

✦　　✦　　✦

Teo felt the *Midnight Glider* start to move as he lay in his hammock below deck. The sailors had been readying the vessel since before dawn. Now that the sun was up, the anchor had been weighed and the ship had hoisted some sail. The destination was the place Teo had heard so much about over the past few months: mysterious Roma, a city known only to the long-distance merchants and the pirates who preyed on them. Roma was the key to everything. There Teo hoped to meet the Papa, the leader of the Universal Communion, whose servants scoured the earth in search of the New Testament. Teo would help him find it. The lost book of Deu would tell the story of Iesus Christus, the Pierced One who died in his service to the Promised King.

Teo dreaded the departure. The finality of departing without Ana was a burden he could hardly endure. To leave these shores was to end a chapter of his life—the phase during which Ana had journeyed alongside him. With a heavy heart, Teo rose from his hammock and opened the footlocker he had been assigned. Among his belongings were the books he had placed in a leather satchel. The sight of the original copy of the Sacred Writing that he and Ana had recovered from the ancient temple stabbed Teo with grief, so he quickly set it aside. Flipping open the Prima, he began to thumb its pages, looking for a hymn that would speak to the emptiness he felt in his soul. He was too weak to rage against Deu anymore; now all he wanted was the comforting presence of the Eternal One.

Instead of a hymn, the divine pages fell open to the book of Jérémie. Reluctantly yet irresistibly, Teo found himself turning to the twenty-ninth chapter. Although he knew the words would pierce his heart, he let his eyes come to rest on his translation of verses 11–14: "'For I know the plans I have for you,' declares the Eternal One, 'plans for peace and not misfortune, in order to give you a future and a hope. You will invoke me and will go away. You will pray to me, and I will grant your request. You will seek me and find me if you seek me with all your heart. I will be found by you,' declares the Eternal One, 'and I will bring back your captives. I will gather you out of all the lands and all the places where I have driven you away,' declares the Eternal One, 'and I will bring you back to the place from which I have made you go into captivity.'"

Teo's mind reverted, as he knew it would, to the day he and Ana made the decision to cross the mountains and leave Chiveis behind. Ana had grieved the loss of her beloved home. In that difficult moment, Deu had led them to the passage in Jérémie 29. When Ana first heard the holy words, she claimed them as a special message from heaven. At the moment of her greatest trial, when the Eternal One asked her to relinquish her parents and her people and her land, Ana had trusted Deu's plans and obeyed him. "I can walk whatever path he lays before me," she had said. And then she did. Through the wilderness. Over the mountains. To Ulmbartia. To Likuria.

All the way to death.

Teo brooded on the word *death*. Such a quiet word—silent and dark and ominous, like a graveyard at midnight. Its quietness came from its resolute will. Once death made up its mind and imposed its permanent sentence, nothing could ever change it. Never in the history of the world had death's steadfast decree been defeated.

Tears came at last to Teo, and because they had been suppressed for so long they came in abundance. He had tried to deny the truth, or rage against it, but it was no use anymore. He finally admitted he had to release his hold on Ana. Sadness engulfed him, the deep sadness that only the bereaved can know. Teo's emotional reservoir had been filled beyond capacity by a sea of grief. Now the dam broke, and the waters came flooding out. Utterly overcome, he fell to his knees and wept in his cabin aboard the ship that would separate him from Ana forever.

O Deu! Why did this have to happen? Teo groaned as he ran to the porthole. The coastline of Likuria was already far away. "No! No! No!" he cried. Though he knew repeating the agonized word wouldn't change anything, he felt the urge to negate a catastrophe of such incredible magnitude. *This can't be happening! I wanted to take Ana with me to Roma! We were supposed to discover the book together! Then we would go home . . . her parents would embrace their only daughter . . . Chiveis would turn to Deu!*

This is all wrong!

I thought our lives were bound together!

Teo pounded the hull of the ship, gagging and choking as he wept. Bitter regret gnawed at him. He couldn't understand how things had gone so far astray.

"I miss you, Ana!" he cried to the strip of land receding in the ship's wake. "I miss you so much! I miss your face . . . your voice . . . your pure heart! I never told you how I really feel!" *O my God, it hurts!*

Teo's voice dissolved as sobs wracked his body. Through burning tears he stared across the water until the land disappeared.

"I'll always love you, Anastasia of Edgeton," he whispered.

Always!

PART THREE

VICTORY

CHAPTER

11

On the little island of Hahnerat the pale man slipped his sailboat into the water under the light of a gibbous moon. It was better to travel by night, Drake believed. The sun was hot during the day, beating down on his fair skin. Recently he had developed lesions on his face and arms, which he attributed to the harsh sunlight. Some of the lesions bled from time to time. They fascinated him. He picked at the scabs often.

Drake made the forty-league trip to his destination in about five hours. During the quiet moonlit journey a dark anticipation began to take hold of him. It had been too long since he had enjoyed any companionship on the lonely island. Gazing at the cliffs that rose from the sea, Drake felt saliva gather in his mouth. Soon he would have the secret pleasure of another companion, the kind he liked best.

Dead.

There's something about a corpse, Drake mused, his heartbeat quickening. *So peaceful and compliant . . .*

A few years ago his strange fetish had found a convenient outlet. The court officials in Manacho wanted to hire a non-citizen for a dirty job: emptying the oubliette of its grisly remains. Word was slipped to a pirate vessel, but no man was willing to take such an accursed assignment. However, the sailors knew the right person to ask. The next time they visited the remote island of Hahnerat for resupply, they informed Drake of the "opportunity."

THE GIFT

Drake made a meager living by managing supplies for the pirates who plied the Likurian sea. He kept accurate records of what items had been left by various ships: extra rigging, nonperishable foodstuffs, kegs to be filled with fresh water, miscellaneous odds and ends. In exchange for his careful stewardship, Drake was allowed a little food on which to sustain himself. It was a good arrangement, one that suited his reclusive personality in all ways except one: he had to leave the island to satisfy his twisted hunger. Graveyards were too often guarded by dogs, but the opportunity mentioned by the pirates had provided a perfect solution. The people of Manacho were fond of their regular executions. They didn't know, or care, what happened afterward to the bodies in the oubliette.

Pirate gossip had brought news of a recent capital offense, so once again Drake approached the oubliette with the rigging system he had invented. He maneuvered the sailboat as close to the cliffs as he dared, then dropped his heavy anchor and made certain its hold was secure. As the sun breasted the eastern horizon he slid into the water and began to swim. A line attached to his waist trailed back to a winch on the boat. He carried a fisherman's net in a compact bundle on his back. A pulley dangled from his belt.

Reaching the base of the cliff, Drake slipped from the sea and worked his way up the climbing rope. It was secured to one of several pitons he had hammered into the rock face above. When he arrived at the entrance to the shaft, Drake attached the fisherman's net to pitons so the webbing loosely covered the opening, then clipped the pulley above it. A line ran over the pulley, connecting the net to the winch on the boat. With his rigging in place, Drake began to ascend the clean-out tunnel.

When the shaft became vertical he reached into a cubbyhole and removed a candle lantern and matchbox. Soon the lantern's yellow flame illuminated the space beneath the floor of the oubliette. The body of Anastasia of Chiveis, the woman executed for regicide, would be on the other side. *It won't be long now*, Drake thought as he crawled into an alcove. *Soon you'll have her. Until then, focus on the task at hand.*

Squatting as he reached for the trapdoor above him, Drake noticed something strange: the iron beam that supported the door was missing. Instead the trapdoor was held shut by a piece of wood wedged into the jamb. Drake worked it back and forth until it was loose, then yanked it out. The door dropped open with a bang, and the woman's corpse tumbled down the incline along with a length of rope. But as the woman flew past, an unexpected sound nearly knocked Drake from his perch.

The woman uttered a delirious cry!

The wheels of Drake's mind began to spin. In the past the criminals had always died by the time he retrieved their bodies. But this time Anastasia's execution must have been delayed for some reason. The woman had apparently been dropped into the shaft only recently—a matter of hours, not days—and so she was still alive.

Interesting . . .

As he considered the matter, Drake decided it would be fun to toy with his new companion for a few days while life remained in her. The feral cats on Hahnerat often enjoyed a little sport before devouring the mice they captured. It would be no different with Anastasia of Chiveis. She would provide some entertainment until he was ready for his deviant enjoyment. Chuckling, Drake blew out the lantern and began to ease down the shaft by the notches he had carved.

At the shaft's entrance the woman lay tangled in the net, moaning and disoriented. When Drake released the net from the pitons, it closed around his victim like a drawstring bag. The line went taut as she dangled from the pulley. One leg extended awkwardly from the net, and her shoe dropped from her foot into the ocean. Drake descended the climbing rope and swam to the winch on his boat. He lowered the woman until she lay in a heap on a boulder protruding from the water. Occasional movements within the net signaled she was alive.

Drake scaled the cliff again and removed his pulley. Returning to his boat, he dragged in the net and hauled the woman over the gunwale. Her brief immersion in the ocean seemed to have revived her, for she sputtered and gasped on the planks, though her words were incoherent. Drake opened the net to take a good look at her. Her hair was ragged in the back, and her sackcloth tunic was threadbare. She wore only one shoe. Manacles bound her wrists, and a cross-shaped amulet hung around her neck. Drake snatched the necklace from her. Opening a flask, he poured water down the woman's throat. She gulped it, then gagged and coughed.

"Do you believe you are alive, Anastasia of Chiveis?"

The woman held her forehead, trying to shake free of her delirium. "Who . . . what . . ."

"You may be out of the hole, but you are still dead," Drake taunted. "In a few days you will lie still. Then you'll be mine."

The woman's eyelids fluttered, and she took a deep breath. She seemed to become more aware of her surroundings, though she was still confused. Drake rose from his seat at the rudder and retrieved a stone jar of gruel. A wooden spoon protruded from it. Drake hawked a wad of mucus, letting it dangle from his lips before it dropped into the pale, lumpy porridge. He mixed it in, then turned to Ana. "Perhaps you are hungry?" She nodded weakly, and he handed her the jar. Drake snickered as she wolfed it down.

To the east, the sun had already climbed well above the horizon. Drake hoisted his sail and took a southwest heading. Soon he would be home with Anastasia, his new companion. He shivered at the pleasing thought of what the days to come would hold.

✦　✦　✦

The lash of the whip was like the sun overhead: merciless and unrelenting. The foreman brought it down for no apparent reason on the shoulders of the men who toiled to move a load of marble blocks down a rough track. It was dangerous work even without the threat of the whip. One misstep could make the sledge lurch, toppling its load of massive stones. The sledge was attached to hemp ropes that ran uphill around a pylon, then down to the strong arms of the "releasers." As the men played out the line, the sledge skidded on top of slick wooden beams. Workers grabbed the beams from the rear of the sledge and brought them around front to be used again. It was a fine-tuned dance requiring perfect coordination. Unfortunately, the men performing the labor weren't coordinated, so they perished in droves. A constant supply of new Defectives was needed to keep the quarry running.

Sol wiped his forehead. Though nights in these mountains were cold, the glare of the sun made transporting the blocks hot, sweaty work. From dawn until dusk the team lowered sledges from the high marble quarry.

Once in the valley, the stone would be transported to the sea a few leagues away. Eventually the material would adorn the beautiful palaces and temples of Likuria. No one there knew what a steep cost in human life had been paid to extract it—and if they had known, they wouldn't have cared.

The labor continued until the sun went down and no more work could be done. Sol followed the men back to their hovels, having eaten only a little bread and some raw vegetables at midday. His evening meal of thin soup wasn't enough to satisfy his hunger, nor to replenish the energy he had expended on manual labor. Many of the Defectives succumbed quickly to malnutrition in the quarries.

After eating his meager portion of soup from a clay bowl, Sol grabbed his dirty blanket and collapsed on the floor of his hovel. He lay on his side, for his back still hurt from the hot irons that had been applied to his skin. He was ashamed to recall how quickly he had cracked under torture. Though he had been defiant at first, the agony of those red-hot brands was more than he could bear. He admitted his association with Teofil and Anastasia, divulging their belief in the true God. Yet Sol prided himself on one thing: he had managed not to inform the shamans about the precious copies of the Old Testament. By breaking early and offering what seemed to be an ample confession, Sol had tricked the inquisitors into thinking they'd learned everything there was to know from him. It was a small victory, but one he cherished.

As night fell and a chill descended, Sol found himself exhausted yet sleepless. The moon was covered by clouds, and the room was dark. A crowd of Defectives wheezed and snored around him. No one had a mattress, though some had woolen blankets. Others lay shivering and exposed each night, their coverings having been confiscated by the foremen as punishment for some supposed offense. One of those unfortunates lay next to Sol now, a blond-haired fellow who worked as a "releaser." He was new to the team. Even in the gloom, Sol could see his eyes were open.

"What's the matter?" Sol whispered. "Can't sleep in such luxury?"

The man chuckled under his breath. "I've slept in better places, and sometimes in worse."

"Worse than this?"

"I was a frontier scout back in Ulmbartia. A few of the nights I spent in the wilderness make this shack seem comfortable by comparison. At least I have four walls around me and no ice in my beard."

"What are you here for? I don't see any defects on you."

The young man remained quiet for a long moment before answering. "They say my inclinations are . . . queer." He paused again. "What about you?"

"My religion is illegal. So I guess we're both 'defective' in a manner other than physical."

"And for that we're sentenced to death."

"We're not dead yet, friend."

The blond man sat up on his elbow. "We're as good as dead," he declared flatly. "What hope is left? They'll work us to death eventually. The only question is how long we'll last in this rotten hell."

"We may die here," Sol admitted, "or we may find deliverance. It's hard to say what will occur."

"What makes you think there's any hope of deliverance? The shamans are in charge of everything. They have absolute power."

Sol grimaced as he worked himself into a seated position. "The shamans don't have absolute power, just the ability to make it seem so. There is only one whose power is absolute."

"And who is that?"

"The God who created this world. His name is Deus, and he's a savior of the oppressed."

The man scoffed. "If he's a savior, he's been absent lately. From where I'm sitting all I see is slavery and abuse."

"Men can be very cruel to each other, no question. The strong prey on the weak. Yet the people of Deus resist this. Often it seems pointless and unproductive—until all of a sudden . . ."

Sol hesitated as a foreman strolled past the hovel outside. They were always lurking around, even at night.

"All of a sudden what?" the blond man whispered when the foreman had moved on.

"People start to *believe*," Sol finished. "Faith catches, and spreads, and people are set free."

The man sat up, then tucked his elbows against his sides and breathed into his cupped hands to warm them. "I think you may possess wisdom, old man. What's your name?"

"I'm Sol."

"My name is Bard." The two men clasped hands. Bard leaned forward and spoke quietly. "So where did you hear about this god?"

"I had a book once, before the shamans got me. No telling where it is now." Sol smiled. "Would you like to hear a story from it?" When Bard nodded, Sol began to recount a narrative from the book of Departure. He described how the people of Deus, the Israëlites, were oppressed by their overlords until a shepherd named Moses was appointed to deliver them. Though Moses was often fearful, he obeyed Deus and acted on his commands. Deus sent a series of plagues upon the evildoers, culminating with the slaying of their firstborn sons. At this fearsome punishment the wicked king let the enslaved people go, and they departed for the wilderness. Then the king had second thoughts. He pursued the people, but Deus led his children through a sea as if on dry land. When the king and his army followed, the waters closed upon the oppressors and destroyed them forever.

As Sol concluded the story, Bard exhaled with his eyes wide. "Do you think Deus would do the same for us? I mean, would he lead us out of here with miracles like that?"

Sol shook his head. "He doesn't promise such things. Yet he is that kind of God. He has the power to deliver his followers—in his own time and way."

"What can I do to call down this power?" Bard asked. "There has to be something! What if I smeared blood on the doors like those people did?"

"Deus isn't manipulated by magic charms. You must wait and believe."

Bard swore under his breath. "I don't have anything to believe in anymore."

"My friend, believe you were created by Deus for a purpose. Believe he loves you, just as he loves the Defectives around us. Deus made them in his own image. For most of my life I didn't understand that truth. But here at the end of all things, I have finally learned to see anew. The Defectives are precious to the true God."

"That's a radical idea, Sol. No one believes the Defectives are good for anything but slave labor. They've never heard anyone say what you just said."

"What would happen if they did?"

"Huh?"

"What would happen if the Defectives thought they *mattered* to the Eternal One?"

Bard laughed. "Then you'd have one angry workforce on your hands! It's despair that keeps them obedient. They believe they're worthless. There's no telling what would happen if they had hope."

"That is what the Exterminati fear most. More than swords and armies and mighty men, they fear the truth."

Footsteps approached again, pausing on the other side of the thin wall. Sol and Bard held their breath until the listener moved away.

"We'd better get some sleep," Sol said as he stretched out. "Come over here and lie close to me. I will share my blanket with you."

Bard balked. "Do you know what I meant when I told you the reason I'm here?"

"Yes, but I don't mind."

"You . . . you would sleep next to *me*?"

Sol threw his tattered blanket over the body of his new friend. "*Si dormierint duo fovebuntur mutuo*," he quoted. "*Unus quomodo calefiet?*"

Bard reclined beside Sol. "What does that mean?"

"It's from the fourth chapter of the book of Ecclesiastes. Surely it is a piece of wisdom that applies to us right now. But come, let us speak of these things no more. The dawn will be upon us soon, and with it will come much toil."

◆　◆　◆

Instead of getting weaker, Anastasia grew strong again.

Drake, of course, did his best to make her life miserable. The pale man with the bleeding lesions was a mocker whose words were spoken with a forked tongue. He treated Ana cruelly, cuffing her with a stick whenever he was displeased. The food he supplied was inadequate. Drake even chained Ana's ankle to a large stone ball. Though it was an encumbrance, she could move around with it better than he knew, for he had underestimated her strength. When Drake was nearby, Ana pretended the stone was heavier than it actually was. He laughed at her efforts and derided her, often tripping her from behind.

Despite the cruel treatment, Ana started to regain her former vigor. More than a week had passed since Drake brought her to the island, and during that time she slept often because there was nothing else to do. She also had plenty to drink. Drake had found groundwater on the island and dug a well, making Hahnerat a valuable supply station for the pirates. The cold, clear water replenished Ana's parched tissues.

Exploring her surroundings, Ana had discovered the oblong island was covered with a pine forest except along the rocky coast. Grapevines and lavender grew in abundance. To the north lay another island, and beyond it Ana could see the mainland shore. Several times she had waded into the sea to test whether escape was possible by swimming. Although the second island seemed tantalizingly close, once she was in the water Ana realized she couldn't swim with the stone attached to her leg. Unlike the wrist manacles whose pins she had tapped out, the padlock on her ankle required a key. Even if she could somehow remove the ball and reach the other island, the mainland looked much farther away. Since Drake kept his boat secured with a thick chain, Ana knew she was trapped on Hahnerat. She had escaped from the oubliette and was grateful for it, but now a new kind of prison entombed her.

Ana had found a few ruined buildings on the island. The most extensive of them was a large complex that Drake described as a monastery of the Ancients. Though it was dilapidated and overgrown, it had obviously been elegant in its day, with several porticoed courtyards and gardens. Drake lived in a little room whose roof he had repaired, but Ana chose to sleep in the monastery's central temple, a spacious hall with stone columns and arches. The architecture suggested it may have belonged to Deu, and that gave her comfort. Near the monastery stood a massive fortress on a peninsula that jutted into the sea. The fortress was square-built and imposing, though now it was just a shell.

As the sun began to set, Ana grew troubled. Nighttime on Hahnerat depressed her. She was forced to come to Drake's firepit for food, and he always drove a stake through her chain so she couldn't leave. Then he would mock her all evening and taunt her with clever words. Only after he had satisfied his need to dominate would he release her to sleep. Though Drake was cruel, Ana was relieved that he displayed no sexual interest in her. She knew he had lusts of a strange sort, yet for now she was glad not to suffer the particular form of abuse so often directed at women.

Ana trudged to the temple of Deu and lay down in her makeshift bed. She had piled palm branches beneath the altar in the apse, then covered them with sheepskin. The glass in the high windows had long since disappeared, and a portion of the ceiling had caved in. Through the opening the moon shone luminous white, shrouded by a halo of clouds. Eventually the night sounds lulled Ana to sleep.

The hour was late when a sudden awareness of evil yanked Ana from her troubled dreams into a living nightmare. She lifted her head and glanced around. Her pounding heartbeat seemed audible in the awful hush. Movement caught her eye. She looked up and gasped. Shadows whose blackness was deeper than the night were filtering through the open windows. At the far end of the hall another shadow billowed through the door, its aura cold and nocturnal and malignant. The shadows could only be seen by the way they blotted out all light. The deadly fog began to fill the room.

"Go away!" Ana screamed. "You aren't allowed in here!"

Despite her threats, the shadows crept closer. Tendrils began to reach toward her. One touched her ankle, its chill palpable. She shook her leg, rattling her chain, and the tendril dissipated. But more came on.

"Deu is the Lord! Get back!"

At those words the shadows retreated a bit. Ana stood up, holding her encumbering stone with two hands. The fog began to creep toward her again. Walking steadily toward the door, Ana chanted a verse from Deu's twenty-third Hymn: "When I walk in the valley of death's shadow, I won't fear any evil, because you are with me." The third time she recited it, the darkness parted, and Ana reached the door.

Then a wicked voice struck fear in her heart.

"We killed your parents," the voice hissed. "We will kill you too."

No! Ana's concentration broke, and she lost track of the verse she was chanting. The dark clouds closed in. She looked back, terrified by what she saw. The shadows had assumed the form of a large, bat-winged monster. Two red eyes gleamed in its head. It uttered a moist, guttural, rasping sound, like the death rattle of a consumption patient. As the spirit began to swoop toward her, Ana fled into the night.

Running as fast as she could with the stone in her arms, Ana left the monastery and took a narrow path through the forest. She didn't have any destination in mind but only wanted to escape the shadows flitting about. Branches clawed at her bare legs. Dread weighed upon her. It seemed entirely plausible that the shadows had killed her father and mother. Though Ana had come to terms with the idea of never seeing her parents again, her escape from the oubliette had reawakened her hope that she might someday be reunited with them. *Are they really dead?* The demon's words had touched one of her deepest fears—a fear she had never acknowledged even to herself.

As Ana rushed headlong through the forest, the chain around her ankle caught on a root, and she fell. Crying out, she turned to face the evil spirit that loomed over her. Dawn was approaching, and Ana could see the demonic shape outlined against the blue-black sky. The morning star gleamed directly above its head.

"Back!" she cried, raising her palm. "You get back, in the holy name of Deu!"

The shadow chanted at her, "No escape! No return! No escape! No return!" The prophetic words sucked the life from Ana. She knew the spirit was right. There would be no return to Chiveis. The demon spoke the truth. It possessed all knowledge. It had all authority. It could make anything happen.

Ana's head spun as coldness engulfed her.

"Leave her alone!"

The speaker's pronunciation was thick and dull, yet the words contained power. The voice was too deep to be Drake's. Ana turned her head from her position on the ground. A bulky figure emerged from the gloom, waving a torch. The black demon dissolved into the forest as the man approached.

The unknown man knelt beside Ana, staring into her face. He was thick-lipped and brutish in appearance, yet she did not sense violence in him. She was not afraid.

"Bad shadow," he said slowly. "Very bad." The man's words were spoken with the deliberate effort of one whose mind is weak. Cautiously he stretched out his hand and laid it on Ana's shoulder. She smiled. The man's bearded face brightened. He hurried off, then returned with a basket. Removing a loaf of bread and an earthenware jug, he placed them on the ground.

"For me?" Ana pointed to herself. The man nodded his large, bald head.

Ana pulled the stopper from the jug and put it to her lips. The wine wasn't an excellent vintage, but it was certainly drinkable. She tipped back her head and guzzled a long draft with her eyes closed. When her thirst was quenched she set down the jug and wiped her mouth, then looked around.

The man from the forest was gone.

✦   ✦   ✦

On a quiet balcony, a middle-aged man and woman stood side by side. Though they were husband and wife, they no longer knew if they were father and mother. The eastern horizon was beginning to lighten, and a breeze hurled ragged clouds across the predawn sky.

"Maybe today," Stratetix said. His voice was thick with emotion. Helena d'Armand slipped her hand into her husband's.

"Yes, my love. Maybe today."

"Let it be so, Deu," Stratetix whispered. Helena nodded as she bowed her head.

After a long silence, Stratetix continued. "Remember the first time she came back? We weren't expecting it, and then suddenly—there she was! I often imagine it will happen like that again." His words were hopeful, yet Helena knew the hope was tempered by a heavy dose of realism. It had been ten months since Anastasia's exile.

"That was a joyous day," Helena agreed, "a day of celebration and delight."

Stratetix chuckled. "I remember how Ana came out on this balcony in the middle of the night. She talked with Teofil out here. I wasn't exactly sure what was going on between those two."

Helena smiled as she squeezed her husband's hand. "I know. You almost got out of bed to spy on them!"

Stratetix glanced at Helena, amused. "A father is supposed to worry about such things," he said.

"Teofil is a good man. You don't have to worry."

At those words a shroud of gloom descended on the husband and wife as they realized they had every reason to worry. Their only daughter had gone with Teofil to a remote hut on a frigid glacier. She hadn't been seen since. Ana's flight was her only option, other than to deny her faith in Deu. Stratetix and Helena admired their daughter's courage, yet it came at a great price. They had endured a gut-wrenching sacrifice when she left Chiveis.

The turbulent clouds continued to swirl in the sky, though most of the stars had faded now. Only one remained, cold and bright. Stratetix felt despair well up. "She isn't coming back, is she? It's futile to hope."

Helena turned to Stratetix and encircled his waist with her arms. "It's never futile to hope. Though we can't know the future, we know Deu holds all things in his hands." She paused, resting her head on Stratetix's shoulder. "Shall we pray?"

Stratetix stifled a sob with a fist over his mouth. "You do it," he said. "I—I can't."

Helena's prayer ascended to heaven from the wooden balcony of the little chalet in Edgeton. She prayed for her daughter's protection from evil, for her faith to be strong, and for her eventual return to the land of Chiveis. She also prayed for Teofil to be a courageous and noble protector. Finally she prayed for her husband and for herself—that they would not give up hope in Deu, the All-Creator, the Eternal One.

When the prayer was finished, Helena looked at her husband. His expression was grave as he stared into the distance. Thick clouds had settled in, covering the morning sky. It would be an overcast day.

"Maybe today," Stratetix said again.

†HE GİF†

Helena took his hand. "Watch and wait, my love."

❖   ❖   ❖

Drake had grown tired of his plaything. The little mouse was starting to rebel against the cat, and it scared him. Mice were supposed to be fragile creatures, easy to dominate. That was what Drake wanted most in his companions: absolute surrender. Their acquiescence made him feel alive and potent and virile. But Anastasia of Chiveis was threatening. Drake decided he would have to do something about her very soon. She must be made docile and submissive. Death was the only way to achieve it.

The woman had run off during the night, but Drake had found her on the west end of the island near the hut where the reclusive simpleton lived. Although Liber was a feeble-minded behemoth who constantly muttered gibberish, he excelled at two things: wood carving and honey making. Somewhere along the way Liber had been taught the beekeeper's craft. Drake was glad for this because the pirates would pay good money for a sweet treat. As for Liber's wood-carving ability, that was no learned craft but an astounding inborn gift. It was difficult to believe an imbecile like Liber could carve so skillfully and in such exquisite detail. The pirates who stopped at Hahnerat—always a superstitious lot—coveted the figurines and pendants he fashioned from olivewood. Drake gave Liber a little food and drink in exchange for his honey and carvings, then resold them to the pirates at a profit. The idiot was an excellent source of income. Beyond that, Drake left him alone.

Anastasia snapped Drake out of his thoughts. "The porridge is ready," she said. "Bring your bowl over here."

After the woman spooned hot gruel into his bowl, Drake took the pot from her and sat under a eucalyptus tree near the craggy beach. When he had eaten two large helpings, he licked his spoon clean and handed it to her with the pot. "You can have what's left," he said. Ana used a piece of bark to scrape the bottom of the pot, eating the last of the porridge while leaving the spoon untouched.

"Look at you, gobbling that slop like a beggar woman," Drake said.

"Your clothes are so ragged they barely cover you. Your hair is filthy, and so are your feet. What a mess! You disgust me." He turned his head away.

"My appearance isn't what matters," Ana replied. "My soul remains clean, and you can't touch that, Drake."

"Oh yes I can." Drake turned back to the woman, staring at her. He pointed a long, pale finger in her direction. "I can drag you down to horror and despair! Your soul belongs to me now. You're all alone, Anastasia—totally and completely *alone*. Do you imagine you can get off this island? Ha! Think again. I'll play with you for a little while longer, and then—" Drake lifted his stout club. "Then I'll knock you down and do as I wish."

His sneer caused apprehension to flicker in the woman's eyes, though she quickly overcame it. "My life doesn't belong to you," she said. "It belongs to my God." The confident assertion infuriated Drake. He leaped to his feet.

"Your God is a worthless piece of garbage! He claims to be loving and good, but where is he now? Is he watching over you? No! You're a repugnant old biddy, haggard beyond your years. I'll never unlock your chains, and you can't fight me. I'm far too strong for you. Soon you'll be dead, and there's nothing you can do about it. You know that in your heart!"

Rage had taken hold of Drake now. Spittle flew from his mouth as he spoke. From around his neck he removed a thong on which a key dangled. He held it up. "Look here! This is the only key to that lock on your leg. What do you think of *this*?" Drake dropped the key onto a rock and began to smash it with the butt of his club. Again and again he pounded the key until it was dented and misshapen. A wild feeling of exultation overcame him. "What do you say to that, Anastasia? Huh? What do you say? Did your big strong God stop me? Did he? Huh? Did he?" Drake felt breathless and jittery, yet strangely jubilant.

Ana didn't answer.

She despises me as a fool.

The realization gnawed at Drake's gut. He wanted to scream but forced himself to regain control. Touching his tongue to his lips, he spoke more calmly. "Let me ask you something—how do you know your God is good?"

"It is written many times in the Hymns and other places in the Sacred Writing."

271

"Maybe those writings were made up long ago by foolish men."

"If the Sacred Writing were foolish, why would so many people have treasured it over the years? And what other book has been preserved through the centuries like this one? Even after the Great War of Destruction, it has been found again."

"There are many old books in the world."

"Maybe. But they don't ring out with truth like this one. The Ancients revered Deu, and I understand why. Even the little I've read about him tells me he's worthy of devotion."

"Curse you, woman, open your eyes! He's a cruel and vindictive deity who withholds good things from his creatures. He delights in destroying their dreams. Why don't you wake up and recognize the truth? Deu is repugnant!"

"You're wrong, Drake." Ana gained a fierceness of her own now. "Your blasphemies won't shake my faith. The Sacred Writing describes Deu's goodness, and I've experienced it in my life. I know it's true. I'm a follower of Deu. I won't depart from him no matter what you say."

Drake narrowed his eyes. "Then you will follow Deu to your destruction, Anastasia of Chiveis."

"My God will protect me. And even if Deu wills that I should die, he will gather me to himself."

"No. He will abandon your soul to the pit, just as he has already abandoned your body. Look around! The evidence proves it. You will perish on this island, forgotten and alone. Your corpse will lie unburied on these shores. You will be ravaged by me until you decay and the seabirds pick the rotten flesh from your bones. Your life is meaningless! You're a speck of dust blown away by the wind." Drake glared at his opponent. "Face it, Anastasia! You are insignificant. No one cares for you—no one at all."

"Deu cares for me. That is the truth. I won't be deterred from it."

"He will do nothing for you. He will let you rot. He is powerless to stop it."

"You're full of lies, you snake! Deu is strong."

"No," Drake belted out. "He's weak. Weak, I tell you!"

"He is the All-Creator. No one is higher than him. He will have the victory."

"What do you make of this then?" Drake reached into a pocket of his leather vest and withdrew the pendant he had removed from Ana's neck. "Look! The symbol of your God is defeat. What other conclusion can there be?"

Drake could see that his words made an impact on the woman. She was uncertain about the meaning of the crucified man, and for once she didn't have a reply. Realizing he had gained the upper hand, Drake decided it was time to act.

He approached Anastasia with his club in his fist. Power coursed through his veins—a strong, vibrant power that boiled inside him and brought a smile to his lips. "Tell me," he asked, "if Deu is so strong, why are you about to die? Is he here with you now? Can he stop me? What do you think? Can he?" Drake brandished his club as he walked forward.

"Get away from me! I reject you and everything you stand for!"

The woman pointed at Drake in an authoritative way that he found unnerving. Somehow her demeanor was far more confident than it should have been. "My God has spoken to me," she declared. "Deu has plans for me. He has promised to bring me back from captivity. So get away from me, or be ready to face the judgment of an angry God!"

"No one shall judge me," Drake snarled. "I am my own god!"

He rushed at Ana, but instead of running away she faced him with her back to the sea. He hadn't expected that. It brought him up short. Ana's voice rang out in the stillness. "'The Eternal One is my light and my salvation. Whom shall I fear? The Eternal One is the support of my life. Whom shall I dread? When wicked men advance against me to devour my flesh, my persecutors and enemies will totter and fall.'"

"Fear me!" Drake demanded, trying to stare her down. She didn't wilt. The woman's serenity enraged him. Drake lifted his club above his head. His arms were long and lean and muscular. The weapon in his hand was thick, and the woman standing before him was defenseless. The feel of the club smashing her soft flesh would be a delight. He would bludgeon her into the state of submission he so desperately craved. His arm began to sweep down.

What happened next reduced Drake to speechlessness. Just as he was about to put Anastasia to death, she slapped him across the face like an old cur dog. A loud smack rang out as her open palm made contact with his jaw. Drake's head was swatted to the side, and a dollop of drool flew from his lips. His cheek stung as if a hot iron had been laid against it. His ears rang, and his head spun.

How dare she!

Confusion boiled up in Drake's dark soul. An empowering presence was within Anastasia, a force he did not understand. He faltered and low-ered his club, stunned that this helpless woman would have the audacity to slap a strong man.

She isn't afraid of me!

It was incomprehensible yet true. The fact disturbed Drake to the core of his being. He backed off and glanced away.

Something in the ocean caught his eye. A sail had come into view. *Pirates!* They were approaching rapidly and would soon come ashore to demand an exact accounting of their stores. Rough men, all of them. Cruel and lascivious. The kind of men who could break a woman's spirit. Shatter it, in fact.

Drake shoved Anastasia to the ground and pounded a stake through her leg chain with his club. "Those men will teach you some respect!" he spat, then hurried to meet the visitors.

◆　◆　◆

Ana watched Drake light two torches and wave them back and forth on the beach. At this signal the pirates lowered rowboats and began to come ashore. They were swarthy men with thick beards and high boots. Evidently their recent plundering had been successful, for their clothing and adornments were finer than what the average sailor could expect to own. Ana reached for the iron stake that had been driven through her chain, trying to work it loose with her fingers. She knew she needed to get out of sight—fast.

The captain of the pirates greeted Drake with a gruff hello. Another man stood next to the captain with a ledger book in his hand. He con-ferred with Drake about the book, then everyone scurried toward the ruined monastery. A clump of boulders and some scrubby bushes stood between Ana and the men. She hunched behind them as she examined the stake. It was driven deep into the earth and resisted removal.

A crew of burly pirates filed out of the monastery carrying sacks and barrels like ants stealing crumbs at a picnic. After loading the supplies into the boats, Drake opened a crate and began to haggle with the men on the beach. He held up jars of golden honey and bartered vigorously. The pirates also inspected small objects and draped pendants around their necks. Drake exchanged some coins with the men.

Ana looked down at the stake with rising anxiety. She tried to push it back and forth to loosen the hole. The stake hardly budged. Normally Drake had to pry it out. She glanced up at the pirates. What she saw made her heart leap into her throat.

Drake was pointing at her, and all the men were staring in her direction. The captain began to march over. Ana did not like the smirk on his face. She had seen that look many times in the eyes of men, and it always meant one thing. She furiously wiggled the stake as the pirates drew near. In the distance thunder rumbled. A cloudburst was moving in.

"Stand up, wench," the captain ordered.

When Ana did not comply, Drake hauled her up by the elbow. Ana felt self-conscious before all the lecherous stares. Her ragged sackcloth garment barely fell below her hips, and much of her body could be seen through the holes. She gathered the rough fabric at her neckline, crossing her forearms in front of herself.

"You see?" Drake said. "I told you she was pretty."

"She's filthy," the captain countered. "Eight scudi."

Drake frowned. "Give her a bath if you need to. I'm sure you could find a man to do it." Coarse jesting erupted from the onlookers. "The rental fee is nine scudi, no less," Drake insisted. "Use her up and bring me whatever is left when you return."

The captain stepped closer to Drake. "What if I decide to take her without paying?"

Though the captain's tone was aggressive, Drake did not back down. He slipped a dank lock of hair from his forehead with a bony finger. "I think you know what would happen. Play dirty with me, Captain, and every pirate in these seas will be after you. The only way my outpost works is if everyone follows the rules. If you break the code, word will get around. You'll be everyone's enemy."

Turning away from Drake, the captain let his eyes rove over Ana's figure. He addressed his men while gesturing toward her. "What do you think, boys? Nine scudi for a few weeks of fun! Is it worth it?"

The rousing cheer was the only answer he needed. Ana's heart began to race. The captain shook Drake's hand, then ordered his men back to the ship with oaths and exhortations about their urgent itinerary. As the sailors moved away, Drake lingered behind, picking at a lesion on his forearm. "You'll have no fight left in you by the time they bring you back," he whispered in Ana's ear. She pushed him aside. Drake laughed as he went to the beach to settle the accounts.

Ana knelt beside the stake and clawed the soil around it. Finally it began to come free. Pulling her leg chain as hard as she could, she managed to slide the stake from the earth. She stood up, terrified, and glanced around. *Now what? Where to?*

Her eyes fell on the ruined fortress on the peninsula. It was the most defensible place anywhere nearby. Ana snatched her encumbering stone and began to lumber down the gravel lane toward the castle, its white ramparts stark against the gray squall advancing over the sea. Though the stone ball was heavy, strength flowed through Ana's body in her moment of need. She had fled halfway to the fortress when she heard shouting behind her.

"Where did she go?"

"There she is! Over there!"

"I see her! Wait here and I'll get her!"

Ana turned to see Drake racing toward her. "Help me, Deu!" she cried as she began to sprint toward the castle, clutching her stone to her chest.

The interior of the castle was made of rough, eroded stone. Ana entered an enclosed yard. The sky began to spit rain. She scurried across the courtyard and reached a door. As she paused to catch her breath, Drake arrived at the entrance, spotting her immediately. The look on his face was pure evil. Ana gasped and ducked into the doorway.

She found herself in a room with a vaulted ceiling. In the center of the room, a waist-high wall formed a rectangle around a small round well in the floor. Openings in the wall gave access to the well, which was surrounded by flagstones and covered by an iron grate. The area above the rectangle was open to the sky, giving the room the feel of an atrium. Ponderous raindrops had begun to speckle the floor beneath the skylight. Ana was beside the wall when a voice stopped her in her tracks.

"What did I tell you, woman? You belong to me!"

Drake's venomous words made Ana recoil. She backed around the corner of the wall, keeping an eye on her enemy as he stalked her. He stood at one end of the rectangle and she at the other. Every time he moved one direction, she moved the opposite way. The game of cat and mouse continued as they circled back and forth around the wall. The rain began to fall harder.

"You can't keep this up all day," Drake growled through gritted teeth. He was obviously frustrated, but Ana knew he was right. The stone in her arms was burdensome. Eventually she would tire, and he would grab her. Then the game would be over.

As Ana moved along the rectangle's long side, Drake unexpectedly darted through one of the openings in the wall. He flashed across the middle, but his foot slipped on the slick flagstones, and he fell on his face. Without stopping he lunged at Ana. She shrieked as she felt her enemy's hand close around her ankle. Though she tried to break free, Drake held her fast. Blood streamed from his nose, reddening his gnashing teeth. He yanked her bare foot to his mouth and bit down hard. Agony exploded up Ana's leg as her enemy's teeth dug into her flesh. She let out a piercing cry.

Drake released his bite and looked up at Ana from the floor. He met her eyes with a malicious grin, enjoying the pain he had caused her. At that moment a lightning bolt flashed outside, and a tremendous thunderclap shook the ancient fortress to its foundations.

Ana grasped her heavy stone in two hands, staring down at Drake. His expression changed. A look of horror flooded his countenance. For a moment everything remained perfectly still.

"You are defeated," Ana declared.

She cast the stone upon Drake's head, and her enemy was no more.

CHAPTER

12

Teo's five-day journey from Nuo Genov to Roma was uneventful. A few merchant vessels appeared on the horizon but escaped before the *Midnight Glider* could engage them. Teo didn't mind. He was content to do nothing but watch the wooded shores slip by as the clipper ship made its way south.

Vanita spent most of the trip in Marco's company, but on the fifth day she approached Teo as he stood at the rail on the main deck. She wore a nice gown and pretty earrings. Though her hair was still short, it had grown out during the past two weeks and was no longer so startling.

"Roma sure is remote," she observed.

"The Likurian sailors think so. They're scared to go far from home. Most never venture more than a day's journey away. Only the bravest men sail long distances."

"Men like Marco. Brave—or reckless."

They stood together in silence, each lost in contemplation. The sun was low in the western sky, its rays turning the coastline a deep russet. After a while Marco noticed the pair and strolled over. Teo turned toward him with a question. "How come there are so few villages around here? It feels like we've left civilization behind. I haven't seen a town since yesterday."

Marco nodded. "All the land you see here belongs to Roma. From the sea it looks abandoned, but believe me it's not. The territory around the city is very productive and has been brought into heavy cultivation."

"Peasant farmers?"

"They work the land, but it's controlled by the nobility. The richest is a pig named Nikolo Borja."

"You'd think there would be other seaports along the coast."

"The nobles want everything channeled through the port of Roma. It's a choke point. All commerce goes through one harbor, and the rich aristocrats grow even richer off taxes and tariffs. Meanwhile the peasants live in squalor and never get to enjoy the goods they work so hard to produce."

Teo glanced at Marco, who was grinning in a roguish way. The expression on his face made Teo smile in return. "So, pirate, I guess it's your job to rob the big men, huh?"

Marco threw back his head and laughed. "Exactly! And it helps the little guys at the same time. When I capture a ship I sell the cargo for a lot less than it would go for on the open market—and still make 100 percent profit. The pirate business is pretty good work if you can get it."

"As long as you don't get killed," Vanita said.

Marco pursed his lips and shrugged. "Violent death is a job hazard I've long accepted."

The lights of Roma's harbor twinkled in the deepening twilight when the *Midnight Glider* reached the end of its journey. Marco ordered the flag of a merchant vessel raised on the ensign staff before entering the port. As soon as the ship was moored, the rough sailors poured onto the docks with a night of debauchery on their minds. Teo, however, had no interest in revelry. He led Vanita to the least seedy inn he could find, hoping it would have rooms decent enough for a lady. The place looked congenial, so he reserved two chambers. In the morning he would hire horses for the trip to Roma, which was situated about twenty-five leagues upriver from the coast. Tilled fields and forests lay between the city and its port.

Teo and Vanita found a table in a corner of the inn's common room. The waitress brought foamy mugs and two platters of food, along with a bottle of amber-colored sauce. Tasting it, Teo discovered the flavor was zesty and salty.

"What's in that sauce?" Vanita asked the waitress.

"Fermented fish guts," she replied. Vanita wrinkled her nose, but Teo laughed and filled a bowl in which to dip his bread.

The meal passed at a leisurely pace. Teo found Vanita to be an excellent conversationalist, a skill she had no doubt learned as part of her elite upbringing. Gone, however, were all the ribald comments she used to make. Vanita was becoming a different kind of woman. Teo was glad to see it.

When the platters were empty, Teo called for the bill and brought out a handful of copper coins. As he sorted them in his left palm, the waitress did a double take. She seemed unusually interested in Teo's counting, then hurried into a back room as soon as she took the payment.

"Something's up," Vanita said, sipping her chicory coffee.

"Let's wait and see." Teo loosened his sword in its scabbard just in case.

It wasn't long before a slim young man in a coarse-spun robe approached the table. "Excuse me," he said. "I have an important matter to discuss with you." He gestured to an empty chair. "May I sit down?"

Teo could see the man wasn't a warrior and posed no threat, so he nodded his assent.

"Would I be correct in assuming you are Teofil of Chiveis?" the man asked.

"Who are you?" Vanita demanded before an answer could be made.

"Ah, yes, I'm sorry." He leaned close, beckoning Teo and Vanita to do the same. "I am a servant of Deus," he whispered. "I'm here on behalf of Ambrosius, the Overseer of the Forbidden Zone. We've been keeping an eye on the docks for a visitor who has"—the man glanced down at Teo's hand—"passed the *test*."

Teo fingered the scar at the base of his thumb from the Overseer's hammer and nail. He examined the youthful visitor's face, considering his response before replying. "What does your master seek? The Forbidden Zone is far from here. Roma isn't within his jurisdiction."

"Indeed the Zone is far, but the Overseer isn't. He has come here at the Papa's request and awaits you in the city. A private carriage will take you there in the morning if you are willing to accompany me."

Teo and Vanita exchanged glances. Events were unfolding rapidly, yet something told Teo they were headed in the right direction. When Vanita offered a confirming nod, Teo accepted the visitor's invitation. The man thanked them and slipped away, leaving Teo and Vanita alone again.

"This might be a trick," Teo said.

"I don't think it is. I think it's the work of your God."

Teo inclined his head, acknowledging Vanita's wise suggestion. "I guess we'll find out tomorrow." He stood up and, after a few words with the innkeeper, led Vanita to her room for the night.

The carriage ride to Roma the next day afforded Teo an excellent opportunity to get his bearings. Approaching Roma from the southwest, he found the city to be much like the Forbidden Zone: a vast metropolis of the Ancients now gone to ruin, with nature having accomplished its inexorable work of reclaiming what had once been an urban area. And yet, unlike the Forbidden Zone, Roma's cityscape wasn't entirely decrepit and overgrown. Whereas the Zone's buildings had fallen into a state of ruin, portions of Roma had been restored—or razed and rebuilt—so that today it was a thriving city once again. While it wasn't as expansive as it had been in ancient times, a central core bustled and hummed with the lively energy of an industrious population. Crowded tenements, busy marketplaces, public monuments, gushing fountains, even lavish palaces—all were part of the vista Teo encountered as the carriage rolled through the streets of the city that would not die.

"Teofil, look at this!"

Vanita stared out the window with her mouth open. Teo leaned over and peeked out, immediately noticing what had captured Vanita's attention. A massive temple rose in the distance, equal to if not bigger than the one in the Zone. Its roof was topped by a dome, while a row of columns lined the building's facade. The carriage turned onto a broad avenue and began to approach the temple head-on. Soon it entered a circular plaza whose colonnades embraced the travelers like a mother gathering her children into her arms. Marble statues of saintly heroes adorned every high place. The driver pulled up next to a colossal stone spike that rose from the center of the plaza. Teo and Vanita alighted from the carriage, marveling at the grand setting.

A figure wearing a white robe descended the steps in front of the domed building, followed by his retinue. As the man drew near, Teo discerned it was the Overseer. The jagged scar on his forehead wasn't obscured by any head covering.

"Welcome, Teofil of Chiveis," he said. "It has been some time since I saw you last, though I did not believe it would be our last meeting." He bowed, then turned to Vanita. "And we welcome you too, Lady Vanita of Ulmbartia. I am called Ambrosius, and I am glad you have come." Vanita returned the bow with an aristocratic curtsy.

"Follow me," said the Overseer. "We must speak of weighty things."

Teo hesitated. "Should we appear out in the open like this? I'm a man with enemies. I don't want to endanger you or your followers."

"Thank you for your concern, my friend, but the Christiani have legitimate legal standing within these grounds. Besides, I think neither you nor I could be hated more than we already are by the enemies of Deus. So then . . . shall we go sit in the shade?"

Teo and Vanita were led to chairs arranged at the side of the plaza beneath the colonnade. The view of the temple was magnificent. After wine was brought, the assistants left the threesome alone. The Overseer gestured over his shoulder at the great building. "This place was even more impressive in the time of the Ancients. Much of the original complex was destroyed during their wars, though the combatants made a pact to protect the basilica itself, along with its chapel. Now it has come down to us. Today the Universal Communion is the guardian of a beautiful shell." He sighed. "Unfortunately, the shell no longer houses the living creature that used to dwell within."

"And yet I believe that life could be restored," Teo said.

The Overseer glanced at him, taking his measure. "Yes, it can, if Deus wills it." He sipped his wine. "The Christiani are few in number. Those of us who exist do not remember everything our forefathers knew, yet we do what we can. We maintain our buildings, we partake of the Meal, we perform the Washing. We also serve the poor—that much we know Deus would have us do! The Pierced One loved the poor and sided with the oppressed. All were welcomed by him: the broken, the needy, the repentant sinner. These are the memories we have retained."

Vanita spoke up for the first time, though her words were tentative.

"I know I'm not worthy to converse with a holy man like you," she said, "but I wonder if I could ask you something?"

The Overseer smiled. "The humble heart is welcome here. Please feel free to speak, Lady Vanita."

"Thank you, sir," Vanita answered demurely. "From what Teofil has told me, it sounds like most of your religion is still a mystery. Why do you hold to it when you don't know all its doctrines? And why do you keep going, especially when you're so persecuted?"

The Overseer folded his hands into his sleeves and was lost in thought for a long time. Finally he looked directly at Vanita. "To answer that question I must tell you the history of our faith." He took a deep breath. "In the time of the Great War of the Ancients, our religion was almost eradicated. The chaos of those days makes it a dark age for us, and we know little of what happened then. What we do know is that Christianism took root again more recently. It grew and prospered until" —the Overseer glanced around, then leaned in—"until forty years ago, when Nikolo Borja came to power. He was only a young man in those days, but even then he was cruel. At his command a great holocaust occurred. The Christiani were wiped out by a secret society of assassins."

"The Exterminati," Teo said.

"Yes. Now they're into the slave trade, but their original purpose was to eradicate the Universal Communion in every land. They did so with vehemence, butchering the faithful. Our books were also collected and destroyed."

"Did no one try to stop them?" Vanita asked.

"The Christiani leadership founded the Order of the Cross, a brotherhood of knights sworn to defend the true faith. Despite their valiant efforts, evil was allowed to prevail, and the knights were killed along with all the rest. In the end no Christiani survived except one man. Such is the tenuous thread by which our faith has clung to life. And yet, my friends, the thread was not broken! Deus preserved our religion."

"So why are you allowed to exist now?" Teo asked. "Why hasn't Borja killed you like he killed the others?"

The Overseer narrowed his eyes. "Borja hates our faith, and he hates our God. He will do everything he can to thwart us through treachery and assassinations. If he had the chance to destroy us openly, he would. It is only the goodwill of the people that allows us to exist."

"The people of Roma support the Christiani?"

"Not really. But as it turns out, they want this grand old building used for its original purpose. They view it like a museum artifact: the vestige of a glorious past they aren't prepared to discard just yet. So when the Christiani began to come back after the purge, Borja was forced to sign a treaty that gave us the legal right to maintain this property as long as we don't proselytize. But there's the heart of the problem. We follow the one true God, so we *have* to win others to him. Therefore we must do our work in secrecy."

"Does Borja know a lone survivor slipped through his fingers?"

"No. He has no idea how the Universal Communion reconstituted itself. He would be surprised to know it was through the tireless efforts of one man."

A light went on in Teo's head. "The Papa!" The revered leader's importance to the Christiani faith suddenly made sense.

"That's right, Teofil. The Papa was just a boy during the purge. Much of what we know today we know because of his memories. As he grew up, he vowed to reestablish the religion of Christianism. Every known believer in Roma owes his faith to the testimony of this one man. He kept the message alive, and through him it spread from person to person."

"But what is the message?" Vanita held out her palms, her face perplexed. "I still don't get it! What's the point of it all?"

"The message, Lady Vanita, is that we are to love the Creator God with full devotion and to love the creatures he has made."

"So that's the sum total of Christianism? Love Deus and do good to your fellow man?"

"We believe this is indeed our *goal*. But remember, we only have partial knowledge. The *means* to the goal has been forgotten."

"How do you function then?" Vanita pressed.

"We live according to what we do know, trusting in Deus even when the way ahead is unseen. That is the essence of faith, is it not? Deus has preserved this religion until now. Will he fail us in the future? I do not think so."

"And you don't mind all this waiting? All the unknown?"

THE GIFT

The Overseer stroked his scarred forehead. "It's true that we don't know all the doctrines of our faith. Yet Deus has given us some gifts. We possess his Old Testament, which describes his holy character. We have the Papa's recollection of the rituals of our faith. We remember the Pierced One's virtuous life—an example for us to follow. We also know there was a glorious king whose power is superior to that of any other. But what is the nature of that power? How can we use it? This we do not know. We believe there must be a way to wield it, if we can only recover the New Testament and learn the king's ways. With that power behind us we will march forth against the enslavers and defeat them!"

The Overseer's voice grew bold, and his blue eyes blazed as he spoke these final words. Vanita leaned forward, riveted by the man's holy aura. Teo could see she was drawn to his profundity and spiritual power. This was a man of Deu if ever there was one.

"I think I understand now," Vanita said. "You believe in the character of Deus himself. He gives you purpose and hope, even when things look bad."

The Overseer leaned back into his chair, laughing gently. "You are indeed wise for one so young, Lady Vanita. Though profound evil exists in our world, we refuse to behave as those who are defeated. Even if our eyes tell us otherwise, we believe our benevolent God is guiding all things. As a matter of fact, we believe he is on the move right now in these momentous times—and that he might somehow use the man sitting at your side."

Teo glanced up from his wine, startled by the remark. The Overseer and Vanita looked at him. Behind them the domed temple of Deus loomed in the Roman sky.

"Tell me, Teofil," the Overseer said, fixing him with an intense stare, "are you ready to meet the Papa?"

Teo returned the Overseer's gaze. "Yes. That is why I have come."

"Then meet him you must. Let us go now and see the great man."

❖   ❖   ❖

The Iron Shield gazed out from a window over the wide city of Roma. He stood in an attic atop the fortresslike chapel next to the Christiani basilica. The smaller structure had obviously been built with military purposes in mind, for its roof was surrounded by a gangway with openings for defense. Today, however, the followers of the damnable god Deus used the chapel only for secret meetings with their leader.

Down in the circular plaza, the Overseer of the Forbidden Zone conversed under a colonnade with Teofil of Chiveis and an unknown woman. The Iron Shield uttered a curse as he observed the scene. Although the Ulmbartian teacher named Sol had been sent to the quarries, and Anastasia had met her end in the oubliette, the tall soldier from over the northern mountains was proving to be a worthy foe. The thought of crushing Teofil's bones one by one aroused the Iron Shield's lust for revenge, but he suppressed that urge, for the Lord Borja wanted information above all else. Vital events were starting to unfold in the Christiani temple complex, events whose secrets could only be gleaned by espionage. Once the Iron Shield had watched and learned all that he could, he would return to a more satisfying method of extracting information.

Staring at the basilica, the dark warrior was reminded of the many nights he had spent exploring its rooftops. The basilica hadn't been difficult to climb, for ladders constantly rested against it and its adjacent chapel. The maintenance of these ancient edifices was an ongoing task, so permanent teams of stonemasons and bricklayers lived in the surrounding neighborhoods. The Iron Shield scoffed as he considered how the workers were pampered by the so-called charity of the Christiani. *What a foolish way to ensure compliance!* In his experience, the carrot was always inferior to the stick.

The ladders and scaffolding had allowed the Iron Shield to explore the basilica under cover of darkness. On moonless nights he crept around the rooftops, taking risks that would have made mortal men tremble. *But we are not mortal, are we? No! We are many!* The Iron Shield felt power coursing through his body as he recalled his dangerous nighttime exploits. Eventually he had found the way into the chapel through its attic. The discovery was particularly important, for it was here that the accursed Papa held court with his henchmen. Now it was time to make use of that discovery.

The dark warrior removed his armor until he was wearing only a fitted tunic and trousers. He tied off a rope and dropped it out a window where it wouldn't be in view of anyone below. Descending the rope, he arrived at a window recessed into an arch. He knelt on the broad sill. A suction cup enabled him to lift out a glass panel he had previously cut. After listening for voices and hearing none, he slithered through the opening into the dimly lit hall.

The chapel was fantastically decorated, though many of the frescoes were now faded and hard to see. The rear wall was dominated by a mythic scene of naked people set against a blue background. The primary figure was a glowing young man with his arm raised. A veiled woman sat demurely at his side. At the bottom of the painting, hideous demons dragged a host of unfortunates down to the underworld. Even the ceiling in this chapel was covered in art. The central panel depicted an old man extending his finger toward that of a naked youth. The whole place sickened the Iron Shield. It resonated with a narrative he did not want to believe—but he did, and it made him shudder.

The windows of the chapel were set high above the floor. Beneath the windows a narrow catwalk ran along three sides of the room. Repairs were being made, so a scaffold obscured the place where the Iron Shield had entered. He lay down on the catwalk and began to meditate. Soon the spirits within him slowed his breathing and lulled his body into a trance. He could remain like that for a very long time—silent, pressed flat, invisible to anyone below. Only when the Christiani archpriest resumed his court would the Iron Shield awaken to listen; and then he would hear whatever there was to know about Teofil's presence in the city of Roma.

❖   ❖   ❖

The rain fell on Ana, soaking her sackcloth shift, drenching her to the skin. Her hair was plastered to her forehead, and water ran in rivulets down her cheeks. She shivered each time the wind gusted. The sky was gray and mottled as the squall passed through.

Limping to the beach on her bruised foot, Ana searched the ground until she found what she sought: the key Drake had smashed with his club. Its shaft was bent, and the teeth were mangled. Though she assumed it would be pointless, Ana inserted the key into the padlock that fastened the ball and chain around her ankle. The damaged key failed to engage, and Ana pitched it away in frustration. Grabbing a rock, she pounded the links that bound her to the accursed encumbrance but only succeeded in sending stone chips flying in every direction. She kept at her task until the rock finally shattered in her hand.

It was all too much. Ana collapsed on the ground, exhausted not only from the effort but from the trauma she had endured over the past several weeks. Her foot throbbed where Drake had bitten it. Rain pattered on her back and shoulders, but Ana ignored it as she fell into a doze that was more like a stupor.

Time passed. The rain slowed, then stopped. Even so, Ana couldn't climb out of her lethargy.

What was that?

Something rustled in the bushes!

Ana raised her head, dimly aware that mud was dripping from her hair but much more concerned about the sound she had just heard. *Did one of the pirates remain behind?* Alert now, Ana trembled at the thought of those lewd men. The squall had driven them away without their slave—but perhaps they had returned?

Ana, how could you have been so careless? Quick! You have to hide!

Unsure where to go, Ana made her way into the forest. She was near the ancient monastery and castle, but hiding in the woods seemed like the best option. Her eyes scanned the underbrush for any sign of an enemy. At last she convinced herself her mind was playing tricks on her. Relaxing her guard for a moment, she was unprepared for the man's voice that spoke behind her.

"Hello," he said thickly.

Ana's only reply was a scream, which the speaker repeated with an equally startled yell. She whirled to see the giant man who had given her bread and wine. The look on his face was fearful, and Ana regretted her response.

"Uh . . . hello," she ventured. "I'm sorry for screaming. I won't hurt you."

289

The man stared at her as if trying to assess the truthfulness of her words—or perhaps to understand them. He was clearly a simpleton.

"What's your name?" Ana asked. The man pointed to himself. Ana nodded with a bright smile.

The man smiled back. "I'm Liber."

"Hi, Liber. I'm Anastasia."

He tried to sound out her name but couldn't get it right. "Stasia!" he cried at last. Both of them laughed.

"What's that?" He pointed to her chain.

"Drake put it on me. I can't get it off."

"I don't like Drake."

Liber picked up a heavy rock. Obviously he had been watching Ana's actions from the forest. She turned away as Liber smashed the chunk of limestone against the chain. It vibrated against her ankle but didn't break. Liber tried several more times, then gave up with a frown. He moved off a short distance and began to mumble meaningless syllables. Ana wasn't sure how to comfort the heavyset man in his disappointment.

"Liber, are you hungry?" she asked at length. He turned toward her, nodding emphatically. "What do you say we eat some of Drake's food?"

Liber's eyes went wide, and he began to wave his hands. "No! No! No!" he groaned as he backed away. "Drake hurts me!"

Ana approached Liber and put her hand on his arm. "Drake can't hurt you anymore. He's—he's gone."

Liber looked skeptical.

"Come on," Ana said. "Trust me. I'll give you something to eat."

She bent to pick up her stone ball, but Liber reached for it first. Their eyes met, and Liber offered a shy smile. He walked behind Ana to the monastery, carrying her burden as if it were a pebble. When she paused at a barrel of drinking water to rinse her bite wound, Liber reached into his bag and handed her a gourd bottle. Ana removed the cork and sniffed the opening. *Honey!* She applied a golden droplet to the broken skin on her foot, then glanced up at Liber. He beamed back at her.

With Drake dead, Ana had no qualms about raiding the pirates' stores. *Tonight*, she resolved, *Liber and I are going to celebrate with a feast.* She gathered the ingredients to make a stew of salt pork, beans, onions, and peas.

At first she considered doubling the recipe, then decided to triple it after taking another look at Liber's large frame. The two of them devoured the hearty stew, leaving nothing behind in the pot. A skin of red wine, liberally consumed, gladdened their hearts as well. Dessert was ship's biscuit dipped in amaretto and slathered with honey from Liber's beehives.

"Thank you, Stasia," Liber said through a stuffed mouth. He grinned, biscuit crumbs clinging to his unkempt beard.

After dinner a sense of peace descended on Ana as she relaxed by the sea with Liber. He lay a few paces away, muttering his strange words to the sky. Ana found herself soothed by the steady chant that tumbled from his lips. Her belly was full, and the wine made her sleepy. She gazed at the stars, thanking Deu for his protection and provision. Even the chain around her ankle wasn't a bother as she pulled a clean sailor's blanket over herself and succumbed to her drowsiness. For the first time in a long while, Anastasia fell asleep unconcerned about what the next day would bring.

✦   ✦   ✦

Teo didn't know whether to look at the side panels or the rear wall or the ceiling. Every surface in the Painted Chapel presented such an astonishing panoply of action and color that his eyes were drawn in too many directions at once. He tried looking at the floor, but even there the intricate pattern of spirals and squares mesmerized him. Finally he turned toward the Overseer—the only person in the whole chapel who wasn't overwhelming. "This art is incredible," he said.

"It was created by a master painter of the Ancients."

Vanita nodded. "He was truly a master."

"Ana would have loved to see this."

As soon as Teo uttered the words, a sharp pang of grief stabbed him. Ana had always been captivated by beauty, especially anything sacred. Teo recalled how awestruck she had been when they first entered a temple of Deu. They found the place by accident after he rescued her from outsiders who had abducted her from Chiveis. *Was it really by accident?* Teo now believed Deu had led them to the temple so they could find the Sacred Writing together. The reminder that Ana was no longer with him ripped open the wounds in his heart. He winced, shaking his head. *Why did she have to die? Why isn't she at my side for this discovery too? My God, I miss her so much!* Teo grunted and tried to push his memories of Ana away but was only partly successful. The pain had a fierce hold on him and refused to let go. He realized he would have to live with an aching, ever-present sadness for a long time.

At the far end of the room, a door opened and a group of men and women entered the chapel. The Overseer led Teo and Vanita through an opening in an altar screen so they could approach the waiting Christiani. Most of them wore brown, so Teo assumed the lone figure in white must be the Papa. He was a short, wiry man, and much younger than Teo had pictured him to be. Although Teo knew the Papa would have to be in his midforties if he was a boy during Borja's purge, he was nonetheless startled by the fit, energetic man who stood waiting near the altar.

As Teo walked forward, the Papa looked straight at him and said, "What do you notice, Teofil of Chiveis?"

Teo hesitated, unsure what he was being asked. "You mean—"

"What captures your attention? There is much here to see. What do you notice out of all that confronts you?"

Teo glanced around. His eyes settled on a triumphant figure high on the far wall. The man in the painting was fair-haired and naked, with only a cloth covering his thighs. His right arm was raised high, and the light of heaven glowed behind him.

"That man is the focal point," Teo said.

The Papa smiled. "Correct. Who do you suppose he is?"

"Because of his prominence, I would assume he's the Promised King."

"Does anything else come to your attention?"

"I could stand here forever trying to take it all in. There's a man holding a human skin. There are people being dragged down to hell. Up there on the left I see people holding the cross of Iesus Christus. Is he in the scene anywhere?"

For a long time the Papa was silent. He had dark, close-cropped hair with a smattering of gray at the temples. His nose was long and aquiline. The man exuded a kind of aristocratic air, though not in a haughty way.

Teo felt drawn to his charismatic personality. But when the Papa finally spoke, his voice was troubled.

"The Pierced One is in the scene," he said. "He is the man you first mentioned, the focal point. That is Iesus Christus. Although you cannot see it from here, he has bloody wounds on his hands and feet. What do you make of that?"

Teo frowned. "It reveals once again that Iesus Christus is central to the Christiani religion. At the same time it obscures the identity of the Promised King. Why isn't he featured more prominently than his servant? The king's absence is remarkable. Where is his throne? Where are the symbols of his power? Something isn't right here."

"Indeed, it puzzles me too. We see the servant, but not his master." The Papa arched his eyebrows and stared at Teo. "Let me ask you this. What do you know about the Promised King?"

"Only what the Sacred Writing says. The ninth chapter of Isaias says the government will be on his shoulders and will have no end. He has many names. He will rule from David's throne and uphold justice forever. The zeal of Deu—or Deus, I mean—the zeal of Deus will accomplish it. That's not exactly how it goes, but I remember the text well enough. And there are many others. I forget which chapter exactly, but the book of Daniel says a king will come down from the clouds 'like a son of man.' Dominion and glory will be given to him, and all languages and people will serve him. His kingdom will never end."

"You know the scripture well," the Papa remarked.

"I spent several months doing nothing but translating it."

"Do you have any idea what it means?"

Teo reflected for a moment. "These prophecies say the Promised King was given an eternal kingdom. If it's eternal, it must mean his power will one day return to his followers."

"So you believe that power is now lost?"

"Yes. Look around—evil holds sway. Our enemies have the power now."

"Why do you say that?"

"Because the Christiani are considered foolish and weak. Borja controls everything. But if we had power, things would be reversed. Instead of being weak, we'd be the triumphant ones."

"Is that what you wish?"

"It is."

"Step close to me, Teofil of Chiveis." Teo obliged, though everyone else in the room remained in their places. The Papa clasped his hands behind his back. "I would like to tell you a story. I will share with you my greatest joy, and then I will describe my greatest distress. But in the end my story will conclude on a hopeful note. Do you wish to hear it?"

"Yes, Holy Father." The Overseer had referred to the Papa this way, and Teo hoped it was proper etiquette for him to do so too.

The Papa waved to his attendants, and they brought chairs for everyone. The stool they brought to the Papa was lower than any other seat. With his already-short stature, he seemed like a child waiting to hear a fairy tale at Teo's feet. Yet it was the Papa who did the talking, and the story he recounted was no myth.

"I was five years old when Nikolo Borja outlawed Christianism. Those were terrible times indeed. I don't remember much about them—only partial images now remain in my mind. I saw killings and burnings and things no child should see."

A shadow descended upon the Papa's face. He bowed his head until he had composed himself, then continued in a sober voice.

"I was the only believer to live through those dark days. At that time I was being trained as a Keeper. That's what we called the boys who were taught to copy manuscripts—Keepers. We learned the art of calligraphy so we could preserve the Holy Book. Unfortunately, I hadn't been taught any theology yet. I only remember what the rituals looked like, not what they signified. We now believe the Washing expresses our desire for forgiveness from sin, and the Meal binds us to Iesus. I recall some things about him—his love, his service to the poor, his healings and miracles. Yet I know nothing of what happened after he perished. Somehow the king triumphed despite his servant's death. The texts you just cited from the Old Testament promised this."

"And there are others," Teo said. "The seventh chapter of Second

Samuhel predicts that a descendant of David will be raised up. He will have a throne before Deus forever."

"That's right. Great power was promised to the heir of David. Evidently the king possessed this awesome power, whereas the servant did not."

"That's the basic issue, isn't it?" Teo could see the crux of the matter clearly now. "Weakness and victory are mutually exclusive. I'm a soldier, I understand that. If you're weak, you lose. Be strong, and you win. It's always like that. Iesus Christus—the servant, the Pierced One, whatever you want to call him—he was murdered in defeat. We mourn for him because he didn't have enough divine power. But the Promised King . . . he triumphed! So the question is, how? That's what we have to figure out. If we could obtain that same power, we could overcome our weaknesses too. We could triumph like the king."

The Papa nodded. "Yes, Teofil. We believe the New Testament will tell us the secret to everything. Then the king's power will be ours, and Borja will have met a force he cannot withstand. We will defeat him with a rod of iron and break him into pieces like a potter's vessel!"

"And you've been working toward this goal since you were a boy?"

"I vowed in my heart as a youth that I would restore the religion of Christianism. Today the Universal Communion in Roma is allowed to exist—against Borja's wishes. As long as we stay quiet, we can carry out our rituals and maintain our buildings. We have some followers in the city, and outside of Roma there are monastic communities scattered around the countryside. There are also some underground believers in Likuria and Ulmbartia and even beyond that."

"Don't forget the Forbidden Zone," the Overseer reminded.

"Thank you, Brother Ambrosius. Yes, there too. And in addition to all this, the Order of the Knights of the Cross has been reinstated, though their number is small. Only a few knights exist among the aristocracy in various places. There is a sizeable group at Marsay, but that city is distant, and I have not been able to establish contact with it. Therefore my ministry is focused on those Christiani whom I know. I send secret messages of encouragement to them, either by faithful couriers or by pigeons if the distance is too great. In this way I provide spiritual direction to my sheep. Much prayer do I expend on their behalf! I am their pastor, and they look to me for guidance. Deus strengthens me for this task each day. Indeed it is my greatest joy."

"You spoke of sorrow as well. What did you mean by that?" Teo hesitated to bring up an uncomfortable subject, but he was finally beginning to understand the Christiani religion and wanted to find out as much as possible.

"My greatest sorrow is what we have already discussed. For forty years I have sought the New Testament of Deus but have been unable to find it. I can recall little of what it says. As a novice Keeper, I had begun to learn the techniques of handwriting and scribal copying, but I was not of age to have entered formal catechesis. Though I often heard the holy scriptures recited in the liturgy, my childish mind did not retain the most important things. That is why finding the second part of the Holy Book is my heart's greatest desire. And I believe we will soon achieve it."

The sound of pebbles falling from a high catwalk disturbed the stillness in the chapel. Some scurrying creature had probably dislodged them, or perhaps they had simply come loose as the ancient building decayed.

"This place is infested with rats," the Overseer said. "It is a sign of the days in which we live."

Vanita spoke up for the first time. "Holy Father, we want to help you find the book. I believe Teofil is uniquely gifted for this kind of task. He is not only strong and brave, he is also an expert in ancient languages." She glanced at Teo. "I'm sorry to say I didn't perceive his worth at first, but I recognize it now. Do you think he can help you?"

The Papa rose from his stool and gazed at the ceiling of the chapel. Finally, with a gleam in his eye, he turned his attention to Teo. "A week ago I had a strange dream. A man who looked much like you appeared to me. That man had three tongues in his mouth. I could see them moving when he spoke."

Teo arched his eyebrows. "Sounds like a hideous monster."

"No. I believe the tongues were symbols. How many languages do you know, Teofil of Chiveis?"

"Well, I speak my native tongue, of course. And I can converse in Talyano, though not always with ease. But I get along."

"Any others?"

"Yes. I can also translate a language the Chiveisi call the Fluid Tongue of the Ancients. We call it that because it's more melodious than our own speech. Few among my people can read it. But I was a professor, and that language was my academic specialty."

The Overseer and the Papa exchanged glances, then the Papa gestured to one of his attendants. The woman disappeared and soon came back with an ironbound chest, which she set upon the altar. After removing a heavy key from within his robe, the Papa unlocked the chest and carried a cloth-wrapped object to Teo. He carefully unfolded the cloths. A slim leather volume was there.

"Can you read this?" the Papa asked.

Teo cradled the delicate book and opened to the first page. The handwriting was faded but legible. Across the top were scrawled the words, *Le journal intime d'un disciple de Dieu vivant dans les jours sombres*. Teo looked up at the Papa. "It says this is the personal diary of a follower of Deus living in gloomy days."

"That is what we thought. The book has come into my hands only recently. I have many monastic brothers scouring the earth for news of ancient texts. The Exterminati seek to thwart them, of course. Three good men lost their lives to bring us that journal. It is a miraculous work of the Lord God."

"And yet you haven't been able to read it."

"Until now. The speech is unknown around here. But you can read it, can you not?"

"Yes, I could provide a translation. Among my belongings at the port I have a lexicon. With its help I could decipher a book of this size within a day."

The Papa's face lit up. "Excellent! I wish you to do that immediately, Teofil of Chiveis. I am certain this is why you have come to us. The diary will lead us to the New Testament."

"What makes you think so?"

Taking the book from Teo, the Papa gently flipped to the last page. At the end of the diary's entries, another hand had written a note in the Talyano speech. The Papa traced the words with his forefinger as he read: "These are the blessed thoughts of my friend Borregard, a noble knight and wandering brother. Together we endured much persecution. Together we evaded the killers of the evil society. Alas! Their poison has taken him to Deus. In a safe and secret place he has hidden the holy scriptures of our faith. Dwell upon his words as he died: 'Whoever would find the heavenly book must recall the saying of the righteous Iesus: *Erunt novissimi primi, et primi novissimi. Multi sunt enim vocati, pauci autem electi.*'"

Teo met the Papa's eyes, waiting for the translation. The slender man holding the book looked straight at Teo and proclaimed, "The last shall be first and the first last. For many are called, *but few are chosen.*" A murmur of awe circulated around the Painted Chapel.

"I don't know if I'm chosen," Teo said slowly, "but I can certainly translate that diary and see what it reveals. I'll get my lexicon and come back to do the job."

"No. You have lingered in this place long enough. To stay longer would arouse suspicion that something important is going on here. Return to the port and blend into the masses. There you are just an anonymous man. No one will know your secret task, and that is our greatest advantage. In the meantime I will have a scribe make a copy of the diary. Tomorrow my brother Ambrosius will come to you with it. You will make a translation and give it to him when you are finished, then burn the copy lest it fall into evil hands."

"I will do it, Holy Father," Teo said.

✦ ✦ ✦

Breakfast at the little inn by the sea was bread, cold sausage, and beer. Teo guessed the lunch menu wouldn't be much different. Dinner would no doubt include beer too. The place offered simple fare for humble people, and that suited Teo just fine.

At this early hour there wasn't much movement along the docks. Teo saw only one ship preparing to leave port, a run-down barque whose men didn't have the look of honest sailors. A few of them sat at a table across the barroom, cursing each other as they devoured their morning meal.

Teo had awoken early and found he couldn't get back to sleep, so he came downstairs for a bite. Perhaps it was just normal restlessness, but he suspected it had more to do with the secret diary he would soon be translating. Once the Overseer arrived, Teo would find a private place to work on the text. By sunset he should know where to find a copy of Deu's mysterious New Testament. For now he amused himself by listening to the pirates' idle chatter. Vanita was still sleeping upstairs. Teo decided he would take her some food rather than let her come down in the presence of such rough men.

The barroom door banged open, and a stocky seafarer with a scruffy beard barged in. From the insignia on his greasy jacket, Teo could tell he was the pirates' captain. The men jumped to their feet with guilty expressions.

"Why are you slugs loafing here while we're getting ready to leave?" the captain roared.

The three men fumbled for excuses, but the captain wouldn't let them speak. His vicious tongue-lashing whipped them into line. As they tripped over each other on their way out the door, the captain turned and bellied up to the bar. "Whiskey!" was his only demand, followed by a slap on the countertop.

From the corner of his eye Teo studied the swarthy pirate. The man wore earrings in both ears, and one of his front teeth was made of gold. Teo smiled as he considered the captain's penchant for finery. It seemed out of place for such a tough character.

Teo finished his breakfast and started to head upstairs. Passing by the bar, he glanced at the pirate one last time. As he was about to turn away, his eyes fell on something that halted him in his tracks.

No! That can't be!

Teo's knees went weak. He rubbed his eyes, then looked again at the pirate to be certain of what he had seen.

Sure enough, it was there.

Around the captain's neck.

A golden pendant of Iesus Christus.

Exactly like the one I gave to Ana!

The implications were staggering. Teo gripped the bar for support. It took him a few moments to collect his thoughts.

Summoning the bartender, he paid for a bottle of the best whiskey available. Vanita's wealth was funding the journey to Roma, and she would consider this money well spent. The pirate captain noticed the expensive purchase, then looked at Teo for the first time.

"Good stuff," Teo said, tipping the bottle. "Have a drink with me?"

The captain scowled, but the fine liquor was too much of a temptation. He slid his empty glass across the bar, and Teo filled it. For as long as seemed polite, Teo made small talk with the foul-mouthed sailor. Finally he pointed to the pendant. "Where'd you get that thing?"

The captain glanced down. "This? It's a little trinket I bought off the fool who runs our resupply station. We're headed there now. I have a debt to settle with that swindler."

"Oh yeah?"

"Yeah! Bought some merchandise off him, then a squall rolled in. Had to leave without my rightful property."

"What was it?" Teo asked, his heart thumping.

"A young whore he had for sale. Dirty little thing. Makes me hot just to think of her."

Teo swallowed his whiskey to hide his astonishment, then asked in a measured tone, "Good-looking wench, was she?"

"You ain't kiddin'. Pink lips, curvy body, long legs. And by the gods, you shoulda seen those—"

"What was she wearing?" Teo interrupted.

"Huh? Oh, some old rag. Rough material."

"Sackcloth?"

"Yeah. Sackcloth and no shoes. And her hair was all chopped in the back like she was some low-class peasant. But there ain't many peasants that look like her."

Teo's mouth had gone dry, and his palms were sweaty. The pirate's crude description sounded like Ana, and the man owned a pendant identical to hers. *Coincidence? Or . . .*

Could she be alive?

Jumbled thoughts rushed through Teo's mind. *The Overseer is arriving today,* he remembered. *I'm supposed to translate the diary.*

But these men are leaving right now to claim a slave that might be . . .

No . . . It probably isn't . . .

But what if it is?

Deu, is this really happening? Is Ana alive?

With cold rationality, Teo told himself there was no chance the unfortunate peasant woman was Ana. Nevertheless, he decided he had an obligation to check out this lead, just in case.

"Where is this resupply station of yours?" he asked, hoping he sounded nonchalant.

"It's an island up north. Why? What do you care about that place?"

Teo poured another shot of whiskey for his drinking companion, who was well lubricated now. "No reason. It's just that I have some business in Manacho." Teo examined his fingernails. "I'm looking for passage. You take fares?"

The captain scoffed. "We don't want no landlubbers on our ship."

"There's a price for everything, Captain."

The remark made the pirate raise his eyebrows. "Twelve scudi," he said boldly.

Teo raised his glass. "Done."

"Alright then, pack up. We leave the harbor within the hour, bound for Hahnerat."

13

The cauldron clanged against the ground outside the shacks in the Defectives' camp, drawing all eyes toward it. Everyone stared in horror as its precious, steaming contents disappeared into the muddy earth. A kitchen slave with a clubfoot stood over the cauldron, his mouth hanging open. The rain that soaked his skeletal body made him look like a wraith from another world.

"Fool!" A brawny foreman marched over and sent the slave sprawling into a mud puddle. "Look what you've done! Curse you and your warped foot!" The foreman raised his club and began to strike the fallen man. A crowd of Defectives watched the scene with fearful eyes. Pleas for mercy rose from the unfortunate cripple as he tried to shield himself from the blows. His pitiful cries were echoed by many of the onlookers. To their simple minds, the violence was disturbing and traumatic.

At the edge of the crowd, Sol whispered a prayer through clenched teeth. "Deus, have pity! Make him stop!"

The fallen man was bloody now, his face slick with reddened mud. The foreman paused and looked at the crowd. "See that?" he cried, gesturing with his stick. "Screw up like he did and it'll happen to you too!" His face contorted into a grimace. "You worthless retards! You're not even human! This is all you deserve!" The foreman gave the man on the ground a hard kick.

Sol could stand it no longer. He stepped forward and stared at the foreman. "They *are* human," he said evenly. "Every one of them."

Though he wanted to say more, the foreman's fierce expression made him hesitate.

"I said they're *not!*" The foreman stormed toward Sol with his club raised. His nose was wrinkled into a snarl, and he bared his teeth like a wild animal. Rainwater dribbled down his face. "Are you contradicting me, old man?"

Sol didn't answer. A breathless hush descended on the crowd of Defectives.

Twice the foreman feigned an attack, pretending to bring down his club on Sol's head but pulling short at the last moment. The action was intended to make Sol grovel. He did not. The foreman uttered a derisive laugh and spun to face the onlookers.

"I could kill him now, couldn't I? I could kill this sorry excuse for a man and it wouldn't matter one bit!" He paced back and forth, staring at the Defectives. Wherever he looked, the frightened slaves retreated from his gaze. "And why is that? Because he's not *human!* He's a worthless piece of trash. Just like the rest of you. Worthless and godforsaken."

"They are not forsaken. The God of heaven loves them."

The foreman whirled toward Sol, and this time he did not hold back. His club swept around in a vicious arc. Though Sol managed to turn away and fend off the blow with his arms, the impact staggered him. He collapsed in the mud. The foreman raised his club again.

"Wait, sir."

Sol glanced up from the ground. His shoulder throbbed where the club had struck it. Bard stood over him, speaking to the foreman.

"I know you could kill him," Bard said, "but this one's a hard worker. Our team needs him to move the marble. If we lose this man it will slow our progress."

"So?"

"The bosses won't like it, and they might blame you. Are you sure it's worth it?"

Sneering, the foreman turned away. He returned to the man who had dropped the cauldron, nudging him with his foot. The Defective's bony limbs barely twitched.

"Look at him! He'll be dead before sundown. And then what? You think your lives are bad now? There's a special place in hell reserved for you. The demons love to torture your kind. Day and night you'll suffer their torments." He brandished his club and thrust out his chin. "Speak up! Who else is ready to contradict me? Go on—step forward! I'll send you to the underworld with my own hands!"

The Defectives lowered their gaze and shrank back. Thunder rumbled in the distance as the rain began to fall harder. The foreman strutted around with his club until the crowd melted away. He cursed and spat on the fallen man, then stalked off.

Only Sol and Bard were left. Sol reached up so his blond friend could help him stand. They did not speak as they approached the crippled man lying in the muck. Sol knelt beside him and took his hand. It was like grasping a handful of twigs.

"Can you hear me, my brother?"

The man's eyelids barely opened. "Am I going to die?" he whispered.

Sol nodded. "I think so."

"I'm afraid."

"Do not fear. What that evil man said isn't true. There is a good God who welcomes all who turn to him."

"Will he save me . . . from the demons?" The man's breathing was very shallow.

Sol bowed his head, unsure how to answer. He wanted to offer comfort, but there wasn't much in the Old Testament about the afterlife. He decided to focus on the character of Deus. "The Creator God made you in his image," he said. "He sides with the oppressed. He is a strong protector. The wicked gods of this world have no power next to his."

The corners of the crippled man's mouth turned up a little, and his knobby hand relaxed in Sol's. His head lolled back into a puddle. He was covered in water and blood. "Deliver me," he murmured. Tears gathered in Sol's eyes as he watched the suffering man exhale his final breath.

With the foreman gone, the Defectives began to return. They stood in a circle, staring at Sol as he held the hand of a corpse. The rain was heavy now. Its steady patter was the only sound in the bleak camp of the enslaved. At last a few of the watchers turned to leave. One after the other, they slipped into the gloom.

Bard's eyes were fixed on the dead man's face. When he finally spoke, his words were bitter: "So much for your mighty God."

He shook his head and walked away, leaving Sol alone in the driving rain.

✦ ✦ ✦

The run-down barque chased three merchant ships and captured one of them during the run to Hahnerat. Teo stayed out of sight during the fighting, which didn't last long. The merchants surrendered quickly to the pirates, losing their cargo, their provisions, their rigging, and even the clothes off their backs. The pirates left the unfortunate sailors in their skivvies with one cask of water and no means of controlling their ship. "That should make things interesting," the captain remarked as he sailed away. His men got a good laugh out of that.

Teo had been assigned to sleep in a dark corner of the ship's hold. Surrounded by frayed ropes and various odds and ends, he whiled away the long hours and tried to avoid the pirates as much as possible. He wasn't afraid of them—they were buffoons mostly—but he didn't want any trouble. He only wanted to reach the island of Hahnerat and find out who the mysterious woman was. Teo steadfastly refused to believe it might be Ana. Though he could have conjured up many joyous scenarios, he knew if he opened his heart to that possibility, the agony would be unbearable when his hopes were dashed. The likelihood that Ana would be waiting for him at Hahnerat was almost nil. Hardening himself, Teo resisted his hopeless daydreams.

Even so, when the ship finally began to near the distant island, Teo realized he needed to make some plans. He sat in his musty corner and considered his next move but couldn't think of a good solution. The pirates expected to pick up the woman and use her for pleasure aboard the ship. Somehow he would have to prevent that. Teo didn't want to see any woman suffer such a fate—and he certainly wasn't going to let it happen to Ana.

It's not Ana, he reminded himself.

But if it is, I'll scuttle the ship with every man aboard before I let them . . .

Quit it, Teo! It's not her!

He reached for his rucksack and stood up. Pirates or not, he needed some fresh air. Teo strapped his sword and ax to his hips, having made a habit of keeping his weapons with him at all times because they were well-made and valuable. No doubt the unscrupulous sailors would try to steal them if they could. The only other items of value he carried were the books he had wrapped in an oilskin inside his pack. Books were precious enough to tempt a thief, and Teo hadn't felt comfortable leaving them behind in Vanita's care. His little library included a lexicon of the Fluid Tongue, the *Versio Prima Chiveisorum*, Sol's Talyano Old Testament, and a treatise he had accidentally brought from Chiveis on explosive powder. However, the book he cherished most was the least valuable of them all: the deteriorated copy of the Sacred Writing from the lost temple of the Ancients. Teo attached deep sentimental value to the book. It was, along with the bearskin cloak folded at the bottom of his pack, one of his last remaining links to Anastasia of Edgeton.

Unless . . .

No. Don't go there.

The sun was shining, and the breeze felt good as Teo emerged onto the barque's main deck. Its square sails were tight and well-trimmed. Apparently the pirates were skilled sailors despite the shabby appearance of their vessel.

After a few minutes the captain spotted Teo and approached. He pointed to a scrubby strip of land a short distance from the ship. "Well, landlubber, we're at Hahnerat. We'll get our woman, then head to Manacho and drop you off. Unfortunately" —the captain looked at Teo with a devious gleam in his eye—"there's been a complication."

"What's the problem?" Teo took a step toward the pirate, staring at him for a few seconds. Men like this understood only power and aggression. They needed to be backed down or they would try to take advantage.

"The Likurian coast guard is on patrol," the captain said. "We don't go anywhere near Manacho when they're around. You're the only reason we're stopping there. It's risky."

"So? I paid the outrageous fare you asked. I don't care about your risk."

The pirate scowled. "I care about my risk. I'm adding a surcharge."

"No, you're not. We agreed on a price, and that's all you'll get from me."

"Five scudi more," the captain said.

Teo threw back his head and laughed. "Forget it, scoundrel! You'll taste my steel if you try. Besides, I don't have that kind of money with me."

The captain's eyes fell to Teo's waist. "I'll take that instead," he said, pointing.

So that's it! He wants my blade! The sword of Armand was worth far more than five scudi, but Teo realized the "surcharge" was simply a ploy to obtain an excellent weapon. He wasn't about to let the pirate have it.

"Unbuckle your sword and give it to me," the captain demanded, holding out his hand.

"And what if I don't?"

The captain stiffened. He was a big man, and Teo readied himself for action. He could see where things were headed. Some of the other sailors began to drift over, sensing imminent violence. Casually the captain removed his jacket and tossed it aside, then pulled on a pair of leather gloves.

"I'll fight you for it," he said, raising his clenched fists. His gold tooth gleamed inside his greasy beard.

Teo saw his chance. "You want to fight me, is that it? What's in it for me?" He looked around at the gathered sailors. "What do you think, men? Shouldn't your captain offer me something in return? I'll give him this fine blade if he can beat me in a fistfight. But if I win, there's something I want from him."

To save face with his crew, the captain was forced to agree. "Alright, what do you want, landlubber?"

"I want your slave woman on Hahnerat. If you lose this fight she's mine."

The sailors erupted in a rousing cheer. The stakes were high, just the way they liked it. Somebody tossed Teo some black gloves like those worn by the captain. He had noticed the pirates wearing them when they brawled, for a hand that couldn't hoist a sail or swing a cutlass was no use aboard the ship. Laying aside his weapons, Teo donned the gloves. He was tugging on the second one when the captain swung his fist and smashed him in the jaw.

Lights exploded in Teo's head as he stumbled backward against the ship's bulwark. The captain barreled toward him, but Teo regained his footing and met the charge with a left jab. The blow halted the captain's advance, giving Teo time to counter with a right hook to his opponent's body. It wasn't fleshy like Teo expected, but thick and firm. Underneath all that pirate couture, the man was a fighter.

"I'm gonna split your skull," the captain growled.

He came in fast, throwing a series of punches that Teo couldn't completely dodge. Each blow felt like a blacksmith's hammer. Teo reeled under the assault while the crewmen cheered their leader. Clinching, the captain gave Teo a fierce shot to the kidney. Razor-edged pain engulfed him. Teo broke the clinch, then immediately attacked with a left feint followed by an overhand right to the mouth. Although the blow split the captain's lips, he refused to go down, countering with a swift jab that rang bells in Teo's head.

The two men grappled and jockeyed for position on the ship's deck. Unexpectedly the captain threw his knee into Teo's gut, knocking the wind from him. An uppercut caught Teo by surprise and made him black out for a moment. Seeing his opponent's defenses were down, the captain pressed his advantage with a flurry of savage punches. Several hard blows connected. Teo felt his knees go watery as he took the pummeling. He shoved the pirate back, shaking his head to clear the fog.

"You're dead, landlubber!" the captain screamed through bloody lips. He surged forward.

Instead of dodging, Teo seized the man's outstretched arm, then threw his shoulder underneath his enemy's armpit and spun around. Bending at the waist, Teo used the captain's forward momentum to lift him off his feet. For a split second the captain was upside down with his legs in the air. Then he hit the deck hard, landing on his back amid a chorus of groans.

Dazed, the captain struggled to his feet. Teo didn't hesitate. He swung a tremendous haymaker that caught the man on the point of the chin. Blood and sweat exploded in the air. When the captain thumped to the planks without catching himself on his arms, Teo knew he was out cold.

The onlookers weren't sure what to say. An awkward silence hung over the crew. Teo strode to the unconscious pirate and yanked off one of his gloves. With his boot knife, he cut a slit along the glove's fingers. Finely ground metal powder spilled out.

"Your captain is less than honorable," Teo declared to the crew. "The knuckles of his gloves were weighted!" He used his toe to roll his enemy over. The captain's tongue dangled out of his mouth, and he emitted a weak gurgle. Reaching into the man's shirt at the neck, Teo removed a golden object. "I claim this pendant as a penalty against my dishonest opponent!" None of the sailors raised a protest.

A voice called down from the mainmast. "Sail ho!"

The first mate jumped into action. He grabbed a swab bucket and doused the captain, who sputtered and sat up. "Sail on the horizon, sir!" the first mate said.

Wincing, the captain shook his head and wiped his eyes. "Coast guard or merchant?"

"Merchant!" the lookout shouted.

"Put on canvas and pursue."

The captain's expression cleared as he seemed to regain his senses. He stood up, turning toward Teo with a malicious smirk. "We're leavin' Hahnerat, landlubber. You mighta won the prize, but I didn't say nothin' about transporting it. If you want that woman you'll have to find your own way onto the island. And off it." The captain's trickery brought guffaws from the pirates.

"Dishonorable from first to last," Teo said.

The captain waved to his men. "Throw this scum overboard!"

Teo managed to snatch his rucksack and weapons before he was seized. The pirates forced him to a gap in the bulwark.

"Good riddance," the captain sneered.

"Same to you," Teo answered, then jumped into the sea.

✦ ✦ ✦

The sunny, blue-sky day was the kind that always made the Overseer anticipate a heavenly blessing. Today the gift of Deus would be obvious:

the secret diary would soon be translated. Ambrosius the Overseer fully expected to know the location of the New Testament by the time the sun went down.

He rode along a little-used track between the city of Roma and its port. His plain clothing would attract no interest, and besides, bandits had been eradicated in the district around the city. It was one of the few perks of Borja's tyrannical rule. Any would-be highwayman was too afraid of being sent to the quarries. It didn't take much to get a man declared "defective" by the Exterminati. Everyone lived in fear of that awful, arbitrary designation.

Not for long, the Overseer thought as he rode toward the port. Soon the power of the Promised King would be harnessed to defeat the evil master of these lands. The satchel hanging from the Overseer's shoulder contained a scribal copy of the diary written by the knight Borregard, who had hidden a New Testament before he died. Almighty Deus, in his wise plan, had chosen Teofil of Chiveis to uncover the diary's long-lost secrets. Excited by that idea, the Overseer urged his horse into a faster gait. It wasn't long before he arrived at the port.

The inn where Teofil was staying appeared to be a decent establishment. As the Overseer dismounted and handed the reins to a stableboy, he examined the building's tidy exterior and well-kept yard. It was a good sign. Although no one here knew about his mission, he wanted to avoid contact with the rough seamen who hung around the waterfront.

"Psst!"

The Overseer couldn't tell where the whisper came from. He swiveled his head but saw no one.

"Up here!"

Ambrosius looked up and saw Lady Vanita Labella standing at an upstairs window. As he started to greet her, she waved him off. "Don't go inside," she hissed. "Meet me at the outhouse."

The Overseer nodded and did as he was told. The structure had two separate privies. He entered one. Soon he heard the door on the other side open and close.

"I'm sorry to meet you in a place like this," Vanita said through the slats.

"Never mind that. Is something the matter?"

"There are Exterminati in the tavern. Two of them. They arrived an hour ago and went into a back room. There's no way out of that room, so I think they're just sitting there waiting. I've been standing in the hall keeping an eye on them until you got here. They must know you're coming."

"Impossible! No one knows about this mission except a trusted few. The Exterminati couldn't have found out."

"Somehow they did because they're here."

"Where's Teofil? He'll protect us."

"That's the other thing I need to tell you. He's gone."

"Gone? What do you mean, gone?"

"He boarded a ship earlier today and sailed away with some pirates. He left me a note explaining it all."

The Overseer was incredulous. "Why would he do such a thing? He's supposed to translate the diary!"

"Don't fault him, okay? He discovered that someone very beloved to him might be—" Vanita hesitated. "Trust me, it's a *long* story. But there's no question he had to leave."

"This is bad news indeed! I'm not a swordsman. I'm not prepared to defend myself against assassins."

"Deus will defend you, Brother Ambrosius."

The Overseer let out a sigh. Lady Vanita was right. He acknowledged her wisdom and silently asked Deus's forgiveness for his lack of faith. Even so, his heart continued to race. "It's not safe to be here," he said. "I have to get the diary back to the basilica right away."

"I know. I paid for a fresh horse already. The boy has it in the stable waiting for you."

"You're a quick thinker, Lady Vanita. And generous."

For a moment she made no reply. Finally the woman spoke solemnly from her side of the outhouse. "I have a lot to atone for."

"Bless you, daughter of Deus."

There was another short silence, then Vanita said, "Go now, brother. Get out of here before you're seen."

The Overseer hurried to the stable and found the waiting horse.

Though he had ridden all morning and was looking forward to a rest, the urgency of the situation made him prefer the trail to the tavern. He rode away from the yard at a slow pace so as not to draw attention to himself. Once he reached the road outside the port, he asked the horse to canter. The leagues slipped by, and an hour later he had neared the city of Roma. The area was remote, for he wasn't following the main road that ran along the river. He passed a few travelers along the way but did not greet them.

As he crested a low rise at the outer precincts of Roma, the Overseer spotted the distant dome of the basilica gleaming in the noonday sun. Relief coursed through him, and he began to relax in the saddle. He decided the Exterminati must have come to the inn only to spy on Teofil. They had no way of knowing about the copy of the diary in the satchel. Though he did not understand why Teofil had suddenly disappeared, the Overseer rejoiced that the diary had not fallen into enemy hands. He closed his eyes and turned his palms toward the sky, holding the reins loosely.

"Great and mighty Deus, I thank thee—"

"Shut up, priest."

An arrow whizzed through the air, followed by the sickening thud of its impact against flesh. The horse jerked and snorted, then tumbled to the ground with a feathered shaft protruding from its flank.

Fear gripped the Overseer as he was thrown from his mount. He rolled over in the dust to see two heavy boots in front of his eyes. Squinting against the glare of the sun, he discerned a giant man towering over him in black chain mail. As the priest tried to scramble away, the man stepped on his robe and pinned him in place. Since flight was impossible, the Overseer waited until he was allowed to stand up. He faced the dark warrior, straightening his shoulders and lifting his chin. Dignity was called for, and courage. *Give me your strength, Deus!*

"There was no need to kill the horse," he said. "That was cruel."

"The horse's suffering will soon be the least of your worries."

"Who are you?"

"We are legion," came the rumbling, echoing voice of the warrior in black. "Now hand me the diary."

✦ ✦ ✦

Teo waded ashore, clambering over the red rocks that lined the beaches of Hahnerat. He held his rucksack out of the water along with his weapons. Kneeling, he opened the pack and inspected the contents. Everything was fairly dry, for the pack was tight and well sealed. The oilskin in which his books were wrapped had done its job. Water beaded up on the outside, but no moisture had penetrated the cloth. Setting the rucksack aside, Teo removed his leather jerkin and linen shirt, then hung them over branches in direct sunlight. He also made sure to dry the blades of his weapons against a clump of grass.

The pirates' barque was now a white dot on the horizon. Teo turned his head and surveyed his surroundings. A ruined castle stood on a peninsula, and a large complex of buildings poked out of the undergrowth nearby. One of the structures was topped with the kind of spire that probably marked it as a temple of Deu. The island was low and piney, and it appeared uninhabited. Teo decided to have a look around.

A narrow trail led into the forest, then opened into a lavender field, although the purple blossoms were not yet in bloom. Teo was examining a faded footprint when he caught movement out of the corner of his eye. He looked up. A young woman stood across the field.

Teo's heart sank. *It's not her.* Disappointment gathered in his gut like a solid lump. The woman was too gaunt to be Ana. Her hair was limp and short, not at all like Ana's lustrous, honey-colored hair. She . . .

Squinting, Teo took a closer look.

His heart began to race.

✦ ✦ ✦

Ana watched the pirate ship sail away, rebuking herself for not having been watchful enough to notice its arrival. The ship had obviously approached Hahnerat and then departed, perhaps because Drake wasn't around to give the all-clear signal with his torches. Ana knew the day was coming when pirates would come ashore despite the lack of a signal. She had scouted two or three hiding places in the woods and had stolen a dagger from the supplies. It hung around her waist on a rope belt.

The afternoon was growing late as Ana made her way back to the beach near the monastery. She thought of that place as her "home" on the island, perhaps because human dwellings were there. However, since the night the demon visited her, she had refused to sleep in the temple of Deu. She slept under the stars now, though fearsome dreams plagued her still.

Ana had been lugging her stone ball for several minutes, so she dropped it while she caught her breath at the edge of a lavender field. She also set down the basket of wild asparagus she had harvested. The fresh vegetable would provide a nice change from salt pork and ship's biscuit.

As she was about to pick up the ball, Ana experienced the eerie sensation of being watched. She glanced up. What she saw made her stomach clench into a knot.

A shirtless pirate stood in the distance, staring at her. Unlike the scrawny Drake, this man was tautly muscled. Though Ana reached for the dagger at her side, she knew she could not overcome a man like him. He started forward, then broke into a run. Ana felt her knees go weak. A terrified gasp burst from her lips. There would be no escape.

The pirate rushed toward her, parting the lavender stalks as he ran. Ana clenched her jaw as she gripped her dagger's hilt. The man would feel the bite of steel before he took her.

Ana watched him draw near. He was incredibly powerful.

And he was coming for her.

◆   ◆   ◆

The closer Teo got to the woman, the less he could contain the hope that swelled within him. He hadn't dared to believe a moment like this could ever occur. Now his defenses crumbled. He discarded his unbelief and let hope have its way.

The woman was thin and bedraggled, but as Teo sprinted across the field he began to recognize her. The way she carried herself . . . her posture . . . the shape of her face . . .

Can it be? Deu, can it be?

He ran. She did not move.

It's her! It's really her!

He was close now, running at full speed. Jubilation overwhelmed him, an unspeakable feeling of exultation and delight.

"Ana!" he cried.

Her eyes went wide. Her expression changed. Her arms reached toward him. She stood motionless in the sunlight, radiant like an angel, waiting for him to come.

✦   ✦   ✦

When the pirate called her by name, Ana swallowed in disbelief.

No!

Is that . . . ?

No! How could it be? It's impossible!

She looked again. The man was only seconds from reaching her. She stared at his face. He was smiling. Ana began to tremble.

Teo!

She dropped her dagger, threw out her arms, and received him.

His coming was like a whirlwind. Teo enclosed Ana in his embrace and gathered her to himself, weeping uncontrollably. She wept too—the pent-up tears of her profound love now flooding out.

"It's you!" he cried. "Ana, I can't believe it! You're alive! Oh, my Ana, you're alive!"

"Yes, Teo, yes, it's really me!"

She matched his hug with a fierce ardor of her own, squeezing him with both arms around his chest. Her face was buried against his neck. Teo's scent was the same as ever: a manly, woodsy smell. It triggered a rush of memories, though in the intensity of the moment she couldn't tell them apart.

He separated from the embrace and gripped her by both shoulders as he examined her face. She beamed back at him, unsure what to say. His expression became concerned.

"Are you hurt? Are you okay?"

That's Teo! His face is all banged up, yet he's looking out for me.

"I'm fine," she said, suddenly self-conscious beneath his steady gaze. She tucked a lock of hair behind her ear and smoothed her ragged shift as if that would matter. "I'm sorry I'm so"—she looked down at her feet—"disgusting."

Teo let out a gasp. "You're not disgusting! You're the most beautiful sight I've ever seen!" He clasped her to himself again. "Ana, I can't believe it's you! I'm so happy . . . so happy . . . ."

He held her for a long time. Ana remained in Teo's embrace, not wanting to be anywhere else in the world. They laughed and cried together, delighting in one another's presence. At last Teo parted from her once more. His eyes were tearful, but his face was joyful.

"We have to do something," he said. "Before we tell our stories, before anything else, we have to pray. Right here, right now we have to thank Deu for what he's done."

Ana knelt, pulling Teo down in front of her. "You go first," she said. "Then I will."

Their prayers ascended to heaven along with the scent of lavender. Teo earnestly thanked Deu for the great miracle he had accomplished. He prayed for Ana's recovery from her hardships and for their future together, whatever that might be. At those words Ana felt her heartbeat accelerate, and she whispered a quiet affirmation to the prayer. When Teo was finished Ana also praised Deu for his abundant grace but then faltered and quickly ended the prayer. Her soul had grown troubled. She sat on the ground and folded her legs beneath herself.

"Teo, there's so much to say."

"I know!" He grinned as he seated himself across from her. "But we're stuck on an island without a boat, so we have plenty of time to catch up."

"Seriously, Teo. We . . . we drifted apart. It was my fault."

Teo noticed her serious mood and looked at her intently. Ana had forgotten how handsome he was, with those gray eyes and his dark, tousled hair.

"I know what you mean," he said. "Somehow we became estranged. I never thought that could happen after all we've been through, but it did. Things got complicated."

"It was more than that. I sinned against you. I sinned against Deu. I've already confessed it to him. Will you forgive me too?" Ana felt tears return to her eyes.

Teo reached for her hand as it rested in her lap. "Of course I forgive you. And I hope you'll forgive me for not being everything you needed."

Ana removed her hand from Teo's and covered her face. "You were everything I could have asked for. I was the one at fault. I just felt so weak. I got caught up in a lifestyle I don't believe in. And I think evil spirits were tricking me. But those aren't excuses! I chose my own path. I became arrogant and sensual and . . . immodest!" She winced. "I feel so *ashamed*."

"Don't be ashamed. You made your confession to Deu. That's enough."

"I can't believe how I treated you! You didn't deserve it, Teo. I'm . . . I'm so sorry."

"It's okay. Remember how you forgave me when I sinned? Well, now I forgive you too."

Ana sniffed and glanced up. "Really?"

"Yes, really! How could I not forgive someone I love as much as you?"

"What about all the terrible things I did? You were so faithful to me, but I kept pushing you away. I even . . . oh, it's awful! I vomited on you!" The memory of the night she became drunk at Count Federco's party stabbed her with remorse. She stared at her lap, unable to endure the thought of having done such a thing. It was embarrassing and repulsive.

Teo patted Ana's hand, and she peeked at him from underneath her eyelashes. He smiled gently at her. "You want to know something? It wasn't as bad as you think. In a strange way I was happy to do it. I wanted to protect you from that shame. I wasn't even bothered by the . . . you know . . ."

Ana put her hand to her forehead and shook her head with her eyes closed.

"I'm telling you, it was no big deal. How about if we just forget it and move on?"

"Can we? Can we truly start over?"

Teo scrambled to his feet. "Sure." He bowed and looked down at Ana as she sat on the ground. "I'm Teofil of the Fifth Regiment," he said in a formal tone. "May I have the name of such an exceptional woman?"

Ana sucked in her breath as she heard Teo's words. They were the words he had used when he first met her. That had been long ago, in a land called Chiveis, a land of unlimited possibilities and unbroken dreams. Ana realized Teo was offering her the ultimate grace: the chance to begin again, to start afresh with nothing between them anymore. His kindness touched her deeply, and a lump gathered in her throat so she couldn't speak.

Unable to convey the words she wanted, she stood up and gazed at Teo with conflicting emotions. She felt an overwhelming desire to be in his arms again, yet hesitated to move. As Teo stood facing her, so lean and muscular and intensely masculine, Ana became aware of a sexual attraction she wasn't prepared to handle. Sensing her confusion, he approached until he stood very close, though he did not touch her. Slowly she bent her neck upward so she could speak into his ear.

"I'm Anastasia of Edgeton," she whispered. "It's nice to meet you, Captain."

He stepped back and caught her eye, smiling. "That's a name I haven't heard in a while."

"Do you miss it?"

"More than you know."

"Why are you so sweet to me, Teo?"

He laughed. "Well, you are extremely lovable."

"I'm not. I'm all dirty, and my hair is chopped, and I haven't shaved my legs in weeks. To top it off I'm wearing a filthy rag with holes in it."

"I can see that. It's quite revealing. Not much left to the imagination."

Ana opened her mouth and crossed her arms over herself. "Teo, what are you saying? Look away if you can see anything!" Though she pretended to be shocked, she knew he could see the little smile on her lips.

"Alright, I'll look away." Teo's expression turned mischievous. "But later on I might peek when you're not watching."

"You're bad!" She swatted him.

"Nah, I'm good," he said with a grin.

She nodded. "You are good, Captain."

For a moment an awkward silence hung between them, until Teo finally said, "Maybe we should get something to eat. I saw a firepit back at the beach, and I brought some supplies in my pack. Are there any rations on this island?"

"Plenty, if you like sailors' food."

"It'll do. Let's go have dinner and tell each other our stories." He started to leave, then noticed Ana bending over. "Hey!" he exclaimed, seeing her chain for the first time in the thick lavender. "What's that?"

"There was an evil man on the island. He put it on me."

"Did he . . . hurt you?"

"Yes, but he's gone now."

Teo's expression grew fierce. "Did he—"

"No, it wasn't like that."

Teo seemed reassured. He picked up the ball. "I'll carry it for you until we can figure out how to take it off." Ana retrieved her dagger and basket, then the two of them set off for the beach.

Dinner that night was a banquet. Teo broke open a couple of store-rooms that had been locked to Ana and found a cache of decent food reserved for some epicurean pirate captain, along with a bottle of excellent brandy. Earlier that day Ana had killed one of the many pheasants with Drake's bow, so she decided to prepare an improvised coq au vin. After simmering the plump bird in red wine with onions, garlic, salt pork, and mushrooms, she seasoned the mixture with thyme, then served it over broad noodles. The wild asparagus made a tasty side dish, while the brandy was a perfect digestif. Teo and Ana laughed as they shared their feast around the campfire.

After dinner, each told the other what had transpired since that awful day in the Manacho courtroom. Though Teo didn't press Ana about her experience in the oubliette, she found herself wanting to tell him a little about it. She said she believed she wasn't in that horrible place for more than a few hours.

"Did you pass out?" Teo winced at the thought. The discussion clearly pained him.

"Actually—" Ana paused before continuing. "The Pierced One visited me soon after I was put in."

"Iesus Christus came to you? You saw him?"

"Yes. At first I thought it was Deu himself. He was so, um . . ." She sought the right word. "I guess you'd say glorious. Very benevolent and wise and powerful. I was sure I was seeing Deu until he reached out his hand. It was scarred, so I knew it was Iesus. He kept me in a safe place for a while. Then the evil man who lived on this island got me out of the shaft and brought me here."

Ana shuddered, prompting Teo to move closer to her as they sat by the fire. He slipped his arm around her shoulders, and she leaned her head against him. For a long while they stared at the campfire, satisfied by their full bellies and their shared closeness.

Teo broke the silence. "Hey, guess what? I translated the whole Old Testament into the Chiveisian speech. In fact, I have it with me."

"The Sacred Writing? You mean I can read all of it now?"

"The Old Testament, at least. We still have to find the New."

"We'll find it, Teo. I know we will. Until then I can read the first part of Deu's book." Having only read excerpts of the scriptures, Ana experienced a sudden thrill at the idea of studying the entire Old Testament at her leisure. Though she wanted to get off the island, the fact that she and Teo could read the Sacred Writing together made the prospect of being marooned much less daunting. Ana resolved to read it as soon as she awoke in the morning. For now, though, she was too sleepy.

Teo and Ana laid out their blankets on either side of the campfire. The crackling flames cast a ruddy glow on Teo's face. They talked quietly as they drifted to sleep. Both agreed the day was one of the most joyous of their lives. They also decided that the bond they shared was too precious to let anything ever come between them again.

A nightmare awoke Ana late in the night. The moon had gone down, but the stars glinted like ice crystals in the sky. She lay on her side facing the campfire, trying to shake off the effects of the bad dream. Though the flames had died to embers, their faint light offered some comfort. The black void at her back felt dangerous and scary.

"You awake?" Teo asked quietly.

Ana was startled by his whisper. She thought he was sleeping.

"Yes. I often have nightmares now."

Teo was silent for a moment, then asked, "Are you afraid?"

"Mm-hm," Ana acknowledged.

"Do you want me to come over by you?"

The words brought a memory to Ana's mind. Teo had asked her that question once before as they lay by a campfire in the Beyond. Ana had declined his offer then, though she wasn't sure why. *Was it fear of intimacy? Feminine modesty? Independence and self-reliance?* Perhaps it was all those things. Now, however, Ana realized she had other desires.

"Okay," she murmured. She wanted Teo close. He came to her with his blankets.

Nestled between Teo and the fire, Ana felt safe again. She remarked on how beautiful the stars were as they swept across the sky in a milky band. Teo agreed. Soon Ana began to grow drowsy.

As she lay with her arm outside her blanket, Teo unexpectedly began to stroke her hand. Ana's heartbeat shot into a rapid flutter. Though she and Teo had held hands before, and had even slept side by side, somehow this felt *different*. The sensation of Teo's caress was tender and warm and even . . . arousing? The tips of his fingers tickled her hand, then her wrist, then up and down her forearm. She stole a sideways glance. Teo's eyes were closed, and he looked as if he was asleep. She began to whisper, "Teo, what are you doing?" but caught herself, afraid to break the moment. His soft touch felt too good for her to do anything to disrupt it. Ana remained quiet and let him continue, until at last she fell asleep under the wheeling stars.

◆　　◆　　◆

The next morning Teo dulled eight pirate knives on the chain around Ana's ankle but only succeeded in making a thin groove on one link. He picked up a rock and raised it above his head. Ana caught his arm.

"Tried that already, Captain." She winked at him, and he set the rock down.

Suddenly Teo's head swung around. He leaped to his feet and drew his sword in the same motion. Ana gasped as he dashed into the underbrush. She heard a squeal of terror.

"Teo! Wait!"

She picked up the stone ball and hurried after him. Teo had corralled Liber and was threatening him with his sword. "No, stop!" she cried. "I know him!"

Teo lowered his weapon. "I heard him sneaking around in the bushes."

Ana went to the terrified man's side. His eyes were closed, and he was mumbling to himself in an indecipherable monotone. "This is Liber," Ana said, switching into the Talyano speech. "He's my friend." At those words Liber halted his muttering and opened his eyes.

"What was he saying?"

"He mumbles like that when he's frightened. He's harmless, Teo. Be sweet to him."

Sheathing his sword, Teo thrust out his hand in greeting. Liber stared at it blankly. Teo took a closer look at the man, then leaned forward and put his hand on Liber's shoulder with a smile. "Hello, Liber. Sorry for the scare. Can we be friends? I'm Teofil."

"Hi, Teofil," Liber replied, still shaken.

The threesome moved back to the open space along the beach. Liber seemed apprehensive. He clutched something to his chest in his giant fist.

"What do you have there?" Teo asked. "Is it something important to you?"

Liber glanced at him and nodded. "Gift for Stasia."

"I'm sure she would love it. Will you show it to us?"

Ana and Teo approached Liber, who held out his fist, then relaxed his fingers. A beautifully carved object lay in his palm. It was made of olivewood, and one end had been shaped into the image of a bird taking flight.

"A key," Ana said. "It's lovely. What's it for?"

Liber pointed at Ana's ankle. "Like the bent one. But straight."

Ana felt her breath catch. "Oh, Liber!" she exclaimed as she looked into her friend's innocent face.

Teo took the key and knelt. It slipped easily into Ana's padlock. With one twist, her chains fell off and she was free. She threw her arms around Liber, thanking him again and again. Teo laughed and clapped Liber on the back. The big man's smile stretched from ear to ear inside his bushy beard.

The rest of the day passed uneventfully. Ana had been marking the time by carving notches on a palm tree each evening. By her count she had been on the island twenty-three days. On the morning of the twenty-fourth, a sail was sighted on the horizon.

"Get out of sight," Teo instructed. Everyone scrambled for the woods. Ana marveled at her ability to run without encumbrance.

The ship anchored a short distance away. A rowboat was lowered and began to come ashore. Teo told Ana and Liber to lie low and remain quiet. The pirates would probably pick up their supplies and leave. Teo studied the rowboat from his position in the bushes. Then, unexpectedly, he jumped up and started pointing.

"It's okay! I'd recognize that handsome rogue anywhere. It's Marco! And look! There's Vanita!"

"What?" Ana was stunned. "Vanita? Where?" She craned her neck.

"In front, see?"

Ana gasped. "What happened to her *hair?*"

Teo glanced at Ana. "You'll have to ask her about that." He started forward, and Ana followed close behind.

The boat reached the shore, and the party of rowers disembarked. Teo and Ana stepped into the open. Vanita spotted Ana and rushed toward her, carrying a small leather valise.

Ana analyzed her emotions. Though she knew Vanita had betrayed her, she couldn't find it in her heart to be angry. Now, at the moment of their reunion, Ana felt nothing but joy at seeing her old friend. She lifted her arms for an embrace, but when Vanita drew near she fell prostrate and grabbed Ana's ankles, crying and shaking.

"Anastasia, will you forgive me? Will you please forgive me?"

"Yes, Vanita, of course!"

"When I read Teofil's note that you might be alive, I hardly dared hope it was true!"

"Deu protected me, and here I am."

"I wronged you horribly! I can only beg your mercy!" She groveled in the dirt.

"What's done is done. I've put the past behind me. Now stand up and hug me properly!"

Vanita rose to her feet, pulling Ana close and holding her tight. She sniffled and whimpered but said nothing. Finally she let go and looked into Ana's eyes. Her expression was earnest. "Do you hate me?"

"Vanita, I said I've forgiven you, and I have."

Ana's words made a visible impact on her friend. She brightened, and a smile came to her lips. "Then can I give you a special gift? I've been dreaming of a day like this ever since Teofil left to go find you. He's not the only one who's missed you all these weeks."

"Okay," Ana replied. "Whatever you think."

Vanita asked Ana if she would meet her in one of the monastery's courtyards in half an hour. When Ana agreed, Vanita picked up her valise and marched in that direction. The pirate captain trailed her with a bulky sack over his shoulder.

Ana arrived at the courtyard at the appointed time. A cauldron of boiling water sat over a fire. Vanita stood beside it, smiling impishly.

"Look what I made for you," she said, gesturing to a water barrel. Vanita lifted the cauldron from the flames and dumped its contents into the barrel. Steam billowed from it as the hot and cold water mixed.

"A bath!" Ana exclaimed.

"And I brought your favorite soaps." Vanita was giggling now, gleeful as a schoolgirl. "All the men are gone. Get in!"

Ana didn't need any further encouragement. She threw away her ragged shift and sank into the makeshift tub, submerging all but her face. The hot water filled the barrel to the brim, a delightful, soothing luxury. Vanita had brought many sweet-smelling lotions, soaps, shampoos, and even a razor. Whenever the bathwater grew lukewarm, Vanita freshened it from the cauldron. Ana stayed in the bath until her fingers were pruned and her skin was rosy.

At last Vanita brought a thick towel and a little keg to step on. Ana stood up in the barrel, her body feeling soft and clean. As she swung her leg over the barrel's rim to climb out, she felt Vanita's finger touch her hip, lightly tracing her scar.

"Anastasia . . . I am truly sorry." Vanita's voice trembled, and she cast her eyes down. "You aren't defective. You're beautiful."

"Actually," Ana said, putting her hand on her friend's shoulder, "I *am* defective. But Deu has made me beautiful again."

◆　　◆　　◆

Teo stood on the deck of the *Midnight Glider* as the sun slipped below the ocean horizon. The light sparkled on the water like a million jewels, but Teo paid it no mind, for Ana was at his side, and she was far more lovely. Vanita had done Ana's makeup to perfection and had cut her hair into a short style that elegantly framed her face. The golden rays of the sunset lay soft upon her delicate skin. Ana wore a gown of iridescent green with fitted sleeves and a deep neckline. Purple amethysts dangled from her ears. They were Ana's favorite gemstone; now they were Teo's too.

Slipping his hand over hers on the ship's rail, he said, "I missed you, Ana."

When she glanced at him and smiled, the sensuous shape of her lips nearly drove him insane. She noticed his sudden desire, and it caught her off guard. Blushing, she uttered a little laugh and seemed to forget what she was going to say.

Teo filled the silence by reaching for an object in his pocket. "I, uh . . . I have something for you."

Ana arched her eyebrows and looked intrigued. When Teo withdrew his gift, she gasped.

He held up the golden pendant of the Pierced One. Ana's face shone. "Oh, Teo, you got it back! That means so much to me."

"Turn around. I'll put it on you—again."

Ana spun to let Teo fasten it at the back of her neck, then faced him, flashing a radiant smile. The pendant rested against the caramel skin between her collarbones. Teo swallowed.

"You look breathtaking," he said.

She eyed him with a coy expression. "You make me feel it."

He stepped toward her. She moved her body in a way that invited him closer. His arms encircled her waist. He could feel her trembling beneath his touch. Ana tilted her head and looked up at him. As her blue-green eyes met his, he sensed the intensity of her affection.

"Teo?"

"Yes?"

"Will you do something for me?"

"Anything you ask."

"It's something I should have asked you long ago."

"Name it."

"Let's find the holy book of Deu—you and me—together."

"Are you sure? As soon as we start looking for it, we'll face opposition."

A smile turned up the corners of Ana's mouth, but her words were spoken with deep sincerity. "Whatever we face, I want to face it with you."

14

The room at Nikolo Borja's palace was expensively furnished and decorated with fine art. Ornate draperies hung at the window. The Overseer might have imagined he was an esteemed guest, were he not tied to a chair with his wrists strapped to the armrests.

The dark man known as the Iron Shield had brought him to the palace after shooting his horse out from under him. The Overseer had been given a little food, and at no time was he abused. Other than being confined to the chair, he had been well-treated. Yet the Iron Shield's words on the road still haunted him: *The horse's suffering will soon be the least of your worries.*

A door opened across the room. The Iron Shield walked in, followed by a short, bald, very fat man whose extravagant attire made him look more like a fop than a gentleman. The Overseer knew it could only be Nikolo Borja himself. The man was as repulsive as descriptions had made him out to be.

"Your hospitality is lacking," the Overseer said, nodding toward his bonds.

"That is because the Christiani are unwelcome in this land."

"Nevertheless, we have a right to be here."

Borja smiled and tucked his chin, making bulges ripple at his neck. "We shall see about that."

"Untie me, if you are the civilized ruler you pretend to be."

"Civilized?" Borja stared into the Overseer's face. "What makes you think I wish to be viewed as civilized?" He scoffed and waved his hand. "No, priest, there is something I desire far more than that."

"To be unjust and oppressive?"

Borja's hand shot out and grabbed the Overseer by the neck. The Overseer struggled to breathe, but the tight fingers did not let go. Borja leaned close until the two men's faces were almost touching.

"To be *feared*," he growled.

After waiting a few more seconds, Borja finally released his grip. The Overseer gulped air and tried to clear away his dizziness. Now he understood the situation. He began to prepare himself for what lay ahead.

The Iron Shield brought a table and set it beside the Overseer's chair. Borja laid three objects on it: a parchment, a quill, and an inkwell. "It is time to renegotiate our agreement," he said.

"Why should I bargain with you?"

Borja smirked. "I shall provide you with motivation soon enough."

"What do you want from me?"

Eyes flaring, Borja pointed an accusing finger in the Overseer's face. "You've been proselytizing! You think I don't see what's going on? We have eyes in every head! We see what you're up to. You and your 'Papa' aren't content to carry out your rituals in your dead temple! No! You must spread your filthy cult among the people. Handing out favors they haven't earned . . . filling their heads full of lies . . . consorting with Defectives like they're actually human! You're disgusting, priest! That scar on your forehead makes you one of them." Borja leaned close again, thrusting his finger under the Overseer's chin. "Before this day is over, there will be even more reasons to call you defective," he snarled.

The Overseer swallowed and blinked his eyes, taken aback not only by the words but by the visceral hatred emanating from his adversary. It was like a solid force—a malignant fist of malice that pummeled the Overseer and threatened to overcome him. He prayed to Deus for the strength to resist it.

"You may not like it, Borja," he said, gathering his courage, "but we have a legal right to exist. You can't prove that any of us has violated the treaty. Some of the aristocrats won't want you upsetting the balance we've achieved here. If you don't release me, there will be legal consequences."

"Ha! So you wish to appeal to the law, do you? Perhaps you forget: your right to exist is dependent on not proselytizing! You have broken that law." Borja poked the parchment on the table with a stubby finger. "When you confess to it, your rights will be altered."

"I will confess to no such thing."

"Oh, I think you can be made to do so."

Borja nodded to the Iron Shield, who approached with a slim knife and a pair of pliers. The Overseer grimaced when he saw the fearsome tools. Beads of sweat broke out on his brow. *Deus, grant me endurance!*

"I'll do it myself," Borja said, taking the knife and pliers from his body-guard. The Iron Shield's hand clamped down on the Overseer's left wrist, which was strapped to the armrest of the chair. Smiling, Borja set the point of the knife against the Overseer's fingertip.

"Cruelty is strength," he said.

He shoved the blade forward.

The Overseer could not help but scream as Borja pried up his finger-nail. Pain like molten fire erupted from his hand and exploded up his arm. Every nerve in his body was seared by the agony. He threw back his head and writhed in the chair.

The Iron Shield laughed. "Nicely done, my lord. May the next nine be just as proficient."

The Overseer panted, unable to breathe because of the intense pain. He could feel sticky blood on his hand but did not dare look at it. Dizziness engulfed him. He thought he might faint.

Borja held up the quill. "Perhaps you are ready to sign?"

"Never," said the Overseer through gritted teeth.

Shrugging, Borja handed the torture implements to the Iron Shield. "Continue until you have obtained the confession. I will see if our guests have arrived."

As the dark warrior approached with the knife and pliers, the Overseer's stomach tightened.

Help me . . . Deus . . . help me . . .

The knife touched the tip of his middle finger. The Overseer clenched his jaw and steeled himself. And then the excruciating pain came again.

On the third nail, he bit his tongue so hard it began to bleed.

On the fifth, he passed out.

A slap across the face awakened him. His head hung low, and his vision was blurred. A throb like a million hammers pounded his hand. The Overseer felt as if a swarm of wasps were stinging his fingertips.

"Look here, priest." It was Borja's voice. "We have some of your friends."

The Overseer squinted through the haze. Sweat stung his eyes. His mouth tasted like blood.

Three figures dressed in ragged garments stood across from him, making whimpering sounds. Their facial features were deformed, their movements jerky. The Overseer could sense the confusion in their childlike minds.

Defectives.

Borja loomed over the Overseer with his hands on his hips. "If your own torment will not cause you to relent, perhaps the deaths of these twisted specimens might make you change your mind."

"Leave them alone, you fiend! They're innocent!"

Borja snapped his fingers. The Iron Shield sprang into action. His mace flashed, and one of the Defectives was knocked across the room. The other two men started to wail. Though they tried to get away, guards held them fast.

"There is no limit to how many I will exterminate," Borja said. "I will keep going until you sign."

The Overseer dropped his chin and closed his eyes. Though the confession might alter the Christiani's legal status, he could not watch the children of Deus be slaughtered one by one.

"Hand me the quill," he said.

Borja turned to the Iron Shield. "Summon the clerks from the League of Merchants. They must witness it."

✦ ✦ ✦

The *Midnight Glider* did not dock in the port of Roma but anchored off a tiny fishing village nearby. Two crewmen rowed Teo and Ana ashore, along with Liber, who had agreed to leave Hahnerat with his new friends since he could no longer obtain food from Drake. Vanita rode in the little boat as well. She had volunteered to watch over Liber while Teo and Ana made contact with the Papa.

All things considered, Teo was in a good mood. Though the plan to translate the diary had been delayed, he felt he was back on track. Ana was at his side. Things were as they should be. Soon they would discover the New Testament together.

They spent the night at an inn on the village's central square. The next morning, the foursome met for breakfast in the common room. Teo marveled at how much food Liber was able to put away. After his isolation on the island, the new tastes were an obvious delight to him.

Teo and Ana departed after breakfast and made their way to the placid river that flowed from Roma to the coast. A riverboat company operated regular trips between the city and the port. Teo purchased two seats under an awning on the rear deck. The boat shoved off, propelled upstream by its crew of rowers. For two hours the forests and cultivated fields slipped by. Eventually, however, the remains of ancient civilization became more frequent.

"We're entering the old city limits of Roma," Teo observed. "Soon we'll reach the modern settlement."

Ana sat up in her seat and craned her neck to look ahead. "I'm so excited to see it!" She glanced over at Teo. "A little afraid too."

"Afraid? Why?"

Ana hesitated, fingering a lock of her hair. "Remember when we had dinner on Fisherman's Isle?"

"How could I forget?"

"I made you swear to find the New Testament that night."

"I know. I've thought of that vow every day since."

"Well, now we're here. This is the culmination of it all. We've waited so long, gone through so much. What if it doesn't turn out like we hoped? What if we never find the book?"

"You're usually so optimistic, Ana. How come you're worried? It isn't like you."

She sighed. "I stayed up last night reading the Old Testament. Not all of it, but a lot. It's obvious there's more to the story. Creation, Abraham,

King David, the prophets—they were all building to something incredible, but now it's been lost. I feel a lot of pressure to recover it."

"Me too," Teo said.

"Yet you're not afraid to fail?"

"I am," Teo admitted, "but that's where faith comes in, I think."

"How so?"

"To me, faith is when you're scared or uncertain about something, but you keep going because you trust the one who's in charge. That's what we have to do here."

Ana nodded. "I've prayed for deeper faith like that. I want to trust Deu. But it's hard! What if we make a wrong decision and blow our chance to find the book? What if the book isn't what we expect it to be? Then do the bad guys win?"

"The bad guys aren't going to win. The New Testament describes the Promised King. He had power from Deu—power we can learn to use too."

"If he was so powerful, why did his servant Iesus die?"

"I guess Iesus didn't tap into the power that the king had."

"But we can?"

Teo smiled as he arched his eyebrows and held up his palms. "That's what we're trying to find out. It's all in the book."

"I hope so," Ana said. "Everything's riding on that." She settled back into her seat.

The riverboat's oars continued to dig into the river. Soon the travelers reached the modern city. Very old buildings, now refurbished, mingled with structures of a more recent vintage. Ana marveled at Roma's ancient grandeur. Teo sensed it too. Roma was different from the cities in Ulmbartia or Likuria. Somehow it felt . . . eternal.

After disembarking at a pier along the riverbank, Teo led Ana toward a distant bridge. The Christiani basilica was on the opposite side of the river. As they wandered past shops and markets, Teo made a point of stopping periodically to let Ana rest her sore foot. The wound Drake had given her had healed well thanks to a honey poultice, so Ana hardly needed the rest, but stopping also gave Teo an opportunity to take note of their surroundings.

After one of the breaks he stepped close to Ana. "Don't be obvious, but do you see that beggar back there?"

Ana slyly glanced over her shoulder. "Yes, I see him."

"He's following us."

"Following us? How do you know?"

"He's been behind us since we got off the boat. When somebody reached out to put a coin in his cup, he ignored it. No beggar does that."

"Who do you think he is?"

"I'm pretty sure underneath those old rags is a shaman."

Ana sucked in her breath. "Those men are awful."

"I don't think he'll try anything in the open, but you never know. What do you say we give him the slip?" Teo leaned close to Ana with a brash grin.

She smiled back. "Lead the way, Captain," she said.

Teo took Ana's hand and darted into a pottery shop. Ignoring the storekeeper's protests, he dashed through a back room and exited into an alley. The pair dodged through the maze of streets, but to Teo's surprise, the beggar managed to keep up. In fact, other figures in similar disguises joined the chase. Teo picked up his pace. Ana stayed right behind him. Rounding a corner, they paused to catch their breath.

Ana peeked around the edge of the building. "They're still there," she said.

"We'll lose them. Come on!"

The land began to rise as Teo and Ana ascended a hill. They changed course at random in an attempt to evade their pursuers. Teo had no idea where he was now. As he emerged from an alley he found himself staring at an immense palace surrounded by gardens. Guards with red armbands stood at attention near the entrance. Though pedestrians milled around the plaza in front of the palace, Teo didn't think he could blend into the crowd before his pursuers caught up with him.

"Teo, look where we are!" Ana's face wore an expression of horror as she pointed at a sign above the palace gate: *Nikolo Borja, Lord of the Pincian Hill.*

"In here, quick!" Teo ducked into a shed in an out-of-the-way corner.

It was filled with bulky objects under tarps. A lavish house stood across from the wooden structure. Ana put her eye to a knothole.

"Unbelievable," she said, turning back to Teo. "It's a brothel."

Teo looked through the hole. A courtyard beside the house centered on a fountain with statues of naked figures in various erotic poses. Overdressed courtesans wearing thick makeup and tall, curly wigs lounged around the fountain or chatted in the courtyard. Delicate, round-bodied eunuchs with pomaded hair ferried the women back and forth to the palace in two-wheeled rickshaws. Teo lifted one of the tarps in the shed. More rickshaws.

Ana peered through a crack in the opposite wall. "The shamans have arrived. How are we going to get out of here?"

"I'll think of something."

"If we go out now, they're sure to spot us."

"We just need a diversion."

As Teo glanced around the shed, his gaze fell on a large water main with a wheeled valve. He instantly recognized what it controlled. Grinning, he caught Ana's attention. Their eyes met. He pointed. A slow smile spread across her face.

"You wouldn't," she said.

"Oh, I would."

Ana came over to Teo and cocked her head as she looked up at him. Her expression was mischievous. "Actually I would too."

Together they began to turn the wheel, opening the valve all the way.

High-pitched screams exploded from the courtyard. Staring through the knothole, Teo saw the decked-out courtesans scrambling for cover as the fountain's heavy spray rained down on them. Their soggy wigs fell to the ground, and their mascara ran down their cheeks as they fled. Rickshaws careened around as the eunuch slaves tried to escort their mistresses out of harm's way. Rough men from the streets added to the pandemonium by teasing and obstructing the courtesans, whose expensive services were the stuff of their wildest dreams.

"Now's our chance," Teo said, encircling Ana's waist as they peeked out the door. "Let's go!"

They dashed from the shed into the hubbub outside. The bewildered shamans looked for them, but Teo used a passing rickshaw to hide from their view. He spotted an alley and scurried into it. After a few more turns he stopped to listen but heard no pursuit. Ana panted next to him.

"There. I told you it wouldn't be difficult," he said. "Have a little more faith in me next time, okay?"

"I did have faith," Ana replied with a smile. "Faith is when you keep going because you trust the one who's in charge."

Teo chuckled. Though he liked Ana's clever quip, he didn't have a quick response. She walked close to him and pointed over his shoulder. Teo turned. The Christiani basilica stood in the distance, its great dome rising into the sky.

"I think that's where our faith will truly be tested," Ana said.

✦   ✦   ✦

Nikolo Borja pulled the last dormouse from a pot of boiling oil and released the tongs so the morsel would fall onto a plate. Although a slave would finish preparing the rodents and distribute them to the guests from the League of Merchants, Borja felt it was good theater to do the actual cooking himself. It gave the appearance of refinement and hospitality. Besides, he liked to watch the dormice squirm when he speared them with his fork.

As the slave served the fried snack to the gathered merchants, Borja stepped behind a podium to deliver the keynote address. The business-men had been discussing financial matters all day; now it was time for something else. The carefully planned speech began by laying a founda-tion of patriotic fervor. Then, after the greatness of Roman society had been extolled at length, Borja launched into a withering critique of the Christiani religion. He cast it as the single greatest threat to the culture and morals of Roman civilization. Nods of agreement circulated around the room as Borja mocked the ancient faith.

A plague, he called it.

The ominous word caught everyone's attention. A hush descended on the crowd as each businessman stopped crunching the little bones of the dormice delicacies and considered the ramifications of what had just been said. Borja waited until the tension was at its highest, then spoke in a conspiratorial tone. "My friends, listen to me. The plague has begun to *spread*."

The spacious hall burst into an uproar. Curses ricocheted back and forth as the audience called for action. Though the shouted solutions were chaotic, everyone agreed on one fact: something had to be done.

The voice of one of the leading bankers rose above the din. "Lord Borja, what makes you say this? How do you know the disease is spreading?"

Borja quieted the crowd with a wave of his hand. Removing a scroll from his embroidered tunic, he unrolled it and showed it to his guests. "The Christiani have been proselytizing! Look here: I have a signed confession."

Again a tumult broke out in the room. The banker stood up from his seat. "Is the document valid?"

Borja signaled two clerks from the League of Merchants to come forward. When they confirmed that the confession was signed by a leading Christiani overseer, the listeners were incensed. The fact that it was signed under physical duress made it all the more legitimate, for it was assumed that torture would force a man to tell the absolute truth. Now there could be no doubt. The Christiani had broken their part of the bargain. Outrage filled the room. Everyone called for punishment.

Borja seized the opportunity. "My brothers, now is the time to crush this corrupted faith. We have let it fester in our midst for too long."

"Tell us what to do!" cried a voice.

"Let us revoke the legal privileges we so foolishly granted to the Christiani. Let us exterminate them from our realm!"

Another merchant raised his hand. "Lord Borja, we should consider all factors before we make a move. A few aristocrats favor the Christiani. They might use their wealth and influence to defend the cult."

"That is true," Borja acknowledged, "and that is why I have called you together today. With the combined resources represented in this room, we could hire the kind of army needed to make any resistance futile."

"That would be costly!" shouted a man in the back. "What's in it for us?"

Borja felt his face flush. Though he tried to hide his fury, he couldn't help but adopt an angry tone. "Forty years I have lived with this bur under my saddle. No more! This confession is all the evidence we need to dissolve the treaty with the Christiani. Gentlemen, I am seeking your support. I ask you to send me mercenaries on the day I cancel the pact. Our troops will seize the Christiani temple and kill anyone who tries to stop us. If some of the local gentry protest, we'll label them conspirators and confiscate their lands. You stand to grow rich off this deal!"

From the murmurs in the room and the crafty smiles creeping across the merchants' faces, Borja could see his words had made a positive impression. He said no more, letting each man's greed take hold of him.

"How would you do it?" asked the wealthy banker. "What's your plan?"

Borja smiled and spread his hands. "I have it all worked out. On Midsummer's Day there will be a great festival in the Temple of All Gods. We will make an offering to the idol of Dakon. By that time I intend to have prepared a special sacrifice for the god. Then I will annul the heresy of the Christiani for a second time—and this time it will be permanent! We will set fire to their temple and burn it to the ground. My assassins will draw their blood throughout the land. Mercenaries will quell any resistance. All you have to do is look the other way until the purge is over. Then you can pick up the spoils for yourself."

"It's too risky," someone yelled.

Vile coward!

Covering his irritation, Borja remained calm. "Yes, there is some risk. That is why I need you to send me troops. Together we can defeat any opposition that might be mounted against us."

He walked forward until he stood in the midst of the seated merchants. Every eye was locked on him. Borja let his voice become sugar-sweet. "My friends, I understand your fears. Like all powerful and respected men, you worry at the prospect of losing your wealth. Let me assure you, no such thing will occur. Yet I sense some of you might be harboring a measure of concern. I would like to put you at ease. To that end I have arranged for some . . . shall we say, some *comfort*."

Borja swept his arm toward the double doors at the side of the room. They burst open to the sound of high-pitched, melodious laughter. As a crowd of voluptuous young courtesans flooded the hall, the men's delighted cries told Borja his victory was complete. Everything had gone according to plan. Laughing to himself, he grabbed one of the girls by the wrist and thrust her to the floor.

It's time to celebrate, he thought. *Let the revelry begin.*

✦ ✦ ✦

Ana approached the Christiani basilica with her eyes opened wide, dazzled once again by the architectural splendor of the ancient religion she now called her own. Like the first time she entered a temple of Deu in a lost city of the wilderness, so now Ana gaped at the great structure rising before her. The dome atop the basilica was an incomprehensible feat of engineering and design. The columns and spires and statues that adorned the building overwhelmed her imagination with their ageless grandeur. Giant letters were carved along the facade. Ana tried to read them, but they made no sense: *IN HONOREM PRINCIPIS APOST . . .* The mysterious letters only added to Ana's sense of wonder. She found herself excited at the prospect of going inside, yet reluctant to do so as well. The interior of such a magnificent temple must be dreadfully beautiful.

She turned toward Teo and caught his sleeve. "It's so immense," she breathed. "I'm in awe."

"There's ancient sacredness here," Teo said. "The temple is old. The Christiani faith is old."

"Deu is old."

"Yeah. 'Before the mountains were born, or you gave birth to the earth and the world, from eternity to eternity, you are Deu.'"

Ana smiled at Teo. "I like a man who can quote the scriptures," she said. Her playful comment made him laugh.

She gestured toward the basilica. "Shall we?" He started up the front steps, and she followed close behind.

They passed through a portal between two massive columns and arrived in a portico with a lofty ceiling. Just as they reached the central bronze door of the temple itself, another door on their right creaked open. "Come this way, pilgrims," said a solemn voice. "Enter through the Holy

Door, for it is a year of jubilee." Ana and Teo glanced at each other and complied.

The interior of the building was even more astounding than Ana had imagined. Her eyes were drawn first to a distant structure, a canopy supported by twisted, spiraling columns. Shafts of sunlight illuminated the canopy from the dome directly above it. Ana's gaze then drifted upward as she marveled at the immensity of the space encompassed by the grand building. At last her eyes alighted on a statue to her right.

"Go see it," said the man in priestly robes who had admitted them inside. "It is a thing of great beauty."

Ana hurried toward the sculpture, her steps quickening as she approached. It depicted a young woman, veiled and demure, with a dead man draped across her lap. He was naked except for a cloth covering his loins. The man's head dangled backward as the woman cradled him with a serene and pious expression.

"The Pierced One," the priest said, "with his mother."

"Oh . . . It's so *moving*." Ana felt sadness well up within her, yet the emotion she experienced was more than pity at Iesus's fate. She was surprised to discover she was powerfully drawn to that sorrowful man. Though she couldn't explain why, Ana found his suffering noble. Somehow it was even . . . triumphant.

Teo walked closer to the statue. "The book of Zacharias says, 'They shall look on me whom they have pierced.' Now here we are, looking at him."

"I think there's another reference to the Pierced One in the Sacred Writing," Ana said. "I read it last night in the Prima. The prophet Isaias says something like, 'He was pierced for our iniquities, he was bruised for our sins. Our punishment was on him, and by his wounds we are healed.'"

Teo turned his head and stared at Ana for a long moment. She couldn't decide whether he thought her statement was ridiculous or profound. Just then the priest beckoned them with his hand.

"My friends? The Papa awaits you. Come."

Ana and Teo followed the bald priest to the far end of the basilica, their footsteps echoing on the marble floor. A chair had been set up beneath a golden window depicting a bird in flight. Ana felt butterflies in her stomach when she saw the Papa waiting for them. The middle-aged man in the chair was slender and handsome, with a regal bearing. He did not smile as they approached.

"Teofil of Chiveis, why did you abandon the assignment I gave you?"

Teo fumbled for an answer, but Ana intervened. "Sir, I can explain. My name is Anastasia of Chiveis. Teofil came to me in a time of dire need. He has restored my life many times, and now he has done it for me again."

The Papa frowned and let out a sigh. "Your care for Anastasia is to be commended, Teofil. Yet it has resulted in an evil turn of events. Brother Ambrosius has been taken captive in Borja's palace. That means our duplicate of the secret diary has fallen into enemy hands."

Teo's jaw dropped at the news. His fingers instinctively gripped the hilt of his sword. "I'll fight my way into Borja's palace! I can find the Overseer and spring him out!"

The Papa waved his hand. "No, Teofil. No one can fight their way into the dungeons of Nikolo Borja. Though you may wish it, now is not the time for daring deeds. You can best serve the will of Deus by translating the diary as intended."

"But what about the Overseer?"

"I will see to him. You have been chosen for a different job."

Teo nodded and bowed his head. "Yes, Holy Father. I have my lexicon with me. If I start right away, I can have the translation for you by tomorrow."

"Let it be so. We will meet again when the task is complete. I will have the diary brought to your chamber. You may go there now."

The bald priest led Teo and Ana to a pair of lodging rooms, then left them alone. As they each stood before their doors, Teo turned to Ana. "Sorry about this," he said, "but I guess I'm going to have to disappear for a while."

"I understand. You're happiest with your nose in ancient books. When you're finished translating, let me know."

"I'll come get you as soon as I'm done." He entered his room.

The rest of the afternoon and the next morning passed without incident. Ana spent most of the time reading the Prima and praying. Meals were brought at appropriate intervals, simple fare served on tin plates.

She was engrossed in a story from the Book of Magistrates about a woman who drove a peg through an evil king's skull when a loud knock startled her. Rising from her bed, she opened the door. Teo burst in, parchments in hand. He didn't look pleased. A jittery feeling took hold of Ana.

"Well? Does the diary tell us where to find the New Testament?" she asked.

Teo shook his head. Ana's heart sank.

"It's nothing but the story of his wanderings."

"Whose?"

"This man named Borregard. He and his friend were running around trying to escape the Exterminati. In the end they got him. Poisoned him. There's a lot about the local topography and plenty of spiritual musings, but he doesn't say where he hid the book."

Ana bit her lip as she considered the matter. "Teo, think about it," she said at length. "He probably wouldn't come out and say where he hid it. Maybe there's a coded message in the diary."

Teo seemed startled at the idea. He rubbed his chin and stared into space, then looked at Ana with a twinkle in his eye. "What do you know," he said good-naturedly. "All this time I've been hanging around you for your pretty face. Now it turns out you have a good brain in there too." He tapped her forehead, but she swatted his hand away.

"Professors always think they're the only smart ones in the room," she said with a huff.

"That's because we usually are." Teo's cocky grin would have been annoying if Ana didn't know he was playing a game. He spread the parchments on a table by the window. "Alright, let's see if we can find a code."

They sat side by side at the table and explored various combinations of letters, looking for repeated words or patterns. For an hour they sifted the pages of the translated diary but could find nothing to indicate a secret message. Teo finally pushed the parchments away and tossed up his hands in frustration.

"The Papa seems to think I've been chosen to figure this out, but I can't make sense of it at all."

"He thinks you're chosen?"

"Supposedly."

Ana located the final page of the diary. "Does he think you're the fulfillment of this prophecy?" She pointed to the words, "The last shall be first and the first last. For many are called, but few are chosen."

"I got that impression from what he said." Teo pounded his fist on the table. "Some choice, huh? All I've been able to accomplish so far is the translation of a travelogue from forty years ago. A bunch of miscellaneous ramblings."

Though Ana heard Teo's words, her attention was focused on the diary's last page. "The last shall be first . . . the first shall be last . . ." She tapped Teo's arm to get his attention, then pointed to the text. "Look! This is exactly how Deu works. He takes the weak and raises them up, and he brings the mighty low. He turns all our values upside-down."

"I know," Teo agreed. "He's not like any god that men would come up with."

Ana met Teo's eyes. "What if this principle were hidden in the diary? Maybe that's how the code works."

"What do you mean?"

"What if you take the first word of each paragraph and make it the last of the message, then the last word becomes the first, and so on. Something like that."

Teo grabbed a quill and dipped it in the inkwell. Sorting through the parchments, he scrawled some words on a blank sheet but soon shook his head. "It doesn't make a message. Just nonsense."

"What if you used the first and last letters instead of words?"

"I'll give it a go."

Teo's quill scratched on the page. The string of letters grew longer. As he worked, he began to get excited. "These are real words, Ana! Words in the Fluid Tongue!"

She leaned close, peeking over his shoulder. After transcribing the letters from the final page, Teo threw his quill on the table triumphantly. Ana looked at what he had written:

bienquesuffoquéeelleachantébienquedécapitéeelleenseigneletroisetleun

"What does it mean? Translate it for me!"

"I don't know what it means, but it says, 'Though suffocated, she sang. Though beheaded, she teaches the three and the one.'"

"That may not make sense to us, but I bet the Papa will be able to interpret it."

Teo rose from the table. "I hope so! Let's go see him."

Collecting the parchments into a stack, Teo and Ana left the lodging room and greeted the warder outside. He summoned a priest, who escorted them to an outer salon at the Papa's residence. It was a plain room, sparsely furnished. The leader of the Christiani religion entered and motioned toward some chairs.

"Please be seated." The Papa glanced at the parchments in Teo's hand. "You've finished the translation, I see."

"Yes. The text says nothing of the New Testament—at least not directly. But we've found a cryptic message encoded in the diary."

"A message? What does it say?" When Teo read the words about the mysterious woman, the Papa's eyes grew wide. He shot up from his chair.

"Suffocated? A singer? Beheaded? It's talking about Holy Cecilia!"

Ana wanted to blurt out, "Who's that?" but her expression must have made it obvious, for the Papa quickly said, "Holy Cecilia was an ancient believer, a patroness of sacred music. Though evil men tried to suffocate her in a steam bath, she survived. She was then beheaded for her faith. When her body was later dug up, it had not decayed. The fingers of her two hands taught that Deus is both three and one. We think the 'three' may be a reference to Deus, the Promised King, and the servant Iesus."

"But how does all this help us find the New Testament?" Teo asked.

The Papa's face grew solemn. "There are Christiani burial grounds outside the city walls. Very old, very dark, very dangerous. The passageways of the dead twist deep beneath the earth. It is believed that the monument of Holy Cecilia lies among the tombs. Today the entrance to that fearsome place is almost forgotten. No one goes there anymore."

Teo rose to face the Papa. "They do now," he said.

345

Ana's eyes flicked toward the ceiling. She smiled. *Good choice,* she told her God.

✦　✦　✦

The young monk with the shaved head dismounted from his pony. He knelt and inspected the ground. "There's a road here somewhere, I think."

"It's there," Teo said, pointing. "See how the cypress trees grow in rows? They once lined a road."

The monk nodded and climbed back in the saddle. After inspecting a frayed map by the early morning light, he led Teo and Ana a little farther. Small buildings poked out of the undergrowth. Most had fallen down, and those that still stood were roofless.

"There's the entrance," said the monk, recognition dawning on his face. "A deacon brought me here when I was a boy so we could pray and remember the departed faithful. I didn't do any praying. I was terrified. A king's treasure couldn't get me down there again."

"A king's treasure couldn't keep me out," Teo said as he swung down from his horse's back.

"Actually the king's treasure is already inside," Ana remarked.

Teo rummaged in his saddlebag and tossed Ana a woolen cloak, which she draped around her shoulders. The temperature in the tombs was known to be cool. She had already changed into a homespun gown like the peasant women wore. Teo had also changed into a more practical outfit of woolen trousers, a thick tunic, and sturdy boots. He expected to get dirty clambering around underground.

The entrance to the tombs was boarded up, but Teo kicked aside the slats and cleared away the boulders and rubble. A staircase led into the inky depths. He tied the end of a spool of string to an anchor point. Lighting two of the torches from his pack, he handed one to Ana.

"Ready?"

Instead of replying, Ana slipped past Teo into the dark tunnel. He tsked and shook his head, then started after her.

A terrified scream echoed up from the depths. Teo's heart jumped into his throat. An explosion of bats burst from the tombs, darting past him with fluttering wings and high-pitched squeaks. Relieved, he hurried down the stairs.

"That startled me," Ana said, reaching out to Teo for support.

"Stay close from now on, okay?"

"Yeah, I think I will."

Teo moved down the nearest passage, playing out the string behind him. It wasn't long before he was completely turned around. If not for the string he would have been hopelessly lost. The hallways were tall and narrow, with niches carved into them to hold the bodies of the deceased. Torchlight revealed that most of the bones had been removed, but here and there the gaping eye sockets of a skeleton stared back in the gloom.

Along the main hallway, small rooms branched off at intervals. Ana stepped into one, and Teo followed. The space was obviously a communal tomb with grave niches on every wall. Decorative images had been painted on the white plaster. In one scene several figures sat around a table with dishes and baskets of bread.

"They're having a supper," Ana said.

"Probably the Sacred Meal. It's an ancient practice of the Christiani."

"I want to understand it." Ana touched the image for a moment before exiting the dark cubicle.

Exploring farther down the labyrinth, they came to the largest room so far. The high ceiling was barrel-vaulted in brick, and the floor was smooth flagstone. Two columns decorated with spiral fluting and ornate capitals flanked each side of the crypt. A large stone panel bore an inscription, though Teo couldn't read it. To the left of the panel, a passageway curved into the darkness.

The air was cool and very still. Teo's oily torch had burned low, so he retrieved another from his pack and lit it from the first. As the flame flared to life, Ana walked down the unknown passage.

"Another room here," she called. There was a pause, then she exclaimed, "Teo! Come quick! I've found something!"

Hurrying into the next chamber, Teo saw Ana kneeling beside a white marble sculpture set into an alcove. It depicted a barefoot female figure lying on her side upon a rectangular pedestal. The woman's head, wrapped in a death shroud, was turned toward the floor so her face was hidden. Both arms rested limply in front of her on the pedestal.

"Look at her hands," Ana said.

"What about them?"

"See how she's holding out three fingers in her right hand and one in her left? I think she's 'teaching three and one' like the message said. I wonder what it means?"

"I have no idea. Maybe we'll find out someday."

Teo reached to the sculpture and brushed away some dirt. A gash encircled the woman's neck. "There's our confirmation. She was beheaded. It's Holy Cecilia for sure."

"That means the New Testament must be hidden around here somewhere!" Ana began to clear the area behind the pedestal. "Help me look for it!"

After jamming the torches into crevices in the wall, Teo knelt beside Ana and joined her in scraping away the accumulated debris. As he wiped the mud from one of the flagstones, he noticed something incised into it: a cross.

"Here it is."

Ana stopped her digging and glanced at Teo. Her long-lashed eyes shone in anticipation of the momentous discovery. For a moment they stared at each other in the flickering torchlight.

"Are you remembering the same thing I am?" she asked.

Teo nodded. "The temple of Deu, when we found the Sacred Writing on the roof."

"You let me draw it out that time. Maybe now it's your turn."

"Back then you were the only one who believed. Now we both do."

Ana smiled. "I'm glad, Teo. How about if we do it together?"

Teo used his knife to pry up the stone. A black space lay beneath. He and Ana plunged their hands into the hole. A jar of clay was there, its lid sealed shut. They lifted it out.

"Do we dare open it?" Ana bit her lip and raised her eyebrows at Teo.

"There's treasure inside. I think we have to." He set down the jar and tapped it with the hilt of his knife. It cracked, and part of it broke away.

Wincing, he gingerly drew out a linen-wrapped object, then unfolded the cloths.

It was a book.

On its cover were three words: *Le Nouveau Testament.*

Ana sucked in her breath. "Is it . . . ?"

"It is."

Teo sensed the presence of an enemy before he heard the footsteps pounding toward him from behind. Dropping the book, he leaped to his feet and drew his battle ax just as a black shadow descended upon him. A mace crashed against the haft of Teo's ax. The violent impact reverberated all the way up his left arm.

Ana shrieked and dodged out of the way. Staggering back from his enemy, Teo shoved Ana out the door of the underground chamber.

"Run! Ride!" he yelled.

There was no time to say anything else. The Iron Shield swung his mace in a deadly arc. Teo ducked as it sliced through the space where he had just been standing. The mace smashed into the face of an icon painted on the wall. Jagged shards of brick rained down. The Iron Shield wrenched the mace from the wall and attacked again. Teo parried with his ax. In the classic move of a Chiveisian soldier, he caught his enemy's weapon in the crook of his ax head, then yanked it from the warrior's hand. It clattered to the floor.

The Iron Shield stepped back and uttered a dark laugh. He wore black chain mail to his knees. His cat's eye, a sickly yellow orb pierced by a slit, reminded Teo of their battle in the sea. Sweat trickled down the man's square jaw. The dancing light of the torches gave him the fierce look of a demon.

"You have led me straight to the prize, Teofil," he gloated. "Now at last I will kill you. My only regret is that I cannot prolong your death. I will have to pour out my anger on your woman instead."

Teo slid the sword of Armand from its sheath and pointed the glittering blade at his adversary. "Your pride will be your downfall, lord of darkness. Come! Test your strength against a servant of the living God."

The Iron Shield reached over his shoulder and withdrew a longsword from a baldric. "Gladly," he snarled, then leaped at Teo like a wolf closing for the kill.

The attack was furious and unrelenting. Teo was hard-pressed to fend off his aggressive enemy, and he had no chance to counterattack as he mounted a desperate defense. Each blow from the muscular warrior felt like the strike of three men, or five, or an entire legion of souls. It was all Teo could do to parry the thrusts with his ax and sword. He knew he could not withstand such a fierce assault for long.

The Iron Shield's sword lunged at Teo's gut. Sidestepping, Teo swept the blade aside with his ax. Then the dark warrior did something unexpected: he smashed his gauntleted fist into Teo's chin. Stunned, Teo dropped his ax and stumbled backward.

The Iron Shield pressed his advantage. Seeing that Teo's left side was now unprotected, he drew back his sword and prepared to bring it around. Teo knew a slashing blow like that would easily sever his arm from his shoulder.

Something flashed in the corner of Teo's vision. He heard a loud crack as splinters exploded against the Iron Shield's forehead. Spinning, the warrior knocked the new assailant to the ground. Teo saw Ana sprawled on the floor, clutching the broken stub of a human thigh bone.

Foolish woman! Foolish and courageous!

Teo sprang into action. Before the Iron Shield could resume his assault, Teo stabbed and forced his enemy to defend himself. Blood trickled into the man's single good eye as he parried Teo's cuts and thrusts. The Iron Shield kept wiping the blood away, but his vision was obviously impaired. The battle had turned.

Suddenly the Iron Shield whirled and grabbed Ana by the arm. She cried out as he put his blade to her throat.

"Give me the book or I'll wash her in blood," he growled.

"No, Teo! Don't do it!" Ana struggled against her captor, but he held her in a vise grip.

Teo knelt by the sculpture and picked up the New Testament, keeping an eye on his opponent the whole time. "Let her go," he said.

"Throw the book over here."

Teo held it low and eyed the Iron Shield. The man would trick him if he could.

"Don't do it, Teo! Not after all this!"

The sight of Ana in the Iron Shield's grip was more than Teo could bear. He pitched the book on the floor, not far from his enemy's feet.

I'll attack him when he reaches for it, Teo thought. *I can make this work!*

The Iron Shield snatched a torch from the wall and shoved it against Ana's back. She screamed as her cloak caught fire.

Aghast, Teo ran forward.

The Iron Shield scooped up the book and disappeared into the shadows with the torch.

"Help me! Teo! Help!" Ana's voice was frantic. Her cloak was ablaze. She was wreathed in flames.

Teo ripped the burning cloak from Ana's neck, its clasp flying across the room. Underneath the cloak, her peasant gown smoldered. She writhed as she tried to get away from the heat. Teo held her firmly and swatted the fabric until the fire was out, then dashed to the hallway. The Iron Shield was gone.

A hole had been singed in Ana's garment. The smooth, white skin of her back was reddened, though not blistered. Teo poured water from his canteen on the burn. Ana arched her body and hissed but did not cry out. He tore a piece of unburnt cloth from her cloak and soaked it thoroughly, then pressed it to her skin as a cool compress. Holding it there, he listened for his enemy's return, but all was quiet in the tunnels.

"Oh, Teo," Ana murmured, "the book . . ."

She turned and looked at him. Though they said nothing aloud, they communicated their grief with their eyes. Ana slipped into Teo's arms, clutching the sleeves of his tunic.

"We lost it," she said, her voice heavy. "We found the book of Deu, and then we lost it."

I lost it, Teo thought.

The remaining torch winked out, and the catacomb went dark.

CHAPTER

15

L iber knew that Miss Vanita had told him to stay put while she went out to buy fish at the village's docks. But Liber didn't want fish. He wanted the new kinds of food. And Miss Vanita hadn't left him any.

The heavyset man rose from his bed in the lodging room he shared with Teofil. Reaching into a pouch on the dresser, he removed a round piece of metal with a picture on it. He knew what it was. Everyone thought big Liber was dull. *Huh! I'm not dull! I know how things work!*

He looked out the window. A road followed the coastline. In the distance ships came and went from the busy harbor. It wasn't far. A man could walk there without much effort. In places like that, people set out food to look at. If he gave them the round metal things, they would let him have their food.

Simple.

Liber put the metal disc in his pocket and closed the bedroom door behind him.

The sun was high and hot when he reached the port of Roma. Many of the pedestrians gawked at him. Before he lived on the isolated island of Hahnerat, people had often been taken aback by his large stature. Their stares did not surprise him. Even so, Liber didn't like the attention. Feeling unsure of himself, he withdrew into his mind and began to utter his comforting, monotonous syllables. Meanwhile, his eyes scanned for food.

At last he saw it: a stall filled with the juicy red fruits he had recently discovered. Stasia had called them "apples of gold." Each was plump and shiny, with a spiky green tuft on top. They were eaten in slices with white cheese and basil. Very delicious. He would need a lot of them.

"I want those," Liber said to the shopkeeper behind the stall. He held up the disc.

The man laughed. "That coin wouldn't even buy you one," he said. Liber didn't understand what that meant.

"I want some," he repeated, reaching for the red fruits.

"Hey, hands off!" The man slapped Liber's wrist. He was just like Drake—a rough, mean man.

Liber brandished the metal piece. "Give me the apples!"

"They're not apples, you freak, they're apples of gold, and you don't have enough to pay for them!"

Liber felt agitated. This wasn't going like he planned. He stomped his foot and grabbed a fruit. The shopkeeper darted around his stall and began to reach for it, shouting curses.

"What's going on here?" an authoritative voice demanded.

Both men ceased wrestling and turned to the speaker. He wore a dark robe with a low-hanging hood that overshadowed all but his mouth. The shopkeeper let go of the fruit and shrank back.

"N-nothing," he said, easing away. "He can have it!"

The robed man approached Liber. "Hmm, what's this? It seems we have a Defective running loose."

The man's words were confusing, but even worse, he radiated evil in a way Liber didn't like at all.

"Go away," he said.

"I think it's you who needs to go away."

The man withdrew a dagger from his cloak and stepped forward. Liber was scared now.

"You will come with me," the evil man said.

I will not!

Liber balled his fist and smashed the man in the face. The man flew backward into the stall, scattering the fruits in a squishy mess.

Terrified by what he had done, Liber rushed from the marketplace and did not look back.

◆　　◆　　◆

Teo pounded his fist against a table in Ana's guest apartment at the basilica. He was grimy from his foray into the underground tombs, and his rough tunic made him itch. Nothing was going right. He stared out the window, his frustration boiling over.

"That book was the key to everything!"

"It's okay," Ana ventured. "At least we're alive."

"It's not okay!" Teo whirled to face her, then immediately softened his angry expression when he saw the startled look on her face. He hung his head and sighed. "I'm sorry. I'm not mad at you, Ana. I'm mad at *myself*. I feel like . . ."

"What?"

"Like I let you down." He stared at the floor.

Ana came to him and put her hand on his arm. "Let me down? Teo, how could I ever feel that way after all you've done for me?"

He shook his head, not lifting his eyes from the floor. "I made a vow to you. I said I would find the New Testament and take its message back to Chiveis. Now that will never happen."

"You don't know that."

"I had it in my hands! I should have been watching for enemies. I should have known the Iron Shield would follow me." Teo smacked his fist into his palm. Despondent, he looked directly at Ana. "It's my fault. I'm a failure."

Ana's eyes widened, and her lips made a circle at his words. "No, Teo! You're not a failure!" Her voice was tinged with emotion. "You'll never be a failure to me."

She moved forward and encircled his chest with her arms. As Teo held Ana's slender form against him, he felt a sense of peace return. She clung to him for a long time, smelling of lavender from the oil they had applied to her burn. Finally she parted and went to her bedside, then returned with the Prima. She flipped it open and placed her finger on the text as she scanned it.

"You know the story of Joseph?"

"Yes. It's in the book of Beginning. He was thrown down a well. His brothers sold him into slavery."

"Right. Joseph was as good as dead. He lost his family, his lands, his people—everything! For a while he was even in prison. But Joseph stayed faithful, and at the right time Deu raised him up to be a mighty king. That's how he was able to save his brothers during the famine."

"So what's your point?"

"Listen to what Joseph said to his brothers." Ana bent her head to the page and read aloud. "'You intended to do me harm, but Deu converted it to good, to accomplish what has happened today, to save the life of a numerous people.' See how the evil circumstances became part of Deu's greater plan? Even though Joseph's brothers meant to injure him, Deu was doing something else—something bigger and more grand. He had purposes Joseph couldn't see until later."

Teo put his hands on his hips and exhaled a heavy breath. He gave Ana a wry grin. "So, Miss Theologian, are you saying Deu wants to overcome my failure by making me a king?"

Ana closed the book and returned Teo's smile. "No . . . I'm saying we shouldn't lose hope when something bad happens. Deu may have purposes we can't see. He's the kind of God who brings victory out of what looks like defeat."

Teo reached toward Ana and put a hand on her shoulder, staring into her blue-green eyes. "Thank you," he said. "I guess I knew that. I just needed the reminder."

She stepped closer, tilting her head to look up at him. "So what do we do next, Captain?"

"I think we ought to pray."

"I was hoping you'd say that."

They knelt side by side in front of the window of the guest apartment with their palms upraised. Each took a few moments to ask Deu to show them the way ahead. Teo's prayers were especially earnest, for he had no idea what path to take.

When they finished praying they stood up. Ana brought out a plate of fruit, cheese, and bread, along with some leftover wine. They sat across the table from each other as they ate lunch.

"Any ideas?" Ana asked.

Teo chewed a slice of dried apple. "I was thinking about how David fought the giant warrior."

"What about it?"

"How he took courage and confronted the giant boldly. He went on the attack because he knew Deu was with him. He took the initiative to face his enemy. Maybe it's time we did the same."

Ana's face lit up. "That's exactly what I was thinking! Why have we been the responders all this time? Borja's thugs keep attacking us and putting us on the defensive. We should take the fight to him!"

"I agree—and I have an idea about how to do it."

"Somehow that doesn't surprise me," Ana said with a knowing smile. "What did you have in mind?"

"I want to free the Overseer from Borja's dungeons. No telling what he's suffering down there."

"That palace looked huge. How would you know where to find him?"

"Last night I was browsing the Papa's library. He had lots of books about Roma—its streets, buildings, infrastructure, urban planning, stuff like that. One of the books showed a floor plan of the palace on the Pincian Hill. It was built long before Borja got hold of it. The dungeons are underground in the south wing."

"The Papa said nobody can fight their way into those dungeons," Ana pointed out.

"Who's talking about fighting? I plan to go in secret. All I need is a disguise that will let me roam the halls without suspicion."

Ana frowned. "Excuse me? Don't you mean *we* need a disguise?"

"Oh come on, Ana! I'm doing this alone. You think I'm going to take you by the hand and lead you into the enemy's lair?"

"You think you could stop me?" she shot back.

Teo acted displeased, though secretly he loved Ana's spirit. "I'm not taking you with me, and that's final," he said.

"You have to take me."

"Why's that?"

"I'm your ticket in. I'm part of your disguise."

"How do you figure?"

Instead of answering, Ana went to a dressing table and rummaged through her bag, then returned with a pair of tweezers. Her smile was impish as she extended her hand and pinched the tweezers in front of Teo's face.

"I hope you're secure in your manhood," she said, "because I'm about to make you very pretty."

◆   ◆   ◆

Teo peeked through the knothole in the shed near Borja's palace. The fountain outside the brothel had resumed its normal flow, and now the courtesans lounged around it once more. As Teo considered his outfit, he was tempted to open the valve again and flee the scene. He felt ridiculous wearing a eunuch's livery, with pomade in his hair and a touch of rouge on his cheeks.

"Do your eyebrows still hurt?" Ana asked.

"They're killing me. I don't know how you women do it."

"It's not easy. It hurts to be beautiful."

Teo turned from the knothole and looked at Ana. Instead of her usual classic attire, she wore a voluptuous dress with a tight-fitting bodice and a low-cut neckline. Her amber hair, normally smooth with a little wave in it, had been curled into tight ringlets. She had smeared more makeup on her face than Teo had ever seen her wear. Ana waved a fan in front of her face.

"How do I look?" she asked in a husky voice.

"I never thought I'd say this, but . . . sleazy."

Ana laughed. "Then I'll blend right in, won't I?"

"I guess that's the point. Get in the rickshaw and we'll go."

Teo rolled the two-wheeled cart into the bright sunshine while Ana sat back and pulled an awning over herself. No one paid them much attention as they made their way to the palace gate. A young guard with a clipboard held up his hand.

"Who are you going to see?" he demanded.

"My mistress only sees the best," Teo said in lilting voice. "He should be on your list."

"Which one?" The guard scanned his clipboard.

"What's the matter? Are you new around here? Who's the noblest man on there?" Teo spoke in an arrogant, contemptuous tone.

"The Duke of Campanya?"

Teo tsked. "Obviously," he scoffed.

The guard inspected Teo more closely. "You don't look soft enough to be a eunuch. You don't act like one either."

Teo put his hand to his chest and affected a languid demeanor. "You think we're all alike? We're individuals, just like you. Some of us are more aggressive than others. But I can assure you, I am what I appear."

The guard squinted at Teo with a doubtful expression.

Teo stepped close to the man. "Are you going to make me prove it? There's only one way you can know for sure."

The guard jumped back, aghast. "Move along," he ordered, waving his clipboard. Teo pulled the rickshaw toward the hilltop palace.

"Quick thinking," Ana said from behind him, "but it's a good thing he didn't call your bluff."

Reaching the palace, they ditched the rickshaw and entered through a side door. They sneaked down a hallway and turned several corners. Twice they passed a group of palace servants, whom they ignored with the confident air of those who are exactly where they should be. Finally Teo led Ana into a stairwell.

"The dungeons ought to be down here," he said. "We need to avoid being seen from now on. There isn't a good reason for a high-class courtesan to visit a jail."

No sooner had Teo spoken than he heard voices and footsteps descending from above. "Hurry! Let's move!" Ana whispered.

The pair scurried down the spiral staircase, passing a window at ground level. The stairs went deep underground until they ended at an oaken door. Teo paused, straining to hear whether the persons above would exit to the main floor. They did not; their footsteps drew nearer. Teo glanced at Ana, then eased open the door. The dark, torchlit hallway on the other side was deserted. Taking Ana by the hand, he slipped through.

"They're coming," Ana said. "We need to hide."

The hallway was lined with doors. Teo tried several, but all were locked.

"They're going to find us!"

Teo grasped a doorknob. It turned in his hand. "Here's one! Come on!" Ana stepped into the room. Teo followed her inside just as two burly men emerged from the stairwell door.

"Did they see us?" Ana's whisper sounded loud in the darkness.

"No, the hallway is too dim. I think we're okay for the moment." Teo heard Ana breathe a sigh of relief.

Reaching for a match in his pocket, Teo struck it and held it up. They were in a storeroom. He lit an oil lamp on a shelf. Stone jars with heavy lids contained moldy, worm-eaten biscuits. Tin plates were stacked next to the jars. Manacles lay scattered on the floor, along with something even more ominous—stout wooden clubs.

Teo put his ear to the door. "I think those guards are gone," he said.

"Look at this, Teo." Ana was reading a log book. Teo peered over her shoulder. The entries were scrawled in the juvenile hand of a barely literate writer. Ana's finger traced the list. "It tells who's been imprisoned here and how much food they're supposed to get. Some of these people must have almost starved."

"Turn the page," Teo said.

Ana complied. "Hey, there he is! The Overseer!" She showed Teo the entry: *Ambrosis, Kristiani preest*. "It says he's in cell 26."

Teo removed a ring of keys from a peg. "They're all numbered. Let's go now, quiet as you can." He led Ana back into the hallway after peeking out to make sure it was empty. Locating cell 26, he unlocked the door, and they darted inside. The room was lit only by a small hole that served as a skylight. Dirty straw littered the floor. A human shape lay motionless in the gloom.

"Brother Ambrosius, can you hear me?" Teo knelt beside the man on the floor. When he rolled over, Teo immediately noticed the jagged scar on his forehead.

"Teofil—is that you?" The Overseer clutched Teo's sleeve with one hand. His beard, normally snow-white, was now filthy and gray.

"Yes! We've come to get you out of here."

The Overseer sat up, and his vision seemed to clear. "I'm weak," he said, smiling ruefully. "The food in this establishment isn't so good."

Teo fished some jerky from his pocket and handed it to the famished man. The Overseer chewed it, eating with dignity despite his hunger. As he ate, his eyes flicked toward Ana, who waited quietly in the background. Teo suddenly remembered their startling costumes.

"We came here in disguise," he said. "This is Anastasia of Chiveis, my closest friend. She is a righteous woman and a believer in Deus." Ana returned the Overseer's greeting with a nod and a courteous word.

When the Overseer finished the jerky, he asked Teo to retrieve a tin pail from the corner. It contained scummy water. The Overseer winced as he tried to use his two hands to drink from the pail.

"Are you okay?" Ana asked.

"They tortured me, but I'll live."

"You were *tortured?*"

The Overseer lifted his hand into the light. Teo recoiled, and Ana emitted a gasp, covering her mouth and turning away. The man's fingertips were a bloody, swollen mess. Where his nails should have been, raw wounds festered.

"Now I am even more defective than I was before." The Overseer did not seem bothered by that fact.

"Can you walk?" Teo inquired. "I think we can get you out of here."

"I can walk, but where could I go and not be noticed?"

"The hallway is empty. If we run into anyone, we'll tell them, uh . . ." Teo thought it over, then motioned toward Ana. "We'll say Borja's courtesan pleased him. As a favor to her, he released you. We're escorting you out."

"Ha!" The Overseer shook his head. "No, Teofil, Borja would never release me. The times are evil, my friend. The Christiani are in danger."

"More than usual?"

"Yes. Borja got an affidavit from me that he'll use to destroy our people. Though I held out under torture, I was forced to capitulate when he began slaughtering the innocent."

"Oh, no," Ana breathed.

"It gets worse," Ambrosius said. "Borja has found the New Testament. I've seen it with my own eyes. The only thing that man enjoys as much as torture is gloating. He stood right here and desecrated the holy scriptures by—well, never mind, it's too crude to repeat." The Overseer grimaced. "Ach! For forty years the Papa sought that book! Now our enemy has it."

Teo felt a stab of shame at the Overseer's words. "Borja might have it now, but we'll get it back."

"Then you'd better hurry. Borja boasted to me about his big plans. He intends to burn it on Midsummer's Day in the Temple of All Gods. The entire priesthood will be there to watch the book be consumed by flames before an idol. Then Borja will dissolve the Christiani treaty and wipe out our people."

"No!" Ana exclaimed.

"I won't let that happen!" Teo vowed.

"You have courage, Teofil, but what can—"

Footsteps sounded in the hallway. Someone was approaching.

Teo ran to the door. "Quick, Ana, over here!"

They stood on either side of the door with their backs to the wall. The latch rattled, then the hinges squeaked as the door swung open. A guard stepped into the room with a tin plate in one hand and a torch in the other. Teo threw his arm around the guard's neck, drawing his elbow tight in a choke hold that would restrict the man's blood flow. In a matter of seconds the guard went limp—but then his tin plate clattered against the stones, and his torch set the straw on the floor ablaze.

"Hey, what's going on?" said a voice in the hallway.

A heavyset man filled the doorframe. Teo socked him in the abdomen and sent him tumbling to the ground, then snatched up the torch. "Come on, hurry!"

Ana had already helped the Overseer to his feet. The trio dashed into the hallway.

"Help! Attack!" shouted the man on the floor. He reached for Teo's ankle, but a swipe from the torch made him withdraw his hand.

"This way to the stairs!" Ana cried.

They headed in the direction of the stairwell but were brought up short by guards advancing from that end of the hall. Teo spun, then halted. More men were coming from the opposite direction.

"In here!" Teo ducked into the storeroom he had used before. Ana and the Overseer followed, then Teo slammed the door and broke the locking mechanism with one of the clubs. The guards began yelling and pounding on the door.

"It'll take them a while to break that down," Teo said.

"But what then? We can't stay in here forever, Teo."

"I don't intend to." He bent to the rear wall and pointed to a line of moist, green algae along the floor. "Look at this."

Ana squinted in the torchlight. "What about it?"

"I noticed it before. Why should it be wet right there? Everything else is dry. There's only one explanation."

The storeroom door shuddered as a guard outside rammed it with his shoulder. It rattled in the frame but didn't budge—yet.

"Stand back." Teo cocked his foot and smashed his heel against the brick wall above the algae. Twice more he did the same. The mortar was old and crumbly. On the fourth try a gaping hole opened up. A cool mustiness wafted into the storeroom, along with the sound of gurgling water.

"A sewer," the Overseer said.

"No, even better—an aqueduct." Teo held up a brick stamped with four letters: SPQR. "In ancient times this was the sign of all public works. It means the Senate and People of Roma erected it."

"How did you know it was here?" Ana asked.

"One of the Papa's books said it ran under the Pincian Hill. When I saw the algae, I knew this had to be it."

After kicking away more bricks to widen the hole, Teo slipped inside, then helped Ana and the Overseer follow him. The tunnel was tight, but they could walk in single file as long as they hunched their backs. A trickle of water ran along the floor. They traveled a long way by the flickering glow of the torch. No one pursued; apparently the storeroom door was holding firm. Occasional holes in the aqueduct wall admitted thin sunbeams speckled with dust. Finally Teo spotted a larger shaft of light ahead.

"We can climb out there," he said.

The three fugitives clambered out of the aqueduct pipe into a deserted area of what had once been ancient Roma. Many tall buildings surrounded them, now thoroughly decayed. Shrubs and vines obscured whatever was left.

Ana approached a marble statue poking out of the ground. It depicted a muscular man with wavy hair. His left hand held a conch into which he blew, while his right hand rested on a horselike creature with wings like the fins of a fish. Water had gathered at the base of the sculpture, forming a deep pool.

"I believe that was part of a fountain," the Overseer said.

Teo nodded. "I saw it in a drawing. Fontana di Trevi. People used to throw coins into it."

"It must have been magnificent in its day," Ana said wistfully. "So much beauty has been lost since ancient times."

Teo dug a pair of copper coins from his pocket and tossed them into the pool. "Here's a wish for beauty's return."

✦　✦　✦

Evening's twilight had gathered in the Painted Chapel when the Papa's messengers began trickling back to their master. All twelve reported good news: the aristocrats to whom they had been sent would attend the secret meeting. Such a momentous convocation had never before occurred. The twelve local Knights of the Cross would assemble at midnight in the sacred chapel of the Christiani. There the Papa would lay out the cold, hard facts.

War was on the way.

Yesterday afternoon the Overseer had arrived at the basilica. The Papa had been delighted to see him, though he was also annoyed that Teofil had disobeyed his orders a second time by entering Borja's dungeons. Nevertheless, the leader of the Christiani had embraced his friend Ambrosius warmly, then sent him straight to a doctor to receive care for his tortured hand.

The information Ambrosius had relayed was shocking. Nikolo Borja planned to burn the New Testament on Midsummer's Day, then use that stunt to galvanize public opinion against the Christiani. He intended to extinguish the Universal Communion once and for all—and the League of Merchants would provide the military muscle to make it happen. Since hearing the terrible news, the Papa had not ceased praying.

Footfalls on the marble floor pulled the Papa's soul from the face of Deus back to earth. The Painted Chapel was dark now, lit only by two candelabras whose waxy tapers had dripped to mere stubs. The Papa pushed himself from the kneeler in front of the altar and stood up, his knees aching. A priest in brown robes approached.

"All the guests have arrived, Your Holiness."

"Excellent. Seat them along the wall. And bring tea! It will be a long night, for we have much to discuss."

"I will show them in."

The twelve men arrived through the chapel's rear door. They craned their necks, marveling at the paintings that covered the ceiling and walls. Most of the knights belonged to the lesser gentry, but a few viscounts and barons were among them, and even one earl. The priest brought a tea cart and made sure the guests were comfortable. When they were settled into their places, the Papa stepped forward to address the assemblage.

"Men of honor and devoted followers of Deus, I welcome you!" Words of greeting echoed from the men in the candlelit hall. "As you know," the Papa continued, "I have never gathered you all at once. I am well aware of the danger in such an undertaking. Only in the most extreme circumstances would I dare to do so. Yet I fear we have reached such a juncture. My friends, I bring you disturbing news tonight. I have learned that Nikolo Borja intends to dissolve our right to exist—and he is backed up by force of arms."

The announcement sent murmurs rippling through the gathered aristocrats. Their tone was indignant. "He can't do that!" the earl exclaimed. "It's outrageous!"

"It is, yet he intends to try. Borja has forced a confession from one of our own. Though its legality is dubious, the people might be convinced by it. Popular opinion is always a precarious thing on which to rely. I fear the situation will be resolved by armed combat. Whoever wins that contest will determine the new scenario."

"Does Borja have an army?" called a voice.

"He has obtained the help of the League of Merchants in hiring condottieri. They will no doubt form a substantial force." The Papa stood before the knights, turning slowly to meet the gaze of each man seated along the wall. "Brothers, this is why I have summoned you here tonight. I need your help. We must have mercenaries of our own."

Once again the twelve aristocrats were thrown into a tumult. They turned to each other in agitated clusters, debating the Papa's request with heated words. Finally the earl stood and spoke. The other knights quieted to hear what he would say.

"Holy Father, you make a valid point. We will indeed require men-at-arms if we are to resist our enemy's designs. But consider the matter from our perspective. We would have to hire troops from the region around Roma, then move them into position and garrison them on our estates until they are needed. Those of us here tonight are men of wealth, to be sure. Yet our costs are high too, and our recent profits have been lean. All our assets are tied up in land. We do not have the kind of liquidity you need—the cash funds to raise an army."

The Papa smiled as he approached the earl, stopping a few paces away. The distinguished, silver-haired man looked back at him, confused by the Papa's mischievous expression.

"My brothers," the Papa said, "did I say anything to you about money?" Silence greeted his question, so he went on. "Hear me now. I do not ask for your wealth, but for your organizational skills and the use of your lands. You have the necessary contacts to obtain the troops, and you have space for their tents and supplies. Yes, there may be some cost to you, but I am not asking you to bear the burden of paying the soldiers or provisioning them."

The knights were dumbfounded. No one spoke for a long moment. At last the earl broke the silence. "But, Your Holiness, this would be an extremely expensive endeavor. Where will the money come from?"

"Deus will provide," the Papa replied. "Just hire the army."

❖   ❖   ❖

"Come on! You can do it! Come to Daddy!" Count Federco Borromo beckoned to little Benito, urging him to take his first step. Benito clung to a chair in Federco's study and gazed at his father, smiling and cooing. His fat legs were wobbly.

Count Federco extended his hand. "Come on! Come on, little man."

In a sudden flurry of exertion Benito trotted three steps and tumbled into his father's arms. Federco scooped him up and kissed his blotchy purple cheek.

"That's my boy! You did it! Oh, Benito, if only your mother could have . . ." Federco stopped and shook his head, dismissing that mournful thought.

Someone knocked, and Count Federco granted permission to enter. The gatekeeper bowed to the count. "Foreign guests have arrived, m'lord. Strangers from far away."

"Did they give you anything?"

The gatekeeper handed his master an envelope with a wax seal. Federco opened it and removed a card. It was blank except for a single sign: a cross.

"Show them in."

The guests were travel-worn and dusty. The leader was a slim man of about thirty years, while his companion was younger and more powerfully built. Federco guessed he was a bodyguard for the journey. The leader stepped forward and bowed. "I bring a message from Roma," he said.

"Hand it to me."

"I beg your pardon—the message is not written but memorized."

Federco nodded, and the man proceeded to speak. After offering the right passwords and countersigns, he recited his message in full. Brother Ambrosius, he said, had been arrested by Borja and tortured. The New Testament had been captured by the enemy. Now the Papa faced his most desperate hour. The Christiani were under attack. A final showdown was coming. Mercenaries were needed—an army of them.

"We have brought pigeons," the messenger announced. "They will fly hundreds of leagues without stopping, straight to Roma. With good winds they can be there in as little as seven hours." After handing Federco a tiny metal tube, he departed with his bodyguard.

The count closed the door behind the men, then walked to the windows that looked out over the terrace. Greater Lake stretched before him, its azure waters reflecting the clear sky above. He cherished its stunning beauty. Nothing was more lovely than the magnificent lake on a warm, sunny day.

Federco's thoughts went to his deceased wife, the Countess Benita. *How she loved the Creator God!* Benita's faith had been strong right to the end. Even as she labored to bring her son into the world and could feel her life slipping away, she had rejoiced in the grace of almighty Deus. "Raise our son to know the Eternal One," she had said, clutching Federco's sleeve. With tears in his eyes, Federco had sworn a solemn oath to his beloved.

"Da-da-da," Benito babbled, tugging the cuff of Federco's trousers.

"My son! Oh my son!" Federco lifted the child from the floor and held him close. Benito squirmed, but his father did not let him go. He looked into the boy's chubby face—a face the shamans dared to call defective. Outrage seethed within the count. "What kind of world is this?" he cried. "It cannot continue!"

Federco set the boy on the floor and went to his desk. Dipping his quill into an inkwell, he scrawled a message on a tiny piece of parchment:

> Greetings to you, Holy Father, in the name of the Eternal One. I have received your emissary. I will send him back to you with letters of credit from the Bank of Ulmbartia. Amount: one million scudi.
>
> Grace be upon you, and on all the brethren. FB

Federco's heart was beating fast as he set down the quill. The amount was almost his entire net worth. Yet, with that guarantee of financial backing, the Papa could immediately borrow from the Roman banks and hire an army. He glanced at Benito, who was staring at a grandfather clock, mesmerized by the swinging pendulum. An overwhelming love washed over the count at the sight of his son.

"Your world shall not be my world," he vowed.

Federco rolled up the parchment and slid it into the metal tube.

◆　◆　◆

Inside the captain's stateroom aboard the *Midnight Glider*, four figures sat around a linen-covered table. Marco had invited Teo, Ana, and Vanita to

dinner, though Teo knew which of the three was the real guest of honor—
and her name wasn't Anastasia. The pirate captain had spared no luxury
for the meal. Fine china, sterling silver, and crystal goblets were upon the
table. The menu was far superior to standard sailor's fare. Even Marco's
appearance fit the occasion. He was impeccably dressed, yet somehow he
still exuded a devil-may-care nonchalance. His cheeks were clean-shaven,
his goatee was combed, and his black hair glistened with oil.

Despite the lovely setting and Marco's fashionable elegance, the
group's mood was somber. It had been twelve days since the Overseer's
escape from the dungeons. When the Papa heard about Borja's evil plan,
he jumped into action. "Teofil," he said, "I'm going to find you and your
companions a place to disappear for a while. Your military skills will be
needed after I've laid some initial plans. For now, though, I want you to
lie low." The Papa sent him to a lonely cottage on the seaside estate of
an earl, where Teo had quickly concluded he wasn't much good at "lying
low." Marco's dinner invitation had offered a welcome respite from the
boredom.

The topic of conversation around the table kept returning to the stolen New Testament. Its loss galled Teo and saddened Ana. Neither could
quit thinking about it. Vanita and Marco strategized with them about
ways to recover the book. Most of the proposed schemes were hopelessly
impractical.

"Maybe you could sneak into the palace as a eunuch again," Vanita
suggested to Teo.

"And go where? I have no idea where the book is hidden. Besides,
they'll be on high alert now. We took a prisoner from under Borja's nose.
He's bound to have tightened security. That palace is locked down like a
treasure chest."

Marco chuckled. "Every treasure chest can be pilfered, one way or
another."

Teo glanced at the handsome pirate. "You have any ideas?"

"When I was a boy, I used to pick pockets outside a whorehouse. The
pimp of that place was rich. Had a lockbox full of gold. I used to look in his
window and dream of stealing it from him, but the box was banded with

iron and was far too strong for me. I could have hammered it for an hour and been no closer to opening it."

Vanita poked Marco in the ribs. "So what did you do, you rascal? Steal the key?"

"The guy was huge and wore the key on his belt. I didn't stand a chance."

"Then did you give up?"

"Ha! Give me a little more credit than that! I used a different strategy—*diversion*. I waited until I saw the guy open the chest. Then I lit a dog's tail on fire and turned him loose in the house. The dog went crazy, furniture flying everywhere, dishes breaking. In all the commotion I dashed in, grabbed a handful of coins, and ran like mad."

Marco paused expectantly. Silence hung over the table.

Suddenly Teo's eyes went wide, and his mouth fell open. "Midsummer's Day!" he exclaimed.

"Now you're thinking," the pirate said.

"On Midsummer's Day the 'chest' will be open, and the 'gold' will be exposed. All we have to do is disrupt the ceremony and snatch the book."

"Exactly. It's all about diversion, as every pickpocket knows."

The wheels of Teo's mind were spinning. "It would have to be something really big. Something that would throw them into confusion and make them afraid."

"How about if you knock over their idol?" Vanita proposed. "The priests would scatter like rats."

Teo considered it. "That's a good idea, but we'd have to string up ropes to do that. It would take too much time. For this plan to work we need to act suddenly. There's no force in the world that could knock over a huge statue like—" Teo paused as an idea came to him. A chill ran down his spine.

The other three figures around the table stared at him, waiting for him to speak. Ana was the first to break the silence. "Surely you're not thinking of . . . Astrebril?"

He glanced at her, excited. "Yes! I have a book about his fire. I accidentally brought it with me from Chiveis."

"Oh, Teo, don't use that terrible powder. It's evil."

"The powder isn't evil. What matters is how you use it. We would use it for good."

Vanita held up her palms, a bewildered expression on her face. "What are you two talking about?"

Ana turned to her friend. "An evil Chiveisian god called Astrebril taught his followers how to make an explosive powder. It's unbelievably powerful. In fact, it destroyed my entire house in a great fire with a sound like being inside a thundercloud."

"Wow," Marco said. "If it could destroy a house, it could certainly knock down the idol."

"Everyone would be stunned," Teo agreed. "We'd have the advantage of surprise. I could run into the Temple of All Gods and grab the New Testament before anyone knew what was happening."

Ana frowned. "It's the enemy's weapon."

"No, it's not! It's just three natural substances. Evildoers may have harnessed it against us, but the substances themselves come from Deu."

"But, Teo, the powder itself is violent. Where would it all end?"

"It would end with us getting back the Holy Book of Deu." Teo found himself a little irritated by Ana's protests.

"Do you know how to make it?" Marco asked.

"I think I could learn. It's all described in the book. You have to mix salt-stone, brimstone, and charcoal. We'd need a lot of those three substances."

"Charcoal is no problem," Vanita said. "Everyone uses it for fires. There's plenty around. I'll buy as much as you want."

"And I can get brimstone easily," Marco added.

Teo was surprised. "Really? Where?"

"Far to the south there's an island with a giant fire mountain. Lots of brimstone there. Traders bring it up to Roma. The launderers buy it for bleaching clothes, and it has some healing properties too. Any merchant ship with a southern flag probably has some aboard. I'll see if I can make a little"—Marco's face turned sly—"acquisition."

"Then that just leaves the salt-stone." Teo turned to Ana. "Didn't you once tell me farmers use it on their crops?"

Ana sighed. "Yes, it's an excellent fertilizer."

"I wonder if any farmers would have some?"

"They might, but not a whole lot. It grows on the walls of cellars and stables and chicken coops. It's a feathery white powder that can be scraped off. It would take a long time to collect a significant amount. However . . ." Ana dropped her eyes and stared at her plate.

"What is it, Ana? Come on, tell me."

Ana looked up and met Teo's gaze. She reached over and gripped his hand. "Are you sure about this?"

"Yes, of course. We have to do something dramatic or we'll lose our chance to retrieve the New Testament before it gets burned up."

"Alright. I trust you." Ana pursed her lips and gathered her thoughts before continuing. "When I went down into the Christiani tombs, do you remember what scared me at first?"

"Yes, a huge flock of bats."

"There was salt-stone everywhere from their droppings. More than we could ever use."

"Great! First thing in the morning, let's start assembling the ingredients. When we have what we need, we'll follow the instructions and try to make the powder." Teo and Marco grinned at each other, but Ana just stared out a porthole at the distant horizon.

Over the course of the next week Teo worked intently on the project. He acquired the salt-stone and charcoal while Marco obtained a keg of brimstone. As Teo worked alongside the roguish pirate, he found himself drawn to the man. The two of them made a good team. While they labored in a remote corner of the earl's estate, the women occupied themselves around the cottage and looked after Liber.

Eventually Teo and Marco managed to perfect a grinding process that would make decent powder. The book from Chiveis, called *The Secret Lore of Astrebril*, said that if the powder was held in a rigid container it would pack far more explosive force. The tighter the container, the more violent the explosion would be. Teo decided to try a sealed clay jar. When he lit the fuse, the effect was enormous: the jar shattered with a loud bang and a brilliant flash of light.

"Imagine what cast iron would do!" Marco said from behind a nearby tree.

"It's time I showed this to the Papa."

The next morning after breakfast Teo led a horse from the stable. A small sack of powder was stowed in the saddlebags. Ana came out to meet him in the cottage's front yard.

"Should I go with you?" she asked as Teo tightened the girth.

"Sure. I'd be glad to have you."

"Aren't you worried the Papa will think the powder belongs to the underworld?"

Teo frowned. "I wish you'd stop saying that sort of thing. I'm no fool, Ana. I'm working hard to get the sacred book of Deu back into the hands of his people. This is the best way."

"So it would seem."

"Look, if you don't agree with what I'm doing, just stay here. I believe this plan is from Deu. If the Papa has any misgivings, he'll say so."

"I have as much at stake in this as you, Teo. I'm only trying to offer perspective."

Ana's tone was firm, but Teo sensed a note of hurt as well. He started to respond, but she began to speak at the same time. They both hesitated.

"I'm sorry I snapped at you," Teo said. "What were you going to say?"

"Oh, let's just drop it." Ana winced and waved her hand.

Teo approached her. "No. What is it?"

"I just . . . I just don't like it when we disagree," she said at last.

"Me either. But we won't let it come between us."

"I know. It's just that . . . well . . . ever since you found me on the island, I've been scared we'll be separated again. I hate the thought of us not being together." Her face reddened. "Obviously that's silly. But I . . . I can't help it."

"It's not silly. It's sweet." Teo smiled warmly. "How about if I saddle up a second horse? Come with me to the basilica, and we'll see what the Papa has to say. Then we can decide what to do next." He turned to go, but she grabbed his sleeve.

"I really do trust you, Teo. You know that, right? I think you're a wise man."

"If I am, it's because I have a very wise woman in my life." He laughed to lighten the mood. When Ana smiled back, he decided to let the matter drop and set out for Roma.

They rode for several hours on a mostly deserted trail. As soon as they arrived at the Christiani basilica Teo requested an audience with the Papa. After a short wait they were shown to the far end of the building where the Papa's throne was located. He sat on it now beneath the yellow window of the flying dove.

"Greetings to you both," the Papa said. "You will be happy to hear that Brother Ambrosius's hand has healed well over the past weeks."

"Indeed that is good news, Holy Father."

"And how may I help you, Teofil? I am told your errand is urgent. That is fitting, for we live in urgent times."

"I come with a strategy for attacking the forces of Nikolo Borja."

"Ah, do you indeed? Battle planning has been on my mind of late as well. The Knights of the Cross are gathering tonight to discuss the matter of troop deployment. In fact, we're meeting at the very estate where you've been residing. As a military man, your insights would be welcome at our convocation."

"I will gladly attend, Your Holiness. And I have a feeling you might wish to give the men a demonstration of a weapon I've developed."

The Papa seemed intrigued. "What sort of weapon?"

"Allow me to show you." Teo set his rucksack on the floor and began to rummage through it.

"You're going to do it *inside?*" Ana whispered.

"On a very small scale." Teo held up a round ball about the size of a cherry. It was made of stiff leather sealed with wax. A fuse poked out of it.

"This secret weapon has tremendous power. I have some thoughts about how we might use it."

"It doesn't look that impressive, Teofil," the Papa said.

"Its force can be expanded by several magnitudes. But even so, watch what this small version can do."

Teo set a household idol of the fish-god Dakon on the floor of the basilica. The Papa leaned forward, fascinated. Teo placed the little bomb between the god's feet and lit the fuse. It began to sizzle and spark. The Papa's eyes went wide.

When the bomb exploded, the sharp report inside the basilica nearly made the Papa leap off his throne. The flash of light, the sudden burst of smoke, the echoes of the bomb's explosion—each made a dramatic impact. The idol of Dakon went skittering across the floor with one of its legs broken off.

"I've never seen anything like it!" the Papa exclaimed. "What is this thing?"

Teo reached for a sack of black powder and handed it to the amazed leader of the Christiani. "It's the mighty provision of Deu," he said.

✦   ✦   ✦

Stasia and Teofil were talking together on the beach. Liber could hear them clearly, though he wasn't interested in their words. He was engrossed with the little brown seashells he was arranging in the sand.

"It went even better when I showed it to the knights," Teofil told Stasia in an excited voice. "You should have seen their expressions! That little idol shot up in the air and shattered when it hit the floor. It was perfect!"

"So they want to use the powder?"

"Definitely. We devised a great plan. The enemy isn't going to know what hit him."

"Well, you're the warrior. I guess you know what you're doing."

"There's a lot to accomplish between now and Midsummer's Day. Three weeks isn't long to make the bomb and put all the pieces in place. There will be lots of strategy meetings. We're supposed to relocate to the basilica. Vanita with you, and Marco with me. I need his help to pull this off."

"But what about—?"

Liber stopped arranging the shells and glanced toward Stasia. He could see she was indicating him with a nod of her head. *People always think I don't know what's going on. I might be slow, but I understand!*

"He needs to go somewhere safe until the battle is over," Teofil said in a hushed tone. Liber pretended not to notice as he organized his shells, but now he was listening more intently.

"Like where?"

"There's a community of Christiani sisters up the shore a ways. They would take him in for a while."

I don't want to go away!

To Liber's dismay, Stasia nodded. "Okay. I guess it's for his own good."

Stasia and Teofil began discussing those boring topics again—wars and powders and other strange talk—but Liber could only think about his own fate. He didn't know if he would like living with the Christiani sisters. The idea was terrifying. As he arranged the shells into a star pattern, Liber asked the Father in the Sky to make him feel calm. His new friends had told him about the gentle Father who lived up there behind the clouds.

"How are you feeling about all this?" Teofil asked Stasia.

Liber frowned. He didn't like how the handsome warrior spoke in such a tender voice. He knew if Teofil made Stasia his wife, she wouldn't have time for a slow man like him anymore.

"Nervous, but trusting Deu," she answered.

"Same here. Let's take a moment to pray." Teofil scooted next to Stasia and lifted his palms to the sky.

"Wait," she said. "Liber should pray with us too."

Liber's heart swelled. *Stasia is so good to me!*

"I don't think so, Ana," Teofil countered. "We shouldn't weigh down his mind with all this. He doesn't need to know about our plans. The idea of a bloody battle will scare him."

The man and woman on the beach debated how much to tell Liber. Stasia was the more insistent of the two. "Liber is one of us," she declared. "Or maybe I should say, we're one of him."

"Yes, but to ask him to pray about this is to lay a heavy burden on his shoulders."

"Deu hears the prayers of the heavy-laden."

Teofil looked at Stasia for a moment, then nodded and gave in.

She waved Liber over. He abandoned his shells and approached the couple. Stasia smiled sweetly.

"Liber, we're going to make a nice home for you with some women who live near here. They're believers in Deu like us. They'll take good care of you."

"Okay," Liber said. He would try to do whatever Stasia asked.

"But first we want you to pray with us," she continued. "Something important is happening, and we need Deu to hear our prayers."

"A big fight. I know."

"Oh, you heard us? Yes, it will be a big fight. You must keep it a secret, okay? It's all going to happen on Midsummer's Day. I want you to pray very hard that Deu's people will win. The sisters can help you keep track of the days. It's three weeks from now. Would you be willing to pray every day until then?"

Stasia looked up at Liber. Her face was so pretty and kind. He sat down beside her in the sand. "I will pray every day," he promised.

Right there on the beach they all prayed to the Father in the Sky. Liber knew his words weren't fancy and smooth, but he prayed with fervor nonetheless. He felt glad Stasia had included him. Teofil, too, had welcomed him with warmth. *These people love me*, he realized.

The next day three sisters in brown robes arrived at the cottage on the earl's estate. They brought an extra horse. After plans were made and Liber's few belongings were packed, the traveling party set out. Liber was surprised to see that Stasia had tears in her eyes. He decided to be brave for her sake and not cry like a woman. But inside he felt sad too.

Liber had ridden behind the three Christiani women for an hour when they stopped for a meal. They had encountered few travelers on the road. Most passed by with a brief greeting, though one strange man had turned his horse and galloped away as the foursome approached. Liber now found a place in the shade. As the kind sisters handed him bread and cheese, his spirits lifted. *Maybe this won't be so bad*, he decided.

Galloping hooves startled Liber. He dropped his bread and cried out. The three sisters also shrieked.

"There you are, you vermin!" The speaker was the evil man with the hood whom Liber had knocked into the apples of gold. Other mean-faced thugs surrounded him. "So you finally decided to emerge from whatever hole you were hiding in! Now you belong to us!"

Terror gripped Liber's gut. He closed his eyes and began to mumble. The rhythmic sound in his head was comforting. Though the syllables held no meaning to him, their monotonous pattern was a refuge.

"Do not think you can elude us, you warped excuse of a man!" the leader screamed. "The stones in the quarries are heavy. You will work hard until the day you die!"

Rough hands grabbed Liber and hauled him up. He begged the mighty Father to protect him, but it was no use. Apparently the Father in the Sky could not hear.

16

The Papa's mercenaries had arrived—strong men, battle-hardened, with swords and axes and bows for hire. Teo stared at their secret encampment in the woods. Would they be enough? In a few days he would find out.

"They look tough," Marco said. "I wouldn't want to face them."

"Borja will have tough soldiers too."

"But they don't know we're coming. We have the advantage of surprise."

"Unless word leaks out," Teo said, drawing a reluctant nod from Marco.

The two men stood at the edge of an opening in the forest. Though the place was entirely covered by a canopy of trees, the understory was sparse, and the soldiers had erected tents across a wide area. A stream meandered through the camp, its water clean, for there were no villages nearby. The forest belonged to a Knight of the Cross who supported the Universal Communion. These were his private hunting grounds, a remote and secluded part of the earl's vast estate. The land stretched away from the sea in a low, flat plain. Few trails penetrated the deep woods.

Teo tied his horse to a tree where it would be out of the way. He would have preferred to let the animal crop a little grass, but the forest prevented its growth, for the trees took everything the thin soil had to offer. The place was unusual. A vast expanse of crumbly pavement lay

just beneath the topsoil. The Ancients' remains were especially numerous here—not only buildings, but rusted equipment and old wheels and
snakelike hoses mingled with the plant life. Teo had passed a peculiar
oblong structure on the way to the mercenary encampment. It was made
of metal, now badly corroded, with flecks of white, green, and red paint
clinging to its exterior. Appendages protruded from it, reminding Teo of
the wings and tail of a bird. One end of the building was pointed, almost
like a nose, and oval windows lined its side in a continuous row. The
whole thing looked curiously like a vehicle, yet Teo knew it was far too
large for that.

Marco snapped Teo's thoughts back to the present. "There's the blacksmith," he said, pointing to a tent at the edge of the mercenary camp. A
forge, anvil, and trough stood behind the tent. Horseshoes lay in a heap
on the ground.

Teo and Marco made their way to the tent, greeting the blacksmith
as they approached. The man's hairy chest was bare, revealing muscles as
hard as the iron he shaped with hammer and tongs. Wiping his hands on
a leather apron at his waist, the blacksmith eyed the newcomers. "What
do you want?" he grunted. "Can't you see I'm busy?"

"We're here to pick up the special commission," Teo said.

"Oh, right." The blacksmith turned and went inside the tent, returning with a sturdy rucksack. He handed it to Teo in exchange for a pouch
of coins, then turned back to his urgent tasks.

Teo waited until he had ridden well clear of the encampment before
opening the pack. He lifted out its contents: an iron container shaped like
a small keg. The keg had a tiny opening on top but otherwise was sealed
tight. An iron plug and a funnel were also in the pack.

"I can't even imagine how loud that thing is going to be," Marco said.
"My men are going to hear it all the way at the port."

"If they do, tell them to cheer, because it's the sound of victory."

Marco glanced up at Teo. "You sure about that?"

"Nothing is certain in life," Teo admitted, "but I'm putting my confidence in Deu. He gave us this gift, and he won't let us down."

"I admire your faith, Teofil, I really do." A sly grin crossed Marco's face. "But I'm going to have the *Glider* anchored offshore—just in case."

✦ ✦ ✦

Liber didn't know what to do when the injured man was thrown over-board. The skinny fellow had reached the point of exhaustion and was useless as an oarsman. The two whipmasters who controlled the crew had tossed him into the ocean, where he wailed pitifully as the ship continued onward. Though the Defective galley slaves pretended not to hear, many of them whimpered and cringed.

"That man needs help," Liber said, terrified at the idea of being left alone in the deep water.

"Ain't no helpin' him," advised the humpbacked rower across the aisle. "The devils have him now."

A whip's sharp report cracked overhead. Liber closed his eyes and pulled the great oar, the chains on his wrists rattling as he labored.

The galley arrived at a harbor late on the third day of travel. Everywhere blocks of white stone were being loaded onto tall ships manned by Defective sailors. Liber was herded into a crowd with other new arrivals. An arrogant whipmaster forced the slaves to march three hours up a mountain valley. The sun had stained the sky red in the valley's mouth when they finally reached a collection of low hovels enclosed by a fence. Men were crowding around a cauldron, each receiving a dollop of gruel in their bowls. Famished, Liber pushed his way forward.

"Where's your bowl, idiot?" the man with the spoon demanded.

Liber stared back. No one had said anything about bowls. The server turned his attention to the next man. Other eager Defectives crowded Liber out.

"I want some!" Liber shouted. His exhaustion and hunger made him mad.

The server jumped to his feet and smacked Liber's face with the spoon. "Then dig it out of your beard!" he snarled. A foreman in the background guffawed.

Liber was too hungry to give up. "Give me food!" he bellowed.

"And what if I don't?"

"Then . . . then I'll tell my friend!"

"What friend?" the server sneered. "You ain't got no friends here."

"His name is Teofil. He's a warrior. He's gonna *fight* you." It was the most dangerous threat Liber could think of.

The server's face turned suspicious. Liber saw his advantage. "That's right," he continued. "A big fight. You're going to lose."

The foreman stormed over, cuffing Liber with his club. "What are you talking about, you dumb ox?"

Uh-oh. Stasia said to keep the fight a secret. Liber clamped his mouth shut.

"I said, what are you talking about?" The foreman struck Liber hard on the ear. "Tell me what you know!"

Liber was afraid now. The blow to his ear hurt, and it had started a trickle of blood down his neck. The foreman brandished his club. Liber raised his arms. "A big fight! A big fight is coming!"

"A battle?"

Liber nodded.

"Where?" the foreman demanded.

Liber remained silent. The club swept down on his injured ear. "Roma! Roma!" he blubbered through the agony. "The Papa!"

Grabbing Liber by his ragged tunic, the foreman drew him close. "You'd better tell me when it's going to be," he said through gritted teeth, "or I'll break both your shins."

Liber thought about how much it hurt whenever he banged his shins on rocks. The threat of the heavy club smashing his leg bones was more than he could bear. Tears came to the big man's eyes. His shoulders sagged.

"Midsummer's Day," he whispered.

The foreman grimaced, then released Liber's tunic and spun away. He marched toward the gate of the Defective camp and disappeared.

Oh no, Liber thought. *What have I done?*

✦　✦　✦

The predawn hours of Midsummer's Day were dark, and the moon was shrouded in clouds. Teo considered that a blessing from Deu.

He stood on the roof of an annex behind the Temple of All Gods. The ancient brick temple was circular in its floor plan and, like the Christiani basilica, was topped by a dome. A ladder leaned against the rotunda's sheer wall, disappearing into the blackness above.

"Here we go," Marco said.

"You nervous?"

"Terrified."

"Me too," Teo admitted. "Maybe that's not a bad thing."

"You go first, *amico*."

Teo set his foot on the ladder's lowest rung and began climbing. A coil of rope was over his shoulder. He was glad it was dark so he didn't have to see how high off the ground he was. Soon he scrambled over the lip of the temple's lofty roof. Minutes later Marco joined him, breathing hard from the weight of his backpack. Both men rested for a few moments as they gazed at the gloomy Roman vista around them. Then, as if on cue, they rose and turned toward the pale, white dome.

The base of the dome was tiered in six levels, but the top portion rose in a smooth arc. Stairs had been carved into the dome all the way up. Teo and Marco reached the crest and dropped to their hands and knees. Crawling forward, they approached the black circle at the dome's high point. It was the oculus—a round hole directly above the great idol of Dakon.

"Now we wait," Teo said. He lay on his back and interlaced his fingers over his chest, hoping to catch an hour of sleep before dawn.

The creaking of a great door awoke Teo from a doze. Servants had arrived in the twilight to prepare the temple for the ceremony at noon. Through a crack in the edge of the oculus, Teo watched the activity below. Men with brooms swept the floor, while others filled a brazier with charcoal. The workers set the brazier on an altar in a decorated wall niche. The giant statue of Dakon gazed upon the proceedings with an expression that seemed more malevolent than benign.

By midmorning a horde of shamans had congregated at the Temple of All Gods. High-ranking Exterminati and aristocratic dignitaries in expensive robes also milled about. Teo's heart began to beat faster. He cracked his knuckles and blew out a breath, trying to calm his nerves. *Everything has come down to this . . .*

"I don't see Borja," Marco whispered.

"He won't arrive until the ritual is about to begin."

The disc of sunlight shining through the oculus crept across the temple floor toward Dakon's scaly feet. Slowly the light made its way up the god's body until his head glowed as if with a heavenly corona. The sun was now directly overhead. It was noon on the summer solstice.

A bell rang out, startling Teo as he watched. Three times it tolled. The crowd within the temple waited in hushed silence as the echoes reverberated around the spherical interior. Then the main doors swept open, and Nikolo Borja entered the hall. He bore a cloth-wrapped object in his bejeweled hands. An awed gasp rose from the crowd.

"Brothers . . . comrades . . . men of distinction, I greet thee!"

Though Borja uttered words of friendly welcome, his powerful aura was intimidating. No one dared respond to his greeting.

"Today I bear ill tidings for those who revere Dakon the Great," Borja continued. "A heresy has grown up among us, a disgusting boil on the face of humanity. Like all boils it must be lanced, so that its filth may spill out and the wound may be healed."

Murmurs of approval greeted Borja's vivid words. He stalked across the marble floor, adored by the crowd. Though the onlookers remained silent, Teo could see how they surged forward in their leader's wake, caught in his magic spell.

Borja assumed his place behind a lectern, illuminated by the radiance from the idol's head. After pausing to let a hush descend on the hall once more, he launched into a persuasive speech of eloquent rhetoric. The declamation began with an encomium on Dakon's virtues, but soon it descended into a tirade against Deus. Borja's vilifying words whipped the crowd to a fever pitch. When he spoke of Christiani beliefs, the onlookers jeered. When he recited the misdeeds of the Papa, the shamans called for blood. When he predicted the destruction of the great basilica, the priests stamped their feet in readiness to pull down its walls. Finally, after decrying Christianity as a vile and sinister religion, Borja declared it illegal. The inflamed shamans pledged themselves to its annihilation.

"And now, my brothers," Borja declared, "we must seek the favor of the mighty Dakon. Only by means of an appeasing gift will we merit his blessing. Today I come with such a gift. Behold! The sacred book of the Christiani!"

Borja let the cloth drop away as he held up the leather-bound volume. The onlookers gasped, drawing back as if the pages themselves contained evil charms. Borja stepped down from the lectern and waddled toward the altar.

High above, Marco laid a box of matches on the lip of the oculus, then checked the strength of the iron bar he had hammered into the roof a week earlier. A rope was fastened to the bar with a sailor's hitch. Marco clasped Teo's shoulder.

"May your God go with you," he said.

Teo nodded. Gazing into the oculus, he swallowed, for his mouth had gone dry. A heavy backpack was on his shoulders, and a torch was in his hand.

Marco struck a match and lit the fuse of a fist-sized bomb. It began to throw off sparks. Next he ignited Teo's torch. When the fuse on the bomb had nearly burned down, Marco tossed it into the gaping maw of the Temple of All Gods.

Nothing happened for a long moment.

But then . . .

The bomb thundered in the confined space, sending shock waves through the building. Although the effect was intimidating, the weapon was designed to smoke rather than destroy. The billowing vapors that followed the concussion caught the shamans off guard. Their screams added to the confusion.

"Now!" Marco cried. "Go!"

Teo pitched the rope's end through the oculus. Holy words sprang to his mind: *The Eternal One is my light and my salvation. Whom shall I fear?* Clutching the rope, he jumped into the smoky temple.

Teo's feet touched the floor just as another smoke bomb from above detonated nearby. The acrid smell of black powder hung thick in the air, and the smoke burned his eyes. Everyone was shouting and rushing around. Teo ran toward the altar. Red-hot coals glowed in the brazier.

Circling behind the altar, Teo found Borja cowering on the floor. The man looked up with bulging eyes. His jowls quivered as he shook his head.

"No!" he screeched. "You can't have it!" He waved his hand and clutched the New Testament to his breast.

"It is not yours to keep," Teo said. "It belongs to the one true God."

He snatched the book from Nikolo Borja.

A massive force suddenly crashed into Teo's back, hurling him across the room. The sound of iron striking iron resounded in the temple. Teo hit the floor hard. His torch and the New Testament flew from his grasp. As he scrambled to his feet, a malignant voice spoke to him, full of deadly power.

"So fate has brought us together once more, Teofil of Chiveis." The Iron Shield lifted his black mace. "This time I will kill you."

Teo's back throbbed. Only the iron keg in his rucksack had kept the blow from snapping his spine. He slid the pack from his shoulders, then drew the sword of Armand. "I have fought you before," he said, "and I am not afraid to do so again."

Smoke swirled in the temple. Torchlight flickered on the evil warrior's face, dancing in his glass eye. With a sinuous motion like a cat, the Iron Shield darted to the New Testament and snatched it from the floor. "Behold, Teofil, you have failed."

"No. It is you who will fail. The victory will belong to Deus."

A shadow enveloped the tall warrior as he inched toward the altar. "Yes, we know," he said in a voice that rumbled from deep within his chest. "But today is not that day."

Blade in hand, Teo stepped closer to the altar. The Iron Shield's flank would be exposed if he made a move toward it. The two men stared at one another, each waiting to see what the other would do.

Teo's rucksack lay near his feet. A long fuse protruded from inside. Before the Iron Shield could react, Teo grabbed his torch and lit the fuse, then pitched the pack against the idol's feet. Though this wasn't the way he had planned things, he judged now was the time for a desperate gamble.

The Iron Shield's jaw dropped. "You'll kill us all, you fool!"

"Throw me the book and I'll put it out!"

"Never!"

"Are you prepared to meet Deus?"

"Deus be cursed to the depths of hell!"

The Iron Shield heaved the New Testament over Teo's head. Borja caught it and plunged it into the brazier. A demented smile was plastered across his face. The book's brittle pages burst into flame.

No! Stop!

Teo dashed to the altar as the Iron Shield moved in the opposite direction. Teo tried to grab the burning book, but the fire was too hot. Already the pages had curled up and turned black. Bits of ash floated on the wafting smoke. As Teo watched in horror, the New Testament was engulfed by the hungry flames.

"You lose!" Borja stood several paces away, clapping his hands and dancing madly. "Look at that book burn! You lose!"

Teo turned his back on the repugnant man.

The Iron Shield knelt beside the pack containing the ironclad bomb. He gripped the fuse in his fist and yanked it out. Teo drew his war ax and sent a steel ball hurtling toward his enemy. The missile took the Iron Shield on the knuckles. Though the warrior's hand was gauntleted, he cried out in pain and whirled to face Teo.

From the roof a bugle sounded—Marco's signal for the Christiani forces to attack.

The Iron Shield's head snapped toward the oculus. Assessing the situation in an instant, he dropped his eyes and stared at Teo. "We will meet again," he vowed, then rushed through the doorway into the battle outside.

Borja's haughty voice made Teo spin around. Four shamans stood next to their leader, each holding a dagger.

"You think we don't know about your pitiful rebellion?" Borja's face contorted into a sneer. "We found out all about it. Your troops have walked into a trap. It will be a glorious slaughter! At this very moment my men are advancing toward your temple. They will kill everyone they find: your mercenaries, your Papa, and yes, even your woman."

Ana . . .

Teo ran to the base of the idol and snatched his rucksack. Though the bomb hadn't destroyed the statue as intended, it was still a powerful weapon that could take out many enemies, perhaps even turn the tide of battle. Teo sprinted out the door with the bomb on his back.

The plaza outside the Temple of All Gods rang with the clash of swords and shields as the mercenaries fought in hand-to-hand combat. A fighter on horseback spotted Teo and charged, but Teo parried the thrust and ran his sword through the man. Yanking the rider from the saddle, he mounted and turned into an alley. With a kick of his heels, he urged the horse into a gallop. Its hooves clip-clopped against the cobbled streets of Roma.

Teo's mind reeled. The New Testament was gone. Everything was in motion now. The final outcome would be decided at the Christiani basilica. There he would make a final stand. If he reached the basilica in time, the battle could still be won.

At the very least, Ana must not fall into Nikolo Borja's hands.

O Deu, Teo prayed, *show us your power! Give us the victory!* Though the urgent prayer comforted him as he galloped through the streets, he couldn't shake the feeling he had been here before.

Teo arrived at the basilica to find a pitched battle unfolding within the arms of the church. As he galloped into the circular plaza with his sword unsheathed, he discerned right away that the Christiani fighters were hard-pressed. Though the Knights of the Cross fought valiantly alongside their troops, the enemy was starting to overwhelm them. Borja's condottieri outnumbered the Christiani mercenaries by at least three to one. Unless some dramatic action altered the balance of power, the outcome didn't look promising.

Surging ahead on his warhorse, Teo dealt a series of grievous blows to the footmen who dared to confront him. He passed the stone spike in the center of the plaza and fought his way toward the basilica. One of the Christiani knights, his silver hair slick with blood, held the portico as a last line of defense. Teo leaned from the saddle and swung the sword of Armand in an arc, severing the head of a man attacking the earl. The earl glanced up from his enemy's fallen corpse and nodded at Teo, letting him pass.

At the top of the steps Teo paused and looked out over the plaza. Many of the Christiani mercenaries had fled the scene, while those who still fought were being forced back. The battle had turned into a rout. Borja had taken the day.

Teo dismounted and ran inside the basilica, slamming the door and throwing down the bar. The Papa was there, as well as the Overseer with his bandaged hand. Other priests, servants, and aristocrats milled around. Off to the side Teo spotted Ana standing with Vanita. Relief coursed through him, though the emotion was fleeting. *She's still in danger*, he reminded himself.

"Listen, everyone!" All eyes turned in Teo's direction, and Ana's face lit up when she saw him. He beckoned the little crowd to come near. "The battle has gone against us. If you have weapons, get them ready. We must fight our way out if we want to live."

"Indeed we must fight!" The Papa's voice rang out in the silence of the cavernous nave. "But let us not forget, brothers and sisters, that we Christiani bear the most powerful weapon of all." Gathering his companions around him, the Papa asked them to kneel. "Each of us must fight in the way he is gifted by the Eternal One. Fight on with your sword, Teofil of Chiveis, for that is the strength Deus has given you. We who are not warriors will fight with words of intercession. Let us all rely on our God in this hour of desperate need."

At the far end of the basilica a figure materialized from the shadows. Sword in hand, Teo ran to meet the intruder but quickly discerned it was Marco. As the pirate drew near, Ana and Vanita also came to greet him.

"There's no time to wait," Marco said. "I've come up through the grottoes. I have horses with me, four good ones. My ship is ready to sail at the port. The cause here is lost. Escape with me now! We must live to fight another day."

Vanita nodded. "It's a strategic retreat. We need to go."

Teo glanced at Ana. Her eyes were closed, her chin tucked to her breast. He touched her shoulder. "Ana? I think Marco is right."

She did not open her eyes. "I have no strength to flee again, Teo. Not again."

"I know it's hard. But perhaps we must accept it like when we left Chiveis."

Ana looked up, pointing to the group kneeling beside the Papa. "What about them? They haven't given up yet. They're still praying."

"Deu has a plan for them, and he has a plan for us. We must walk the road he has laid before us."

Tears gathered in Ana's eyes. "This isn't the future I imagined," she whispered.

"Me either. But we must step into it nonetheless."

"Must we?" Ana turned toward Teo and gripped his leather jerkin in her fists. Her face betrayed her anguish. "Must we always lose? Always flee?" She shook him by his garments, staring into his eyes. "Where is Deu's *power*? Tell me that, Teo! Where is it?" Ana dropped her hands and threw back her head, lifting her voice to the ceiling. "Tell me, Deu!" she shouted. "*Where is your power?*" Overcome by tears, she buried her face in her palms.

Teo stood in the basilica with his bloody sword, unsure what he should do next. His gaze moved from Ana's weeping form to the wide, expectant eyes of Marco and Vanita.

It's up to me to make a decision, he realized. *Whatever I decide now is going to determine life or death.*

So be it.

I'm in your hands, Deu.

He looked directly at Marco. "Give me your matches. And another fuse."

As Marco fumbled in his pockets and handed over the items, Ana lifted her face from her hands. "Wait a minute, Teo. What are you doing?"

"Cutting off the head of the snake." He turned to go.

"But you'll be killed!" Ana grabbed his sleeve. Teo wrenched himself from her grasp and started running toward the basilica's front door.

"Stop! Wait!"

He ignored her desperate pleas and kept going.

"Teo! Come back to me!"

This time Teo could not give his usual answer.

✦ ✦ ✦

Everything was quiet. The sounds of battle had died down outside. Ana pressed her ear against the door of the basilica, straining to hear what was happening. Fear gripped her. *Will I ever see Teo again?* She didn't know.

When the explosion came, its force physically knocked her from the door. Ana staggered back, her ears ringing. The deafening concussion shook the very foundations of the Christiani basilica. She held her skull in her hands and shook her head. It was all too much. The tightness in her chest made her feel she might suffocate. Ana was at the end of her strength.

Help me, Deu! Protect Teo! Oh please, Deu . . . please . . .

Vanita came and stood next to her, slipping her arm around Ana's shoulders. "I'll stay with you until the end," she said.

The sound of men in the portico startled Ana back to reality. She heard shouting, followed by a tremendous boom as something heavy smashed into the door. The Christiani who had taken refuge in the basilica cried out, and many turned to flee. Again the men outside rammed the door. The hinges snapped, then one of the great bronze doors tumbled to the floor with a deafening crash.

From out of the swirling dust Nikolo Borja pranced into the hall, backlit by the dazzling sun. He was even fatter than Ana had imagined. The obese man was sweating in his engraved silver breastplate, which looked ridiculous on someone so obviously not a warrior. From his belt hung an ornate dagger that surely had never seen service in battle. Even so, Borja seemed to relish playing the role of conquering hero. His face wore a look of arrogant disdain.

"So, Papa, it has all come to this. Welcome to the day of your final defeat."

"Victory belongs to Deus," the Papa replied.

Borja smiled. "Is that so? Come here and behold the 'victory' of your God." He walked out to the barrel-vaulted portico, beckoning the Papa and the Overseer to follow. Ana and Vanita went too, but Marco hung back.

Teo!

He was held by two strong shamans, his wrists bound in manacles behind his back. The Iron Shield stood nearby. Teo's face was blackened by soot, and a line of blood trickled from his forehead.

Borja spread his arms toward the plaza encompassed by the circular colonnade. The Christiani mercenaries were gone. A silver-haired aristocrat lay dead on the steps. Only Borja's troops remained—thousands of them. A deep crater was gouged into the plaza's pavement. Smoke and dust still rose from it.

"Your weapon is fierce, Papa, I grant you that. It will be my pleasure to wring its secrets from you. But as you can see, your great hero has failed." Borja punched Teo in the abdomen, doubling him over. Teo winced as he took the blow but straightened again without replying. Borja snapped his fingers. The Iron Shield stepped forward.

"Hurt him," Borja said. "Hurt him hard."

The corners of the Iron Shield's lips turned up in a smirk, and his cat's eye made his face appear demonic. He brought out a small, evil-looking knife and moved toward Teo while the shamans held him in place.

Ana's breath caught, and her knees went weak. *No! Deu, help him!*

Teo stared into the dark interior of the basilica. Ana's eyes flitted to where he was looking. Marco was there, holding one of the smoke bombs. A match flared. Marco lit the fuse and rolled the bomb onto the portico.

"Look out!" Borja shrieked, covering his body with his fleshy arms.

Everyone stood frozen as the bomb's fuse hissed and sparked. Ana's heart pounded in her chest. Adrenaline rushed through her body, preparing her for instant action. *Run to the horses*, said a voice in her head.

The moment hung suspended. The bomb stopped rolling. For a split second everything was silent.

Then it happened.

The bomb's fuse fizzled out.

What?

Ana stared at it. The little round ball sat on the marble pavement of the portico. A tendril of smoke wafted from the fuse.

The Iron Shield snatched the bomb and hurled it away. He ran to Marco and seized him by the neck, shoving him to the portico floor, kicking him in the ribs. Marco grunted and rolled over.

Turning toward Teo, the Iron Shield grabbed a fistful of hair and yanked his head back. The warrior's teeth gnashed in Teo's face. The knife glittered in his hand.

"I believe it was your God who said 'an eye for an eye,'" he snarled.

Teo struggled, trying to get away, but he could not. The point of the knife moved toward his face.

"No! Leave him alone!" Ana started toward him, but Borja caught her arm, wrenching it behind her back. She cried out.

Teo turned and met Ana's eyes. She knew why. He wanted to take one last look at her before he was blinded.

"I love you," she mouthed to him.

At that moment the shout of a mighty host descended upon the holy place. All eyes looked up at the sudden, deafening noise. The Iron Shield ran to the portico's main portal and looked out. Borja uttered a cry of confusion and dismay.

Ana darted to another portal. Thousands of men streamed into the plaza, an army too large to comprehend. They wore ragged garments, sometimes just loincloths. Their weapons were sticks and hammers and pickaxes. Something about the way the men moved caught Ana's attention. Their motions were jerky and awkward. She gasped as she realized what she was seeing.

Defectives!

"Rally our troops!" Borja screamed to the Iron Shield. "Lead a charge! Kill them!" His face turned red, and his eyes bulged as he watched the mayhem in the plaza. The Iron Shield instantly obeyed his master's command. He drew his mace and leaped into the fray.

Though the Defectives were ill-equipped, they made up for it with courage and sheer numbers. When one of their men went down, three more sprang into his place. They fought without fear, unleashing their righteous anger against the army of their oppressor. As the mercenaries were knocked to the ground, the Defectives dropped their primitive weapons and picked up the swords and shields. Borja's forces could not withstand the fierce onslaught of so great a company.

Staring at the unbelievable scene, Ana noticed a blond-haired man leading the Defectives in battle. His movements weren't awkward; they were the smooth motions of a warrior who knew how to wield a sword. Beside him fought a giant man with a dark beard and a bald, bloodied head. He used a shepherd's crook like a scythe as he cleared a swath toward the basilica.

The man looked up, and Ana recognized him. She called his name: "Liber!"

When Liber spotted Ana he became a madman. He swung his staff in great, furious arcs, knocking foes aside as he barreled toward her. Reaching the steps, he mounted them swiftly. Ana had backed up into the portico for safety. Liber ran to her with his arms outstretched.

"Stasia!" he cried.

Ana leaped toward Liber, but not so she could return his embrace. She snatched his crook and brought it down hard on a figure behind him. The staff made a dull thud as it struck flesh. Borja howled and collapsed to the ground, clutching his shoulder. His dagger clattered across the portico's marble floor.

"Keep your hands off my friend, you backstabber!" Ana shouted.

She brandished the staff as she towered over the fat man. Borja stared up at her. His face streamed sweat, and his breathing was labored. Ana feinted toward him with the stick. Borja squealed like a pig and squirmed away on his rump.

"Aaargh!" Borja's mouth contorted into a grimace. His pudgy hand clawed at his left arm. The blood drained from his face. His body convulsed, then his eyes rolled back in their sockets.

Ana reeled, horrified by the gruesome spectacle. The man slumped over, his head lolling in an unnatural way. He emitted a raspy gurgle. Dark fluid ran down his chin. Ana covered her face and turned away.

A voice in her ear made her jump.

"Ana, quick! Help me take off these handcuffs!" Teo touched Borja's corpse with the toe of his boot. "The key is right there in his pocket."

Disgusted, Ana started to kneel, but Liber intervened. He plucked the key from Borja's trousers and handed it to Ana, who opened Teo's cuffs. Teo immediately drew his sword and ran to the central portal but stopped short and stared out at the plaza.

"It's finished," he called over his shoulder. "The mercenaries have gone."

"Victory!" the Papa shouted. "Deus has given us victory!"

Teo turned toward Ana, and she ran to him. She could hardly believe what was happening.

"Anastasia!" shouted a voice.

Ana released Teo to see who had called her name. The blond warrior she had noticed before ascended the steps to the portico. Though he was gaunt, Ana now recognized who it was.

"Bard, I can't believe it's you!" Ana greeted him joyfully. She had never thought she would see the Ulmbartian army scout again.

"It's me, alright. And look who I've brought with me!" Bard turned and gestured behind him.

Now it was Teo's turn to be stunned. "Sol! You're alive!" He embraced the white-haired teacher. Teo seemed genuinely moved as he hugged his friend and clapped him on the back.

The Papa and the Overseer approached the jubilant group. "Which of you can tell me what's going on here?" the Papa asked.

Sol faced the Papa. "Your Holiness, the army you see before you has come from the marble quarries. Long have these slaves been oppressed by vicious cruelty, but Deus came to us at last. We finally found our strength and rebelled against our overlords. Our numbers were too great for them, so they fled. Then one of our brothers informed us of a great battle that would take place on—"

"Midsummer's Day!" Liber shouted in his thick voice.

Sol smiled. "Yes, Liber, on Midsummer's Day. Everyone wanted to be part of the fight against Nikolo Borja, who had oppressed us for so long. We sailed to Roma on the quarry ships and marched straight here. Every man and woman you see has come willingly to serve the cause of Deus."

The Papa was astounded. "The marble slaves know about Deus? They are Christiani?"

"Yes, Your Holiness, the slaves have become Christiani. In fact, they now know more about Deus than you."

"That does not surprise me," the Overseer interjected. "Deus is close to the afflicted."

"Indeed. But I am talking about more than intuitive knowledge. These so-called Defectives have learned a great secret, one that turned their beliefs on end. All their lives they've been treated as worthless. The Exterminati beat them down and terrified them with stories of torment in the next life. They had no hope—no hope, that is, until they learned about the son of Deus."

"Deus has a *son?*" Teo's mouth hung open.

"Yes," Sol replied, "and he is none other than Iesus Christus. The Pierced One and the Promised King are one and the same. We had it all wrong, Teofil. We assumed the Promised King couldn't be Iesus because he died in defeat. But as it turns out, weakness and victory aren't opposites at all. In the strange wisdom of Deus they're bound together."

"So Iesus was a martyr king?" Teo asked. "A king who was killed but remained true to his principles?"

"No. It is true Iesus died a shameful death. For a time it looked like a defeat. However . . ." Sol paused, overcome by the gravity of the moment. He had to collect his thoughts before continuing. "The truth is, the Pierced One did not remain in his grave. On the third day Deus raised him again to new life. Iesus came forth from his tomb and walked on the earth once more, then ascended into the sky, alive and victorious forever."

"This is incredible!" The Papa grasped his forehead in a gesture of speechless awe. He staggered as he tried to take it all in. Slowly a smile crept across his face. "Yet it makes perfect sense," he said at last. "Deus is a God of deliverance. He gives victory to the weak. How beautiful that his own son should demonstrate this truth in such a dramatic way."

Sol nodded. "The scriptures say Deus has chosen the foolish things of the world to confound the wise."

"I don't remember that," Teo said. "Where did you read it?"

Sol flashed Teo a mischievous grin. "In the New Testament, of course."

"What? How? I saw it burned to ashes!"

"That does not stop our God. He has led us to another version."

"Another version?" Ana stepped forward and stood next to Teo. "Show it to us!"

"My dear Anastasia, you and Teofil have had it in your midst all along, yet you did not have eyes to see it."

Ana and Teo exchanged glances. She had no idea what Sol meant.

The old man summoned Liber to come close. *"Dixit ei Iesus ego sum resurrectio,"* Sol said.

At those words Liber closed his eyes and began to chant—not in his normal voice, but with an eloquence that took Ana by surprise. The syllables rolled off Liber's tongue like honey. He even trilled his r's like some patrician from long ago. "*Dixit ei Iesus ego sum resurrectio et vita,*" he recited in a steady, pleasing cadence. "*Qui credit in me et si mortuus fuerit vivet, et omnis qui vivit et credit in me non morietur in aeternum.*"

Sol translated on the fly. "Iesus said to her, 'I am the resurrection and the life. He who believes in me, though he is dead, shall live. And everyone who lives and believes in me shall not die in eternity.'"

As Liber chanted and Sol translated, Ana felt her world shift on its axis. It was as if the disordered pieces of her life suddenly clicked into place like the tumblers in a lock when the proper key is inserted. Now she understood the New Testament did indeed contain power—not mystical empowerment against human enemies, but a message of hope that vanquishes the greatest enemy of all. Whoever believes in the resurrection of Iesus will live forever. That, Ana realized, is true power.

Teo could contain his astonishment no longer. "Sol, are you telling me Liber has the whole New Testament *memorized?*"

Liber stopped chanting and grinned at Teo. "My pretty words," he said. "Each has a shape and color." He was obviously pleased with his accomplishment.

"That's hard to believe," Teo said.

"I know," Sol agreed. "But sometimes those who appear weak-minded have a remarkable capacity for memory or music or calculations. Liber was an orphan raised by the Christiani. His amazing memory was noticed early on, and they began teaching him the holy words. He has perfect retention."

"I know this man!" the Papa exclaimed. "When I was a young Keeper, it was rumored there was a boy whose memory was like no other. He could store words in his mind like grain in a silo. I had no idea he survived Borja's purge."

Ana approached Liber and put her hand on his arm, looking up at him. "Liber, I'm so proud of you. You have a divine gift, and you've used it well." The big man beamed at Ana's praise.

Sol lifted the flap of the satchel hanging from his shoulder and displayed some parchments. "I've already started transcribing Liber's words, but I could certainly use some help from my brightest student." He caught Teo's eye. "The Chiveisi need their own version, don't you think?" Teo could only gape at the wonder of it all.

The Papa stepped forward and took charge of the day's chaotic events. He strode to the portico's central portal. The Defectives milled around the plaza. Smiling, the Papa lifted his hands to them.

"Hail to you, brothers and sisters! I welcome you to Roma in the name of Deus and his son Iesus, the Promised King!" A cheer went up from the crowd.

"Until now you have been known to the world as Defectives. Today I lift that accursed name from your shoulders. You are victorious heroes! You have been chosen by Deus for this hour! And so, my friends, I bestow upon you a new name. From now on you shall be called . . . the Beloved!"

The cheer that arose at these words was even more boisterous than the one before. The Beloved embraced each other as they celebrated their new name. Many wept openly, and some even danced with the abandon of the innocent.

As Ana gazed out over the plaza, she found her spirit deeply moved by everything that had transpired. She bowed her head. Though her eyes were squeezed shut, tears welled from them and rolled down her cheeks.

Someone came and stood next to her. Anastasia felt a rough hand slip into hers. She looked up, expecting to see Teo.

But on this day it was Liber.

◆　　◆　　◆

Rain pattered against the windows of the convent by the sea. The hour was late, and all the sisters had retired for the night. Liber, too, slept upstairs. Only Teo and Ana were awake in the common room with its massive fireplace.

"The fire's dying down," Teo said.

He got up from his seat and stirred the coals with a poker, then added a log when a gust of wind rattled the glass panes. Unseasonably cool air had rolled in with the summer storm. Once the fire was going strong, Teo turned back to his chair.

"Sit by me," Ana invited.

She scooted over on the little settee in front of the hearth to make space for him. There wasn't much room, but Teo didn't mind. He thought Ana looked very beautiful in the fire's soft glow. He slid next to her and propped his feet on a hassock. The warmth radiating from the fireplace felt good on the soles of his bare feet. Ana also wiggled her toes toward the dancing flames. Teo's bearskin cloak covered their legs. She reclined against his shoulder, then swiveled her head and looked up at him.

"What next, Captain?"

"I guess we'll stay here for the time being. I want to translate the New Testament as fast as possible."

"How long will it take?"

"Sol is making a text in the Old Words from Liber's memory." Teo shook his head in amazement. "I can't believe after all our searching, Liber had it in his head the whole time!"

"I know. We just didn't bother to ask." The two of them grinned at each other, then broke into laughter at the astounding things they had experienced.

"Shh! You'll wake the sisters," Ana said, touching Teo's lips with her finger.

"I doubt it. I can hear the housemother snoring."

Teo's comment made Ana laugh even harder. Their amusement was a mixture of irony, jubilation, and relief after so much distress. They enjoyed the shared moment, until finally it passed and their laughter died down.

Teo heaved a sigh. "So to answer your question, I don't know how long the translation will take. Sol has to go from the Old Words into Talyano. Then I can take it into Chiveisian speech."

At the mention of her homeland, Ana's mood turned from carefree to pensive. Her eyes narrowed as she stared into the fire, lost in thought. Teo waited for a while, then ventured a question.

"Do you ever think about going home?" He was unsure whether Ana wished to talk about that subject, yet he didn't want to dodge it in case she did.

Ana's gaze remained fixed on the crackling logs. At last she turned to Teo. "Did you know it was exactly one year ago today that we left Chiveis?

I remember because it was the day after the summer solstice. That was a difficult time for me."

"So then . . . you do miss home," Teo said lamely.

She nodded. "Yes. I can't deny that. But at the same time, I *am* home. I've learned to be like a twig on a flowing stream. I go where I'm taken by Deu, and where I'm taken, that's where I'm supposed to be."

"I think I know why Deu led you from Chiveis. He had people he wanted you to meet. You have a gift I've never seen in anyone else."

"Oh, Teo, I'm nothing special."

"Yes, you are. You draw people to yourself, and you change them in the process. Look at Vanita. She used to be a social climber. Beautiful but empty. Now she's transformed. Back there at the basilica she stayed by your side until the end. You showed her a different way to live."

Ana dropped her chin and fiddled with her skirts. "I don't know. Maybe. In any case, I'm glad Vanita is at peace." A smile broke across Ana's face. "Can you believe she's going to sail around like some kind of pirate queen of the high seas? I think she's going to shave Marco's profits to zero! She'll make him sell his loot so cheaply to the peasants, he'll barely clear enough to keep the *Glider* shipshape."

Teo chuckled. "Yeah, Vanita seems very happy with Marco." He paused, growing more serious. "What about you, Ana? Are *you* happy?"

The question made Ana sit up and turn toward him on the settee. She bit her lip and considered her reply. "Yes, I'm happy. Deu has blessed me."

"I wonder if"—Teo swallowed before continuing—"if there's something that would make you even happier."

Ana looked at Teo from underneath her eyelashes. A little smile turned up the corners of her mouth, and color rose to her cheeks. "Yes, Teo. There is one thing I want very much."

Inexorably they moved toward each other. Ana's lips were parted, and her breathing was rapid. Teo closed his eyes, sensing her desire.

A fist pounded on the front door. Ana jumped back at the sharp sound and let out a little gasp.

The wind howled around the eaves. Upstairs several of the sisters opened their doors, and the housemother hurried into the common room. Teo and Ana stood up from the settee.

"Who is it?" the housemother called.

"Sorry to disturb you so late at night," replied a muffled voice. "The Papa has come to see you."

✦   ✦   ✦

Teo and Ana shared a late breakfast the next morning with the Papa and his small retinue. The housemother kept fussing over her esteemed guest after the meal, trying to make him comfortable. He thanked her, then asked if he could speak to Teo and Ana privately. They went outside to some benches under an umbrella pine.

The Papa shook his head at Teo with an appreciative smile. "Much has changed since you arrived in Roma, Teofil of Chiveis. Much has changed indeed."

"For the better, I hope, Your Holiness."

"I should say so. Things could hardly be better for the Christiani. We have opportunities now I could never have dreamed of before. And that is why I wish to speak to you—to both of you, in fact."

Teo nodded. "We're listening."

Ana felt a little nervous, but she gave the Papa her full attention.

The Papa rose from his bench and stared across the sea, then turned back to Teo. "Take a look at this." He withdrew a scroll from his sleeve. "I'm curious if you can read it."

Ana peered over Teo's shoulder while he scanned the scroll. She was surprised to discover she could read it too. It was written in a language much like the speech of Chiveis.

"I can read it," Teo said. "It's essentially my native tongue. The text says wisdom consists of two parts, knowledge of ourselves and of Deu."

The Papa's face lit up. "Excellent! So you could speak this language if necessary?"

"The dialect is a little different, but yes."

"In that case I have a mission for you." The Papa's tone was matter-of-fact.

Ana's heart jumped. *A mission? What does that mean?*

Folding his arms across his chest, the Papa resumed his seat. "Let me explain what I have in mind. As you know, the Beloved came to Roma from their enslavement at the marble quarries. One of those slaves was from a very distant place, a place known to me only by reputation until now. It's called Marsay. The slave confirmed what I already suspected: Knights of the Cross live there, men who speak a tongue similar to that in which Borregard's diary was written. Furthermore, those Knights are in contact with a people upriver from them. The text I just showed you comes from these upriver folk. The Knights believe they are open to receiving Christianism, although no formal contact has been established with them yet. So, Teofil, I think you can see the strategic role I'd have you play here."

"Because I know these two languages?"

"Yes. And because you are a warrior who can travel great distances, confront dangers, and overcome obstacles. It's hard to doubt Deus has appointed you to the task I have in mind. Only you can do it."

"And what exactly is that task?"

"I want you to become my liaison to the Knights of Marsay and bring me copies of whatever religious texts they may have. I also want you to journey upriver and explore the possibility that the people there might become Christiani."

Ana could remain quiet no longer. "That would take a long time," she said, trying to keep her tone neutral.

"No question. The seas would close for the winter before Teofil could return. He would not be back here until the following spring." The Papa looked at Ana and addressed her with tenderness. "I know this would be difficult for you to endure. And yet I must forbid you from going with Teofil on this mission, if indeed you are inclined to do so. He must not be double-minded for this task. Your role is to wait with holy patience, trusting in the care of Deus. I do not know you well yet, Anastasia, but from what I have observed, you are a woman of righteous character who could do this thing I ask."

Ana remained silent.

The Papa stood up. "My friends, I shall take my leave now. You must consider my request and come to a decision regarding it. I will return to the basilica, for I have much to do in these exciting times. If you decide to take up the yoke I have laid upon you, come see me and we will begin to make plans."

As the Papa rode away with his retinue of priests, Ana found herself distressed.

"Let's take a walk," Teo said, heading toward the beach. Ana slipped off her sandals and followed him.

They walked for a time in silence. The sun's warmth felt good on Ana's shoulders, but her heart was in turmoil. At last Teo stopped walking and turned toward her. She met his gaze, dreading what he would say.

"I believe this mission might be from Deu. I'd like to know if you think I should go."

Ana felt tears well up, but only for a moment, and then they receded. She straightened her back and lifted her chin. Teo stood there, waiting for her answer, looking down at her with his gray eyes.

"You are the bravest and most gifted man I have ever met," she said. "For that reason I dare not keep you to myself."

He stepped closer to her, much closer. "I will stay if you ask me. Just say the word."

"Why would you do that, Teo?" she whispered.

He slipped his arms around her waist and brought her near. Laying his cheek against hers, he asked, "Don't you know?" Ana's heart raced at the ticklish feel of his breath in her ear.

"I do know. But say it to me."

"I choose you, Anastasia of Edgeton. You are beautiful to me. I want no one but you."

Ana felt Teo's mouth trace the edge of her jaw. The caress of his lips was maddeningly light and elusive. She shivered and exhaled, overcome with desire. Wrapping her arms around his shoulders, she pulled him against herself. He kissed her softly on the throat, then along her shoulder, which was bare in her summer dress.

"Teo, I love you . . . I always have . . ." Her voice was breathy, but she couldn't help it.

"Tell me you want me to stay with you," he said.

"I want you to stay," she answered, "but Deu wants you to go, and I want that even more."

He came to her then, kissing her with a passion she was more than willing to return. The intimate touch of their lips thrilled her in that quiet, lonely place. The kiss was soft at first, but it quickly swelled to something more exhilarating as ardor took them both. When they finally parted, Ana's heart was racing, and she felt dizzy and weak.

"Can I ask you something?" Teo's voice was playful.

She nodded.

"Was that your first kiss?"

Ana peeked up at Teo, suddenly feeling shy. "Yes," she admitted. "Was it *yours?*"

She asked it impulsively, though she already knew the answer was no. However, Teo surprised her by replying in all seriousness, "Yes, it was."

She looked into his face. His expression was earnest.

"My first true one," he said.

Ana remained in Teo's embrace as she stared out over the sparkling ocean that would soon carry him away. Her head rested on his shoulder, and his hands were clasped at the small of her back. They stayed like that for a long time, enjoying the warmth and oneness that bound them together.

At last Teo sighed. "It's decided then. I'll go on the Papa's mission. I would have stayed if you had asked me."

"I wouldn't have asked it. There is no better path than the one the Eternal God lays before us. I release you with my full blessing."

Teo separated from Ana so he could look at her face. His fingers stroked her cheek. "My beautiful, sweet Ana . . . I'm going to miss you while I'm gone."

"Me too," she said, laying her head on his shoulder again. "But I know you'll come back to me. You always do."

EPİLOGUE

Footsteps sounded in the hallway, and the woman who heard them knew whose they were. She strode across the room. The messenger stopped just outside the door. Before he could knock, the woman grasped the knob and flung it open.

A fair-skinned man stood there, one of the many priests of Astrebril. His face bore a startled expression. "You were . . . expecting me?"

"Of course. The Beautiful One reveals his mind to his servant." The woman seized the priest with her eyes, but he could not endure the stare and was forced to look away. "Has the party arrived at the gate?" she asked.

"Yes, Your Eminence."

"Very good. Welcome them and make them comfortable, for they have traveled far. I will greet them shortly."

The woman spun away, dismissing the priest by slamming the door in his face. She crossed to a vanity table and seated herself in front of a mirror. Jars of powder and small tins of cosmetics lay scattered on the table's surface. She whitened her face, then reached for a lipstick. After painting her lips glossy black she rose from the vanity and turned toward the door. It was time for the visitors to meet the High Priestess of Chiveis.

In the entry hall of the Capital Temple a party of men waited, wrapped in dark robes and even darker power. Crystal goblets of wine had been given to them. The men stood in a huddle conversing in hushed tones.

The High Priestess swept into the room, her gown floating behind her. As she entered the hall, one of the men, taller than the rest, turned to face her. He wore chain-mail armor, and his right eye was yellow like a cat's. His steady gaze stopped the priestess in her tracks. The man's potency leapt across the room, grasping at her like a fist. His presence stirred the priestess like nothing in her prior experience. She wanted from him what she had never wanted from any other man.

The High Priestess resumed her stride toward the visitors. The black-robed men circled around their leader. He put his hands on his hips. She stared into his face, and he returned the steady gaze.

"I welcome you to Chiveis in the name of Astrebril the Great," she said.

The man in armor stepped forward and clasped a fist to his chest, then knelt before the High Priestess with his head bowed low. "I thank thee, O servant of the Beautiful One," he intoned. Though his words were thick with a foreign accent, she could understand his speech.

"Rise."

The man stood.

"What is your name?"

"I have no name. Men call me the Iron Shield."

"Astrebril told me you would come. He did not say why. Speak now, and be plain about your business."

"I come to you on the heels of a defeat. My liege lord was killed at the hand of my enemies."

"And how does that concern me?"

"My enemies are yours as well—Teofil of Chiveis and his woman Anastasia."

The High Priestess drew back with a hiss but quickly regained her composure. "How can that be?" she snarled. "My general told me they fled to a frigid glacier where no one can live."

"Somehow they survived. They crossed the ice and arrived in Ulmbartia. There they began to spread word of . . ." The man paused, unsure of the proper term.

"Christianism," she finished, drawing a nod from the Iron Shield.

The High Priestess clenched her fists, digging her nails into her palms. She wanted to shatter something, to lash out, to abuse the innocent—anything to cool the rage that seethed inside her. The scent of Astrebril's threefold powder would have been a comfort, but it could not be had at the moment. She fingered the iron collar around her neck until at last she could speak. "What do you want from me?" she asked the dark warrior.

"I come from Roma," he answered. "Perhaps you know what that means."

Roma?

The announcement shocked the High Priestess. Roma was a city of legends. *Was it even real? Did it still exist after so many years?* No one had come to Chiveis from Roma in how long? A century? Maybe two?

And yet an emissary from Roma had now arrived. He stood before her, right here in the Capital Temple of Astrebril. It could only mean one thing.

The Iron Shield leaned close. The High Priestess let him come. "I wish to renew the Pact," he whispered.

The words brought a smile to the black lips of Astrebril's favorite queen.

STUDY QUESTIONS

1. Why is the novel called *The Gift?* What "gifts" can you identify in the narrative?

2. Consider the situation with the bottle of medicine in chapter 2. Teo makes a heroic run to fetch it, but the necessary medicine was with Bard all along. In what way does this parallel the larger themes that emerge through the narrative?

3. In this story Teo and Ana both serve as Christ-figures. How does Teo exemplify the Incarnation in Part One? What does Ana teach us about the Cross in Part Two?

4. Why does Ana get caught up in a fast lifestyle? What delusions does she believe? What is the source of her confusion?

5. Why is Dohj Cristof driven mad by Ana?

6. What theological themes are represented by Ana's encounter with Drake on Hahnerat? Hint: what do the names of these two characters mean (an Internet search can be helpful here)?

7. Who is the main villain in this story? Why do you think so?

8. In your opinion what is the most exciting scene in the book? The most saddening? The most romantic? The most mysterious?

9. By the end of the story, is Vanita Labella "saved"?

10. What does the Overseer reveal about the nature of Christianity?

11. In the Chiveis Trilogy many of the locations are actual places. For example, Roma is obviously Rome. Can you identify any specific locations within the city? Thinking further afield, where is Nuo Genov? The Domo in the Forbidden Zone? Greater Lake? Manacho? The newly-discovered pass that Ana crosses while injured? The island of Hahnerat?

12. What meaning do you discern in the names of the book's three acts (Solidarity, Extravagancy, Victory)?

13. When does Teo become aware he is in love with Ana? When does Ana realize it in return?

14. Why is Teo so committed to building and using the gunpowder bomb in Part Three?

15. Summarize the theological theme of the book in one sentence.

Coming in June 2012

Book Three of the

CHIVEIS TRILOGY

For more information, visit www.Chiveis.com

THE SWORD

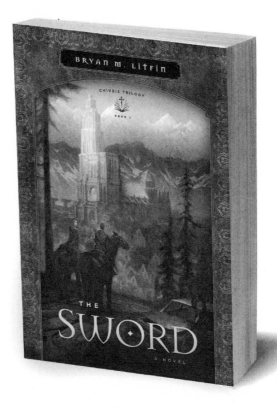

If you enjoyed reading *The Gift,* be sure to check out book 1 in the Chiveis Trilogy.

CHIVEIS TRILOGY